i

Isle of Orainn

Louise Furley

Isle of Orainn

ISBN- 978-1-7349807-4-5 (paperback)
ISBN- 978-1-7349807-3-8 (eBook)

Cover image by Deusol

ALSO BY LOUISE FURLEY

Isle of Orainn

Prologue

Breathy filigrees strumming twilight and shadows drifted away as she softly ended the song. The applause was sparse, sporadic at first as the dazed audience in the tavern realized she had finished singing. It took a moment for them to fumble from the entranced state she'd lulled them with her poignant voice.

Just turned 17, Indiana Kolbi's voluminous green eyes glossy with the pleasure of singing, tensed in wariness as the crowd's enthusiasm intensified. The clapping now almost deafening, intoxicated patrons exuberantly called out for more. Poised for flight, she hovered on the slightly inclined stage within reach of grossly drunken, horny men already struggling to get out of their seats to get at the teen.

Petite and shyly delicate, Indiana had the pert curves of a girl on the cusp of womanhood with the promise of the curves growing lush while the rest of her frame remained slight. The sapphire sequined dress she wore clung to her burgeoning figure to just below her willowy thighs. Light strawberry blonde hair rippling with golden highlights and deeper amber strands curled and waved down her back.

Before the first bombed, fat-bellied man reached her, Indiana glanced around for the manager, the bouncer, the bartender, anyone to come between her and the grasping crowd. But as usual, Mr. Johnson had displayed her up on the stage and left her to fend for herself.

Indiana suspected that the manager told the bouncer to let things run their course, not get involved. Sally, one of the barmaids told her that Mr. Johnson said having men fight each other over his beautiful starlet might increase business with the drama. Jealous Sally had snorted rudely proclaiming Indiana was not even close to pretty, much less beautiful.

Nonetheless, Indiana spun around and fled towards the back of the bar and down a hall. She reached the employees' exit, shoved the door open and ran out. The door closed automatically behind her. She hoped she had disappeared too quickly for the men hopped up on drugs and alcohol to catch where she went.

Outside, the night blanketed the shaken teen as she moved away from the back door into the darkened alley behind the tavern. The bar on a decrepit street blended with equally slovenly businesses. Which was how she was able to get hired to sing in a bar at her minor age.

Her father died when she was an infant, and a few years ago her mother had vanished. Of course, she'd done it before. Got high with one of her new paramours and forgot she had a young daughter alone at home in a cruddy apartment on a mean street in Savannah.

Normally Raeleen would return in a week or so when the drugs, and the man, ran out. But this time, she didn't come back. Indiana had to drop out of school to find jobs to feed herself and keep up the rent on their tiny squalid apartment.

Lucky for her there were a lot of employers out there willing to hire someone off the books and ask no questions, like her age, SS# or require identification to rake their leaves, pick fruit, or man a market booth.

She struggled while working several jobs and studying for her GED, her dream was to one day go to college and have a real career. She started at the Noir Den Saloon when she was 16. Mr. Johnson paid her cash, gave her a fake ID, and said he didn't care how old she was as long as she could pull in the crowd. And she did.

People paid to hear the young girl with the golden voice and the face of an angel serenade them. The drunker they got, the better they liked her. The happier they were, the more they drank, and hence the more money they spent.

Indiana had learned to judge the time between when her set ended and how quickly the customers comprehended it and would gather their wits before coming after her. She had scoped out which of the various rooms in the rear of the bar she could quickly hide in, or if the way was clear, to scurry out the back.

Her timing was the only thing thus far that had enabled her to remain a virgin. An un-raped, as yet, virgin. How long she would be able to keep herself safe was tenuous. As long as she stayed smart and quick she would survive. But, every night she sang was one more falling domino closer to her being assaulted, or worse, kidnapped and sold in the sex slave market Sally had told her about.

Poorly lit, the dank alley was layered in rank filth. Asphalt broken up in big chunks shambled over most of the worn tar, the walls of the buildings slimy with God knows what that had been thrown, pissed or puked on it. The dumpster was at one end but its putrid smell lingered near where Indiana hovered against a clammy wall in the shadows.

She waited until she determined no one had followed her out there and she could slip back inside, discretely grab her purse and slide back out unnoticed. A few clickety steps in her kitten heels to the door, she reached for the handle, and heard cursing.

Slinking back into the shadows, invisible in the dark she held her breath, every muscle tensed. Two men entered the alley dragging another man between them. Their voices and scuffling footsteps echoed spookily through the bricked corridor raising the hair on the back of her neck.

"Fuckin' A," one of them complained. "Ol' Carlo shoulda laid off the carbs, man, he weighs a ton. It'll be a bitch to get him in the dumpster."

"Huh," the other man grunted. Dragging the unconscious man down the foul alley, the pair kicked trash out of their way, beer cans clanked, clattering metallically as they tumbled along the uneven tar. Plastered against the mildewed wall, Indiana held her breath in the shrouded dark, not daring to make a sound. When they reached the dumpster, the man they hauled moaned.

"Aw crap, Apollo, he's still alive. You pussy," one of them growled, "you pullin' your punches with those brass knuckles you wuss?"

"Fuck you, lay him down." The two men grunted as they dropped the guy heedless that he thumped bone-cracking hard on the ground. The man called Apollo pulled a revolver out from under his jacket, twisted a long cylinder on the end, held the barrel to the unconscious man's temple and fired several muffled pops, the body jerked then lay still. No more moans.

Jumping shocked with each shot, Indiana clamped a hand over her mouth to stifle her screams; her stomach retched threatening to expel the ramen she'd had for dinner.

The men huffed and grunted as they lifted the corpse over their heads and tossed it into the dumpster. It barely made a sound as it landed on trash and sunk beneath the lighter garbage on top. Slapping their hands on their pants to wipe off the dirt of the deceased, the men's remorseless grumbles diminished as they traveled back down the alley.

Their stomps startled a rat, it skittered across her foot, Indiana shrieked and leaped back. One of the men turned, she saw his face clearly under the street lamp at the end of the alley. A coarse white face, mean slash of lips, tuft of yellow hair above his sharp chin, and spiked blond hair shone in the illumination.

With a frightened squeak, she turned and sped down the back of the alley, racing to where she parked her car. Instantly, she could hear cursing and stamping footsteps chasing down the alley after her.

Her heart racing, Indiana ducked her head down to blend into the dark mosaic of parked vehicles in the back lot as she rushed to her car. Her purse was in the bar but she had a spare key over the back tire. Skidding to her bare knees when she reached the old black Corolla, Indiana fumbled, patting frantically under the wheelbase.

"*Thank God,*" she cried when her fingers touched the tiny metal box. Snatching the key out of the box she jumped to her feet, shoved it in the lock, hopped inside, stabbed it in the ignition, fired it up, and was backing up as the men burst across the parking area charging right at her.

Her heart banging up her chest and into her clenching throat, Indiana stomped on the gas pedal, flooring it.

Muffled pop-pops of the silenced firearms, bullets pinged into the metal frame of the rusted car, a side window shattered, glass flew everywhere. Ducking her head, she smashed harder on the gas and the car fishtailed, narrowly missing the men as they dove out of the way, and she tore down the street.

Her pulse ratcheting crazy, panicked breaths slamming against her ribs, Indiana sped recklessly down the eclipsed streets, one after the other trying to think what to do. Her purse was back at the bar, if the men went inside and asked about her they would quickly figure out who she was, and her address was in her purse, she couldn't go home. She had no friends or relatives.

She considered the police, but, she was working illegally, underage in a saloon that served liquor, they would toss her into foster care. She knew what happened in foster homes, and she'd already had her fill of her mother's pedophilic boyfriends. The police would most likely arrest her.

She didn't have a driver's license, and she had no way to prove what she saw. With her luck, the police would accuse her of the murder and claim she invented the two assassins to cover her crime.

Murder! "Oh my gosh," she heaved, wiping at her sweating forehead. Sprinkles of glass shook off the back of her hair. It was sinking in. She'd seen a man die tonight. Executed in cold blood. And the killers would be coming after her as a witness to the ghastly deed.

The Corolla wound aimlessly through the night as her frazzled brain ran in circles more and more frantic, her terrified mind clamoring *what to do, where to go?*

Chapter One

Six years later

Humming a sweet lullaby, Elizabeth Westcott carried the folded blanket and towels still warm, fresh from the dryer up the stairs. She quieted as her heels trod over the carpet lest she wake the baby.

Inside the pink and yellow ruffled nursery, Elizabeth set the towels on the dresser and turned to the crib. Over the crib, a mobile of pastel Winnie the Pooh stuffed animals twirled slowly tinkling a hushed melody to aid in sleep, not hinder it. Baby Brie was so easily awakened, and so hard to settle back down.

Elizabeth tiptoed to the crib, her motherly smile gentle, peaceful, so loving, she bent over quietly- "What the-" Elizabeth gasped, her hand going to her throat. The crib was empty. The doctor said no pillows, toys or blankets for safety, so Elizabeth could see instantly that the bed was bare.

"How on earth-" She stood and stared blankly; then blinked rapidly as if her eyes tricked her and the six-month-old baby would magically appear. Shaking her head out of her stunned muse, Elizabeth crouched and looked under the bed, behind the door, in the rocking chair. By the time she reached the closet, her heart was hammering up her throat blocking her windpipe, throttling her dizzy with panic.

She flung the closet door open, and prayed. Eyes wide, she scanned the inside, and groaned in disbelief. The maids were not due until four, and there was an hour window between the two nannies' shifts. "No, wait," she murmured. Her smile shaky, she breathed deeply to control her panic.

"Of course, Stedman just came home early and picked Brie up and took her downstairs…for her bottle…or, took her for a walk. Yes that's it!" She hurried out of the room and down the hall to search all of the other bedrooms first.

They were empty. She ran down the carpeted stairs to check the den crammed with over-stuffed furniture and books, no one there, she rushed through the living room, morning room, and the salon and on to the barren kitchen.

As she dashed to the window, her stomach clenching in anguish flared into abject terror. Seizing nerves of hopelessness rushed towards an explosion of horror in her head.

Peering out the window she saw Stedman's car wasn't in the drive, the kitchen door was open, and the empty stroller was folded beside the door.

Panicking fountains of screams roiled up her chest, choked through her lungs and gushed in raging grief as they writhed with shrieking despair throughout the neighborhood.

Chapter Two

"C'mon Velvet, get yer arse in gear, order's been up five minutes!" the barking shout came from the kitchen.

"Oh dear." Jesselin Judan covered her mouth with her hand. Worry in her soft girlish voice, she advised, "Gee, Velvet you better high-tail it, Cook sounds angry."

"Ha!" The waitress in her early thirties rolled her eyes, set a hand on her portly hip and made a shooing motion with her other hand towards the kitchen. Looking anything but like a woman named Velvet, she was short and rotund with pale skin. Her uniform was dove grey with a white lace collar and apron, both of which clung quite snuggly to her very round figure.

With a smug shrug, Velvet tossed back a long, thin, light brown braid, the tip brushing her corpulent ass. Her wide mouth turned up in a playful grin, she said with a saucy wink, "Oh hon, he's always like that. Terse and bossy, that's why they call him, Sarg. Cook was in the army, what," she snickered, "like a thousand years ago and he still likes to bark orders at everyone. He'll get over it."

In her plain face, almost pretty with plump cheeks yet pointed chin, Velvet's light brown eyes twinkled with constant mirth. Nothing, absolutely nothing ever fazed the calm, mildly sarcastic young woman. Her ultra-confident, pleasant and casually blasé attitude attracted her fair share of customers. Regulars asked for her station. She was snarky witty and nothing upset her.

Jesselin, on the other hand, small, almost wispy yet with killer curves she kept under cover, fussed with the end of a long curl. Eyes the color of spring darted nervously from the coolly smug Velvet to the barking cook.

True to Velvet's words, Cook, aka Sarg, resembling an aged Popeye, growled and grimaced, cursed some more in a country-ish accent then went back into the kitchen. No one else in the bistro paid him any mind.

A pleasant looking woman in her sixties fluffed the side of her curly, grey silted brunette hair and tsk-tsked. "Oh Velvet," she scolded the waitress, "do get along. Stop teasing him. He's likely to have an apoplexy." She and Velvet shared a grin.

Clarie Barton and her husband Finnlan owned Divine Bistro. Still softly attractive with pretty blue eyes, her friendly, kind personality never changed no matter how stressful the situation. Clarie was the grandmotherly type that hovered over everyone at holiday dinners pushing more food on them.

"Velvet!" Cook shouted from the kitchen, and Velvet rolled her eyes. She hollered back, "God-doggit, Cook, keep your pants on, I'm coming!"

A tall man in a suit and tie with a stiff spine, straight black hair combed starched to the side, an austere countenance tightening his long face, Benoit Sloan approached with a frown. "Now, then, what is going on here?" His crisp voice scolding, "What's this bickering? The shouting?" Wrinkling his snooty nose, the manager shook his head and rebuked, "This is a place of business, you people must-"

"Sloan," a cheerful voice interrupted him. "Stop bellyaching. Let 'em play, these people are my people, I am captain of this ship."

The restaurant manager's lofty brows arched. "Ship?"

The chipper man, Finnlan Barton grinned. "Yeah. I grew up bottle-feeding on the first Star Trek. With all their fantastic adventures, they were my heroes, comrades that loved but bickered with familial goofiness but always came through when it mattered, and always, always, had each other's backs."

His wife Clarie tittered smiling, patting his shoulder affectionately. "Ah, and I suppose you are Captain Kirk?"

Nodding with a big grin, his thumbs tucked into the waistband of his belt, he agreed, "Yes, of course I am. I am the leader, passionate yet aggressive, brave and clever, I-"

9

"You!" she laughed. "I recall Kirk as a trim, muscular, charismatic sexy young man, while you-" her teasing grin rolled down his pudgy body, the grey hair waving around his ears but thinning on top.

"Me?" He frowned, lips pushed out. "I am the perfect, epitome of James T. Kirk."

She laughed. "Yes well, you are charismatic, and I certainly find you sexy," she stroked his round cheek. "Well, what about me?" she asked. "Who am I then on this Divine Ship?"

Finn pecked his wife on the cheek. "You, my sweet are my Lt. Uhura."

"What!" Clarie's brown brows slivered with grey drew down in insult. "Your secretary? A Receptionist?"

Her jolly husband wrapped an arm around her plump shoulders, smiled with the adoration clear in his merry blue eyes, "Ah, but, sweetheart, she had the most important job as Communications Officer, and," he wriggled his eyebrows in a cheeky leer, "she and William Shatner were secret lovers. During the noon break I will show you-"

"So," another waitress joined the game asking, "who is your Spock? Your First Commander?" Laverne 'Bubbles' Evans, forty-ish, also a shade overweight, came up tying her apron behind her back.

"Hmm." His finger to his chin, Finn considered her question. His eyes flitting around the bistro lighting briefly on each employee, then he grinned. "That of course would be Benoit Sloan," he nodded to the stiff manager who frowned at him.

Nodding cheerfully, Finn said, "Yes. Cool, aloof, straitlaced, bossy, a genius with a bit of that snobbish bladed nose in the air." He laughed at Sloan's pursed lips, and lowered brows like black wings over annoyed eyes that yet held a miniscule spark of humor at the teasing.

Velvet announced, "I want to be Chekov!" They all turned to her with amused denial.

"Uh," Laverne, her sassy voice mocking, advised her, "first of all, you are female, and not an Asian, and really, he was a, don't take offense now, sugar, but he was thin and wiry, a swordsman warrior, and you," her gaze teased at Velvet's short, round figure.

Velvet tossed back her long braid with a sniff. "Listen toots, a girl can be a warrior too you know. And," she smirked saying, "under all this…voluptuous meat," she grinned at the laughter breaking out in the gathered group, "I am a lean, mean, fighting machine, um, in here," she pointed to her head," and they laughed louder. "What about you, Bubbles?" Forehead wrinkling quizzically, Velvet asked, "Where does the nickname Bubbles come from, anyway?"

Laverne snipped her a naughty wink answering, "Why, from my dancin' days, girl. I made a mint as an exotic dancer. Yeah," she grimaced at their looks of disbelief. "I didn't always have an extra 30 pounds on me, and I wasn't born 40 ya know. And I had these, natural, big for the days before implants," she put her hands under her hefty breasts and pushed them up.

"Stripping paid the rent in those days. Anyway," Laverne said, "I wanna be Christine Chapel, the nurse. She was ballsy with a deep voice, and hot," she patted her thick dark curls and flapped her lashes.

Finn said, "Yeah, yeah," pleased that they were playing. He motioned to the kitchen. "Cook is McCoy 'cause he has that country accent, he keeps everyone healthy with his cooking like the doctor Bones did with medicine-"

"And, he's as crabby and annoying as McCoy was too!" Laverne joked, they all laughed.

"That leaves Hayes the bartender as the ship's chief engineer," Finn said.

Clarie commented, "But he's a bartender, and black, engineer Scotty was white and-"

"True." Finn nodded cheerfully. "But he has a Scottish accent, and, you all know he's the one that fixes everything around here that breaks. The plumbing in the bathroom that can be shaky, the creak in the front steps, the main oven that quit working."

"And," Velvet restated, "he has the Scottish accent!"

Jesselin stood off to the side, smiling at their playfulness, but had no idea what they were talking about. Star Trek, the early ones were well before her time, and she was too poor to have satellite for cable to catch reruns.

Glancing at the shy girl, Clarie said, "Hey, what about our sweet little Jesa? Who would she be?"

"Hmm," Finn pondered as he studied the petite Jesselin they had nicknamed Jesa, then snapped his fingers. "She's gorgeous and blonde, well, strawberry blonde, like Janice Rand was who played the yeoman. She has that hint of a southern accent that she tries to hide, yep, she would be our yeoman. She was Kirk's," he smiled paternally at her, said, "I mean *my*, personal assistant."

Jesa looked in bewilderment at him and the rest of the giggling group. All were laughing except of course Benoit Sloan who stood stiffly and aloof as always, pretending he wasn't engaged in the game. Although secretly, he liked being identified as Spock. The Vulcan was always his hero. Logical, reserved, brilliant of course, and often saved the day.

The phone at the desk rang; Finn ambled over and answered it. Velvet left to collect her order, and everyone else chatted while setting tables.

The front and most of both sides of the Bistro were floor to ceiling glass that let in an abundance of sunshine. In the summer, a jumble of colorful flowers cascaded around the building. A faux loft in the rear lent a very high ceiling, and with the enormous windows, there was an impression of open space and comfort.

Under lilac luminosity, white-clothed tables scattered the main dining room leading all the way back to the curved recessed wall where paintings decorated the wood-trimmed alcove beneath the loft. A huge stone fireplace anchored a corner where Finn had set up a cozy seating area. Two small divans and several comfy chairs semi-circled the fireplace where people could visit, enjoy just a cup of coffee, peacefully read a book, or surf the net.

In winter at night, through the vast windows, patrons enjoyed the view of cool silver moonlight glinting off abundant piles of glistening white snow, a contrast to the black night that nested the restaurant.

In the warm seasons, the back of the bistro opened to a patio with round tables topped with cheery umbrellas. Beyond the patio, Saoire Hill gently sloped down to an open grassy area like a small park, surrounded by trees and a view of a picturesque bridge that crossed a narrow stream. A few hundred yards past the park was the ocean.

As Finn hung the phone up, he noticed early customers starting to enter the bistro for the dinner hour. "Everyone," he announced, clapping his hands to get staffs' attention.

"Ah." His eyes traveled over the group attending to him. "We've all heard about the missing baby, little Brie Westcott," everyone nodded suddenly solemn. "Well, apparently the FBI is sending a man to assist the local police since the island is so remote and such.

"That was Chief Taggart McKabe calling. It seems that all of their officers are out on jobs, the taxis are closed up in the station for annual inspection, and the rental cars have all been taken by the nonlocal snowbirds that are preparing to leave for the winter season before the peninsula is washed over by the squalling sea and closed off from the mainland."

"So? Why are you telling us this?" Clarie asked, her blue eyes warm on her husband.

"Well…" His gaze flitted to Jesa who was slipping pink camellias into white vases on the tables. "They need someone to pick up the FBI guy at the harbor and, well, like I said, there are no people or cars available to retrieve him. The police station is just down the block, and," he glanced around as the staff scattered to prepare for the customers coming in the door. Sloan was at the desk gathering menus and greeting the guests. "We all are about to be too busy to help, but," his eyes landed again on Jesa. "I can spare Jesa to go."

Clarie looked over at the slender girl, frowning. "Are you sure? She's so new here, she doesn't really know her way around, and to set her up to be alone with a strange man-"

Finn patted her arm. "She is a clever girl, she'll find her way. And, honey, he's the FBI, she will certainly be safe with him." Pulling bills out of his pocket for gas, he called to the young woman busily tucking the last of camellias into the bud vases, "Jesa, dear, can you come here?"

Jesa looked up at the bistro owner with a pretty smile and started towards him.

Chapter Three

Frustrated that she could not find her way through the winding maze of streets to the wharf, clutching the directions in her hand, Jesa swung the steering wheel of her tiny, ancient Epic back and forth over the hodge-podge of crooked lanes.

"One would assume," she grumped, "that you could see the entire island from up on the Commons." But in fact, the way the smaller hills rolled down the mountain and the roads curved down and around dense timberland veiling the descending land, the harbor wasn't visible until one was almost upon it.

Of course she hadn't wanted to admit to Mr. Barton that she was terribly directionally challenged. If there was a fork in the road she would invariably take the wrong one. Glancing at the crumpled directions again, she tossed them on the seat and peered over the wheel.

Finally, through the open window, she could hear the surf pounding as the advancing winter forced the high, heavy punishing seas at the peninsula. In a few weeks the strip of land at the north harbor leading to the mainland would be completely washed over, impassably flooded, and then turn icy. The ice would not be solid, yet still extremely dangerous due to the continual pummeling of the sea that was turning the peninsula into an island.

Throughout the winter the land would be virtually closed off from the rest of the world. The severe weather and dramatic violence of the ocean would make Orainn essentially impregnable.

The island was shaped like a hilly seal. With the head spreading down and out to wide flaps at either side, and the broad, hi-topped belly, then growing narrower down towards the feet. The rough ocean around the perimeter of the land would crash the shore so ferociously there would be no safe access for boats.

The few beaches would be critically flooded and too dangerous to attempt mooring. Since there was no airport, it would be tremendously difficult and perilous to leave, or approach the Isle of Orainn. The Irish name for the isle, depending on who was doing the telling, meant either 'gaze in wonder,' or 'watching us closely.' Jesa hoped it was gaze in wonder because watching us closely gave her the creeps.

On the choppy water, the colossal ferry, fishing boats and a few yachts jounced erratically, swaying and bobbing jaggedly over bigger and bigger rolling swells that walloped in with the cooler wind. The wind had picked up as the temperature dropped, Jesa watched people in jackets bustling about loading boats with suitcases and boxes.

Other boats were depositing supplies for those that stayed the winter on the island. The hum of conversations, shouts, noise from motors rumbling, the roaring surf crashing against the pier added to the rousing hubbub.

Following the road that wound to the busy wharf, she sighed in relief that she'd made it, then her stomach fell. Surely the man in the immaculate suit standing on the walk with the cross expression, tight lips and hands clenched on his hips in impatience, wasn't the agent she was sent to pick up. But Jiminy Christmas, she bit her lower lip, he matched the description she was given.

Parking the car at the curb, she put her hair up in a knit cap to keep the bitter wind from flapping it around her head, and pulled on sunglasses to protect her eyes from the stark winter sunlight, glaringly bright as it ricocheted blindly off the water while submerging into the horizon.

Two suitcases at his feet, the man looked around, down at his watch, huffed an annoyed exhale then looked around again.

Taking a deep breath, Jesa got out of the car and warily approached him. She moved slowly, he was an intimidating male. Taller than Mr. Sloan, and a lot bulkier, at least his shoulders were. The black suit stretched across the very broad shoulders, every time he lifted his wrist to look at his watch a glimpse of gold flashed, and a huge bicep bulged against the suit jacket.

15

To Jesa he looked really strong, powerful, standing with arrogant confidence, dark hair waving over his forehead. It looked neat, but like he worked at it, like any second it would spring untamed and flop in his eyes. He was handsome in a tough, rugged he-man in a suit kind of way.

A shiver rippled through her when she got closer and saw his eyes. The displeased orbs were dark, ruthlessly hard, cold, maybe cruel, and definitely uncompromising. If there was a lick of kindness or compassion lurking in the enigmatic depths it was deeply hidden.

"Um, sir, I-"

Without moving his head, his eyes lowered with impatient irritation, barely acknowledging her, he muttered, "No thank you, Miss, I don't want to buy anything." He appeared built like a boxer but perfectly comfortable in the suit, he certainly had the cool superiority of an FBI agent.

Now that she was closer, Jesa could see scars carving parts of his face and near his temple, they only added to his already menacing aura. Her brows rose in puzzlement, then lowered in understanding his wrong assumption. "No, sir, you don't under-"

Now he lowered his head and glowered at her like she was an annoying buzzing gnat he wanted to flick away. "Miss, I am not interested in," his contemptuous glare raked her body insinuating that was what she was selling, he sneered, "anything you have to…sell. Now, take off, I am waiting for a ride." He jerked his head from her and continued scanning the dock.

Sighing heavily, her lips bunched in consternation, Jesa said nervously, "I, Mr. Koffi, am your ride. I mean your driver," she blanched at the aggravated look of disbelief he shot her. Sucking in another deep breath, she tipped her head to look way up at him. "I mean, that is if you are FBI Agent Tristan Koffi, I was sent to pick you up."

His eyes widened in incredulity. Again his gaze insolently raked her, then flit to her crappy little car, and back to her. His condescending, "That's Tristan*o*," twined with another aversive pan of her face and petite form. He groused coldly, "Are you even old enough to drive?"

An affronted gasp choked out, "Of- of course I am."

16

His insulting gaze studied her face, eyes narrowed at her high round cheeks rosy from the cold as if he didn't believe her. Behind the light sunglasses her large eyes were slightly visible but the color was undeterminable. Then, seeing her ire at his insinuation that she was a little girl, he snapped rudely, "You don't fucking look it," grabbed up the handles of his suitcases and stalked to her car.

"And you have a potty mouth," she mumbled under her breath.

He turned his head with a frown. "Pardon?"

She shook her head, murmured, "Nothing," and opened the trunk that creaked on the way up. He glared at the crummy vehicle, more of it was rusted than not, and looking like it was on its last legs. "What the hell kind of transportation is this piece of shit?"

Offended, she smiled weakly at the faded blue car. Then, she raised her tiny nose and snipped, "It's *my* kind of transportation, and it's not a piece of...well, it's a little old, and maybe dented and rusty and stuff, but...it's mine," she ended fiercely with her bottom lip thrust out in a pout. "Excuse me for not bringing the limo around, but it's in my garage along with the Porsche and Beamer getting a tune up."

His mouth twitched at her sarcastic anger, the way she defended her piece of crap car. He tossed his suitcases in the trunk, closed it, then climbed awkwardly into the passenger side trying to tuck his long legs into the miniature cramped vehicle. His knees practically hit his chin.

Grasping the lever under his seat, he slammed the seat back as far as it would go. Shifting to get his large frame comfortable, he announced testily, "You are late. Twenty minutes late. Is that what I am to expect from this pokey backwards, one-horse island?"

Her cheeks flamed. "I'm sorry. I'm new here, only been here a few months. I got lost." Climbing in the driver's side, Jesa had to crank the ignition several times before it caught. Pulling away from the curb, the car coughed and rumbled along the wooden planks of the wharf and out of the harbor, leaving boat horns blaring and hectic activity behind them.

Her voice stiffly polite, she asked, "Do you want to go to the hotel where you're staying or to the police station?" She hoped it was the station, she knew where that was.

17

Shooting her an irritated glare, his eyes taking in her delicate form in holey jeans, scuffed ankle boots and oversized flannel shirt, he sniped, "The station. What the hell, if you've only been on this water-logged rock a couple of sorry months, why on earth did they send you to retrieve me?" His voice riddled with condescension, he asked, "Where are the damned police?"

He spoke in such short pompous clips Jesa couldn't tell where he was from. The resort island had only been in existence for less than forty years so most adults came from somewhere else. The bulk of them originated from Washington, Oregon, or northern California so the majority sounded similar, but there were sprinkles of Southern, Eastern and Midwestern accents.

Mouth a hard line, he reached under his butt and pulled out the crumpled directions. Unkinking the paper, he studied it, then said curtly, "These instructions are quite clear; I don't see how you could have a problem finding your way here."

Swallowing her hurt feelings, trying to smile politely, she replied, "They sent me because everyone was busy."

"Huh," he snorted, "the only one expendable. In this entire town, you were the one they could spare to send for me? A rowdy teenager?" One brow raised in contempt, his lip curled in a sneer at the hair tucked up in the knit hat, a few loose tendrils of light color wisped around her heart-shaped face. His dismissive gaze that stroked down her body again indicated how little he thought of her, but his inspection paused at her chest.

The shirt was two sizes too big, but her breasts on the slight frame were clearly full, they bounced gently against the soft flannel as the car jostled along curvy roads. Koffi jerked his eyes away and glared out the front window.

Another insult, Jesa flushed, her fingers gripped the steering wheel. She retorted indignantly, "I am not a teenager." She shot him a withering scowl, then seeing the stern set of his austere face, she bit her lower lip and gathered in her temper. Glancing at him she said, "You need to put your seatbelt on."

"I'm fine, honey," more condescension, he contended, "how bad can an accident on this grassy rock be?"

"But sir-"

"Just drive, girl, let's see this bucket of stones."

Taking yet another deep breath, she smiled slightly, totally unaware that her two front teeth slightly larger than the rest of them gave her a youthful yet sexy look. "Really, Mr. Koffi, this is a lovely island, it is not backwards or- or one-horse, whatever that means." She stepped on the gas and roiled around the twists and turns so fast, he was tossed side-to-side so hard he grabbed at the dashboard.

"Shit, girl, slow it down!" he barked as his elbow smashed into the side door, his knees bumping into the dash. The countryside whizzed past. Green grass turning into winter straw rolled into a vast valley spotted with knots of houses scattered in clusters of neighborhoods.

Buckling his seatbelt, he glowered at the fairytale resort town of quaint homes, pastel-colored chalets with white gingerbread trim. Some were mansions with fancy curlicue trimming on their three-stories, other domiciles just simple bungalows.

Smoke curled from stone chimneys like spiraling grey fingers poking up from a textural painting of cottages, rolling green hills and tall trees upwards to the blue heaven. The autumn had struck so fast and brief the enduring scent left over from warm summer days of apples, raspberries, sweet cherries and a hint of peppermint lingered in the mind.

The little car whizzed down and around the valley, over small rippling hills then chugged through increasingly dense woods heading up the square-topped mountain like a volcano, that was the center of the island. Along the way, pockets of neighborhoods or single bungalows peppered sparingly amongst the trees. As the resort grew, homes had sprung up here and there without geometrically planned patterns of neighborhoods.

Koffi was shaking his head the entire way muttering his skepticism that the crappy vehicle would make it. "Hell, for someone who doesn't know her way around you certainly drive as fast as humanly possible, isn't there a speed limit on this-" he broke off as she yanked the wheel careening out of the way of an oncoming truck. Sticking a finger in his collar, he pulled at it, unbuttoned the top button and tugged the knot in his tie loose.

Her shoulders relaxed some, she slowed a little, answering him, "Oh, I know where I am now, we're almost to the Commons. I get nervous when I drive, I don't do it much. I live close enough it's only a couple of miles walk to the Commons." She didn't mention she needed to conserve her gas as she barely made enough to live on as it was.

Settling back in the seat with one arm braced on the door handle, his knees pressed against the dash, he mumbled, "Commons?"

"Uh huh," she nodded. "Commons Square it's called. It's the epicenter of the island. The square, flat top of a big hill, or actually mountain. It's an uneven mountain. Miles steep on one side, the other side slopes short and more level. Only the steep side is accessible by car, the ocean cuts off the short side's borders.

"There's one high school, middle, and elementary school combined, down by the southern harbor along with the hospital. Fishermen's homes, boutiques, marinas, grills, finer restaurants and grander homes skirt the water, while most of the businesses like shops, grocer, pharmacy, bookstore, pet shop, the police and fire stations, a couple of restaurants, a few B&B's, and other stuff surround the square in layers of streets.

"There's a park with statues and fountains in the center. Velvet told me they hold concerts there in the summer. It's where they'll be lighting the Christmas tree."

He turned his head a hair to study her. Her round cheeks were pink, even behind the shades her eyes glowed with vitality and youth, her plump lips were turned up in an anticipatory smile.

She glanced at him then back to the road. She was surprised; he didn't appear bored with her conversation. Maybe he was just getting the lay of the land. So she continued, "On the east side of the commons, the hill is much less steep and grass slopes down to the far seawall. There's another park there called Pipistrel Park with benches and a pretty bridge that arches over a stream. The elderly people like to sit and feed the birds and watch people sauntering around the park and up the shorter, walkable side of the hill to the Commons."

His head swiveled as he took in the town. Trees scattered the uneven land, their colored leaves sprinkling the ground. As the car ascended the mountain and they came in sight of the Commons Square, Koffi observed children running, chasing each other with happy squeals. One had a kite snapping and soaring in the crisp breeze.

Bundled up young mothers strolled after them, visiting while pushing strollers.

An air of earthy Pacific Northwest dallied, carefree decorative flags in front of shops flapped in autumn wind. The small town feeling blended nicely with the hipper yuppies, the very wealthy, local families as well as tourists enriched, all adding to the old timey, tranquil, happy, Rockwell impression.

When stressed, Jesa drove like a maniac in a hurry to get parked. Since they were nearing the station she calmed, slowing down. The agent was able to take in the view of shops with valances over charming glass fronts that had baskets still filled with dying summer flowers lining the walks.

Finally she came to a screeching halt in front of a brick and brown stucco one-story building. They'd arrived, alive. She parked and turned off the engine. She wanted to drive off as soon as his heel hit the ground, but he might need to be transported elsewhere. Reluctantly she'd go in with him to make sure he was staying there.

He sucked in a deep breath, then exhaled long and relieved. Forking thick fingers through his wavy hair, he chided, "Shit, girl, you are a terrible driver!"

"I am a woman, sir, not a girl." Pushing her door open, Jesa got out. "And," she rebuked him, "you're welcome for the ride." Flouncing into the station, she realized he'd never even asked her, her name. Boor.

Chapter Four

The inside of the police station was larger than expected. A woman came out of a doorway with files in her hands as Jesa and Tristano Koffi entered. There were a dozen desks piled with papers and computers, posters about the dangers of drugs and crime covered the walls. The room was cluttered yet remained professional. A television monitor up on the wall showed an Amber Alert in effect for the missing baby, Brie Westcott.

"Hello there." The woman set the files down and greeted them with a friendly smile. "How can I help you?"

Tristano stepped forward leaving Jesa to hover near the door, where she removed her sunglasses but kept the hat on figuring she was soon going to be back outside.

All formal and authoritative, holding out his badge, he introduced himself. "I am Special Agent Tristano Koffi of the FBI. Our powers that be decided we needed to lead your local-"

"That's assist, Agent, we lead, you assist," an officer stated firmly as he came in through the front door right behind them dropping his jacket on the coat rack by the door. In a deputy's uniform of light brown shirt and dark brown slacks, gold emblems on the sleeves, with sandy hair and friendly blue eyes he appeared around Koffi's age.

Tristano turned to the officer, his dark eyes narrowed. They appraised each other, neither offering their hand to shake.

Then the officer's gaze landed on Jesa and his brows rose, pupils sparked. His smile showed many white teeth. "And are you an agent also, Miss...?" He stepped closer to Jesa who shyly lowered her eyes with a shake of her head. This time he held out his hand. "How do you do, I am Deputy Ronan Roarke." One sandy brow arched with the side of his mouth curving up as he waited for her to introduce herself.

Awkwardly gaping at the handsome officer with gorgeous blue eyes, Jesa blinked, opened her mouth, but before she could speak or shake his hand, Tristano stepped between them. "She is not an agent, she is a driver," he said drolly, "and I use that term very loosely. Can we get on with the-"

The door opened again and another man entered. He was older, around fifty with a heavy face and tired eyes; they flicked from Ronan to Tristano. Unzipping his brown leather jacket, his smile polite he said, "Ah, you made it."

Tristano flashed a dry look at Jesa still standing near the door with her head lowered, muttered, "Barely." They shook hands. The older man said with a Texan accent, "I'm guessin' ya'll are Agent Tristano Koffi. I am Chief Taggart McKabe."

A snort came from the side. Ronan derided, "That's *Special Agent*, Chief, you know, like on NCIS?" The chief frowned at him, Tristano's face remained implacable, the woman laughed, and Jesa looked confused.

The chief was tall like both the other men but huskier. His brown hair under the black cowboy hat grazed grey at the temples, and his five o'clock shadow was stippled with grey. Removing his jacket and the hat, he set them on the coat rack and smiled wearily at Jesa, "You the one Finn sent to pick him up? Jesa Judan?"

She nodded shyly, recalling the rude agent thought she was so insignificant he hadn't even bothered to ask her what her name was.

The older woman said kindly to her, "I'm Willie-Jean Parrish, welcome to Orainn, I heard you've only been here a few months." Tall and gangly, her short brown hair curled around the friendly fortyish face. A civilian employee, she wore a white blouse, and a black skirt that went past her knees, and short heeled pumps.

"Yes, um, Mr. Barton was so kind to hire me to do jobs around the bistro. I know he really didn't need the help, but," she shrugged embarrassed and said, "no one else was hiring and I really needed a job, he found places to fit me in."

"Yes, he's very good at helping people." Willie-Jean smiled. "It was quite obliging of him to send you today, we are short-handed to be sure."

The chief's smile broadened. "Well, I thank you, little darlin' we appreciate your assistance. We're a bit in the weeds here at the moment. With the mainlanders leaving there have been tons of accusations of theft, and brawls at the harbor, domestic quarrels abound with the stress of packing and such."

He tiredly dragged his sleeve across his forehead. "It's damned ridiculous. Everyone always gets all stirred up as the winter comes bringing the dangerous weather and so many people leaving."

"Yeah, we're busy, but hell, Tag, we don't need the damned FBI's help," Ronan complained, his riled eyes trained haughtily on the agent.

Straightening his spine into a steel rod, Tristano ground out through a clenched jaw, "I am not here to help, I am here to run this investigation. You will follow my instruct-"

Ronan got in his face and retorted, "Like hell I will, you listen here-" they about bumped chests.

The chief shook his head and rolled his eyes. "Pull 'em in boys, this ain't no pissin' contest." His lips bunched, he nodded to the Willie-Jean and then Jesa. "My apologies, ladies." He turned towards a hallway. "Come everyone, let's go to the conference room." He said to Jesa who started for the front door to make her exit, "Don't leave, darlin', I think you should come too."

Her cupid lips parted in confusion, why would he want her there? But she followed him out of the bullpen area.

Inside the conference room, scraping wooden chairs with leather seats up to the nicked and scratched table, they sat down. As they settled, other officers receiving the call to attend the meeting wandered in. Taking their seats, Ronan and Tristano glared at each other.

Ronan scowled at the chief. "Come on Tag, you know how the FBI is, they gobble everything up and keep everything a big dark secret. You know they won't divulge a single thing to us-"

Interrupting him, Tristano set a forearm on the table, and said coolly, "I believe it's the other way around, you locals stomp all over evidence, don't know your asses from a-"

"That's enough," Chief McKabe ordered, breaking in, his tired voice calm yet firm. "Thanks, Willie-Jean," he said as he accepted a cup of coffee from her.

Two female deputies came into the room chatting away. When they saw the group already congregated, they quieted. "Caitlin, Tahni," McKabe said to them, "find seats."

In her late thirties, Caitlin Saunders was more muscles than soft curves, her dark brunette hair cut short; she nodded to McKabe and sat down between two male deputies.

Tahni Genarino, tall with light toned hair, a fair butterscotch color, wore her uniform a size too small to outline her voluptuous figure. Her sultry gaze traveled the people in the room; she skipped over Jesa like she was invisible and halted abruptly at Tristano.

Broad lips already in a flirty smile turned up. Seductive lids lowered over dark sapphire eyes that streamed across the agent's huge shoulders, widened at the powerful chest and lit on his harshly handsome face. She stared at him, willing him to look over at her. His eyes remained trained on the chief. More officers piled in and sat at the table.

When everyone quieted, McKabe said, "Now," he leaned forward and eyeballed each officer there and Tristano, "this is the way this is gonna go. Ya'll will work together," he sighed while the bickering picked up with the other officers adding their complaints to Ronan's about the pushy FBI being involved.

He gave them a minute to get their bitching out, then, he held up a beefy hand. "Again, enough. Everyone be quiet, slap them flappers shut." He waited until they settled down again. The deputies glared at Tristano who stared impassively only at the chief as if they were inconsequential and didn't rate his attention.

McKabe went on, "Now, as I was saying, you will work together. To keep everyone abreast of all the information, keeping everything cross-referenced so no one thinks anyone is withholding information," he paused with a Cheshire smile, "I have a plan."

Their brows arching with prepared objections, the group remained silent and questioningly attentive to him. He settled his husky bulk back in the worn leather chair. "I need to check with Finn Barton, but," drumming thick fingertips on the table he smiled at Jesa.

All curious eyes followed his consideration of her, saw her perplexity, and flipped back to the chief.

His attention back to the rest of the group, a serious, no fooling around determination in his voice, McKabe stated, "To keep everyone abreast of everything going on in this investigation so there are no accusations of everyone not being 100% forthright with all the information, I will have a neutral third party be involved in every aspect." His eyes hopped back to Jesa.

The rest of the table, slowly catching his drift, looked one-by-one to the young woman who really wasn't paying much attention since it was police work and nothing to do with her. Then, feeling all eyes on her, Jesa looked around and then to the chief who was still smiling at her.

"Uh…" her skin paled as it was dawning on her that somehow the chief wanted to involve her. "I'm not sure, um…" her brows knit as she worked to comprehend what he was implying.

"It's perfect!" McKabe announced jauntily as if the subject was already closed. "Yes," he said, nodding at her, "I will get the okay from Finn to borrow you, as you said, he isn't dependent on you being at the bistro."

"But-" there it was again, as the FBI agent had said, she was expendable, unnecessary. She bit her lip to disguise how bad it made her feel. As worthless as a stray cat like her mother had called her and treated her.

Leaning forward with a frown, Ronan barked, "What the hell, Tag, you aren't suggesting that she-"

Shaking his head, Chief said, "Oh no, I'm not suggesting, I'm ordering. As a neutral party, Miss Jesa will be at all the interviews and information gathering until the conclusion of this investigation. She will maintain her own notes, and," his eyes tapered with authoritative command looking pointedly at each and every one of them, "every single bit of new information garnered where she is not present will be immediately proffered to her. Then she will forward it to Willie-Jean who will disseminate it to everyone else."

The crowd broke out in loud debate.

"It's downright ridiculous, Chief," one of the deputies sputtered, "not only is she a civilian but she's- she's, well, she's just a girl-"

"Hey!" Both female deputies complained in unison.

Jesa's lips tensed at the remark. "I am not a-"

"Quite," Tristano Koffi broke in over her, "it is insane. She is just a child and you could be putting her in harm's way, you can't be serious-"

McKabe narrowed his eyes at the agent, "Ah, but I am. With no dog in the show the *young woman* will be completely impartial. And you all will be fully acquiescent to my orders. Anyone," he glared at Tristano and then each of the officers, "not 100% on board with what I am ordering, the way I, as head of this island, have laid it out, can leave Orainn," this aimed at Tristano. At Ronan's smug smile, McKabe said, "Or find another job." Ronan's face hardened.

Pleased with himself, the chief smiled cheerfully. "And, as I was saying, it's perfect. Because for now, there isn't a vehicle on this island available for Agent Koffi to use. So," he inclined his head at Jesa, "she can drive you and also be on scene. Every piece of information will stay tight with one person in charge of it all, seeing as we're so short staffed that solves another issue. You see," he sat back, twined his fingers and rested them with satisfaction on his stomach smiling at everyone, "two birds, one stone, perfect, eh?"

Deputy Tahni Genarino said quickly, "I'll drive him! Chief, I can take care of Agent Koffi-" Speaking all at once, everyone talked over her, still voicing their dissidence at the FBI being present, and their dismay at civilian Jesa being involved in police work.

Tristano stood up, slamming his palms on the table, blazed angrily, "Perfectly ridiculous is what it is."

Ronan jumped to his feet. With his exasperated disapproval, his Boston accent thickened. "On this I agree. That is the wickedest stupid idea, she can't do this-"

"Damn straight." Tristano nodded in agreement. "She is too young, too inexperienced, and hell, McKabe," he grimaced, "apparently you have never been at her mercy when she was behind the wheel!"

Jesa's affronted gasp burst out and she leaped up as well. "You men are just crying because I'm a woman, and I'm young, and you don't think I can do what needs to be done. Well," fuming, her mouth set, she crossed her arms over her chest. Cheeks red with pique, she snapped at Tristano, "I got you here in one piece, didn't I?"

Everyone still yammering, the females interjected their own insult of the implication that they were not as not as good as the men. The arguing grew louder. Both hot with anger, Tristano and Ronan got in McKabe's face, but the chief climbed slowly to his feet and hitched his belt up.

"We are done here. I will call the Westcotts and see if we, that is you three," he nodded to Tristano, Ronan and Jesa, "can interview them tonight. Koffi and Roarke will take lead," he eyeballed each man sternly, declared, "equal lead, on the investigation."

Ignoring the continued protests, he said calmly, "Now then, you all can wait out in the lobby. Willie-Jean will give you your specific directives, and directions for you Jesa, to the Westcotts' while I call Finn and then the parents." No one moved. He made sweeping motions with his hands. "Go on now, scoot, everyone back to work."

The room cleared except for the chief, Tristano and Jesa. Tristano started, "Listen, Chief, you really can't have her involved like this. I mean, we don't know who the perps are, what, I mean," he glanced with insinuation at Jesa, "she's new here, no one knows her, what if she is involved-"

"Oh!" Jesa squawked. Gathering herself up as tall as she could get on her petite stature, rising up on her toes, hands on her hips, she stuck her furious face in his. "How *dare* you imply that I would steal a baby!"

"You-" Tristano broke off mid-word, his face went completely blank, but something odd flickered in the dark eyes as he stared at Jesa. It was the first he'd seen her eyes, and, his gaze swept up to the knit hat she wore. Thicker wisps of strawberry blonde hair slipped out curling around her face and a few spiraled down and over her shoulders.

When she turned to the sheriff to voice her complaints, Tristano discreetly slipped his phone out partially from his pocket, pushed a few buttons, glanced down at it, then slid it back in his pocket.

"Sheriff," Jesa started, "he can't talk to me like-"

"Okay, okay," McKabe sighed, putting his hands up between them to separate them. He turned his angry glare on Tristano. "That is enough of that shit, Agent. Jesa, darlin'," he turned to her, his face softened, "the county will pay you for your work. Trust me," he winked at her, "you will earn much more than doing odd jobs at the bistro.

Now, go get the directions and a map from Willie-Jean. Oh, and ask her for a pad and pen so you can take notes. We will see if we can get an iPad or something like it for you to use." He waited while she scowled at Tristano and he scowled back. Then, she spun and stomped out of the room. Both men watched her little round bottom twitch irately as she left.

McKabe took a deep breath, "Now," he said, letting it out. "I know you FBI guys like to be in charge, but I run the show on this island, and I think this neutral young woman will keep everything on an even footing. She won't be in the line of danger as she will always be with one of you, and hell, son, you saw that pure innocence shining out of those emerald eyes, there's not a deceitful bone in that curvy little body, eh?" He put his hand on Tristano's arm. "I'm real serious on this, Koffi, things will be done my way or the high way. You got that, son?"

A vein pulsed over the scar at his temple, but improbably, Tristano's face had lost all his objections and anger, the dark eyes were calm. To the chief, it appeared he was almost smiling, as if oddly pleased at the outcome. Pushing his suit coat aside, Tristano tucked a hand in a pocket of his trousers and said without a hint of rancor, "Of course, Chief, I will abide by your orders."

McKabe studied him for a second seeing if there was any sign of disagreement or possible sham in the agent. But Tristano stared coolly at him with direct eye contact. Satisfied he would be in obeisance with his orders, the chief nodded. "Fine then. Go ahead and join Jesa. I will call the Westcotts and tell them you are on your way."

"Of course." Tristano inclined his head slightly in respect, then pivoted and left the room.

When he was finally alone, Chief McKabe sank back down on his chair with a long, heavy exhale. He sure hoped he had made a good decision. "Hmm," he sighed, "time will tell." His instincts already uncanny were honed from years of experience, he seldom made a mistake.

Out in the other room he could hear the officers discussing the particulars of the kidnapping.

"Huh," one of the men sneered, "Brie? Isn't that a cheese?"

Rolling his eyes, McKabe sighed again and pushed to his feet, he needed to make some phone calls.

Chapter Five

In the front room, deputies mingled, discussing the latest events. Eyes shifted like second hands on a clock at Jesa. Willie-Jean supplied Jesa with a notepad and pen and a cell phone. She told her tomorrow she could provide her with an iPad.

At Jesa's protest that she couldn't afford the phone or the iPad, Willie-Jean tsked, "Dear, we have plenty of them. We get them in for new officers. You'll need the iPad to organize and disseminate the information you gather. You absolutely need the phone, you have to be available," she glanced over at the snort from the agent glowering out the window.

"Huh, more like so she can call when she gets lost," Koffi rumbled.

Ignoring him, Jesa accepted the phone from Willie-Jean with a murmured, "Thank you."

Willie-Jean told her, "All the numbers you could possibly need are programmed in it, and I added the agent's," she motioned with her head to Koffi, who snorted again, like, 'don't do me any favors.'

The curvaceous deputy with the butterscotch hair made her way through the throng of gabbing officers, crossing the room to where the agent stood. "Hey," Tahni's voice weighed with practiced husky sexiness.

Placing herself in front of him, she boldly clipped his tie with two fingers and stroked them down the front of his chest. Tilting her head coyly, she cooed, "Hey there, Mr. FBI Agent-man, I'm Tahni. My, what a hard chest you have," her body wriggled with her throaty giggle. "I'm looking forward to working," she moved so they were almost touching, "closely with you."

Tristano didn't lower his head, his eyes dipped briefly to the pretty deputy with the inviting eyes. He said nothing, just coolly watched her paw his chest.

"So," Tahni simpered, bending her head back, lids low in a sultry pose. "Like I said, I can drive you around. I saw that girl's shitty car parked out front. I have a Nissan SUV, plenty of room for big ol' you," her interested gaze tracked down his long legs.

Rolling her eyes at the woman's blatant unprofessional behavior, Jesa walked over to the door, said over her shoulder as she strode out, "If you're coming, Mr. *Agent-man*, the bus is leaving."

Without a word to the prawning deputy, Tristano turned, uncaring of Tahni's frown and trod over to follow Jesa out the door.

When they stepped outside, the wind whipped even more briskly almost blowing Jesa's knit hat off her head. She made a grab for it while juggling the pad and pen, phone, map and directions, at the same time, Koffi snatched her keys out of her hand.

"Hey," Jesa squawked, "give me my keys!"

Having to wrench open the rusted passenger door, he gestured for her to get in. Making it sound like it was McKabe's order, Tristano said, "The chief would want me to drive, Miss Judan, we will arrive to our destination without getting lost, and in one piece. Hop in," he waited with that arrogant glinty smile of his.

Jesa glared at him, looking from the keys in his hand to his smirky face. He was too big, there would be no way she could get them from him. If she stood arguing about it she would only look juvenile. Huffing her annoyance, she slid inside her car, and he closed the door, trotted around to the driver's side.

Reaching inside first for the seat adjustment lever, he shoved the seat back as far as it would go and then climbed in. Even all the way back, his knees embraced the wheel and his head brushed the top of the car. He snagged the map and directions from Jesa. Ignoring her squawk of complaint, he opened the map spreading it over the wheel, and set the directions down on top of it.

"I can't believe GPS doesn't work that great on this rock," he remarked dourly. He'd been stunned when Willie-Jean had confirmed what Jesa had told him.

"You're driving," Jesa said, "I can look at the map and navigate." She held her hand out for the map.

Tristano glanced at her. She had pulled the hat off and finger-combed her long strawberry curls. The sharp wind struck deeper roses in her cheeks and reddened the tip of her small nose, the green eyes shone with the cold air and exhilaration of the meeting they just left.

"Hmm," he made a sound as if he was considering it, then laughed cocky. "Na, Miss Judan, I would like to get there tonight, not at Christmas, or by leaving a trail of run over mailboxes." Grinning at her affronted gasp, he turned the car on, cranked the heat and drove down the street.

Mouth pouty, Jesa gave him a snooty look. "Everyone calls me Miss, why do you all assume I'm not married?"

A mocking sound from Koffi, he twisted his head briefly towards her, then said, "Maybe because you look like you just came out of the schoolroom."

Lips pushed out further, brows down, Jesa said, "I will have you know-"

"Here," he said, tossing the map in her lap, "you study this, figure out the way to the Westcotts'." One big hand covering half the wheel, he bit back a grin at her huff at his way of getting her to shut up.

He had reviewed the map and memorized the directions, so along the way he never asked her where to turn, which way to go, and ignored her when she tried to tell him to go opposite of the way he went. If he followed her directions they would have already driven off the west seawall into the Pacific.

After a mile or so, Tristano pushed and clicked buttons on the heater, growling, "What the hell is the matter with this thing? There's no heat coming out."

Jesa shrugged. "The heater doesn't work. I've been saving up to get it fixed."

Tristano stared in disbelief at the girl. She'd put a jacket on but it was chilly inside the vehicle. The warmth of the sun gone, the blustering wind blew right through the rusty holes. "I'm in damned Hillbilly-ville. How much you need to get it fixed?"

Her mouth pursed then flattened. Turning to face him, she said between tight teeth, "You may be the big boss of this investigation, and you may be able to boss me around regarding the job, but, my personal life and possessions are outside your purview. Do not bring it up again."

Taking in her heated cheeks and flashing eyes, half his mouth hitched up in a snicker. "Purview? Oo," he mocked, "did I just walk into a hifalutin dictionary out here in Jed Clampett land?"

She opened her mouth to retort, saw his mocking lifted chin and shut it. He was trying to push her buttons. They were silent the rest of the way.

Reaching the Westcotts' home, Tristano parked behind the two police cruisers in the driveway. He stood outside the passenger side of the scrappy Epic watching Jesa struggle to get the rusted door open. Stifling his amusement, he gripped the handle and easily jerked it open.

Face hot with embarrassment, without a word she got out, made her way up the driveway and tromped up the few steps to the house. He followed her with a shake of his head and a slight grin. When they rang the bell, a deputy opened the door. Koffi had been briefed that the deputy would be there to give the Westcotts protection, and was also assisting another deputy set up tracers on their phones.

Tristano flashed his ID. "Special Agent Tristano Koffi," he announced to the deputy. Inclined his head to Jesa, "Miss Judan."

"Yes sir." The deputy introduced himself, "Deputy Gomez. Deputy Osborne is inside. There was a problem with the tracers Osborne initially set up. He's brought new ones and is installing them now." He stepped aside to let Tristano and Jesa enter the house.

The home was a huge, luxurious, white brick two-story mansion. Stedman Westcott was a broker at the satellite exchange in town, and he did quite well. It was assumed the baby had been taken for ransom.

"Anything yet?" Tristano asked the deputy quietly as Gomez led them from the open vestibule and through the house.

With a sad shake of his head, Gomez replied, "No sir. The phone has barely rung. Chief McKabe advised the Westcotts to ask their family and friends not to call and tie the lines up." His mouth tugged, shrugging one shoulder he said baldly, "They are to tell their family and such if they have info about the kidnapping to contact the police immediately, not waste time discussing things with the Westcotts."

Tristano nodded as they entered a large drawing room. To the left of the chicly designed room were two enormous arched windows bordered in mahogany, and to the right of the windows showcased a black and gold fireplace with family photos arranged on the wide marble mantel.

The walls ivory, black-framed furniture with vivid, red leather cushions matched the splash of red in the abstract painting over the mantel. The sofa and several large, matching chairs faced each other in front of the fireplace. The carpet, a duskier shade of ivory than the walls had threads of red and beige woven through it.

Elizabeth and Stedman Westcott sat on the sofa watching Deputy Osborne tinkering with their landline. Both Westcotts' cells lay next to it on a large, glass coffee table. At the newcomers' entrance, Stedman rose. Elizabeth, dabbing at her red dripping eyes, stared at the floor, her chest hitching with her weeping.

Tristano approached and said with quiet authority, "Mr. Westcott," he held out his hand. "I am Special Agent Koffi with the FBI, and this is…" he motioned to Jesa at his side, "*Miss* Judan." The side of his mouth twitched at the sound Jesa made.

Wearing a buttoned-down blue shirt and tie, and sharply creased black pants, Stedman nodded. "Agent Koffi, Ms. Judan," he shook Tristano's hand and inclined his head politely to Jesa.

"Yes, um…" Jesa clutched her notepad to her chest. "Please call me Jesa, I am so sorry to hear about Brie's…abduction. We hope to find her and bring her home."

Tristano wound his fingers around her arm and gave it a squeeze. "Ah, yes, that is, we will do everything we can to find your daughter." Canting his head slightly he gave Jesa a small frown.

The doorbell rang drawing everyone's attention. Deputy Gomez went to answer it, and returned ushering Deputy Ronan Roarke in. While they were distracted, Tristano whispered in Jesa's ear, "Do not speak. You are here to take notes. You are not the police and may give an incorrect impression, we can't make promises we might not be able to keep."

Scalded by his scolding, putting her in her place, Jesa bit her tongue and lowered her eyes to hide her reaction.

The men gathered in a circle, Jesa went and sat down beside Elizabeth but kept a distance so she wasn't intruding on her grief. Holding her pad on her lap with both hands, she turned to Elizabeth with a compassionate, soft smile. Without a glance in Koffi's direction, Jesa disregarded the dictatorial agent's instructions, and said, "Mrs. Westcott, I am so sorry for the horror you are enduring, if you need someone to talk to, or pray with, please know I am here for you."

Patting her eyes with the sodden tissue, Elizabeth wiped her nose, her watery smile tremulous she said, "I...I ...thank you, Officer."

"But I'm not an," Jesa looked at the pretty woman with wide blonde curls that danced on her shuddering shoulders. Knowing she was a mother of an infant, Jesa had expected her to be dressed a bit on the domestic side. She was surprised to see she wore a short skirt and the yellow scalloped blouse was cut relatively low, almost scandalously low.

Elizabeth wiped at the mascara that ran under her eyes. Her lipstick was shiny. A tiny smudge of scarlet on her teeth indicated she had recently applied, or re-applied the lipstick. Even as she wept, Elizabeth opened the purse she clutched on her lap and took out a compact. Studying her reflection, she fluffed her blonde curls.

Because Tristano's mouth straightened into a tight frown at Jesa, a repeated admonition for her to keep quiet, she didn't correct Elizabeth's wrong assumption that she was an officer. But she patted her hand gently then stood up and moved a few feet away.

Ronan, Deputy Gomez, and Stedman Westcott assembled where Deputy Osborne was working on the phone. Seeing the others occupied, Jesa stuck her tongue out at Tristano. His brows arched at her impudence, then lowered back down in warning over dark eyes as formidable as chiseled cinders.

Jesa's cheeks flamed at her behavior, she must look farcical. Here he was, face grave with the seriousness of the case, standing tall and broad shouldered in an impeccable suit and tie, and she was half his size wearing jeans and a worn jacket, and she was making juvenile faces at him. No wonder he treated her like she was a child. But darn wasn't the arrogant man irritating.

"So," Tristano murmured and moved to stand in front of Elizabeth on the couch. Stedman stood kitty-corner to his wife near the glass and marble coffee table. "Mr. and Mrs. Westcott, can you tell us if you have

35

any idea of anyone that could have done this?" He nodded his head at Jesa.

She blinked at him, then started. She forgot she was there to take notes. She pulled the pen from her pocket and set the point on the pad ready to write. Tristano took out a small tape recorder from his pocket. He turned it on and set it on the coffee table. All eyes went to it.

"It is necessary for the accuracy of our notes, we can replay things later, maybe have fresh ears listen that might pick up on something we missed. So, Mr. Westcott," Koffi drew the young husband's attention back to him said, "you were telling us if you know of anyone that would want to extort money from you, or hurt your family."

A gagging sound burst from the couch as Elizabeth clutched her throat. "Hurt? You think they will hurt my Brie? Oh Stedman," she cried.

Her husband rushed and sat down beside her with his arm draped around her shoulders. "There, there," he frowned at Tristano, "no one said she would be hurt. Maybe they just want money, we will pay, and Brie will come home." He patted her arm and rebuked Tristano, "Agent, really, is it necessary to upset my wife? You can see how distraught she is."

His face a mask of naught emotion, voice just as blank, Tristano replied calmly, "If we are to find your daughter, Mr. Westcott, we have to ask questions. We are seeking leads. Now, can you answer my question?" Catching Jesa's wince at his coldness to the bereft couple, he reminded her, "Notes, *Ms.* Judan."

"But the recorder-"

Koffi stated crisply, "Can malfunction. Your job is to take notes, please do so." He had also told her on the ride over to write down any observations she made of the people, the surroundings, their words, the way people looked at each other, especially when they don't realize they are being observed.

As a non-officer, people thinking she was incidental and unimportant may say things in front of her that they wouldn't with LEO, that is Law Enforcement Officer's ears around. He'd made her feel like a negligible flowerpot. "Sit down, Ms. Judan, so you can write," a harsh note marked his voice.

"Here now." Ronan stepped forward with a glower. Seeing Jesa's cheeks pink from the reprimand, he said, "Calm your liver you gump, lay off the girl, there's no need to be discourteous."

His body stiff, Tristano barely turned his head to the deputy. "She has a job to do, as do we. Again," he addressed Stedman, "anyone come to mind?" The tension in the room intensified with the agent's cold admonishments.

Everyone now even more on edge, Stedman blinked at Koffi. The suffering father was attractive with chestnut hair combed straight back off his forehead, at such a young age lines already lanced his dark blue eyes. Hands on his trim hips he coughed, cleared his throat. "Ah, let's see," he considered the question. "There are of course occasionally disgruntled clients that lost money, but, no," he shook his head thoughtfully. "I can't think of anyone that would do this, take an innocent child and-" At his wife's sob, he patted her arm making shushing sounds.

Ronan asked, "Have you received any threats recently? Any damage to your vehicles? Graffiti on your house? Hang up phone calls? Any strangers in the neighborhood? Think of any maintenance people, phone, cable company, anyone that is not normally around. And, the servants, have any of them been caught stealing, brought friends around, or not shown up for work? Nanny issues? Currently, we brought in the staff you listed and they are being interviewed at the station."

Both Westcotts' foreheads wrinkled and their eyes moved back and forth as they reviewed the past weeks in their minds, trying to remember anything that could have been perceived as unusual or a threat. Sharing a glance with his tearful wife, Stedman shook his head. "No, we can't think of a thing."

"Ah." Tristano shot a discrete look at Ronan.

Ronan slanted his head to him then said calmly to Stedman, "Um, Mr. Westcott, I could use a glass of water…" He waited until Westcott nodded, "Of course, come this way." Ronan followed Stedman down a long corridor heading to the kitchen so the couple could subtly be questioned separately.

When they left, Tristano perched on the thick arm of the cushioned chair Jesa was sitting on. Ignoring her edging away from him, he said calmly, "Mrs. Westcott, please don't take offense, these are standard questions we have to ask." He paused while she wiped her eyes and turned to him. "How is your marriage? Any, ah, changes lately?"

She pondered with her blonde brows low. "No, I mean, there are no changes. Stedman works very long hours, actually, we don't really see much of each other." A hint of bitterness underscored her tone. Realizing this, she sat up straighter, blinked a few times and said firmly, "No, our marriage is just fine."

"Finances? Any issues lately with money? Late notices in the mail, anything like that?"

Elizabeth's face darkened. Forehead furrowing, she tossed her yellow hair back with her nose raised. "Of course not. What a thing to ask," her lids lowered, she tipped her head up regarding him with indignation.

"Who pays the bills, Mrs. Westcott? Are you involved with any of that?" Tristano's expression remained blank, voice even, nonjudgmental or accusatory.

Rolling her eyes with an annoyed sigh, Elizabeth shook her head with a stiff smile, then swallowed her pique and smiled sweetly up at him. "No, Agent Koffi. Actually, Stedman takes care of all the finances, I unfortunately have no head for figures, keeping track of money."

A short laugh, she went on, "He makes it and I spend it. Isn't that the way it's supposed to be?" Her head cocked, the smile turned coquettish with a few batted eyelashes. "Don't tell me you make your wife pay the bills?" Although she'd had a baby six months ago, her body was trim, she crossed shapely legs, the skirt rose exposing part of her thigh.

Before he could answer, shaking her head with a crafty smile, her candid eyes frisked his brawny body, she said, "No, not an arrogant dominating alpha like you, you would want control of..." she almost sounded like she was flirting, "everything. Isn't that true, Agent?"

Expression implacable, his jaw flexed and cheeks sharpened. Not responding to her question, Tristano bulldozed right on. "What about, difficulties?" He paused to take the sting out of his words, "Ah, affairs? Either one of you-"

"No!" Elizabeth spurted angrily, all flirtatiousness gone. "No, of course not, we are good, very good, there are no problems in our marriage." She sniffed in irritation, smoothed her skirt down to cover her thighs. "He works hard to support his family, and I take care of our home and baby."

His face a blank veneer, Tristano said, "Of course. I wasn't implying anything, as I said, these are standard questions we have to ask." He was quiet a moment letting her settle back down.

Jesa got up from her chair and sat beside Elizabeth on the couch. Writing some notes, she absently patted Elizabeth's shoulder unconsciously comforting her.

Tristano's eyes on Jesa, he asked Elizabeth, "How about anything strange that has happened? Any unexpected guests? People in the neighborhood you've never seen before? I understand there is an ebb and flow of people leaving the island, and boats filled with winter supplies arriving with strangers on them. Anything seem…amiss?"

Her lashes fluttered as the pretty woman thought. Shaking her head, the blonde curls swept over her shoulders. Using her pinky she pushed a few strands that stuck on her lashes, then, her head listed thoughtfully. Eyes lowered in remembrance, she replied, "Oh, wait, now that I think about it," her red lips thrust out as she thought back.

"Yes?" Tristano inclined his head to Jesa to make sure she was writing. Jesa tore her focus from Elizabeth and attended to her pad.

Crushing the wet tissue in her hand, Elizabeth plucked at her skirt. She uncrossed her legs then crossed her ankles and moved her legs to the side. Surprisingly, she wore very high heels inside when she was obviously not going anywhere.

She said, "When you mention stranger, well, Stedman and I had a party a few nights ago. Most of the people we knew, but some guests had brought along friends. There was a group doing a shoot on the island. They were photographing models for some magazine or something. There were three models," she dissed sourly, "if you can call those lollipop sticks models, all huge heads and no bodies. Anyway, with them, there was this oh, fashion designer he said he was. They were partly his concoctions, the bikinis the girls were modeling."

When she paused, Tristano prompted, "Yes, go ahead, what about this designer?"

"Well," she sniffed with a shrug, "he got stinking drunk. Maddened his models with slurry filthy talk and a few gropings, they slipped around trying to avoid him. Later, one of the nannies came to me and said she'd gone into the baby's room to check on her and she found the designer in there. I mean," her forehead drew down, "he had no business, no reason to be in there. The nanny said it was odd because he seemed to have the side of his head against one of the walls near the crib. Stedman sent a security man to retrieve him."

"What did he say when he was brought back downstairs?"

One shoulder rose dismissively. "Oh, he said he was looking for the bathrooms. We have so many in the house. But the nursery hardly looks like a bathroom for heaven's sake." Beside her, Jesa scribbled away on her pad.

"I see. What was his name?"

"Oh, dear." Elizabeth's eyes closed as she tried to recall. "Um, let me see, it was Emile, no- no, it was Niles something, oh, Ninacola I think it was. Something like that."

"Do you know the name of the magazine?"

Elizabeth's eyes were the color of plums, whether they were natural or contacts wasn't detectable, they turned up as she tried to recall. "Oh," she sighed, then smiled at Tristano with a shrug. "I really can't remember. I didn't care enough to ask. Stedman might know." Her expression stiffened, lips thinned, "He spent plenty of time talking with the models."

Tristano kept his expression flat, not acknowledging the resentment that had crept into her voice, but Jesa paused with her writing. Just then Ronan and the husband returned.

Jesa moved from the couch giving Stedman the space to join his wife. But he stood a few feet away with his hands in his pockets. A hardening of his jaw coincided with the tugging of the side of his mouth as he contemplated his wife. Stedman's long sleeves were now rolled up and his tie loosened.

Ronan came up alongside Jesa and gave her a warm smile. "Hey, sweetheart, how's it going?" She shyly smiled back up at the good-looking deputy in his brown uniform but said nothing.

"Well, then, that should do for now. We'll be on our way," Tristano said, picking up the recorder from the table, he clicked it off and handed it to Jesa. They started for the door when Tristano hesitated, turning back, he said to Mr. Westcott, "Sir, your wife was telling us about an incident regarding an out-of-town designer that was at your party last week?" He caught Stedman's peculiar gaze at his wife.

Still looking grimly at his wife, Stedman crossed his arms. Resting an elbow on his arm, he rubbed his chin, question in his expression.

Ronan stopped and set his hand on Jesa's lower back and whispered in her ear. Tristano's eyes narrowed at them, but he said politely to Stedman, "There was something about this man being found in the baby's room?"

Not remembering at first, then he blinked, said, "Oh yes, yes. That goofy skinny guy wearing plaid pants and striped shirt. Hell," he shook his head with wry mirth, "they say anything goes these days, but seriously? He looked like a geek with mismatched clothes and the big glasses that made his eyes real big. Flying hair sticking out everywhere. Right honey? Wasn't he a dork?"

For the first time a genuine mild smile lifted Elizabeth's face. "Yes, but I really paid him little attention; he was obviously not someone to be known." She smiled at Ronan and Tristano. "If you know what I mean. He was clearly a nobody."

"Hmm, yes," Tristano murmured noncommittal. "Anyway, Mr. Westcott, do you know the name of the magazine they were doing the shoot for, or where they are staying?"

Stedman replied, "Sure. They're staying at the Hotel Clasibella down the bottom of the hill where the Pipistrel Park is. It's less than a mile away from the park overlooking the water. They had to hike down from the Commons as there's no vehicle access to the park. They used the ornamental bridge for photos and also did some scenes by the ocean."

Elizabeth's head jerked to her husband with a frown. "How do you know that? You're at work all day."

A bit sheepish, his neck reddened, Stedman answered, "Uh, yeah, well, we grabbed a couple of quick lunches at the bistro. You could see the shoot from up there."

Looking down at her pad while she scribbled notes, Jesa commented, "You really can't see clear to the bridge from inside, you would have to be way out on the back patio to see to the water."

His wife's eyes narrowed further. "What were-"

"Ah," Tristano cut her off with a stern look to Jesa who looked up in time to see it. "Anyway, Mr. Westcott, do you remember the designer's name or the name of the magazine?"

Ducking his head, Stedman stuffed his hands in his trouser pockets and bumped his shoulders. "The guy's name is Niels Normandy. The name of the magazine is 'Flaunt This.' Uh, you want the girls' names too?" He dodged the sharp glare from his wife.

"Uh huh," Koffi said with a nod. "How did they end up at your party?"

Nervously rerolling his sleeves, avoiding looking at his wife, he admitted, "Ah, a couple of times we trotted down the hill and watched them film up close. We, uh," he glanced at Elizabeth then quickly away at the infuriated storm brewing in her pretty face.

"We all got to talking, and, uh, I invited them. I mean," he shrugged, "they were visiting and didn't know anyone here, and, uh, well, the girls were shivering in their bikinis, I was just trying to be friendly..."

Keeping his mouth flat as if he fought to keep a straight face, Tristano said to Jesa, "Give him your pad, Ms. Judan," to Stedman, "go ahead and write down their names and everything you can remember about them."

While they waited, Ronan spoke quietly with Jesa. Elizabeth scowled at her husband as he wrote the names down, the red in his neck squirmed up to his ears with her staring daggers at his back. Tristano coolly watched everyone, filing away all his thoughts and images.

When Stedman handed the pad back to Jesa, Tristano said, "All right then, we will of course be in touch. Deputy Gomez or Deputy Osborne," he nodded to the man working on the landline, "will let us know if you get any calls or think of something pertinent that could help. They will also guard you, you need to stay safely inside your home. Oh," he pulled Jesa's keys out of his pocket, "we know Brie's foot and fingerprints are on file with the hospital but we need a picture of her. The most current you have."

Jesa bit back a grin. Everyone was looking curiously at the big tough G-man holding the sparkly pink key ring.

Throwing a dirty look at her husband whose neck still heated red, Elizabeth said, "I'll get one." She stalked in a snit of petulance out of the room, her high heels clacking hard on the tiled floor in the hallway, indicating Stedman was in for some heavy chewing out when they were alone.

They all waited in silence until she returned and handed the picture to Koffi. He tucked it in a pocket inside his coat, and Deputy Gomez saw them to the door.

Outside on the step, Ronan pulled Jesa nearer to him and offered, "Listen, it's late, why don't you let the agent take your rattrap to his hotel and I'll give you a lift home."

Surprised, Jesa gaped at him, her mouth open, not sure what to say. She looked to Tristano; he was facing away as if he could care less what any of them did. Her mouth pressed, she said, "Fine. That's a great idea. Can you find your way, Agent Koffi?" she asked with derisive sweetness.

His face the normal mask of blankness, Tristano replied, "Of course, Ms. Judan, I can read a map." He twisted the car key off the pink key ring and handed the ring to Jesa. His eyes flicked to Ronan. "Remember we have to meet early in the morning and prepare for the press release."

His gaze veered back to Jesa. "No late night, I will pick you up at seven." Without waiting for her response, he spun and tramped to her car, folded his long body and climbed in smoothly. As he drove off, Jesa called out, "Wait- my address, don't you need my-"

"Don't worry, sugar." Ronan slid his arm around her and walked to his cruiser and opened the passenger side for her to get in. "He's FBI, trust me, he already knows where you live."

Misgiving crimping her forehead, Jesa slid inside the cruiser. It could be true, Koffi had been tapping at his phone in between interrogating the Westcotts. Who knows what information he had been gleaning?

Ronan hopped in the driver's side and chatted nonstop all the way to her miniature cottage. When he stopped in front of the bungalow, just as he put the car in park Jesa jumped out before he could turn the engine off. Through his open window, he said quickly, "Hey, hon, wait a sec, let me walk you to the door."

Shaking her head with a small smile, Jesa said, "No, I'm fine, it's only a few steps," and she turned towards the house.

"But, wait- Jesa," he leaned out the window, "I could use a cup of coffee, what do you say-"

Looking away from his disappointed handsome face, she waved over her shoulder and tossed back, "Sorry, I'm fresh out, see you at the station in the morning! Thanks for bringing me home," she rushed up the step, hurried inside and quickly closed the door.

Inside the safety of her hut nest, she leaned her back against the door, held her breath and tensely waited. When she heard his truck drive off she let out the retained breath. The deputy was very good-looking with his thick sandy hair and sparkling blue eyes, shoulders like a linebacker, he was really a hot guy. But, she moved slowly to the front window, pushed the curtain aside just an inch to peer out and make sure he was gone.

There was no way she could date a man, especially one in law enforcement. She couldn't build a relationship with him on lies, and she couldn't stick around forever, she'd been found before and barely gotten away in time. No, shaking her head sadly, she headed to the tiny kitchen to make a cup of tea; there would be no handsome prince for her, ever.

Chapter Six

Agent Koffi was supposed to pick Jesa up in the morning but Willie-Jean called and informed her he had been told by Chief McKabe he wanted him to be at the press conference hours before the scheduled event to supervise the setup, the media, prep everyone involved, and help the Westcotts rehearse their pleas for the safe return of their baby.

Willie-Jean said, "The chief thought things would keep on more stringent guidelines and timelines if the FBI agent was organizing and running the conference. Agent Koffi had to be at the auditorium by 5:00 AM, so, Chief sent Deputy Genarino to come and get you, Jesa, honey. Don't forget your pad and pen, okay?"

Holding the loaned cell to her ear with her shoulder, Jesa chowed down a bowl of cereal and gulped a quick orange juice. Through a mouthful of Fruit loops, she mumbled, "Lorda mercy, okay, yeah, sure. When should I expect her?"

"Well, she should actually have been there by now. Agent Koffi said he wanted everyone in place and prepped before the media flocked to the stage. She isn't there? She should be in a cruiser…"

"Maybe she got a little lost?" Jesa offered, setting her bowl in the sink and turning the faucet on to rinse it.

"No, Tahni has lived here for years; she knows the island like the back of her hand. But she really should have been there by now, oh dear, I'll call Agent-"

"No, no, Willie-Jean, don't do that, I don't want to cause a disturbance." She made a sound in the back of her throat. "I won't be missed anyway. Don't worry, I'm sure she'll be here any sec-"

45

"Wait," Willie-Jean said. Jesa could hear her talking to someone on another phone. She got back to Jesa, "I dialed Officer Genarino on my cell. Oh honey, I'm sorry, Tahni said she got caught up in something," under her breath she muttered, "more likely under someone." She cleared her throat. "Uh, so she forgot, anyway, she said give her 20-30 minutes and she will be on her way. Jesa, dear, I'm so sorry-"

"No, no," Jesa sighed, used to being overlooked. "It's not your fault."

Willie-Jean replied, "I know, but, you know Agent Koffi, he's so, you know…tough. I hate for him to be mad at you for throwing a wrench into the works."

"Huh," Jesa grunted. "I don't think I'm important enough to be a wrench," then she laughed pushing aside the self-pity. "Don't worry, everything will be okay."

"It's actually Tahni's fault, but that woman always manages to slide out from under a stinking pile of poop without getting any of it on her. All right dear, I have to go, the lines are ringing." Willie-Jean hung up with a hasty goodbye.

"Goodbye," Jesa said to the dead line and stuffed the cell in her pocket. She picked up a small backpack, put in the notepad and recorder, added her fake ID and stolen SS card and tossed in a ten-dollar bill, all the money she currently had, and went to stand by the window.

The cottage was a one bedroom with kitchen, living room, and even had a tiny morning room to enjoy a good book. An old grill sat on a few slates out back and Jesa had hoped soon she could afford maybe a steak and could grill it and watch the sun set over the Commons. The bungalow was in a good location to view up where she could see a microscopic part of the Square through the trees.

She glanced at the clock. She was going to be so late. As much as she had demurred to Willie-Jean that it was no big deal as she was nobody to the investigation, still, Willie-Jean was right about the agent. Koffi had such a hard, even ruthless glint in his dark eyes and strong jaw that gave her a quiver of nerves. He'd been so cold and threatening ever since she'd picked him up at the wharf, she hated to be the brunt of his wrath.

He had fists the size of footballs and looked like the type that knew how to use them, without hesitation. Not that he would hit her...really. After all, he was the police. No, he was an FBI agent and she saw enough TV to know they often ran outside the box, stepped over the legal line. She could picture the tough, powerful, arrogant man in a fury lashing out at her with his fists just for being tardy-

That's it, she needed to go. She'd grow antsy waiting for Tahni Genarino, maybe she'd run into her along the way on the road. Tossing on a jacket, she locked the door and started up the street.

A resort town, the homes had sprung up as the population grew so the neighborhoods were a medley of mixed potpourri, some cottages clustered together, others were spread wide apart. Fishing charters, whale watching excursions, hiking, extravagant hotel views on the seaside, art galleries, much of the island's income was in tourism. A good many residents were extremely wealthy, or retired so they didn't require employment.

After a few minutes, Jesa traipsed past the small houses on her street and turned onto one of the roads that led up to the Commons. Thankfully it was a gently sloping incline so it wasn't too arduous to travel.

Down by the shoreline the residences started flat along the seawalls like grouped rustic fishing hamlets. Grand mansions and A-framed red roofs mingled with squat shacks. Some homes had sea nets and lobster traps strewn about in their back yards, all sizes of boats and orange buoys bobbed behind houses on the water. Above them, more dwellings were gathered in loose constellations, groves of trees bracketed everything; cottages and woodlands staggered asymmetrically up the hill.

At dawn and dusk this time of year the marine layer mist rolled in completely enveloping some parts to almost total invisibility, only tips of chimneys or treetops could be seen. The fog cloaked wide sections of the mottled buildings and the dark green forests.

Higher up, the forest was denser, then closer to the top of the hill the trees pared back and the cottages started again. Jesa's bungalow was in those stacked clusters. The Commons commanded the land above.

It was getting chillier every day, she should have brought her mittens, but she'd been in such a hurry to avoid the agent's anger she rushed out without them. Air puffed white from her mouth with her increasingly strenuous breaths, the wind struck at intervals slapping her face raw and kicking up her hair.

Jesa moved faster hoping it would warm her up. It was only a couple of miles to the Commons. She was now traipsing along an area that was wooded on both sides, there were no homes, although in the summer up ahead there would be fruit and vegetable stands.

In a dark suit and dark blue tie, Agent Koffi glanced to the main door. As each minute passed, he looked there more and more frequently. Around him surged mild hustling chaos. As much as he'd tried to rein everyone in, the rural folks were all atwitter with the unusual goings on and ran around in excitement not listening to instructions.

Reporters that had traveled from the mainland gathered in front of the small stage chattering while setting up cameras and microphones. The local radio station's news personality had center stage and was conferring with Chief McKabe.

Deputy Tahni Genarino followed Koffi around like a horny voluptuous shadow. He kept sending her on errands to keep her from pawing him. Deputies wandered around trying to corral people and keep a semblance of order. Tristano impatiently jerked his phone out and called the station.

Willie-Jean's cheerful voice answered, "Orainn Police, how may I help you?"

Without preamble he barked, "This is Agent Koffi, where the hell is Ms. Judan?"

There was silence, then he heard the receptionist catch her breath, the cheerfulness faded. "Uh, well, sir, Chief McKabe sent Deputy Genarino to pick her up. Tahni said she was running a little late and should be there by-"

"What the fuck-" Tristano snapped. "Genarino is here." He clicked his phone off and yelled, "Deputy Genarino, get over here!"

A huge smile lit up the face of the pin-up woman with the butterscotch hair braided around her head. She hurried through the growing crowd to him letting her body jiggle as much as possible in hopes of using her body to hook in her claws and reel the barbarous agent in.

When she reached him, face riling dark, Koffi snapped, "Where the hell is the girl?"

Looking confused, Tahni blinked sapphire blues at him, asked, "What girl?"

Biting back his ire, his voice taut with the struggle to harness his impatience, Tristano said tersely, "Ms. Judan, you were to pick her up. Where hell is she?"

Red flushed over Tahni's face, her eyes flashed with annoyance. "Oh really, she's just a nuisance, I have more important things to do than-"

"*Fuck,*" Koffi barked and turned from her swiping his phone. He had been avoiding calling her, but now he dialed Jesa's number. It rang, no voice mail. He dialed again, it rang, and rang. He called Finn Barton at the bistro.

"Yello, we're Divine today, how about you?" Finn greeted in his normal buoyant manner.

"Mr. Barton, this is Agent Koffi, I'm at the community center. Ms. Judan is expected here and her ride didn't show, she doesn't answer her phone, do you-"

"She's probably on her way, Agent," Finn told him.

"I have her car, she has no vehicle-"

Finn spoke over him, "She'd walk, Agent. She walks here all the time to conserve gas. I mean," he chuckled, "she doesn't say that but we know that's why. It's a few miles, we tell her she shouldn't but," he chuckled again, "that girl is as stubborn as a salmon swimming up-"

Koffi shoved his phone in his pocket. Throwing on his trench coat he stalked out the door. The cold wind bunted his body like an icy fist as soon as he opened the door.

Pulling on gloves, he hopped in Jesa's piece of crap car and drove towards the main road that led to her house. He'd studied the map, memorized most of Orainn Island, the many tributary roads, and knew where Jesa lived.

Actually, he had passed by there on his way to the hotel last night telling himself it was so he could find it easily in the morning. Seeing no vehicle in the driveway, he hadn't felt any relief. Roarke could have brought her to his place. Streaking away, feeling like a stalker he'd driven straight to his hotel.

Tristano's room was in the front on the third floor of the Copper Candle Hotel overlooking a fountain with vintage white wrought-iron chairs set out on varnished pavers for the guests' use.

The hotel was painted soft beige, with more decorative wrought iron, white columns, and a white slatted railing like a picket fence that surrounded all floors of the building. Quaint wide shutters painted crayon colors like in the Caribbean framed mullioned windows. In the back courtyard, if it was warm enough to swim, a blue pool shimmered invitingly.

Winding down the hill, Tristano passed colorful cottages. Autumn had come in an instant; many yards still had withered flowers in their yards. Leaves dropping from the trees tossed around in the wind like confetti in a fan. The forest of dense fir trees crept in on the sides, craggily eating up the worn tar and pebbled narrow curving road.

A heavy mist still lingered making the border of trees blurry, and thick fogginess impaired the view up the road making it like driving through a serpentine, hazy grey tunnel. He thought, the girl was insane to be walking on this blind lane deathtrap.

After a mile he spotted her trudging up the hill like an apparition emerging from the clouds. Her strawberry blonde hair was like a beacon. It might be on the cusp of winter but the morning sun was wintry bright and it sliced through the fog shining off her vibrant hair like a wind-whipped brilliant river.

He pulled up by her on the other side of the narrow road. The dumb bitch didn't even look at him, her hands were shoved in her pockets, her head bowed against the blasting wind.

"Dammit," he cursed a blue streak and rolled down the window. Yeah, rolled, the damned car had no electric nothing. He stuck his head out the window and shouted, "Girl!" Of course she kept going and didn't look up. He turned the car around and drove alongside her and stopped, "Ms. Judan, get in the goddamned car!"

Now she heard him, her head jerked up. Eyes rounded in surprise at seeing him. She stopped walking but didn't move towards the car.

50

Patience never one of his virtues, he barked at her, "Get in the fucking car; we have to get to the goddamned press conference." He leaned over and shoved the passenger door. It stuck, he gave it a hard shove and it opened with a groaning squeak.

She blinked at him, strands of curry golden hair swirled around her head. "Oh," her voice held trepidation, but she didn't dare defy his order. Clearly he would come out and get her if she didn't do as he said. Sweeping the backpack off her shoulder she climbed in the car. As soon as she closed the door to the brutal wind and buckled her seatbelt he took off.

Holding the backpack on her lap, Jesa turned to see his angry profile and stammered, "Wh-why uh, aren't you at the community center?"

Big hands gripping the wheel he tossed his head at her, raked down her shivering body and then back to the road. "Because you are part of the team, and you weren't there. What the hell is the matter with you anyway? Leaving the house in this chill, no hat, no gloves, walking that narrow, winding, fog blinded dark road alone."

Jesa rubbed her freezing hands together, kept her eyes aimed out the front window. "I don't have a hat on because it's in here," she nodded at the knit cap stuffed between their seats. His frown deepened realizing she didn't have protection for her head because he had commandeered her car.

She said, "My ride didn't show up, and I was," the words *afraid of your wrath* hung in the air but she didn't say them. "I didn't want to be late. It's no big deal, Mr. Koffi, I walk to work all the time."

"Huh," he grunted, "and home in the goddamned dark too I bet. Here," he tugged his gloves off and tossed them in her lap, ordered, "put those on, don't argue."

Her lips pulled in, she said with chagrin, "Some people have to work with what they have, Mr. Koffi." Reluctantly pulling his big gloves on her small hands, forgetting the way he made her feel nervous, she chided, "Jeepers you have a filthy mouth. Your mama never wash out your mouth with soap?"

His face impassive, the vein at his temple beat, he stared wordless at the road. They were almost to the community center where the press meeting was being held. His silence unnerved her, but assuming he had

51

just happened to be passing by, she asked, again, "Really, why are you out here, how come you're not at the conference?"

Facing the road, he said blandly, "I told you. Because one of the team didn't show, and I understood she was foolishly trotting up several miles along a dangerous piece of road, in the dark, in the cold, and if she didn't get abducted, raped and murdered, she'd likely die of hypothermia."

Brows high in disbelief like he was making up ghost stories for around the campfire, she spouted, "Oh poo, that's silly. This is a resort village; nothing's going to happen to me. You didn't need to-"

"Ms. Judan, I am a Federal Agent and in charge of this investigation, I will even override Chief McKabe if I have to. Everyone is my responsibility. I came to retrieve you, I did, and we're here."

Tristano parked the car, turned off the ignition. As he opened his door, he said, "Magical land or not, an innocent baby has been stolen, do you really think there is no evil here?" Without waiting for her to respond, he got out.

He came around to her side while she fumbled trying to push the cantankerous rusted door open. He grabbed the handle and jerked it open. Snagging her pack off her lap, he wrapped his fingers around her arm and helped her out.

As Jesa stepped out, the wind shoved her back against the car. On top of the hill without the blocking trees the wind had full range to blow. His trench coat whipping at his ankles, Tristano rolled his arm around her pulling her from the vehicle, bundled her against him and closed the door. She held her hand out for the key; he stuffed it in his pocket and drew her to the Center.

The wind bashed at them, tried several times to rip her from his arm but he held her tightly and propelled her inside.

As soon as they cleared the doorway, Tristano shut the door against the nasty wind and handed her the backpack. A few people glanced over at their abrupt entrance.

Clasping the backpack against her chest, Jesa said breathlessly, "Um, thank you for coming to get me. You really didn't have to." Her eyes dropped to his pocket. "And if you would give me my car back I wouldn't have to walk."

Face blank, he said, "Rumor has it that you would be walking anyway." They paused just inside the door, he glowered down at her. "The phone McKabe gave you would be more useful if you answered it or at the very least programmed the goddamned voice mail."

Her cheeks reddened more than from the wind. "It was in my backpack, I didn't hear it ring. And, well, it's really not, it isn't mine. I will be returning it, no one is going to want to have to record over my-"

"Really, Ms. Judan, does everything with you have to be a fight? Just do it. Put the damn thing in your pocket and when I call or text and if you don't answer, I expect you to respond immediately to my message. Regardless of where you are or what you are doing. Am I clear?"

Lips bunched with her frown, Jesa turned to walk away from him, but he caught her arm and held her. She looked pointedly at his hand around her arm and up to him; he didn't release her.

Jerking her head to toss her long hair back, she pulled off his gloves, handed them to him and said, "Mr. Koffi, you are not my boss, not my sergeant, stop barking orders at me. Now, we have jobs to do, let go of me."

His fingers only wound more tightly around her arm as she tried to pull from his grasp. His grip remaining just shy of painful, he leaned his face so close to hers she felt his breath warm on her skin, steel stabbed at her from his dark formidable eyes.

Koffi's voice was just as hard and sharp. "We need to come to an understanding, Ms. Judan. I *am* in charge of you and don't you even think otherwise. You will not ever hesitate to follow my directives. You will set up the voice mail today. Furthermore, from now on, since you can't be trusted, I will be your ride, everywhere. To and from, everywhere. You want to go to the store or the movies or whatever, you will call me and I will chauffeur you."

"But it's my car-"

"As the law, I am appropriating it. I will keep if filled with gas. Since no one on this rock has an iota of responsibility, I will be your ride everywhere. We already have a kidnapped child; I don't need another little girl missing on my watch. I repeat, you call me if you need to go anywhere, at all. You do not trot around the fucking countryside alone, especially in the dark. If I catch you again, trust me, there will be

53

punishment, Ms. Judan, you hear me? Errant children that risk their lives recklessly get spanked to teach them not to do it again."

"What! What?" she sputtered aghast at the audacity of his dictatorship.

That's it." He held up a hand to stop her protest. "Done with the discussion. You heard me, you have been warned. Now, go stand beside the Westcotts so they feel someone is with them that is not instructing them endlessly on what to say and how to look. You are good with the compassion shit, go do it with them."

"But, you can't- I don't-"

As usual, he cut her off, "Go, Ms. Judan, do as I say. You can comb your hair on the way to the stage." He calmly stared down at her, she glared up at him. Jesa broke eye contact first, and with a huff she turned, and flinched as if he'd smacked her on the butt. He hadn't, but, she peeked over her shoulder, he was staring blankly under hooded lids at her, one side of his mouth edged up.

Teeth set, she fisted her hands, after his threat of a spanking, the smack was definitely implied. "Oo, the nerve of the man!" Swinging her head in a tiff, she stalked off towards the stage, remembering halfway there about his rude comment to comb her hair. "How dare he talk to me that way!" Unzipping the backpack with indignant fingers, she pulled her brush out and brushed the wind from her tousled curls.

The chief, Mayor Mountayne, the Westcotts, Deputy Ronan Roarke and a few other deputies gathered on the stage. Tristano Koffi stood to the side, his quiet authoritative voice directing the conference. Reporters, cameras, and microphones semi-circled the stage.

As soon as the cameras came on, Jesa inched until she was way off, as out of range of the cameras as she could get. The last thing she needed was to have her face pop up on national news. Koffi was signaling her to go back beside the Westcotts, but she pretended she didn't see him. Instead, she stood in the shadows of the curtains and observed the crowd.

Chief McKabe started the conference off explaining what had happened and describing the hell the Westcotts were going through.

Most of Orainn was crammed into the community center mixed in with local reporters, and the mainland reporters.

Taut with the strain of being involved in the investigation and being on stage with all the cameras, when, there in the crowd Jesa saw Velvet from the Bistro gleefully waving at her. A smile softened the constriction in her face at the waitress' grin. She wore her grey and white uniform, tight on her fat-padded, ultra-hourglass figure, the brown hair in a thin braid down her back. The end swatted across her wide butt when she moved.

Then Jesa could see many of the Divine Bistro crew was present. Laverne grinned standing beside a stoic Mr. Sloan. The manager managed to give Jesa a brief bow of acknowledgement. Even the oldest waitress known to mankind affectionately called Grandma, with crooked arthritic feet tendered a wrinkled smile at Jesa. Jesa felt the knot in her belly unwind just a hair.

Finn and Clarie Barton were there as well. He had his arm around his wife and both beamed up at Jesa. With all their support she was able to look around more comfortably. Relaxing a bit, she lowered the backpack off her shoulder and set it on the floor.

On the stage, Stedman Westcott had his arm wrapped tightly around his weeping wife. They took turns begging into the microphone for whoever took their daughter to please return her unharmed. Half the crowd was crying along with Elizabeth. So far, no ransom had been demanded. That was even scarier, at least with a kidnapping for money there was a chance the baby was still alive.

Her attention meandering, Jesa only had a partial view of the Westcotts. Looking directly into the main camera in front of them, Elizabeth wiped at her tears, but her eyes flicked continuously off to the left side. Curious, Jesa figured it was a relative or close friend she looked too, it was a young man that seemed to draw Mrs. Westcott's attention.

As soon as Jesa noticed him, he disappeared, blending into the crowd. Jesa barely caught a glimpse of dark hair before he was gone. Elizabeth's gaze hovered at the spot where he'd disappeared.

"So," Chief McKabe's Texas-accented voice brought her attention back to the event. He had answered the few questions he could, and said 'no comment' to the ones he couldn't. "That is all we have for now, folks. We have a reward offered for any credible information in the location of Brie Westcott. If you want to remain anonymous, that's fine.

"We just want to bring this young child home safe and sound to her parents, and we can sure use all the help we can get. So," McKabe smiled his natural good-ol' boy smile, "if anyone thinks of anything they remember seeing, or hearing, or knows anything about this kidnapping, please," his voice dropped to stoic seriousness, the smile gone, "please do not hesitate to contact us. Even the tiniest bit of information can be valuable. Thank you." He bowed, nodded to the reporters, motioned to the deputies to escort the Westcotts off the stage and to take them out the back way.

The auditorium burst with loud conversation and speculation. Reporters yelled out questions but the law had no answers yet. Jesa followed the Westcotts out and found Ronan at her side. His big grin was contagious. "Hey Jesa, how you doing? This is crazy stuff, huh?" He cupped her elbow with a strong hand and guided her through the people flocking around the Westcotts.

Slipping her backpack over her shoulder, Jesa tugged trapped strands of hair loose from under the strap and agreed. "I've never been involved in anything like this before, it's intense all right." She lifted the rest of her thick hair to slide the backpack on more securely, the strawberry curls shifted and tumbled down her back.

Ronan moved his hand from her elbow to her lower back subtly moving closer to her. "I saw the Big Bad Wolf bring you in. Must be hell, Little Red Riding Hood, being jammed up inside your little car with him all snarling and snapping, huh?"

Jesa giggled at the image, and Ronan drew her closer and grinned. They waved at a couple of deputies that were leaving. The Westcotts were talking with McKabe and the mayor. Ronan laughed, "Yeah, bet he has those big bad teeth sharpened and ready to bite you with my dear," he growled showing his own canines, and they both laughed.

"Hey, Jesa," Ronan lowered his head to speak more quietly and gave her a little squeeze, "what say you and I hop down to the Black Rooster Tavern and have a couple of drinks? You know, unwind, take a breather, maybe get to know each other a little."

"Deputy," Jesa reproached him with a smile, "it's not even noon yet and you want to have a drink?" She quipped, "Should we perhaps stop at an AA meeting on the way?" She was hardly aware she snuggled into him. He was big and warm, his beefy muscular arm held her, and there was no denying how attractive he was. When those gorgeous blue eyes gleamed at her she felt her insides tingle.

Squeezing her tighter to his side, the deputy looked down at her, bringing them into a personal private bubble with his big body wrapped around her smaller form, "You teasing me?" He nudged her hair with his nose. "Ah, babe, you smell sweet, fresh." Shaking his head and sniffing her hair again, he said quietly in her ear, "I was thinking coffee or a soda, maybe a milkshake. Let's sneak out the side door, no one will notice us missing-"

"We are all going to the station for debriefing," Koffi's cold voice interrupted them.

Jesa jumped, pushing away from Ronan, but the deputy held her with a firm grasp. Feeling awkward cuddled up with the deputy, a little breathy she said, "Oh, I'm not needed am I?"

Koffi's dark stare lowered to Ronan's hand on Jesa's back. Tough facial features harshly obdurate, his cool voice a hard band of uncompromising authority he informed her, "You will be present at all meetings. They've found the designer. They're bringing him to the station for us to interview after the debriefing.

"Everyone, including you, Ms. Judan," the satiric tone slight but evident, "are to be present." The hooded, inscrutable eyes glinted down at her, square jaw set tight, no smile lingered waiting to break free.

Jesa backed away from him and bumped into Ronan who only wrapped his arm more tightly, possessively around her. The men were almost equal height. Ronan leveled his direct gaze at Tristano, a hard edge to his voice, he said, "Fine. We will meet you there. Come, Jesa, my cruiser is out back." He turned her to face the back door.

Tristano's chilled voice stopped them, "No. She rides with me. You Orainn people are too irresponsible, you would take her to some bar in the boondocks and forget where you left her."

"Hey! I am not a-"

Ronan's sandy brows jumped to his hairline first with anger, then they lowered in mirth. Butting over Jesa's indignant retort, he sneered with clear contempt of Koffi, "Hardly, Agent. It's highly unlikely I would leave a beauty like our Jesa here anywhere, ever." He gave her a brief cuddle and started to move her to the door.

Her feelings about being talked about as if she were again, a child, and one with no sense, pushed her lips out, disturbed brows dropped between her eyes. She opened her mouth in retort but Ronan moved her along.

"I said," Tristano's voice dropped several degrees, "I will take *our Jesa* to the station." His expression revealing nothing but iron ice, he ordered Jesa, "Ms. Judan, go to the front door, I will meet you there as soon as I have a quick word with McKabe." The three of them glowered at each other.

Always the peacemaker, Jesa broke first. She let out a loud exhale heavy with irritation, pushed from Ronan's grasp and started towards the front entrance.

"Do not leave the building, Ms. Judan," Tristano called after her, "wait for me inside at the door. Remember the forceful wind." He saw her shoulders stiffen, then she trod out to the front.

"You speak to her like she's a child, Agent," Ronan said, anger bubbling beneath his words. He forked annoyed fingers through his sandy hair mussing it. Fingers can't be annoyed of course, but they sure acted like it.

"She *is* a child, Deputy." Tristano watched long strawberry curls passing through the crowd that was dispersing. The reporters were closing up their equipment, the noise level from various conversations was still rumbling loud.

Ronan crossed his arms over his big chest shifting the radio attached to his shoulder. Grinding his jaw, his lower lip pushed out in disagreement. "She is a woman, Agent, a grown woman. She can't be but less than ten years younger than us."

Koffi's eyes shifted from the front entrance to Ronan where they rolled down his body and back up. His strong face remained impassive, yet he still gave the impression he found the deputy in some way, deficient. "There are chronological years, Deputy, and there are years of experience. She is as naïve and green as a newborn lamb."

Shaking his head, Ronan said, "I don't think so. She's guarded, true, but there is something, she's been through something, you can see the," he shrugged with a crooked grin. "I hate to be cliché, but there is something haunting buried deep in those cock-hardening green eyes."

Tristan's lip curled with distaste. "At the moment, Deputy, Ms. Judan is a colleague, you will refrain from talking about her like she's a whore off the street."

A humorless chuckle sniggered out. Shaking his head, Ronan dropped his arms setting his hands on his hips over the thick belt that carried his weapons. Expression hardening, he said, "Knock that chip off your shoulder you asshole, that's not what I meant. I meant she-"

"I don't give a fuck what you meant, Deputy. Get to the station," Tristano commanded then pivoted on his heel and strode over to where McKabe and the mayor were still speaking, leaving Ronan turning outraged red with his handsome mouth hanging open.

Chapter Seven

Willie-Jean passed out chips and sandwiches. Chief McKabe sat at the head of the long rectangle table waiting for everyone to get something to drink and find a seat. He noticed Agent Koffi came into the station toting little Jesa. A quirk tugged the edge of his mouth. They both looked peeved, and didn't appear to be speaking to one another. The chief muzzled his smile. He figured there would be drama putting the two together.

Koffi barely constrained the rage that only McKabe saw because of his years of experience as a policeman studying people. To others, it would appear Koffi had a stick up his ass, but McKabe could tell he was a powerful man keeping the leash on what McKabe believed was a violent fury that ate at him. The chief had seen men like him before. Men so fierce, their rage so overpowering they deliberately sought out brawls to relieve some of the consuming tension.

But even so, he wasn't worried paring Jesa with him. Koffi would be a ruthless brute to other males, McKabe would bet his life the agent would never harm a woman. He now knew Koffi had an agenda, a different reason for being on the island besides the missing baby. He would bide his time watching it play out.

Koffi chose a seat right next to McKabe, Jesa sat as far from the agent as she could get. McKabe's mouth quirked again. Yin and Yang for sure, he thought. Hard, tough, aggressive, the cold, domineering agent was the opposite of Jesa Judan. She was petite, really on the delicate side as much as she tried to fight it, hide it. Her mannerisms were innately graceful. He had observed her interact with people. He

60

had previously seen her at the bistro although she hadn't noticed him. She was tremendously kind and compassionate.

When a customer was way out of line letting loose their crossness on a server, Jesa somehow had a way of subtly sliding in and quietly calming everyone. His eyes flicked from her to the agent. Koffi's face was a rock, he appeared to be patiently waiting for the meeting to begin, but his eyes flit around the table under those low hooded lids like black bees hopping from flower to flower, repeatedly landing back on Jesa.

Silently, McKabe chuckled. Koffi thought he was hiding his surreptitious glances at the girl, but again, the chief was well honed from his years on the force. Of course with the agent's usual implacable expression, it was too hard to say why he kept staring at her. Could be because he felt it was inappropriate that she was there. Could be he was attracted to her or felt protective, or could be he thought she was the culprit they were searching for. Could be another reason altogether.

Koffi didn't realize it, but McKabe read something in a flash of expression the agent probably was unaware of. Koffi studied Jesa, not quite like a hopeful lover, but sort of suspicious...hell, the sheriff couldn't put his finger on it. He let his gaze hop around the room at the rest of the team.

Tahni Genarino sat between the two men, Koffi and Roarke. Hmm, McKabe bit back a smile, that should keep everyone on their toes. They would flay sparks off each other, keep the adrenalin flowing and their interest in the case high even when things lagged. McKabe had wanted to put Jesa between the men, see what would happen when he paired up the all-hard-edges agent and the soft, sweet beauty, with the dashing handsome deputy on her other side.

Darn, he was such a romantic at heart. He would have enjoyed watching Koffi hassle Jesa just to poke at Ronan and stir him up. But Tahni had muscled in and Jesa had chosen to sit at the opposite end of the table.

Orainn was lucky to have a good-sized police force. During season there was such an influx of tourists that many officers were needed to keep the island safe. Deputy Morgan Martschmidt's task was to canvass the docks asking around to see if anyone noticed someone leaving with a baby. If so, he was to get names and check them out, see if the child was truly theirs.

Deputy Tom Christensen had been busy questioning the Westcotts' neighbors, Deputy Granger Wate was looking into the Westcotts' finances. Deputy Carl Johnson and Deputy Caitlin Saunders had been interviewing the Westcotts' relatives as well as the people where Stedman works, employees as well as clients.

Deputy Tahni Genarino had telephone duty. Tahni spent the morning calling the pharmacies to see if anyone was purchasing infant items including diapers, formula, and the grocers to see if baby food was bought, and she had to follow up with every single family whose name came up to verify the child they had was their own and not the kidnapped Brie Westcott.

Because they needed the help, McKabe wasn't suspending her for her insubordinate behavior. He had ordered her himself to pick up Jesa and she had flagrantly ignored it because she was wet for Koffi. If Jesa had been injured in any kind of way while under the law's supervision, there sure would be hell to pay. He decided he would watch and see how Tahni progresses before determining a sanction.

Other deputies were out and about on the island just searching for the baby, canvassing different neighborhoods to see if anyone saw anything, knew anything.

"Okay, take notes," McKabe said loud enough to stall the chatter at the table. When they were quiet, he said, "Anyone have anything to contribute? Jerry, let's start with you." He nodded at the deputy. Most of the deputies made notes on their phones or iPads, a few like Ronan and Morgan handwrote their notes. They both complained regularly when they were forced to type up event reports or respond to emails, neither one had patience with computers.

Jerry Osborne had pale skin, red hair, orangey actually, with matching eyebrows and a bucketful of freckles. He replied, "The two cells and the landlines are hooked up for tapping and tracing. I installed security cameras on the outside of the house to capture anyone approaching. Gomez is at the Westcotts' now, Donnie Gable will relieve him in an hour."

He shrugged one shoulder. "But, so far, nothing. Since the media release, friends and relatives are calling. There're been a few hang-ups that frustrate the husband. We told the Westcotts to keep all calls brief. We also put a CSA outside of the residence to keep reporters, friends, neighbors, and relatives away. After lunch I'll go back and review the tapes, see if anyone appeared out of place, maybe lurking suspiciously around the property."

"Good. Keep in mind, our perp could be a friend or neighbor." The chief looked around, "Well? What else?"

Morgan Martschmidt flipped through a small notebook. Shrugging one shoulder, he said, "I got a list of people that said they saw someone that was acting suspicious, and also several sightings of baby Brie," his eyes flickered down the list. He sighed and looked up at McKabe. "So far, the reports I checked out were frivolous, unsubstantiated, or even a couple of jokers that just wanted to seem important. One idiot was trying to prank his brother."

"Jerk," Deputy Caitlin Saunders grumbled.

Morgan's lips twisted in disgust. "Yeah, there's a ton of 'em out there. I have more to check out, but judging by the information provided, they aren't going to be any more credible than the others."

Nodding, McKabe progressed to Deputy Christensen. "Tom? Anything to offer?"

One of the older officers, Christensen's thick mop of hair was almost all grey. Scanning his notebook, the side of his mouth tugged in with a shake of his head. "No, like Morgan, nothing substantial. The neighbors are pointing their fingers at each other. I asked if they thought either of the Westcotts were involved in," he smiled slightly, "extracurricular activities, but they clammed right up on that. I don't know what that means. I'll go back and push some of them harder."

So far nothing was surprising McKabe. "Yep," he said. "I figured that if anything was a real threat, the person seeing it would have come right out and said so. No one wants to think a dangerous criminal is prowling through their neighborhoods. Willie-Jean reported the CSA's on the phones are basically fielding crank calls."

At Jesa's puzzled look, he smiled kindly at her and explained, "Community Service Aids, darlin'." To the rest of the group he said, "They also reported a few crazies calling the station with sightings of baby Brie." Bowing his head over his twined hands on the table, he shook his head with an annoyed condemning frown.

Morgan asked, "What did they say?"

McKabe's mouth pursed then thinned with his aggravation. "One claimed to have seen the baby being transported to a waiting alien ship." He spoke over the trickling of laughter, "Another said she was a zombie princess and she had been returned to her own kind, another said they'd heard a pack of dingoes snuck in the window and stole the baby. Which would be interesting since the nursery was on the second floor, and there are no dingoes on the island. Some people watch too much TV." Shaking his head, he smiled grimly, then said to the deputy a few seats down, "So, Grange, what about you?" He nodded to Deputy Granger Wate who was investigating the Westcotts' finances.

Wate tucked his long lean legs under his chair, his shoulders bowed as he bent his lanky body over his notes. He scratched at dark whiskers on his chin with bony fingers. "Well Chief, Stedman Westcott is doing a stellar business with his stocks and shit," a wry chuckle wriggled out of his stretched torso. "I checked their bank statements, credit cards. They spend right to the very limit of their income. Elizabeth fills her days with lunches and shopping, online too, a lot."

He flipped a page in his notes. "Stedman likes the bigger, high-end expenses like the Mercedes, Corvette, and a couple of other ultra-expensive vehicles in their four-car garage. But," he snapped the notebook closed, "they are paying their bills on time. When I've exhausted everything I'll go to the bank and micro-rummage through every check they've written, or cash withdrawals for the past year."

"Alrighty. Carl? Caitlin?" McKabe glanced at the pair. Neither reviewed their notes. Caitlin smoothed a strand of short dark hair off her brow and reported, "They have no relatives that live permanently on the island. I called the ones I could locate on the mainland. They really didn't want to talk about the Westcotts, surprisingly kinda loyal for relatives."

"Yeah, I got the same thing," Carl Johnson noted. "The people Stedman works with pretty much keep to themselves; they're too afraid of their commodities information getting pilfered. They all claim Stedman works hard, describing him as aloof, even pompous for a young guy. They say he's normally staid, serious. However," a crooked smile crossed his dark-skinned round face. A hulking African-American, his shaved brown pate reflected the ceiling light. "A few hinted that maybe he's not actually having an affair, but, the way he flirts around with the waitresses where they lunch, no one would put it past him. But I got nothing concrete; no one wanted to say anything out loud. They all valued their jobs."

"Huh," Ronan grunted in vague agreement. "I got that vibe from him when I interviewed him at their house." He twiddled a pen in his fingers occasionally tapping the end on the table. "Although, when I asked about any affairs, either him or the wife, Stedman grew quiet, almost sullen. But, like everyone else, there was nothing solid there, he denied anything was going on then closed up, and quickly left the kitchen where we were talking."

"Agent?" The chief turned to Koffi sitting near him.

Tristano ran a palm over the dark hair waving over his head, his callously carved lips pushed out; otherwise his face carried zero emotion. Everyone was in uniform except Jesa who wore jeans and a blouse, and Koffi had on a dark suit with white shirt but today he lacked a tie. He had clearly shaved this morning, but his dark afternoon scruff and tanned skin cut a raw masculine contrast with the severe white shirt. Instead of loafers like Stedman Westcott had worn, he preferred dress boots.

His deep baritone rumbled in a cool, assertive undertone, "Stedman is the only child of a very wealthy family. Elizabeth's family is of an old aristocratic ancestry but they ran through their wealth and are virtually penniless. They get the big invites to all the soirees in town, here and on the mainland because of their blue-blooded names." He paused, clasped his hands and set them loosely on his lap.

His gaze never wavered from McKabe as he spoke. "Mrs. Westcott became extremely distraught when I brought up affairs, and," he glanced at Ronan who smiled, "she got really heated when it was mentioned that Stedman was fraternizing with the models that were doing a shoot here." He explained about the magazine gig, and that the designer was being brought in for questioning.

McKabe glanced down when his phone buzzed. He said to Koffi, "He's here, CSA Smart has him in an interview room when you're ready." He nodded to Deputy Genarino and asked her, "Tahni, how is your task going?" There was censure in his voice. The sexy deputy's eyes were burning a hole in the side of Tristano's head as if she was willing him to look at her. His attention never veered from the chief.

Tearing her eyes away from the agent, Tahni's laborious sigh held the weight of the world. Glancing down at her scrawled notes then her phone, she sighed again." Damn," she moaned, "there are a lot of children coming and going on Orainn."

Everybody remained quietly concentrated on her, waiting for her report. Another sigh of penance and she ran her finger down the middle of her notebook. "I called most of the grocers, shops, and the pharmacies and received a list of names of people purchasing anything deemed for a young child or infant." Her aggrieved sigh reflected in her rumpled face like a whine.

"Deputy," McKabe warned.

Tahni stirred herself, tucking away the self-pity for the tedious job assigned to her. "Uh, yeah, well, so far everything checks out. I have some people already moved to the mainland to check on, and a few more shops, but so far," she shook her head and shrugged, "nada." She tilted her head back and gave McKabe a beleaguered smile, then turned her attention right back to Agent Koffi.

McKabe said to her, "I want the hospital and day care centers, the schools, all checked out as well, Deputy." His implacable gaze didn't waver at her rolling eyes and pained sigh.

"Okay," she groaned, and made notes.

Resisting rolling his own eyes, or barking a sharp reprimand at Tahni, the chief turned and smiled at Jesa. "Darlin'? You have any observations you would like to impart?"

The focus on her brought a darker pink to Jesa's naturally rosy cheeks. She squirmed in her seat. "Um…" her eyes darted nervously around the room before lowering to the table. Shaking her head, the long flaming curls danced around her shoulders. "I…" her lashes fluttered as she appeared to be about to say something, then her voice firmed, "no, I didn't really notice anything."

The chief stared at her for a minute. It looked like she was holding something back, but, he let it go for now. When she became more confident, more comfortable in her position she would likely offer her thoughts. Rapping his knuckles on the table, he looked around at everyone, "All right then, good work. Take a bit of a break, and then everyone head back out and resume your assignments." To Koffi, Ronan, a smile to Jesa, he said, "You three can go start your interview with the designer."

Ronan hopped up and trod right to Jesa. Pulling out her chair, he grinned as he helped her up. He asked her, "Is this exciting for you, Jessy?"

Jesa moved from his hand that went on her lower back, frowning at the nickname. "It's just Jesa, Deputy, Jessy makes me feel like a cowboy," her mouth softened and turned up to take the rebuke out of her words. "You know, like Jesse James?"

Ronan put his palm on her upper back and stroked it down to the inner curve of her spine and left it there as they walked out of the room. "Okay, we'll stay with Jesa. What's that short for, like Jessica?"

Agent Koffi stood in the doorway of the conference room watching the pair stroll slowly down the hall. He could still hear them talking. He stepped back inside the room to have a brief word with the chief.

"It's actually Jesselin," Jesa spelled it out. A fleeting smile twitched, lifting her full lips, she admitted, "I don't care much for that either. Sounds dippy like a hayseed or something."

"You're nuts," Ronan teased, tugging one of her long curls, "that's a really pretty name. Like you." He set his hand back on her and squeezed her waist. "Jesa's a cute name but Jesselin is more for a gorgeous super model or something."

She laughed at him in self-disparagement, "That's certainly not me."

The deputy leaned in, bent his fair head close to her and whispered, "Sugar, you could give a super-model a run for her money any day, and win hands down."

Rolling her eyes in disbelief, Jesa swatted his arm. "Don't be silly," she laughed, and walked with him to where their person of interest waited.

Chapter Eight

A guard stood outside the closed interview room. Ronan nodded to him, and he opened the door. Ronan ushered Jesa inside and as the guard was closing the door, Tristano stepped in. The room was small with a table and two white plastic chairs. A thin man with big glasses and wild hair sat at the table. He looked alternately angry and terrified.

Ronan moved forward and said, "Mr. Nor-"

Tristano cut him off as he stepped in front of the deputy, "I am Special Agent Koffi with the FBI, this is Deputy Roarke," he nodded to Ronan ignoring the deputy's pissed expression. He didn't introduce Jesa. Last thing he wanted was for a suspected kidnapper, a possible felon to know Jesa's name. Jesa stood near the door looking like she wanted to bolt. She had removed her notepad from the backpack, which she left out in the other room; she had a death grip on the pad clutched to her chest.

Niels Normandy set his long thin hands like twigs on the table, and went to push up to his feet. Skinny face flushed, beads of sweat trickled down his temples, he snarled belligerently, "I don't know who the fuck you people think you are, and what the fuck you think you are-" his body was turned towards Jesa at the door.

Tristano stepped in front of him, dark eyes flashing a glare, he commanded, "Sit. Down."

Normandy took one look at the male who towered a foot over him with shoulders like steel beams, black eyes radiating threat, and he plunked back down in his chair. Pushing wild flopping hair off his forehead, he cowered back from the agent, ducking his head as if he thought Koffi was going to belt him.

"Now then," Tristano set a rugged palm on the table and leaned into it. "Tell us why are you here on the Isle of Orainn?"

The designer's gulp rolled over the lump of his large Adam's apple in his thin throat and he audibly swallowed. He dragged his twiggy fingers through the wild hair and stammered, "I- I, we- we- uh, are here to do a fa- fashion shoot. Uh, I mean we were, we are pretty much done."

Ronan had moved to stand at the table opposite to Normandy. He asked, "Fashion shoot for what?"

Hemmed in by the two huge bruisers, the designer sat back in his chair, his gaze bounced from Koffi to Ronan to Jesa where his lids lowered slightly and his pupils dilated.

"Normandy!" Tristano barked slamming his hand on the table so hard the designer, and Jesa, jumped. "Answer the question," he demanded.

His attention back on the agent, Niels Normandy gulped hard again, coughed while loudly clearing his throat. Wiping spittle from his mouth with his hand, his words stuttered out anxiously, "Uh, a- a magazine. Flaunt This. I'm here with- with three models and a photographer. We took some shots down the hill by the bridge, near the creek. I mean, uh…" he stuck a bony finger inside the collar of his plaid shirt and tugged at it. He had on plaid pants too but they were a different design and color than the shirt.

Looking meekly from Ronan to Tristano, he asked, "Did we break some law or something?" Blinking rapidly he spoke faster, "I mean if we did we didn't mean to, I'll pay whatever fine there is." His head jerked as he looked back again from Koffi to Ronan. When his view moved to Jesa, Tristano made a small sound deep in his throat and Normandy jerked his attention back to him.

"You were at a party, Mr. Normandy." Tristano slid a hip on the table and set a hand on his thigh. "At Stedman and Elizabeth Westcotts' home Saturday night a week or so ago."

69

"Uh," the designer murmured, nodding with vague confusion. His eyeballs hopped from Koffi to the deputy and back, he'd taken the hint to not look at Jesa. "Yeah, sure, we were invited."

"By whom?" Ronan inquired.

Normandy's pale blue eyes were large and blurry behind the wide glasses, they flicked to the deputy. "Oh, Stedman Westcott invited us. During one of our shoots I guess he was lunching up on the hill, the Commons I think they call it. He and a couple other fellas came down to watch. I mean," a shoulder drew up, he gave a little giggle. "The models are of course gorgeous," his gaze slipped to Jesa and it rolled from her soft face and down her body-

"Normandy!" Koffi slammed the table again.

The designer jumped and thrust his gaze back to the agent. "Uh-uh, yeah, anyways, the fellas watched the shoot, the broads were in bikinis. I mean," he snickered, "tits and asses hanging out everywhere, what red-blooded male wouldn't be sitting there with their tongues wagging, huh?" His smile more a leer, he swiveled his head from Koffi to Ronan and back seeking agreement.

Tristano's face froze like iron rock. A scar lanced near one cheek of his ruggedly hewn features. The onyx eyes glittered, his lips pressed together. He stared at the designer like he wanted to smack him. "The party at the Westcotts'," the agent's voice as hard as his face, grew harsher, "you were found in the baby's room. What were you doing in there?"

His puffy lips pulled in, Normandy's eyes shifted back and forth and then lowered. Again he jumped when Koffi hit the table. "Normandy, look at me," Tristano ordered the skinny guy who was now shaking. Niels raised his trembling eyes to the lupine agent. Tristano repeated louder, "Why were you in the baby's room?"

Clearing his throat noisily, the designer tugged at his collar again, his nervous gulp gurgling noisily. His voice thinned, came out strident with his nerves, "The, uh, bathroom, I was looking for the bathroom."

"The nursery," Ronan said, setting his palms on the table and leaned forward towards Normandy, "is on the second floor. There are several bathrooms on the first floor." Already a big man, in the brown uniform with the wide belt packed with weapons, the radio at his shoulder, heavy boots, broad shoulders hunched over with his blue eyes firing menacing bullets, the deputy was an intimidating figure.

Both hard lawmen moved closer to Normandy, uncomfortably penning him in, confining him with their brutish dominating presence.

Shrinking back, Normandy gulped, then chuffed. "Yeah, well, they were all occupied and I had to go bad, ya know. I drank a lot that night." The designer's blurry eyes behind the thick lenses wobbled from Koffi back to Ronan then dropped to the table. His knobby fingers splayed on the tabletop as if they were stuck to it like a lizard with suction cups on his fingertips, like he was trying to hold himself together.

Shifting to stand up straight, Ronan crossed his burly arms, the big biceps flexing under the short-sleeved shirt and said, "Still, there are several bathrooms upstairs too, it doesn't explain why you were in the nursery. In fact, there's a bathroom right next to the baby's room. Again," placing his knuckles on the table he bent over into the designer's personal space. Although they were separated by the table, Normandy cowered back from him. Eyes tapering irascibly, Ronan demanded loudly, "Why were you in the baby's room?"

Mouth hanging open, his pale eyes huge behind the round glasses, Normandy blinked. Comprehension wrestled his face into shock. "You- you-" he looked from one to the other in stupefaction. "This is about that kid, that baby that got snatched!" He blinked faster. "That was," his brow furrowed, "ah hell, I haven't been watching the news. I've only heard bits and pieces here and there."

He pushed his glasses down and pinched his nose, then levered the glasses back up. The big blurry eyes wide, he said, "That was Stedman Westcott's baby? The stolen kid was his?" Shaking his head from side-to-side, he pushed the glasses on top of his head shoving the wild hair back, brown strands stuck up willy-nilly, and he rubbed his eyes, then fidgeting with them, he lowered the glasses again.

"Yes," Koffi snapped. "Answer the goddamned question." His dark gaze leaped to Jesa and narrowed at her shaking her head silently scolding him. He pointedly motioned his head to her pad indicating she should be taking notes, not policing his language.

One finger digging in the inside corner of an eye under a lens, the designer sighed. "I didn't know it was their kid. Listen," his brows lowered, tongue swept around his dry thick lips. "I had to piss, that was it. I was trashed, could hardly walk, I got lost in the enormous house and stumbled into the kid's room.

"I didn't know it until I saw the crib. By then there was some bad-assed security guard hauling my ass downstairs and he kicked me out. That's it." He folded his arms across the scrawny chest and sat back with a nod of his head, hair flopped forward slapping his glasses.

"We were told you were leaning the side of your head against the wall." Ronan's arched brows indicated how bizarre he thought that was.

Normandy blinked at him for a second then shrugged a thin shoulder. "Yeah, well, I told you. I was fucked up," he threw an apologetic glance at Jesa. "Sorry, Miss."

Repositioning the glasses on his nose, he continued with a weary exhale, "I was staggering on my feet, I was using the wall to hold myself upright. That's it. Nothing nefarious, people. You don't think someone would have noticed if I had a baby tucked under my arm like a football and was tearing out the backdoor with it?" His snort sardonic at their ridiculous questioning.

Ronan said quietly, "The baby wasn't taken that night; it was almost a week later."

Normandy sat up with a smug grin. "See then? It clearly wasn't me. Now," he snuffled indignantly, "I want to leave or should I call my attorney?"

Koffi shifted his hip off the desk to stand. He set his hands on the back of one of the chairs, arms rigid, his shoulders hunched, he and Ronan shared a look.

The deputy paced to the door, his arm brushed Jesa's arm as he opened the door. Tristano tugged the hem of his suit coat down, straightened his cuffs and said, "That's all for now, Mr. Normandy. I am ordering you not to leave the island until I give the okay."

His brows shot up to his high hairline, Niels spurted, "What? No, the weather is reckoning, soon the connecting landmass will be impassable. I can't get stuck here all winter, I have things to do, places to be, you can't-"

"Yes I can. If you try to leave I will have a warrant for your arrest issued and your ass hauled right back here and locked in a cell, treacherous weather or not. There are deputies stationed at the wharf, you can't get on the ferry or take a bus back to the mainland without being seen. You stay here, you understand?" He calmly perused the designer who glowered ferociously at him, then wilted under the iron face staring with ruthless coldness back at him.

Normandy nodded weakly, his murmur meek, "Yeah."

Tristano turned and saw Ronan was already ushering Jesa out the door. Sighing heavily, he waited until the guard came back down the hall to retrieve Normandy. The affronted designer glared hostility at him as he left the room.

By the time Normandy was hustled down the corridor, and Tristano stepped outside, he saw the hallway was empty. Lips tightly compressed, his forehead furled. Striding down the hall he muttered out loud, "That little girl better not have blown off my orders and left with that ego-bloated deputy."

He made his way to the main room of the station uncaring that the officers avoided him. Most of them resentful, thinking the FBI agent considered himself above them refused to make eye contact with him. The testy agent strode over to the front desk, and disregarding that the two women were in a conversation, broke in impolitely. "Ms. Parrish," he said tersely.

Willie-Jean was speaking with Caitlin. She looked up and smiled when Koffi approached. "Hey, Agent Koffi, how are things go-"

He snapped, "Where's the girl?"

The receptionist blinked at his surliness, "Girl?" she parroted. Caitlin gave him a dirty look for his arrogantly interrupting them.

Mouth ground tight in a scowl, Tristano growled, "The girl, Ms. Judan, where is she? Did she leave?"

Her lips settling into a friendly smile, Willie-Jean cocked a brow at Caitlin then replied to the agent with the calm, patient voice of a kindergarten teacher, "The young woman has not left the building, Agent Koffi. Maybe the chief wanted a word with her?"

"Uh huh." The scowl still there, Tristano asked, "The blond deputy, Roarke, is he still here?"

Her smile broadened displaying nice teeth, Willie-Jean said helpfully, "Yes, he's still here somewhere."

Pivoting, Tristano turned from her and stalked through the room and down the hall towards McKabe's office. "Damn that girl, where the hell-"

Blam!

He didn't see the ladies' room door open or Jesa step out and he bashed into her so hard he fell off-balance and slammed them both into the wall knocking her notebook flying out of her hand.

"Ah, fuck," he cursed, his body pressed hard against Jesa's soft curves. She gave a tiny squeal when she hit the wall and the air knocked out of her lungs.

Tristano's nose landed in her hair, his forearms flat on the wall, his fingers splayed. *Fresh, like apple blossoms,* he dug his nose in deeper and inhaled. His broad chest flattened against her full breasts, he could feel them. Soft plump mounds pressing into rock-hard pecs, another part of his body was hardening, still, he didn't move.

Jesa gasped and squirmed. Tristano groaned at her curves rubbing over his chest.

"Mr., uh, Agent Koffi," her voice a whisper from his big body crushing her petite softness, she couldn't draw a deep breath. And he still didn't move. Their hearts crashed in rapid rhythm against each other. She brought her hands up and clutched at his jacket sleeves, her hands too small to wrap around his huge biceps. Pushing him was like pushing at a Mack truck. "Agent, please, I can't breathe."

His palms staying pressed against the wall, his chest brushed against her bosom before he leaned back a few inches and looked down at her. She raised her head, their eyes connected, mouths so close their breaths met. His dark eyes grew as black as burnt coals, sooty lashes and low lids hooding them as they trolled to her lips, he slanted his head and lowered it-

"Jesa!" The irritation harsh in his voice Ronan tramped down the hall towards them.

His hands still on the wall, elbows bent, Tristano didn't look at him, he was staring down at Jesa's flushed face, her dazed eyes heavy-lidded crescents. She blinked hard and her lids flew up. Her fingers gripping his sleeves and pushing at the same time, she whispered huskily, "Agent, please."

Tristano straightened his arms and stepped back from Jesa, freeing her body plastered against the wall. Eyes round like green saucers, her cheeks turned beet red and she hurriedly edged away from him. He calmly smoothed his jacket, not acknowledging the pissed off deputy stomping towards them, fire blazing ire in the blue eyes.

"What the hell is going on here?" Ronan snapped as he reached them. He had changed into jeans and a flannel shirt. He set his hand on Jesa's shoulder, inquired softly, "You okay, honey? Did he hurt you? It looked like he was touching you, ah, inappropriately?" His angry glare swerved from Jesa to Tristano so hot it could have burned Koffi's skin. Tristano's black brows arched with amusement at the furious deputy.

"No." Her voice soft with a slight tremble, Jesa said quickly, "We-we ran into each other, literally, it was an accident." Disconcerted, she combed her fingers through her hair pushing it back off her shoulders. Frowning at Tristano, she rubbed her chest, sore from their collision. Both men's gazes followed her movements. "Geez, Agent Koffi, you crushed me into the wall like a bull flattening a marshmallow."

One brow rose, Tristano's mouth turned up at a corner, his eyes darkened as they roved down her body. "Hmm, a shapely marshmallow," he murmured. Bending over, he grabbed her notebook and handed it to her.

"Anyway," Ronan growled, his hand on Jesa's shoulder he maneuvered her closer to him. "Chief wanted to know what we thought about Normandy." Lips pursed at Koffi, he turned his head to smile at Jesa and affectionately lifted a tendril of hair off her cheek.

"Other than his kaleidoscopic clothes making me want to puke with dizziness?" Tristano scoffed disdainfully. "Why he was in the baby's room is certainly suspicious, but it doesn't prove he took her, she was still there days later."

"No, but he could have been casing the place, seeing where the nursery was, where the doors and windows were located. Even maybe leaving a window unlocked to gain entrance later," Ronan said.

"But Mrs. Westcott said the kitchen door was wide open, why would he go in that way if he'd left a window unlocked?" Both men turned to Jesa. Her clothes had become twisted and disheveled from Koffi's big body smashing her into the wall.

Fixing her blouse, she tucked it in and said, "Of course walking in through the kitchen door would be much less noticeable to a neighbor than if he climbed in a window. Or, maybe he was telling the truth and was just really drunk and wandered in there by accident like he said."

The men's expressions were relatively blank as they watched her fix her clothing, but it was clear they felt the designer was up to something. "Anyway," Ronan said, "we're done for the day. Come on, Jesa, I'll take you for some seafood at the Crab Pit."

He stroked his palm down her arm and took her hand. Smiling mockingly at Tristano, he said, "Unless Special Agent Koffi wants to knock you around some more." His smile widened at Tristano's frown. "Let's go," he said, and before Jesa or Tristano could respond, Ronan pulled her down the hall and to the front room.

They greeted Willie-Jean who was tidying things up before leaving for the evening. Ronan helped Jesa on with her jacket. She picked up her backpack she'd left at Willie-Jean's desk and stuffed the notebook into it.

Ronan shrugged into his own jacket, and with his hand firm on her back, he opened the door for Jesa to pass through.

"Jesselin," Tristano's imperious voice stopped her. Ronan's head fell back, his eyes rolled with a groan. The agent didn't come up to them; he stayed by Willie-Jean's desk looking starched and impeccably urbane in his expensive suit. "I will pick you up at seven tomorrow morning."

Ronan grinned a leer at him. "I can bring her in." His insinuation that he might be staying overnight brought a flush to Jesa's cheeks.

Koffi's jaw worked, he said to Jesa, "I will be there at seven. Do not leave until I get there." Dark eyes warning, he reminded her, "And, keep that phone in your pocket. Always."

"Agent-" as Jesa started to speak, Ronan gave her a gentle push out the door. He brought two fingers up in a sarcastic salute to Koffi as he closed the door behind them.

Chapter Nine

Down by the thunderous coast the smoky sky pitched into the squalling sea. White frothing crest of surf glowed as it surged and crashed over the pie-shaped branny shore. Muted lights fought the windy dark, casting hazy spheres in the murk, but they only spackled the crown of the surf and the wings of swooping gulls. In the faded distance, the lighthouse's revolving red beacon swept an arc over the rumbling sea.

The Crab Pit stood on thick beamed stilts in the thrashing water. Under turquoise awnings, windows encircled the building that was surrounded by a wide deck offering outside seating overlooking the ocean. On nicer days, the sun would be shining down on lively hungry customers enjoying a spectacular bird's eye view of the ocean.

Today, the restaurant's deck was deserted, the blustering wind and torrid sea having chased the guests inside. In the eve's gloom, foreboding clouds reflected against the just as black and unruly sea.

Ronan wrapped his arm around Jesa as they hurried through the gusty threatening night and into the restaurant, closing out the roar of the wind with the heavy oak door. They were quickly seated and ordered their food. The Crab Pit was rustically paneled with rough wood and planked flooring. Pictures of fishing boats, bounding fish, and proud fishermen holding up their trophy catches hung slapdash on the unvarnished walls.

The large windows giving a 360 view contrasted the warm, bright and cheery indoors with the dark and thundery outside. The atmosphere simple, the noise level high with banging loud music, cadent chatter, and wooden tables covered with newspaper as customers gleefully hammered their crabs into submission.

When Jesa took a huge bite of her burger, the tomato slid half out the other end, Russian sauce leaked down her fingers. Every other bite she licked a gooey finger.

Sitting opposite her, Ronan dipped a hunk of crabmeat into a ramekin of melted butter. He lifted the crab and tried to get his mouth under it before the butter dripped off the meat. He didn't make it, half the butter dribbled down his chin.

Jesa giggled and handed him a napkin off the pad the server had set beside the bowl for the shells. "You know, Deputy, the crab actually has very little taste, it's the rich butter that has all the flavor."

Chewing, he moved his head back and forth in delight, nodded, swallowed. "Whatever, it's damned delicious." He stabbed his fork into another chunk of pink and white meat and sunk it to soak in the butter. Satisfied it was totally saturated with butter, before he propelled it in his mouth, he said, "It's Ronan, Jesa. Heck, we're practically co-workers."

As he chomped the crabmeat, his blue eyes streamed over Jesa's pretty face, her long strawberry blonde hair was tied back in a fat messy braid. Ketchup from French fries dabbed one corner of her mouth, the Russian dressing spotted her chin. She wiped at it with the back of her greasy hand.

Laughing, Ronan leaned over the table and dabbed at the ketchup then the sauce with his napkin. Jesa licked her lips and giggled. "I'm kind of a slob." She blushed and used her own napkin to clean her face. Opening a towelette and wiping her fingers, one shoulder bumped up embarrassed. "Sorry."

Ronan chuckled. "Actually, it's kind of sexy watching you eat. You're so…elegant, feminine, but you eat with gusto. And the gooey stuff," he grinned, "only makes me want to lick… it all off… every inch of you."

The blush bloomed brilliant, her eyes lowered to the table, Jesa grabbed her soda and drank it so fast she choked. Soda spurted out of her mouth as she tried to control the coughing.

Ronan got right up and pulled the side chair close to her, sat down and patted her back. "Hey, sugar, you okay?" He tried to sound worried but his voice shook with laughter.

Mortally embarrassed, Jesa hid her face with her napkin. Taking a deep breath, it whooshed out. "Yeah, I'm okay, just," the napkin covered her face she muttered, "mortified. Geez, everyone is gawking at me like I'm a silly fool."

Ronan slipped his arm down around her shoulders, "Naw, they're staring because you are one breathtaking woman." He tugged the napkin down. Tossing it on the table, he drew her close and slid two fingers under her chin, lifted it. "So gorgeous," he murmured as his lips descended to hers, "I find you too hard to resist," and he covered her mouth in a hungry kiss.

Jesa spread her hands on his chest and turned her head from him. "No, Ronan, I mean," the blush darkened, "people are watching us, we're in public."

He kept hold of her chin trying to recapture her lips. "They're just jealous, babe, come on, just a quick kiss to hold me." He gripped her chin, lifted it and dipped in to kiss her, but she shrugged away from him, keeping her hands up between them.

"Really, Deputy, no, please." Her eyes darted around the room self-conscious at his PDA.

"Okay, okay," he gave in, and sat back with a smile. "Not the place. I'm sorry, you are such temptation on a platter, I couldn't wait." Sitting casually, he crossed an ankle over a knee and slid a hand under her hair to caress her neck, "I'll be good, wait until we're alone. And," he reminded her with a tap to the end of her small tilted nose, "it's Ronan. Okay?"

She moved from his hand stroking her neck and shook her head. "No, Ronan, please, I- you're moving too fast. I- don't want a- a relationship. I mean," she took a breath, "it's not you, I just can't-"

He rolled his arm behind her setting it on the back of her chair and put a finger on her lips to shush her. "Hush babe, I'm sorry, I unnerved you moving on you so fast." He slipped his fingers under a thick curl, lifted it, then set it behind her back. "We have all the time in the world, but," his brows drew down between his eyes. With an underlying tinge of jealousy he said, "You were letting Agent Koffi practically screw you up against the wall and you balk at a tiny kiss with me?"

Jesa's lips pressed in consternation at his crudeness, her forehead furrowed in dispute. "No, we told you. I came out of the bathroom and we didn't see each other. He was walking quickly I guess, and just crashed into me. We, I mean, he," her head whipped back and forth in denial, the blush spread.

Her palm flat on her forehead she shoved her hair back in vexation at the thought that the brusque agent had appeared to be about to kiss her. That was ludicrous, he would never- "For heaven's sake, Ronan, Agent Koffi is the rudest, bossiest, grimmest man I've ever met, who doesn't hide his dislike and disdain for me. I would probably turn to stone if he kissed me!"

Appeased, Ronan chuckled and sat back. "More like black ice. As hard and cold as he is his dark touch would turn you into an icicle." They laughed together, the tension broken. The blond deputy said with an affable grin, "Hey, when the winter season is over how 'bout we go on a helicopter ride? The island is so cool from a satellite view."

"Really?" Jesa was intrigued.

Buoyed at her interest he told her, "There're a few helicopters that come over in the spring. I can pilot it, so it can be just you and me. Romantic, huh?"

"You can fly a helicopter?"

His grin big and boastful, he replied, "Yeah. A lot of us deputies got licensed. It helps to get from one side of the island to the other quickly in an emergency. If we need to get someone to the hospital in a hurry, things like that. We've used it to search for missing hikers, boaters and stuff."

"Wow." She was impressed. "I'd love to go for a ride, it sounds exciting."

Over dessert of chocolate cake, Jesa skimmed her fork over the top of the thick rich frosting and languidly licked it off with closed lidded moans of delight.

Beside her, Ronan sipped at a beer and watched her. Every couple of minutes he squirmed and discreetly adjusted his jeans. Unaware of his intense perusal, Jesa asked, "There have been no ransom calls from the kidnappers. So, if not for ransom, why would someone steal a baby?"

He held the bottle's neck between his thumb and fingers and tipped it, took a swallow, shrugged and set the beer down. "There are lots of reasons. Like, if parents couldn't have one of their own, and aren't eligible for adoption, maybe they have criminal histories or are too old, they'll buy one through the underground black market. Or, it's been known for a single woman trying to hold onto a husband that wants kids and she can't have one of her own, so she fakes it.

"Then there's the financial aspect of course. Not for ransom but, hell, I hate to say this," he paused, stared down at his beer where he started picking at the label. "Children are often stolen to sell, to, ah, sick, perverted assholes. There's also the selling of the body parts, that's big money-"

Clapping her hands over her ears Jesa cried, "Enough!" Closing her eyes against images of tiny children being gutted, sounding as if her heart was being ripped out of her ribcage she said, "I can't hear any more. I'll never be able to sleep tonight." She looked up at Ronan with tears in her eyes. "Ronan, how can people be so horrible?"

"Ah, well, the world is made up of all kinds of freaks. That's why I do my job," he patted her hand that rested on the table then kept his hand over hers. His broad shoulders straightened, he said modestly, "I have to protect the innocent, bring in the bad guys, and rescue the victims. Sure," he lowered his head shaking it regretfully, going on, "there tends to be more failures than successes, but," his lungs filled with air then emptied, he turned his head slightly to look at her from the side.

Shoving a flop of dark yellow hair off his forehead, his voice sad, he sighed. "I still get up every day and put one foot in front of the other and do my job the best I can."

Jesa patted his arm. "You are a good guy, Ronan, one of the good ones. You make me feel safe just knowing you're out there trying to put the bad guys away."

Her eyes wide and warm expressing how proud she was of him, with her hero gaze and praise, his chest puffed out in pride, he bent to kiss her, she turned her head and his lips ended up on her cheek.

She tugged her hand out from under his, dabbed her napkin at her lips, folded it and set it on the table. Her smile soft, sweet, she said, "Um, you know we have to get up early, we should really get going."

He smoothed her long curls off her shoulder and tried to wrap his hand around her neck to pull her close, but she twisted away, picking up her purse.

His crooked grin resigned, Ronan sighed again. "Okay, you're right, the big bad wolf will be knocking at your door." He picked up the check and took out his wallet.

Jesa opened her purse and set her ten-dollar bill, all the money she had, on the table.

One brow quirked at the money, Ronan opened his mouth but she was busy shuffling out of the seat. "Jesa, hey-" he quickly threw money down and stood up as she was walking away from the table.

Jesa threaded her way through the tables with Ronan on her heels. At the door, he reached his long arm out in front of her and pushed the door open, holding it while she walked through.

The wind had died down some but the air was biting. "Listen, Jesa," he started as they walked to his truck, he opened the passenger door and helped her up the high step. His hand on the door he said, "I asked you out, that means I pay. I didn't expect, I don't want your-"

She smiled at him. "It's okay, Ronan I'd like us to be friends. All right?"

Ronan flattened his lips to keep from scowling, kept his sandy brows even, hiding his anger at her clearly putting up walls. Seeing his dissatisfaction anyway and pretending she didn't, Jesa put on her seatbelt to stall any further discussion. He closed her door and climbed in the driver's side. They drove in silence to her home.

He parked in the gravel driveway, when he went to turn the ignition off; she set a hand on his stopping him. "Thank you, Ronan for a fun time. But, I can walk myself in, and it's late." The way he'd tried to kiss her in public there was no doubt to Jesa that he would pursue more once they were closed inside her home, in complete privacy. She opened her door and slid out, catching the frustration on his handsome face.

He said quickly, "Jesa, listen," and leaned over towards her bracing his hand on the seat. "Give me just a minute-"

Shaking her head, she said, "We have to leave early tomorrow, I'll see you at the station. Good night, and thanks for a really nice time, Ronan." She quickly closed the car door and hurried inside the bungalow.

As before, she pressed her back against the door, and waited.

He sat in his truck not moving, obviously contemplating whether or not to give in to his desire to push her, talk her into letting him inside. Her shoulders humped rigidly near her ears, preparing to have to anger him further by rejecting him.

Hearing the truck back down the drive and head out to the road, her chest fell as her breath released in relief.

Chapter Ten

The next morning, pulling her jeans on, Jesa grabbed a pale blue t-shirt. The shirt fit her very snuggly so it made a good underlay for the soft white sweater with the deep V-neck. She stuffed her feet into ankle boots then pondered her reflection in the mirror over the old, banged-up dresser.

Drawing a brush through her long curls, she frowned when she realized her hands were shaking. Large green eyes stared unhappily back at her. She never was good at hiding her feelings. Fear, sadness, loneliness, all gleamed at her like pages in a book.

Last night at the restaurant rolled through her head. A smile brightened her melancholy expression; she'd had a really fun time with Ronan. The smile dimmed as she set the brush down. The deputy was gorgeous, and he made it clear he was interested in her. As just a sleep-buddy or more she wasn't sure.

It didn't matter, she turned from the mirror with a glum sigh. She just couldn't take the chance of getting involved with any man, especially a deputy. And that thought brought her to why her hands were shaking.

Agent Koffi was coming to pick her up and she needed to be ready. Last thing she wanted was to incur his impatient displeasure. Jesa admitted it to herself; the harshly chiseled, growly man frightened her. Darkness glimmered in his cold eyes. It was as if something terrifying wanted to climb out of them and it took all his effort to keep the monster submerged. Yeah, she was afraid of him, but...she slipped her jacket on making sure she had her hat and mittens.

When his body was smashing her into the wall, she still thought he had been about to kiss her. And, a shiver ran through Jesa's slim body, she had felt drawn. Her chin had tilted up, eyes closed and lips parted as if he had some sort of mystical control of her. A wizardry spell making her respond to him against her will.

But why? The gruff, domineering agent surely would have no interest in her when women flocked to him like flies on a horse. Plus, he constantly demeaned her by calling her a girl, and was snappy rude with his commands to her like she was his foot soldier, or something beneath him.

Picking up the backpack, she shook her head with a goofy grin at her ridiculous fantasies. She snatched her keys off the table with a firm sure movement. It was silly, she was attracted to Ronan with his light hair and devastating blue eyes, and his delightfully mischievous manner. No way did the brusque, overbearing, scary agent hold any interest for her. Ronan's soft locks curled hippy-ish over his collar compared to the agent's neatly styled hair, cut arrow straight across the back of his thick neck.

Ronan's off-duty attire was washed-out jeans and flannel shirts, a relaxed contrast to Koffi's expensive suits fitted perfectly to his muscled build. His idea of relaxed was no tie. Sure, if you took the cold ruthlessness and the crude and brutal demeanor away, even with the dangerous looking scars Koffi could be considered handsome too. He was villain dark to Ronan's hero light.

Jesa wanted to stay in the light. Ronan's lips were soft while Koffi's were- goose bumps ran up her arms at the thought of being intimate with Agent Koffi. Not surprising, her body quivered with bone-chilling fright, but also inexplicable arousal tingled through her. She rubbed the goose bumps off her arms.

A snort of self-ridicule Jesa chastised herself, "Where did that arousing thought come from? What do I know about…sexual feelings?" Always hiding, constantly on the run, pushing aside men's passes so they didn't get too close, she'd never had the time to kiss a lot much less ever to have had…sex.

"It must be this island," she thought, "some of the romance is just filtering onto me. The heated desire in Ronan's arresting blues must be getting my libido stirred up-" then glittering, hooded obsidian eyes, seething with mystery and danger sparred in her mind with the breezy fairer, impish orbs of the deputy's. She pictured Koffi's lips bearing down on hers, her body tingled more sharply-

Flummoxed and confused with her disturbing imaginings, Jesa stomped across the kitchen floor, telling herself that her reaction was her fear of Koffi. Tugging on her hat and mittens, her mouth pulled in at a corner. Funny that thinking of Ronan in that way didn't cause the same fearful arousing reaction. Of course, that's because she wasn't afraid of him. She felt relatively safe with the buff deputy. Her body was confusing arousal with fright, just nerves, how foolish of her.

She reached for the doorknob resolving to not allow Agent Koffi to intimidate her. No, she was a grown woman, shrugging her backpack on, it was irrational to be afraid of the agent, she opened the door and squealed.

Koffi was standing on her stoop with his fist out about to knock. "Shit, girl, way to give a guy a heart attack. I didn't think you knew I was here."

"Uh," the gulp wriggled down her tight throat. "I didn't. I was coming out to wait for you."

Brows drawn down, he reached around her closing her door. "Why would you wait out-" the stoop wasn't that big, his muscled chest brushed against her, Jesa shrank from his strapping body. She lurched backwards, and stepped right off the edge of the porch.

"Fuck!" Tristano threw his hand out, snagging her arm, he jerked her back up so hard she stumbled forward in danger of falling the other way. He rolled his arm around her back catching her up against him.

Holding her in a close embrace, he grumbled, "Geeze, what the hell is wrong with you?" He ran a hard hand down her trembling back to steady her.

Gaining her balance, and flooded with embarrassment, Jesa pushed at him to let her go. The agent curled his thick fingers around her arms and held her still, forcing her to look up at him. Her head tilted up but she kept her eyes averted.

His dark gaze prodded her like a finger under her chin pushing her face up higher. Her eyes lifted to his, he plumbed their depths quizzically. Deep voice rumbling, he growled, "Jesselin, are you afraid

86

of me?" A flicker of fear rippled over her pale face and disappeared, but it had been there. "Dammit Jess-"

She wrenched from his clutch, stumbling again, but she managed to stay on the steps down to the ground where she backed away from him. Lips pushed out defiantly, lids lowered to hide her emotions, she jerked on the backpack strap, said stiffly, "Of course not. Don't be ridiculous. Shouldn't we be going?" She turned on her heel and marched to the car.

Koffi strode after her. Reaching the car first he yanked the passenger door open and stood back for her to get in. When she balked, he caught a strap of her backpack pulling it right off her shoulder.

Her plump lips pushed out further. "It's my car, I want to drive." She started to move around him to go to the driver's side but he blocked her.

"We discussed this already, girl. McKabe would want me to drive. It's cold, get in." Face a block of unyielding rock, he stared blankly at her, he wasn't giving in.

"That's just- just stupid. Why would the sheriff- hey!" Koffi grasped her arm and about lifted her into the car. Pushing the backpack onto her lap, he closed the door in her irate face.

The smirk not really hidden, he trotted around the car and hopped in behind the wheel. "Here," motioning between the seats to a carton holding cups and a bag, he said to the petulant woman, "I brought you a coffee. There's cream and sugar in the bag if you want."

Cranking up the car, he glanced at her; a slow grin curved the side of his face. She was sitting with her arms crossed, lips still pushed out in a pout glaring at the windshield.

The warmth in the small car was a welcome respite to the bitter morning air. Jesa exhaled exasperated and accepted the coffee. Removing the lid, she took out a couple of creams and sugars from the bag and added them to the hot brew, stirring vigorously in her annoyance.

With a small chuckle, he drove down the street heading to the main road leading to the Commons, then he sobered. "I don't want you waiting outside for me, Jesselin. It's cold and your cottage sits back from the road somewhat isolating it. No one would see if you were attacked."

"What?" Her lashes flew up flabbergasted. "That is preposterous. Good heavens, I told you this is just a sleepy little resort town, no one is out to get me," she was unnerved to find her voice shook. He wouldn't know the reality of what he was saying. But, no, she was safe here on Orainn, no one could possibly find her, track her here.

"Brie Westcott-"

"I know, she's been kidnapped," her voice heavy with her sigh of his continuing to throw that at her. "But that is just an anomaly; she was taken for- for ransom. I am poor as a church mouse, I haven't got anything anyone would want." Nothing except her eyewitness testimony.

Turning his head towards her, Koffi's gaze roamed down her body, his lips compressed. "Don't sell yourself short, little girl, you have plenty that a man could want to take."

Brow furrowing into a frown, she said, "What on earth could I-"

"Never mind. Just do as I say. Don't wait outside for me, and don't wander around this wooded area alone. You are well aware there are transients on this rock, people are coming here on vacation, half the population is temporary, the land is abundant with strangers. That's it, we're done with this conversation, don't argue with me."

Her mouth hung appalled at his bossiness. Seeing the granite jaw set, the edges working, his inflexible eyes on the road they traveled, she closed her mouth knowing it would be futile to argue with him.

They drove in silence, until Jesa sighed. Her good nature couldn't keep her anger up. "What are we to do today, Agent Koffi?"

Dark brows knit down, he shot her a quick glance. Deep voice starting aloof, dictatorial, eased off, he took a breath then said, "Jesselin, we are basically colleagues, for now. It would be more appropriate if you called me Tristano." At her silence, his glance over again caught an unreadable look creasing her face. "What?"

Jesa said nothing, just shook her head. Nose in the air, arms crossed she said to him with a haughty sniff, "You must stop calling me girl. It is not only incorrect; it is insulting to an adult woman to be called that. I am not a girl."

A chuckle eked out and he shot her a quick grin. "Hmm. Coulda fooled me. You sure as hell aren't the opposite." His gaze roved over her face. The large vibrant eyes, cheeks rounded like apples, gumdrop lips, his eyes shifted to her chest, he didn't look like he agreed with her, but he shrugged with indifference. "All right." His big hand curled over the wheel was confident as he steered them up the winding hill.

"You didn't answer me, Agent Tristano, what are the plans for today?"

He arched his neck and looked up at the ceiling in incredulity. Cranking his head back and forth to crack his neck, he looked over at her shaking his head. "Just Tristano, Jesselin, leave off the Agent."

Jesa watched the baring trees and evergreens out the side window. It was contradictory for him to insist she call him by his given name like they were equals when he was always playing the big boss issuing instructions and commands to her. But, she'd learned disputing his orders got her nowhere. "Okay." She turned to him, "I go by Jesa, not Jesselin." When he made no comment she turned back to the window.

As he pulled up and parked by the police station, he said, "We are interviewing the models that Normandy guy was photographing." By the time he got around the car, Jesa had only budged the door open about two inches. Tristano gripped the handle and opened it with one jerk. Jesa slid out and he slammed the door shut and started walking, but Jesa stood frowning.

She stared at the car, then it dawned on her what was different, her lips compressed. Rushing after him, she yelled, "Hey!" His long legs made quicker work of the walk than her shorter ones did, she had to jog to catch up to him.

When she reached him, she grabbed his jacket sleeve trying to make him stop. He did, smiling at her in amusement. Brows lifted, he asked, "Problem?"

"You- you-" Anger roiled up her throat, "The heater was on in the car. You had it fixed when I precisely told you not to!"

Bending his head closer to her, he stuffed his hands in his pockets and gave a look like, 'seriously? You're upset about that?' But instead he just shrugged. "Yeah. It's no big deal, woman, don't get your panties in a twist. I'm driving it, so I get to do with it what I want. You can't make it through the upcoming harsh winter here without the heater, and Finn Barton told me you barely make enough to pay rent and feed yourself. So, get off your high horse and live with it." He swiveled from her and started traipsing back up the walk.

She hustled after him calling, "Wait, Agent," he moved faster. Huffing to keep up with him she puffed, "I will pay you back. Tell me how much it cost and I'll write you a check."

Ignoring her, he grasped the handle to the station door and swung it open. As she sputtered, he put his hand on the small of her back and pushed her inside. Then when she gathered her wits to lambast him, he chuckled and strode off down the hall to the sheriff's office. Jesa had no choice but to scurry after him, her face pinched with frustrated indignation.

McKabe was standing outside his office with Deputies Morgan, Jerry, and young Donnie Gable who had been babysitting the Westcotts. The word was out that the models were in the station; half the deputies had already stopped by for one reason or another.

"Hey, we've been waiting on you, the ladies are here." McKabe nodded at Tristano, smiled at Jesa with a paternal wink. "Ronan's already in there. Let's go." He held an arm out for them to follow him.

Jesa's phone rang. She stopped to slide her backpack off her shoulder, took the phone out and slid her finger to unlock it. "Hello?"

Tristano stayed with her while the others went on ahead. His brow creased when Jesa kept repeating, "Hello? Hello?" With a "Humph," she clicked it off and dropped it inside her pack and started walking. Koffi strode up next to her. He asked, "What was that all about?"

Bumping one shoulder airily, she responded coolly, "It was nothing, just a hang up. I've had a few, must be I have someone's old number." She walked with her head down trying to hide the worried expression on her stiff face under a curtain of long flaming curls.

But Koffi saw it. "What? What's wrong, Jesselin?"

Shaking her head she shrugged it off. "Nothing, I told you. Just a wrong number."

Tristano caught her arm holding her back, insisting, "Jesselin, tell me-"

Ripping her arm from his clutch she said tartly, "I don't like to be called Jesselin. My name is Jesa," and she stomped into the room only to come to a dead halt. Her eyes widened. Inside, a ton of male deputies and other men in the local area had crowded into the room each jostling for position to get near to the three models preening amidst the throng.

Holding central court was as per cliché, a blonde with classic features, a spicy brunette, and a redheaded African American. They were all well above average height and stick-thin.

Caitlin came over and stood beside Jesa and filled her in. "The redhead with the updo is Ashanti." The girl had smooth cocoa skin and she was the only one with any semblance of a body. Her breasts were small but she had a narrow waist that swelled out to a donkey round butt that judging by the skintight bandage dress she wore, she knew was her best feature, that and her exotic, slanted golden eyes.

Caitlin went on, "They're all from LA. The blonde with the cheekbones is Chantal." Chantal's straight hair was swept back off her forehead to hang board-stiff like a yellow whiskbroom across the back of her bony shoulder blades. Quite flat chested with boyish hips, her lack of curves didn't slow down the male salivation. Probably due to the tiny cheek-exposing shorts and braless cropped top she wore.

The deputy lowered her head to speak more quietly in Jesa's ear. "The one with the baseball boobs that are sitting oddly on either side of her chest, skinny hips and pin-thin legs, is Sierra." In a miniscule skirt, Sierra parted her zigzag chocolate brown extensions to one side so they puffed high on her crown to tumble over one shoulder.

"Uh huh." Jesa nodded at the madness in the room. Closest to the girls, Jesa saw sandy blond hair a head above the rest. Ronan was there. Agent Koffi bent his head and spoke quietly in Jesa's ear, "Put the fucking phone in your pocket," and he left her side muscling through the small crowd to reach the models.

Her lips pushed out in an abandoned pout, not that she ever expected anything different, Jesa slipped out of the room. The corridor was clear, she traipsed down the hall to one of the back rooms. Lifting the backpack from her shoulder, she set it on a table and took out her pad. With nothing else to do, she reviewed the notes she'd made. She'd add more information that various deputies had forwarded to her and then she'd send them on to Willie-Jean to disperse.

She had no idea how much time had passed when she heard a sound behind her. Slipping the pad back in the bag, she turned. Tristano stood with a shoulder braced against one side of the doorframe watching her. As if he wasn't there, she continued fussing with the backpack, shuffling items around inside.

"Jesselin," the imposing baritone carried quietly across the tiled floor, "we are about to begin the interviews. Are you ready?"

She blinked at him as if surprised she was included. The harsh face cracked a rare smile, he held a hand out to her and said, "Come."

Jesa hesitated, the sting of not belonging, not being attractive or exciting enough to hold a man's interest for more than a heartbeat like the models, still stabbed at her gut. Sure, she didn't want the attention, but still… Koffi had only sought her out likely on the sheriff's bequest.

Tristano undoubtedly hated to be the one to have to leave the models and come and wrangle up plain Jane Jesa. Customers at the saloon had told her she was beautiful, but they were drunk. Women like Sally, and her own mother Raeleen, incessantly reminded her that she was just on the right side of ugly. Her lungs emptied with a dismal sigh, stringing the pack over her shoulder she moved dejectedly towards him.

His enigmatic eyes never revealed his thoughts, but his mouth pulled in with benevolent concern. Jesa's face was like a musical sheet with all the notes crisply perceptible, her misery penciled all over it. "Hey, Bitty bit, what's going on? What's wrong?" He tried to put his hand on her shoulder but she ducked around him.

Hurrying out to the corridor she tossed breezily over her shoulder, "Nothing. I'm as happy as a pig in sunshine."

Perplexity in the slant of his head, Tristano traipsed after her.

Chapter Eleven

They went to Interview Room 1 where Chantal Erikson lounged back in a chair. Crossing her long, long legs pushed the tiny half-shorts up higher exposing most of one of her ass cheeks.

The curl lifting a corner of her burgundy-slicked lips indicated she was well aware of it. One sharp elbow draping nonchalantly over the back of her chair drew the crop-top up to reveal the bare under swell of her braless small breasts. The girl knew how to work what she had.

In jeans and a blue-striped oxford shirt, Ronan half sat on the edge of the sturdy wooden table. He was shaking his head, he broke off what he was saying when Koffi and Jesa entered the room.

Chantal's vast eyelashes swept down disdaining Jesa as nonexistent, but widened, then fell half-mast in sultry notice at Tristano in his custom-made suit. The suit was dark with a white shirt, and subtle grey and black striped tie.

Blunt-straight blonde hair scraped across the model's bony shoulders as she shifted in her seat exposing more bare cheek-skin and fluttered those extra-long lashes at him.

"Hey Jesa." Ronan slid off the table and went to her. "Where have you been? I looked for you-"

"Let's get this interview started," speaking over him, Koffi set his hand on Jesa's lower back and moved her into the room. The room was small but had three chairs and the table. Tristano pulled out a chair and nodded to it for Jesa to sit. "You need your notepad," he said.

Jesa blinked, she kept forgetting she had a role there. Setting the pack on the floor, she removed the pad and pen. Keeping her eyes on the pad, she flipped a few pages over and laid it on the table. Last thing she wanted to see was the deputy she was attracted to flirting with the model. But, Ronan sat in the third chair dragging it closer to her. "Sugar, I-"

"Ms. Chantal Erikson," Tristano's gun-smoke curt voice interrupted him again. "I am Special Agent Koffi with the FBI, this is Ms. Judan, and Deputy Roarke. We are here to-"

"*Agent*," the word dripped silkily over her tongue that was sliding around her parted wide glossy lips. This time the model cut him off. Leisurely trolling her eyes over his harsh face, down the rugged body in the expensively cut suit, pencil-thin brows arched blatantly exhibiting her interest in the tough agent.

Such a husky voice from such a skinny body indicated heavy cigarette usage, she purred, "Normally I would be furiously appalled at being hauled down here like a common criminal, but," her sexy gaze lavished bold desire as it rolled further down to his fly, where it paused, and she took a deep breath.

"Since I get to meet a real live G-man," she licked her lips and shamelessly looked him over again, she purred, "I can forgive the insult."

Observing the brazen seductress, Jesa's cheeks bloomed with red seeing Chantal's pointy chest stick out further with her deep breath, and her hard little nipples poked through the thin material of her top. Swallowing down her embarrassment, Jesa averted her scandalized eyes to her notepad. Her cheeks darkened at Chantal's knowing snicker.

Not wanting to see the two men with their tongues hanging out drooling over the sexy model, Jesa kept her head down fussing with her pen.

His voice surprisingly frosty, Tristano said, "We have some questions for you, madam. The more quickly we get them answered the sooner you will be allowed to leave."

Chantal's provocative gaze rose to his dark eyes, a slow simmering smile spread over her thin face. "Hmm," she simpered, "as long as you leave with me, I'm game."

Ronan stood up shoving his chair back. "Ms. Erikson, how long have you lived in L.A.?"

Her beguiling eyes rolled up to the big deputy, the lustful smile didn't diminish. "Ah, this island is rife with brawny hunky men." Lids fell and lifted, she turned her perusal to the deputy. "We were in a personal discussion before we were interrupted. We can-"

"Ms. Erikson," Tristano did not hide his irritation, he ordered, "Answer the question."

She slowly re-crossed her legs revealing she was commando under her shorts.

Shades of Sharon Stone, Jesa's face turned tomato but she noticed both men kept their eyes fixed on Chantal's face.

The model's regard returned to Koffi. Seeing his features hard and unyielding, lids narrowed in impatience, she sighed. Lifting her arms she smoothed her palms over the stiff do, groused, "Oh, these small towns, the men are such puritans. Fine. I have lived in L.A. all my life."

"Thank you," Tristano said stonily. "How long have you known Niels Normandy, or worked for him?"

"Huh," she sniffed, her big lips pursed in annoyance. "I do not work for him. Sierra and Ashanti and me were hired to do this one shoot. I've only worked *with* him once or twice before but a large fashion company hired us all, Niels included."

Rolling his wide shoulders back, Koffi pushed the sides of his jacket back and set his hands on his hips. Even with a belt his slacks hung slightly from his lean hips. "So, how well do you know him? Be specific."

Her brows daggered down. "If you mean have we fucked, no. He's a squirrely little man, I wouldn't let him touch me with a ten foot-"

"He said be specific, Ms. Erikson." Ronan also sounded irritated with the vain model. "How long, how well do you know this designer?"

Her eyes flit to him, she smiled with a slight shrug. "I barely know him. The other two jobs we didn't even share more than a couple of words, mostly posing directions from him. This entire shoot we girls conversed, gossiped you know," she swung the crossed long leg, patted her hair. "You know, juicy gossip makes the world go round."

"Yeah, tell us about Normandy," Ronan asserted.

"Fine, fine." Rolling her eyes with a huff, her lips twisted, she said, "We pretty much avoided octopus hands Normandy. Ya know what I mean?" She looked from Ronan to Tristano who both stared stone-faced back at her.

"So, you're saying you really don't know Normandy that well?" Ronan asked.

Her gaze slinked back to him, one bony shoulder bumped expressing her annoyance. "No. And I don't care to. He's a cheap no-name designer trying to get himself out there. He's talentless. Oh, he has some skill, the bikinis we shot were pretty nice. Showed a lot of skin," she laughed, "can't beat that, huh?"

She twisted her hips further almost completely baring one butt cheek and peered up at Ronan then Koffi with one brow raised in daring. Her thin face frowned at Jesa's cough, then she glared at Ronan's snickering clearing of his throat.

"You all attended a party at Stedman Westcott's house around a week ago." Tristano waited for her to flick her attention back to him.

"So? We are gorgeous models," she responded with zilch modesty. Sniffing with conceit, she examined her manicure. "We are invited to tons and tons of parties. In mansions, on yachts," her vapid eyes shifted to Jesa with an egotistic jeer, indicating the younger woman would never have the same opportunities.

Tristano said, "Mr. Normandy was found lurking in the Westcotts' baby's nursery. Have you any idea why he would be in there?"

Chantal got slowly to her feet and stretched with a loud yawn. Reaching her long arms over her head she bent her elbows dropping her hands behind her head. The crop top crept up so far her ribs jutted out of her midriff, and the brown areoles became visible. Bored with the conversation, her arms fell at her side, not bothering to tug the shirt back down, it bunched over her tiny breasts.

"No, I have no idea why the idiot would be in there. He's probably some kind of child pervert, I mean, he gropes us every chance he gets, and just look at him," her sneer contorted her face ugly. "It's not like any normal female would go out with him. Certainly not one of us, we are so out of his league we're in the stratosphere. Now, her on the other hand," she dipped her head at Jesa.

"Thank you, Ms. Erikson," Tristano said abruptly and took a few steps to the door and opened it. He stood beside it, staring coldly at her. Chantal stood flapping her long lashes in astonishment at him.

"You- you want me to leave? Don't you have more questions for me, handsome?" She snaked her elongated, skinny body over to him. Fingers like sharp pens with blue painted tips pecked then settled on his arm. "Maybe you and I could-"

The agent stepped aside and motioned for her to leave. "We have enough, thank you for your time." He turned his back to her and said to Jesa, "You done with your notes, Jesselin? We need to interro- uh, move on to question the others."

Not used to being denied and dismissed with such rare indifference, Chantal parted her burgundy lips apparently to make an offer to Ronan, but he shook his head with an unpleasant crooked grin, blue eyes twinkling a mock. Snapping her blonde head with an indignant huff, the next sound was her furious six-inch heels clicking angrily down the hall. Shoes have no emotion of course, but if they did, hers would be spitting spurned fire.

Koffi, Ronan and Jesa interviewed the other two models with the same useless, vain, results. Their forward brazen invitations to both men were also rebuffed. Afterwards, everyone ended up in the big conference room, the models holding court again with men swarming them, giving them the love and lust they didn't get from the agent and the deputy.

The three interviewers settled wearily on chairs off to the side of the room, away from the commotion. It was warm in the room, Tristano took off his jacket and loosened his tie. Ronan rolled up his long sleeves. Jesa pulled the white sweater off and twisted to lay it on the back of her chair. When she turned back around, both men had strange looks on their faces. "What? Is my shirt dirty?" She looked down at the snug T.

A sound croaked in his throat, Ronan stuck a finger in the top of his shirt and tugged at it like it was too tight. Yanking his blue eyes up from their latch on her chest that rounded out plump in the t-shirt, he coughed, "Ah, you," he grunted down another cough, "you usually wear really baggy stuff that don't show your figure. And, I'll say, sugar," a lopsided grin broke across his handsome face, "you have one damned helluva figure." His gaze traveled back down as if by magnet to her full breasts, his pupils pulsed inside the sky blue irises.

Tristano jabbed his elbow in his arm.

"Hey, ow, you shiesty jerk." Ronan glared at him rubbing his arm, he groused, "What the hell, asshole."

Getting to his feet, Koffi left them and strode out of the room.

His hand still rubbing his arm, Ronan shook his head with a grimace. Sandy hair flopped over an eye; he shoved it back in irritation. "Guy's an asshat igit," he muttered. The buzz of conversation regurgitated through the room as people rooted about vying for the models' attention.

Tossing her bag over a shoulder, Jesa stood up purposefully.

Ronan asked, "Where you going? You following that alpha-jerk?"

Jesa gave him a half smile at his rivalry behavior. "No, I'm going down the street to the bistro. I haven't seen my friends for a few days and I kind of miss them."

Ronan jumped up claiming, "I'll go with you."

"Roarke." Caitlin Saunders had just entered the room. She walked over to the couple but her absorbed appraisal was taking in the scene. Men were falling all over themselves trying to hook up with one of the girls.

Chuckling, Ronan said, "You wanted something, Cat?"

The female deputy was as enthralled with the models as the men.

Chuckling again, he said louder, "Earth to Cat, Earth to Cat, come in, Cat." He and Jesa grinned at each other.

Deputy Saunders made no secret that she preferred playing in the lady pool. Never looking at him she mumbled, "Ah, Roarke, the chief wants to see you, wants your dissemination on the women." She almost stumbled in her haste hurrying over to join the pandering crowd.

Ronan laughed. "Good luck to her. If I were her, I'd try for Ashanti. Soon as you whipped that sweater off, the model's eyeballs blew out of her head and she's hardly looked away since. I hope Cat likes dark meat, 'cause that girl is cookin', eh?"

"Huh?"

Ronan touched Jesa's cheek, keeping his fingertips there for a moment until the heat of her shy embarrassment warmed his fingers. "Wait for me, sugar, and I'll go over with you."

She ducked from his hand and adjusted the strap of her pack to fit more comfortably on her back. "No, that's okay, I'll catch up with you later. Agent Koffi said we were done for the day."

Ronan tucked his fingers in his jean's pockets, hunching his big shoulders, his smile coaxing. "Come on, honey, wait for me and we can catch dinner at the bistro or the Shipwreck on the water. They have great food."

Jesa took a step away from him. Her soft voice apologetic, "No, I really want to go spend some personal time with my friends. I'll see you tomorrow, okay?" She was surprised to see his attractive face crestfallen at her rebuff. The guy was a block of gorgeous and muscle, he could have any girl on the island he wanted including the models who had all shown interest in him, why would he care about her?

She decided he has probably slept with all the available women here and she was someone new. Well, he had at least three other new females to get to know. She headed for the bistro without considering how she would get home. She'd walked numerous times in the dark before, it wasn't a big deal.

Chapter Twelve

The restaurant was busy but everyone greeted Jesa joyfully with open arms. Velvet gave her a huge hug. "We've sure missed you, hon. Your sweetness is addicting, even the customers ask about you," she patted Jesa's shoulder with a pudgy hand.

"Jesa!" Lavern threaded through the tables filled with customers. Wiping her hands on her apron, she hugged the petite young woman. "Where you been, girl?"

Velvet said with a snicker, "Where you think, Bubbles, she's being carted around by two of the hunkiest men to ever skate on this rink of a rock. If she's smart, and I know she is," the waitress winked, grinning wickedly, "she's banging at least one, if not both of 'em. Which one, Jes, give us the dirt!"

"Velvet, gosh." Jesa turned bubblegum pink. "I never, it's only been a few days, I'm not, you- you-"

"Okay sweetheart, calm down, everyone knows you're a good girl. But hells bells, you gotta do them, make us married chicks proud! Let us live vicariously through you!" Velvet laughed and Lavern grinned while nodding in agreement.

Ducking her head, Jesa said, "Stop, Velvet, please." To hide her embarrassment she partially turned her back to the rotund server, and was stunned to see Elizabeth Westcott. "Is that, I mean, Mrs. Westcott is here, I thought they wanted her to stay home and wait for...um."

Laverne gave Jesa another hug then trotted off to pick up an order.

Velvet looked over where Elizabeth was in the back alcove under the loft chatting with a young man. "Oh yeah. Apparently the Westcotts got bored sitting home, and Deputies Gomez and Osborne escorted them here for dinner. Stedman is down the street talking to Sheriff McKabe, he should be here any minute." She set the backs of her hands on her big round hips, her fingers curled out. "Any word on the baby? How's the investigation going?"

Jesa's plush lips tugged in woefully at the corners. "Not good. There's been no ransom demand, no calls from the kidnappers. No one except a few nuts claiming to have seen little Brie. Oh Velvet," she sighed sadly. "That poor baby, those poor parents," she watched Elizabeth still in the clandestine alcove talking with the young man. From what she could see, he was good looking with dark hair, and... Jesa's brows lowered, and the couple appeared quite...friendly.

The man's mouth was near Elizabeth's ear, her head was angled close to him, and she was...giggling. Jesa considered going over and speaking with the young mother-

"You order your dinner yet?" The familiar dark growl rumbled behind her. Jesa swung around to see Agent Koffi.

"I...I, what are you doing here?" She inched back from him but stopped at his frown.

One hand shoved in his trouser pocket, he palmed the other over the top of his hair. He'd lost the tie but had the suit jacket back on, he must have left the trench coat in the car. The starched white shirt a sharp foil to his tanned skin, early evening stubble spread dark across his hard jaw.

"I had to look around for you, *again*, Jesselin, and eventually ran into Roarke in McKabe's office and he..." his mouth twitched dryly, "reluctantly told me you came here." Hooded eyes shadowed, cloaking his thoughts, he said with soft accusation, "How had you planned on getting home? What part of I told you that 'I will take you everywhere' didn't you grasp?"

Struggling to keep still even as his powerful body loomed over her, Jesa stiffened, pursing her lips. He did it on purpose, she was sure. He thought it was amusing to intimidate her. Well, she was not playing his games.

Ignoring his comment about how she was getting home, she snipped, "Okay, then, you found me. So, you can go on now about your business, I'm sure you have things to do, models to date, reports to fill out, people to boss around."

His dark brows rose satirically at her, hard mouth sloped in a laconic smile. Tucking his hand in a pocket he shrugged his thick shoulders equably. "Nope, got all my business done. There's nothing else to go on at the moment, and I'm hungry. Let's get a table, I haven't been here, it looks nice. Kind of rustic cozy chic, yet," he looked around, "it feels open with all those big windows."

He took in the glassed front and sides. Outside the panoramic windows colorful autumn leaves chased each other in swirls. The tables were teeming with merry customers, mostly merry anyway. The flickering fireplace, and the amber hued wooden beams and braces made the room warm and inviting.

Jesa said, "No, I- I'm not hungry," then her head jerked back to the alcove, Elizabeth and the young man were gone. "Agent Koffi, did you know the Westcotts were here?"

He rifled a few fingers though his short wavy hair not looking pleased. "Yeah. It was against our advice, but I guess they were going stir crazy, got cabin fever. We put a detail on them," he nodded to a table where Elizabeth was sitting down, and Stedman was shaking out his coat and laying it on the back of a chair. One of the mainland reporters that was still milling about on the island, and the mayor were with them.

"Let's see about that table." Ignoring her demurrals, Koffi pulled her with him to the hostess desk.

"Baby," Clarie Barton declared and hugged Jesa with affection. "We've missed you, honey." She smiled at Koffi, "Who is your friend?"

"He's not my friend," Jesa said quickly. Tristano squeezed the hand he had wrapped around her wrist. "I mean, he's the man from the FBI, you know, the one I was sent to drive around." A twist to her lip she murmured, "Which has turned out to be more the opposite actually." Koffi squeezed her wrist harder, whether in humor or annoyance Jesa wasn't sure.

Observing Jesa's unhappy expression, her smile polite, tone open and friendly, Clarie held her small hand out to him and said warmly, "I'm Clarie Barton, pleased to meet you."

Koffi squeezed Jesa's hand so hard she blurted the introduction, "He is Special Agent Tristano Koffi, Clarie, with the FBI," she tacked

102

on redundantly and yanked her hand from his grip catching his imperceptible smile.

He shook Clarie's outstretched hand with a slight bow. "Pleasure to meet you, Mrs. Barton. I like your bistro with the light and openness, and the amber wooded ambience."

Her laugh as friendly as the rest of her, the older woman admonished, "Just call me Clarie, please, Agent Koffi."

"Okay, Clarie, I am Tristano, although," his eyes slanted to Jesa, "some people can't seem to remember that. You and your husband own the Divine Bistro?"

"Yes, yes," she nodded cheerfully, "for nigh on 16 years. We love the bistro as much as we love Orainn. Welcome to our island, well, peninsula still at the moment."

"Thank you, Clarie. At the risk of stating over-worked platitudes, from the little I've seen, Orainn is a quaint, picturesque village." He set a hand on Jesa's waist holding her in place with an almost proprietary touch. "Ah, Jesselin and I would like a table for dinner if you have one available?"

Clarie's gaze flit from him to Jesa and saw the color rising in Jesa's cheeks. "Oh, of course. We have a few open tables. Mr. Sloan is in the kitchen, I'll seat you myself."

Koffi gave her another slight respectful bow. "Thank you. Jesselin?" He moved his hand to her lower back nudging her forward to follow Clarie.

Digging her feet into the floor Jesa whispered fiercely, "No, I can't."

He bent his head so no one could hear their conversation. "Why the hell not? It's been hours since you ate."

Her face heating in an uncomfortable blush, she muttered, "I," damn she didn't want to tell him but he was staring at her and obviously not going to move until she responded. Exhaling, Jesa tried to wriggle away from his hand on her back to no avail. She spoke so quietly her words were almost inaudible, "I had only planned to come and say hi. I…don't have enough money…" Keeping her head turned from him, she strove harder to break his grip but didn't want to cause a scene.

His fingers wrapped around her waist with an eye-roll and exasperated sigh. "Jesselin," sounding harsh, he stopped and cupped the side of her face forcing her to look at him. A kind smile lifted his full lips, such a rare thing to see, Jesa blinked rapidly thinking it was her imagination.

"First thing," he said, "I don't think that as an employee Barton would expect you to pay, and second," he bent over bringing their faces mere inches apart. "I have money, we fibbers aren't destitute you know. Now," seeing the color deepen in her cheeks, he spoke quickly feeling her shaking her head in objection at his paying.

"Enough, Jesselin, you are being too melodramatically prideful. Just," he moved so his lips were against her ear. Wisps of her hair fluttered as he said, "Let's consider this a business dinner. Will that mollify your pride?" Obviously struggling not to grin at her, his lips pressed together in a straight line.

She uttered, "But-"

He tugged her, forcing her to move with him and not letting her protest further. They followed Clarie who had stopped and waited for them with a puzzled look.

"Um…" Clarie's smile faltered. "Is everything all right?"

Tristano's mouth turned up in a natural smile. "Yes, Clarie, we're right behind you." He motioned with his arm for the pretty, matronly woman to go on to the table.

Her gaze went from him to Jesa who looked perturbed and didn't make eye contact with her, and back to Koffi's confident, authoritative nod. "Uh," she stammered, then smiled widely, "okay, follow me, Jesa honey, and Agent Koffi."

Her fingers flew to cover her mouth with a giggle. "I see why Jesa has a hard time calling you Tristano. You just, um, ooze commanding FBI agent. I don't think I can comfortably call you by your first name." She turned and started down an aisle.

Koffi bent and whispered in Jesa's ear, "But I expect you to call me Tristano." Her hair rippled with his breath, his mouth was so close to her ear. His big hand heating the inner swell of her back, she stiffened under it. Jesa dragged her feet, but his palm was like an iron plate and he easily moved her along.

He took her bag from her then helped her off with her jacket and set both their coats on the booth seat, then she slid in to sit next to them. Tristano sat opposite her with the white and gold speckled tabletop between them.

Clarie handed them each an open menu. "There you go, order whatever you want, you know your money isn't welcome here." She gave them both a huge grin. "I'll send Velvet right over." She smiled warmly at them then left them alone.

Knowing what was on the menu, Jesa just laid hers on the table and glanced around the room. Several customers waved at her bringing a pleased smile to her taut face.

"Ah, that's better, little one. Finally, a smile out of you."

Jesa turned her attention to Tristano and saw his gaze intently roving over her face, shifting from her eyes to her lips and back. He said, "You know the menu, tell me what's good."

Shrugging out of his suit jacket, he set it on the seat beside him then unbuttoned two of the top buttons of his shirt. Jesa could see a bit of dark hair beneath the open buttons, and she unwittingly stared at it. Until she heard his low chuckle and her eyes jerked back up to him. The side of his mouth nicked up in a casual grin, which lifted higher as her cheeks turned rosy.

The dining room lights dimmed and the recessed lights came on. They emitted an elegant purple glow that reflected on the windows and the glasses on the tables making them sparkle with purple luster. The lower illumination made Tristano's own dark eyes shine like mysterious black lacquer. In a conversational note he asked, "Do you have a boyfriend, Jesselin? Have you had a lot of boyfriends?"

Her brows lowered, she replied tartly, "That is not any of your business."

Tristano's grin deepened. "Hmm, said so primly, that means no. Tell me about you and Roarke-"

Velvet came to their table. "Hey, Jesa honey," she greeted, leaned in and gave her another quick hug. "Like I said, we really miss you!"

Jesa reared back in surprise. "Oh? Are you that busy? Mr. Barton assured Chief McKabe that I wasn't needed. Should I come back? Tomorrow for the lunch crowd-"

Koffi's forehead creased in a frown. "No, Jesselin, you-"

"Oh honey." Velvet laughed. "It's not your work I'm talking about, we miss *you*, you silly goose!" Her grin teasing and warm. "You gonna introduce me to your handsome friend?" Her thin lips curved up with slight flirtation at Tristano.

Seldom having any close friends for any length of time, Jesa was socially awkward. Again not introducing him, she rattled off, "He's not my friend. He's the FBI agent I'm supposed to drive around. He-"

Tristano held a hand out to Velvet, she shook it cheerfully. He said coolly, "Tristano Koffi, please call me Tristano," his eyes darted at Jesa and he raised his chin reminding her that he wanted her to refer to him by his given name.

"Ah, you are so lucky, Jesa." Velvet winked at the agent. "Well, you can certainly be *my* friend, Agent Koffi." Her smile turned sly, lids lowered, she exclaimed, "I mean *Tristano*," drawing his name out in a long sexy sound. Then the waitress winked at Jesa. "But he's yours, hon, no touchy on my part!"

"Um, he's not, uh, mine." Feeling more uncomfortable by the minute, for heaven's sake everyone was acting like they were on a date. Disconcerted at the insinuation, Jesa sputtered, "What's the special tonight?"

Chuckling at her friend's discomfort, Velvet said, "We have Veal Escardaro with pearl onions and garlic potatoes, and the Gorgano Pasta. You know with chunks of sausage, shrimp, roasted peppers, oodles of yummy stuff."

"That pasta thing sounds good," Tristano said looking at Jesa.

She closed her menu, and nodded. "Okay, I'd like that, please."

"Make it two." Tristano smiled at Velvet.

The server hadn't taken out an order pad or anything to write their order down. She said, "It comes with a dinner salad and Jake will be over with the warm rolls, butter, and olive oil with seasonings. Would you care for an appetizer?"

Tristano looked to Jesa with an arched brow. Jesa shook her head. "Heaven's no, I'll hardly be able to finish what I have!"

He said to Velvet, "Not tonight, thanks."

"Okay, what would you like to drink?"

Before Jesa could speak, Tristano said, "May I see your wine list?"

"It's on the back page of the menu," Velvet indicated with a motion of her hand.

"Oh." He flipped the stiff page and perused the list. He looked up at Jesa. "Do you have any preference?"

She blinked at him, shook her head. "No, I mean, I don't really drink, I think I'll just have a soda."

"Hmm." He closed the menu and handed it to Velvet. "Bring us a bottle of the Rishéau, and two glasses."

Velvet nodded with a sly grin taking both menus.

Jesa said, "But, no, I don't think-"

But Velvet swung away, tossing over her pudgy shoulder, "Chill, girlfriend, it's time you lived a little." With another saucy wink, she left them.

A different server brought a tray with the wine along with glasses of water with lemon in them. Setting the tray on a stand beside the table, he settled a white tablecloth over the booth, then placed cutlery rolled in napkins, and set the bottle, wine and water glasses and bucket down.

Opening the wine, he poured a thimbleful into Tristano's glass. While awaiting Tristano's approval, he visited with Jesa. As soon as he left another employee stopped by. They weren't left alone for a minute until their dinner arrived.

Again another different server set their plates down, and said jauntily, "Real good to see you, Jesa," a nod to Tristano, "and uh, sir. Bon appétit," with a slight bow he whisked away.

Refilling Jesa's wineglass, Tristano said, "We haven't had a second to ourselves, next time I take you out it'll be at a place where no one knows you." He refilled his own glass and set the bottle in the wine bucket on the table and immediately stuck his fork in his pasta. "Damn, this looks good, smells amazing," he twisted the fork in the noodles wrapping a bundle around it.

Her eyes on her wineglass, Jesa's brow furrowed, she had drunk an entire glass of wine and hadn't realized it with so many people stopping by to greet her. Her head shot up. "Go out?" She shook her head. "We are not out, we will not be going out again, we are-"

"Wow." Chewing, Tristano licked his lip. "This is great, Jesselin. Go on," he gestured with his fork, "eat up."

"Wait, Agent," she started again but he waved his hand at a passing employee. "Hey, son, can you bring us some grated cheese? Thanks." The young busser nodded in affirmation and took off to get it.

"Agent," she tried again, setting her palms flat on the table beside her plate. "Listen, we are not-"

"Eat up, Jesselin, it won't taste as good cold. Here," he added more wine to her glass.

She had taken several nervous gulps, again not realizing how much alcohol she was imbibing. Now, feeling slightly lightheaded, she couldn't remember what she was saying. Jesa lifted her fork and gave a mushroom a taste. "Mmm." She nodded, chewing lustily. "Yeah, you're right, Agent, this is delish," and she stuck a sausage.

Once she got involved with her food, Tristano watched her enjoying her dinner. "I guess you don't have a boyfriend since you went out last night on a date with Roarke. So, how did that go?"

Her fork paused halfway to her open mouth. Setting the fork down, she prevaricated, "It, no, it wasn't a- a date, I mean, we, just, ah…"

Buttering a roll, he said, "He drove you there, pulled your chair out for you, paid for dinner and drove you home. That's generally called a date. So, how did it go? Was he a gentleman, or did he steal a kiss, try to take advantage…" watching her hedge then balk, he innocently chomped half the roll in one bite.

"Agent Koffi," she replied, her cheeks darkened with anger. "That is certainly not your business, and," she grabbed her wineglass and drank a good portion. The wine was going to her head, she set the glass down too hard and it nearly spilled. Frowning at the glass, she said frostily, "He did not pay for my dinner. I paid for it. Can we change the subject?"

Both brows swung up. "You paid?"

"For my half. Agent Koffi, can we please-"

"What the hell kind of gentleman is he that he made you pay half?"

Rolling her eyes, Jesa said, "He didn't *make* me pay. In fact he was upset that I did."

Lips jutting out, black brows lanced in censure he asked, "So then why did you? And why did he let you?"

She pushed her empty glass at him. "I'd like some more, peeze, I mean puhlease," giggling at her slurring.

Tristano leaned back in his chair, said, "I think you've had enough. You're kind of a lightweight in the booze department. That'll make some guy, Roarke for instance, a happy man that you're such a cheap date."

"Hey," she scowled at him complaining, "that's not true, or nice, or," then went to lift the bottle out of the bucket herself but it slipped out of her hand making her giggle some more.

When she went to lift it again, Tristano set his hand over the bottle with a smile. "No, Bitty bit, you've had enough."

Her lips bunched in a scowl. "You are not the boss of me, Agent Koffi. And," her nose in the air she said with a sniff, "he didn't *let* me pay, I put the money down and got right up and left the table. He hadn't much choice. He kinda didn't like it." Remembering his sulky pout she giggled again.

"So," Tristano drawled, buttering another roll, "why did you insist on paying for yourself? I mean, he makes a good wage and you can barely get by."

Her plush lips bunched harder and the scowl returned. "Like I said, Agent Koffi, what I do is none of your affair."

His scowl matched hers as he drained his wine. "Jesselin, I've asked you to call me-"

"Jessy honey! You're here!" A heavy woman with a heavier man behind her shrieked and plopped down beside Jesa on the seat. "We have missed our shy little miss with her sweet smile."

That was the end of Jesa and Tristano's conversation as more people stopped by throughout the rest of their dinner, and dessert. Tristano excused himself to go to the men's room. Instead, he sought out Finn Barton.

The jolly owner shook his hand. "Good to see you, Agent. You taking care of our Jesa?"

Tristano smiled in greeting while he pulled his wallet out of his pocket and opened it. "Trying to, sir. Like you said, she's one mulish female." He took out two, one hundred dollar bills and stuffed them into Finn's shirt pocket. Surprised, Finn pulled them out and looked at them. "What's this for?"

"For our dinner. No," he held up his hand with a brief shake of his head. "You can comp Jesselin's meal, but not mine. I can't accept a free dinner."

Admiration softened the owner's pleasant face; he held the bills out for Tristano to take back. "But this is way too much, your food wasn't nearly this much."

"Keep it." Tristano stuffed his hands in his pockets. "I'll leave more for the server." He turned his head to see the booth where he'd left Jesa. She was giggling, her cheeks rosy, several employees were sitting with her. "I better get her home." His eyes slid over to Finn. "Ah, I didn't ask, she is old enough to drink, right?"

Finn laughed out loud, his head bobbing in affirmation. "Yeah, but not by much. We wouldn't have served her alcohol if she weren't, or sent her off to retrieve you," he peered a stern look at Tristano over his reading glasses. The smile came back lighting up his cheery face. "You take care of our girl now, you hear, Agent?" He clapped Tristano on the back.

Already starting back to the table, Tristano mumbled, "I plan to."

Back at the booth he discretely shoved bills into Velvet's hand and said, "We should head out, Jesselin."

Her big green eyes were shimmering, half hidden by drooping lids from the alcohol. Her head tipped unsteadily up to him, lips pushed out with a whine, "But, I'm not ready to go," a giggle slipped out with a cheeky sing-song, *"Secret Agent Man,"* she dissolved into more giggles and the people sitting with her laughed.

The woman next to her got up. Tristano reached over Jesa and picked up her jacket. He grasped her arm pulling her to her feet. "Yes you are," he said, and helped her on with her jacket.

Slipping her arms in the jacket, she flipped her hair out from under the collar and whined, "I wanna stay longer, I can walk home, you can just go on."

He didn't bother disputing her foolish words, just handed her, her bag, grabbed his own jacket and escorted her away from the booth. It took forever as they wound their way through the bistro for everyone to bid her goodbye and tell her to come back soon. As an afterthought, he was invited back too.

110

He held her arm tightly as she tripped and stumbled, giggling in the cold air all the way to the car. After helping her in and getting behind the wheel, he turned the key starting the engine.

Driving down the dark winding road, he commented, "For being here such a short time, you are well liked."

Her head lolled, she shrugged unevenly. "Um, well, really, it's just that the bistro is such a nice, wonderful place to work it brings out this...joy. I think, uh, the contentment spills over onto the staff." Brows drawing crookedly together in thought, she said, "Agent Koffi, I've seen Mrs. Westcoot, something's not right," a big yawn overtook her, she didn't finish the sentence.

"Yes? What about Mrs. West*cott*?" He chuckled at her slurring. When he was met with silence he glanced over. Jesa was curled up against the door, her head on the window, fast asleep.

She didn't wake up until he pulled into her driveway, the tires crunching on the gravel, he put the car in park and shut it off. When he pushed his door open and the cold air rushed in, Jesa sat up, blinked hard to clear her boozy brain. Seeing him about to get out, she said quickly with a shade of nervous forestalling, "We have an early start tomorrow, I guess you should head on home." She pushed at her door but it didn't budge open.

His mouth twitched but he got out and came around and wrenched the rusted door open for her to climb out.

Her head crooked back so she could look up at him. Afraid he would follow her inside she said, "Agent Koffi, I have nothing to offer you to drink, and I'm really tired, and you need to go on home."

"Hmm," he murmured then bent, clasped her arm and pulled her out. She clutched the strap of her bag and moved away from him, her boots scraping on the gravel driveway. "Agent Koffi, listen-"

His voice quiet with a hint of amusement he said, "Jesselin, you can't get the car door open on your own, and I always walk a lady, even if she's not my *friend*," his wily smile deepened bringing a dimple to one of his cheeks, "to her door. Heaven forbid you trip on a crack or a wild dog attacks you on my watch."

Her onerous rebuttal on parted lips and her vexed expression made him laugh. Then her eyes narrowed at him, pointing at his face she slurred with an accusatory tone, "Hey, you have a dimple, Mr. Secret Agent Man."

"Uh huh." Tristano cupped her elbow and walked her up to her front door. "Make sure you drink a big glass of water and take a couple of aspirins before you go to bed." His humor diminished at her unsteady gait. "I should have been more careful with you, I didn't know you hadn't had much alcohol before. Maybe I should come in and make sure you get settled okay."

Shaking her head vehemently, she mumbled, "No, you can't come in." Suddenly afraid he might force himself inside, she sobered. Turning to face him she put a hand on his chest. "Please, don't. I'll be fine."

His expression thoughtful, Tristano scrutinized her. Taking in her sudden anxiety that he would go inside her place, he backed off, sighed. "All right. I will call you when I get home. Keep your phone in your hand, and if you don't answer, I will be back and I will come inside. You got that, Bitty bit?"

Lips tight, she nodded firmly trying to keep her balance. He took her keys from her and unlocked the door. "Hey," she slurred, "bitty bit, I remember one of my teachers saying that. It's…" she blinked, "southern." Blinking more slowly as her lids grew heavy, she mumbled, "I think." When he pushed the door open, she practically leapt inside to partially close it on him, make sure he stayed out.

"Uh, okay then, thank you, Agent for, um, uh, thanks. I'll see you early tomorrow, right?" She closed the door to his amused smile. A few seconds passed before she heard his footsteps moving away from the door. A moment later the car rumbled off down the street.

Twenty minutes passed, a man kept to the shadows a house over, observing. "Fuck," he cursed under his breath as a police car drove slowly past her place, someone always seemed to be with her, or driving by her home as if checking on her. Hell, he'd follow her, keep surveillance, when he was sure no one was around, or possibly coming back to check on her, then he'd strike.

Chapter Thirteen

The sun was barely painting the tree trunks yellow when Tristano's fist lightly knocked on her door for the third time. He didn't even try to stem the smug grin that softened his tough face at the sight of Jesa when she opened the door only a few inches and peered out at him from under very puffy lids. The strawberry curls were wild and tousled around her sleepy face. Bleary green eyes shaded with a hint of red scowled at him as he pushed the door open forcing her to stumble back, and stepped inside.

Trying to block his entrance, she said, "No, you can't come in, don't-" But he was already closing the door on the brisk wind behind him.

"You are not ready," he said, eyeballing her attire of a tank top and shorts. Her feet were bare, she tried to comb her curls with her fingers but couldn't seem to manage it. "Hmm," he murmured, "as much as I like that outfit," his gaze stroked over her bare shoulders, down her chest where his pupils heated at the half exposed, obviously unfettered rounded breasts. His gaze roamed down further to the slender, girlish legs that were mostly visible in the small shorts. "That what you wear to bed?"

Her response was a grunt and a yawn. He smiled; she was clearly hungover. "Did you drink the water and take the aspirin like you said you were doing when I called last night?" The slight nod she gave him seemed to take all of her energy.

His smile lengthened as he held out a bag. "Here, I brought you sustenance. Get a little nourishment and caffeine into you and you'll soon be feelin' finer'n a frog's hair split four ways."

The inane words coming from the harsh man were weird, but strangely familiar, she stared groggy-eyed at the bag. "Huh?"

"Food," he said, traipsing across the tiny living room. Glancing around, he complimented, "Looks fairly comfortable." An old divan had a crocheted blanket laying rumpled over the back of it, two unmatched cozy chairs set in front of it. The rug was softly worn, low morning light streamed through the picture window brightening the pale walls.

With quick experienced observation, Tristano noticed there was nothing personal at all in the room. No photos on the tables, nothing on the walls. He went straight to the compact kitchen ignoring her protests.

The kitchen was white and yellow wallpaper, with ancient appliances. He set the bag on the counter and lifted a box out of it and set that on the counter.

Jesa trailed in resentfully behind him. "Agent Koffi, what do you think you're doing? You need to go back out to the car and wait for me there. I'll be ready in just a second." Seeing him in his precisely perfect suit, faintly striped grey and white shirt, cufflinks blinking out with his every other move, the black and white paisley tie neatly knotted at his throat, and polished black dress boots, she glanced down at her thin shirt, shorts and bare feet, and winced.

Ignoring her demands, he thrust a cup of coffee at her making her have to take it or it would drop. "You probably should drink it black to get your engines revved, but I got you cream and sugar the way you like it. Here," he pulled out a wrapped sandwich and shoved it into her other hand. "I stopped at the bistro and Barton had the cook make us a couple of egg and bacon sandwiches. Eat up," he commanded cheerfully.

At the pained look on her face, he worked to keep the smile off his. She protested, "Agent, I have cereal, I don't need-"

Frowning at that, he scolded, "Sugary cereal is not sufficient fuel for a body to function properly." The frown intensified, he asked, "Why is it so cold in here? Aren't you freezing in that," his eyes dipped down her barely clothed body then snapped quickly back to her face. His complexion peculiarly darkened. The suit he wore was lined so he was warm enough to have left his trench coat in the car.

Her frown matched his. "I had a quilt around me before you so boorishly forced your way inside. And, I conserve energy, my ah, ecological footprint you know, being responsible by keeping the heat, ah, low." Her eyes darted away from his. She set the sandwich down and busily poured two creamers and two sugars into her coffee; stirred with the swizzle stick and sipped. The stiffness in her face melted. "Ahh, oh, Agent, that's good. You're right, I needed that."

"You mean you're conserving your money, not the electricity, Jesselin."

Prideful stiffness returning to her soft face, she grabbed up her sandwich and coffee and turned from him. Rounded butt in the tight shorts shimmying as she padded across the cold tiled floor to a doorway, she said crossly, "I told you what I do is none of your business, especially my finances. I'll shower and dress as quickly as I can." She disappeared into the doorway.

"Yeah, don't bother changing on my account," he muttered, his hooded eyes on her pert bottom. He knew everything about her finances, he'd dug into every nickel and dime of hers as soon as he'd realized who she was.

While she was absent, he took the opportunity to rummage through her kitchen. He checked every cupboard, every drawer, the miniscule pantry. There were only things there that would come with the rental of the house, plates and flatware. Her cupboards were painfully bare, containing mostly cheap ramen and the like, the fridge held nothing but a small jug of milk and a few condiments. A half loaf of bread and a jar of peanut butter set on the counter next to the cereal she was about to consume before he arrived.

He wanted to search her bedroom and bathroom but he needed a time when she would be away from her home, and in a safe place. Which at this point, he didn't trust anyone but himself to keep her safe, or keep an eye on the girl that managed to disappear in a moment's notice.

By the time she returned, yawning and trying to drag a comb through her wet tangles, he had examined every inch of the kitchen, living room and front closet and was standing nonchalantly sipping his coffee and munching his sandwich. He was relieved, and partly disappointed to see she'd replaced the shorts and tiny top with jeans, ankle boots covered her little feet, and for once she wore a sweater that fit.

The soft yellow firmed over her high full breasts tight enough to outline their plump shape yet loose so their movement was noticeable. He jerked his gaze up to see her face wrinkle in pain as she ripped the comb through her hair, he ordered tersely, "Come here."

Her eyes rolled warily up to him. He repeated with a lighter tone, "Come here, Bitty bit." When she moved a little closer to him, her body rigid with suspicion, he took the comb from her. "Sit," he ordered, pointing at a stool near the counter. Watching him carefully, Jesa did as he said. When she sat, he grabbed the stool and turned it around. She grasped the stool seat with a gasp, "Hey! What are you doing?"

"Hush, sit still." Tristano set a big hand on her slim shoulder holding her in place with her back to him. Then starting at the bottom, one lock at a time, he drew the comb through, gently untangling the tresses.

"Agent-" she tried to turn around. He put his hand back on her shoulder stilling her with an admonishment, "Don't move," and he tugged a snarled tangle hard. "Hey! Ow," she squawked, "that hurt."

He bent and whispered in her ear, "That was for calling me Agent." She tried to turn again to berate him, but he chuckled and prevented her from moving.

With a huff, Jesa sat still until he set the comb down on the counter. When she heard him rustling in a drawer, she cocked her head. "What are you looking for?" He didn't answer, just picked up tresses and twisted them, pulling on the locks for a few minutes.

He announced, "There, you're ready, get your jacket and things and let's get going."

She jumped off the stool and her hair swung around. Looking up at him with astonishment, she said, "You braided my hair. Pigtails."

"Yeah." He grinned and tugged at one.

"But," she objected, yanking it out of his hand, "I'm too old for pigtails."

Tristano said with a playful grin, "They're cute," and he strode out of the kitchen into the living room. He waited at the door while she grabbed her jacket and backpack. She didn't even bother arguing about driving, she knew it was a losing battle, and resisted rolling her eyes when he ordered, "Put your phone in your pocket."

As they drove up the hill, Jesa asked, "What's the plan for today, Agent?" She yelped when he reached over and yanked on a pigtail.

"Tristano," he said, a roguish grin came with the reminder. He told her, "The hotel room the models are staying in was broken into last night while they were out partying. Orainn's CSI's are there now doing an inspection. I doubt there's anything we can do, but we'll stop by."

Tristano parked in front of the stylish Hotel Clasibella near the park down by the water. The wind had lessened but the temperature was colder than it had been all week. Behind the ritzy hotel the ocean brooded dark and churning, but the sun forked through the storm clouds letting in tunnels of light.

Koffi held the door for Jesa to enter and he followed her inside. A deputy stood by the front desk, Koffi went right over to him.

"Agent," the deputy greeted with a nod to Tristano then Jesa. "It's 259, up the grand staircase and to the right. The women are being situated in another room. Room, ah," he glanced down at papers in his hand then said, "256."

"Thanks." Tristano led Jesa up the wide, curved stairs.

A white banister wound with the carpeted steps. Over the royal blue staircase an enormous chandelier glinted colored lights from the crystal and topaz drops clinging to it. Down the hall they saw an open door with a deputy standing just outside. Suite 259 was imprinted on a gold plate on the door. The deputy greeted the couple and stood aside as they passed through into the three bedroom suite.

Inside, the opulent room was a mess. Drawers had been upturned in every room scattering clothes, shoes, makeup, all of the models' belongings had been strewn all over. "Don't touch anything," Koffi warned Jesa. Wearing plastic booties, a fortyish man knelt by one of the bathrooms twirling a dust brush on one of the tossed drawers. He looked up at Tristano's voice.

"Got anything?" Koffi asked him flashing his ID.

"Deputy Stamms, sir," he introduced himself, his gaze sliding up and down Jesa several times until Tristano cleared his throat. A slight shake of his head, Stamms said, "Not much, don't expect much. So many prints smeared on top of each other. The three models apparently have had," his eyes flit to Jesa, "a lot of company. A constant parade of male company judging by the vast assortment of big prints. Even after daily cleaning, there're prints on top of prints. I really don't expect to find anything clear enough to match up with the data base."

He set the brush down in the pot of dark powder. "There aren't any security cameras, as they don't expect a lot of crime waves here on the isle," he chuckled then straightened his mouth at Koffi's hardnosed expression.

"Yeah, uh, anyway, it looks like the burglar used a flat-edged pry bar to crack the door open. It's not here, he must have taken it with him. The deputies did a quick canvass. A maid says she saw someone acting suspiciously in the night. The girls didn't get in until, ah, around five a.m. and discovered the mess. With," he sighed, "a freak load of screaming and cursing, crying and threatening to sue everyone and everything on this, and I quote, 'Pissy piece of shit island.' The maid is in with the models and Deputy Gunderson down at room 256. So far nothing's missing that they can tell 'cept a small frivolous notebook one of the girls had on her nightstand."

Jesa made notes, and the CSI went back to his work. Tristano led Jesa down the short hall. They came across a second tech working away in one of the bedrooms. She also hadn't offered any encouragement that they'd find anything useful. Tristano poked his nose in the closet and under the bed, the bathroom cabinet.

Emerging back to the living room, Tristano gave a quick look around, thanked the deputy then ushered Jesa out and down the lushly carpeted hall. He opened the door to suite 256 without knocking and they went in. The room was done in luxuriant ivories and soft blues with crimson embellishments.

At their sudden entrance, Sierra Santiago unwound her uber long legs from a sofa and stood up. Her painted face blotchy and puffy from all night partying, she spouted, "This is a bunch of bullshit, Agent, we expect compensation immediately! You will find the perpetrator of this fucking crime and shoot him! Kill him, avenge us!"

Half exposed baseball breasts sitting oddly on her chest jiggled with her outraged infuriated tirade in a mostly unbuttoned white blouse.

Messy zigzag extensions shook with her movements down to her boyish hips.

"Yeah." Chantal unfolded her equally lengthy legs and moved to stand close to Tristano. She ran a fingertip down a lapel on his jacket. She cooed, "You'll find the criminal, for us," sidling closer she tipped her neon pink lips up to him, "for me. Won't you, handsome FBI agent? I'll...reward you..."

The third model stayed sprawled on a sofa. Pushing inches long nails up at her red hair that was sinking out of its updo, Ashanti complained, "And while you're at it, you tell that manager we insist he put us up in a grander suite. This one only has two bedrooms. How can he expect us to survive in only two damned rooms?" Her glare landed on Jesa, narrowing her eyes, she sneered at the younger woman's cheap jeans and soft yellow sweater. "Pigtails? Really? What are we, in the wild wild west? Or kindergarten?" She laughed along with her snickering friends, enjoying the pink that climbed Jesa's neck.

"Hell," the deputy staying with them grinned and said, "I think they're cute. And damned sexy. Hot. In fact, Miss," his eyes latched onto her bosom mounded under the braids in the yellow sweater, "later you and I can get together, I'll show you what I can do with those braids." He flashed wide teeth at Jesa, but Tristano broke in with a *back-off* glare and said sharply, "We will speak with the maid, now."

The maid sat in a chair by the window. Her eyes downcast, hands folded tightly in her lap. Tristano approached her, without preface he said quietly, "Come with us."

She hesitated then stood up, her face fraught with trepidation. The white pantsuit she wore was shiny, wrinkle-free polyester; the rubber-soled shoes would be noiseless as she worked.

"No, hey, wait." Chantal clutched at Tristano's arm to stop him. "You need to interrogate us, take me first." Pouched lips pursed out in a sulk. "I left you many messages, you haven't returned my calls. But," she smiled artfully, raising her head high so their mouths almost touched. "I forgive you. I'll-"

The model's overwhelming perfume savaged his nose, her breath of booze, food and cigarettes could kill maggots. Tristano said to Jesa, "We're going down the hall." He turned his hard face, a cold slate of politeness away from the model and said to the maid, "Miss?" inquiring her name. In her thirties with short dark hair curled behind ears that stuck out, she raised dark eyes to him then quickly lowered them. "Vanessa, sir, Vanessa Chalia."

"Okay, Ms. Chalia, come along." Ignoring the background noise of Chantal's strident pleas for him to stay, Tristano cupped Jesa's elbow and gestured with his head for the maid to follow them.

Several doors down the thick blue carpeting, the deputy that was with the CSI while they conducted their examination of the break-in, walked with them and opened the door to 355, an unoccupied room, and told Koffi to go ahead and go in.

"There you go, sir, you'll have some privacy," and the deputy ambled on down the hall back to the room the models were ensconced. At the same time, a deputy stepped off the elevator. Koffi indicated to him to come over.

"Sir?" the deputy asked.

"Just stay here by the door, Deputy, I'll need you to stay with this woman," he glanced at the maid, "when we're done with her." The deputy nodded and took his place just outside the door.

Inside, Tristano motioned for Jesa to sit on a chair, and he indicated to the maid to have a seat on the small divan. The room was lavish with ornate furniture and decorated in peach and gold with gilded paintings on the walls.

He nodded to Jesa to get out her pad. Waiting until she was ready, Tristano glanced around the room then turned his commanding attention to the maid. The edges of his hard mouth barely ticked up in cordiality, he said, "Ms., ah, Chalia," catching her cringing from him, he glanced over at Jesa, who frowned at him.

Jesa put a finger and thumb to the corners of her lips and pushed up forming a huge smile.

Tristano's brows tugged down. With a sigh, he forced his mouth to curve more warmly at the frightened maid and attempted to soften his rough voice. "Ms. Chalia, your manager said you told him you saw someone acting suspiciously around the time of the break-in. Can you tell me what you saw?" He kept his arms at his sides to appear as innocuous as he could to ease the maid's fear.

But he was nevertheless a big man, tough and powerful, his voice dark and cold, face a dangerous harsh rock. She kept her head down, mumbled, "No, I…didn't see anything, Mr. Reynolds made…made a mistake."

"Ms. Chalia," iron grated in his tenor, he had no patience for noncompliant witnesses. "This is a robbery investigation, you can be subject to being charged with obstruction, even accessory after the face if you protect this person."

"But- but, he- he could come after me, he saw me too, I…I think," the maid stuttered, her head jerked anxiously towards the door as if itching to flee. Perspiration beaded along her hairline, her rapid blinking was in tandem with her frantic shallow breaths. Clasping her hands together, she raised them in front of her mouth, pleaded, "Please, do not put me in jail, I- I am claustrophobic. Miss," she turned to Jesa's soft face, away from Tristano's grit teeth, angry flexing jaw.

He opened his mouth to speak more severely to her to force her to answer him when Jesa said softly, "It's okay, Vanessa. No one is going to hurt you, you are not going to be arrested, I promise you," she cast a reproachful glare at Tristano, then smiled with sincerity at the maid.

"Vanessa," she said softly, clutching her notebook she bent forward to be closer to the maid. "You could maybe really help us a lot. Your information could be very important; we can't do this without you. We need your help." Her smile friendly, she nodded gently in supportive encouragement to the woman.

Vanessa raised her eyes to Jesa's pretty face and warm smile and nodded back to her. Looking at Jesa and not Tristano, she said faintly, "Um, okay." Taking a deep breath, she exhaled and told her, a slight tremble in her voice, "It was around two in the morning when the people in room 250 called requesting extra pillows. I dropped them off and was almost to the elevator when I saw this man at the end the hall. At the time," her face flushed, eyes dropped, "I am so sorry," she raised her anxious gaze back up to Jesa.

Her reassuring smile offering a safe, nonjudgmental environment, Jesa nodded, encouraging her to continue.

Vanessa darted a quick nervous glance at Tristano, feeling more comfortable when she saw he was watching Jesa, not her, she said to Jesa, "I did not notice at the time that he might have come from room 259 where the models were staying. I mean," she shrugged and her cheeks darkened, "there were a lot of gentlemen going in and out of there. Like, a lot. *Dios mio*, the baskets overflowed with the used condoms, you know?"

Tristano cleared his throat, Jesa bit her lip forcing herself not to blush. "Uh, okay, so, go on, Vanessa."

"Well, it was not until my manager spoke to me, asked me if I saw anything. I said no, at first," her brown eyes bounced to Tristano and right back to Jesa. "Then he told me the models were out most of the night and did not return until after five and that their room had been ransacked. That is when I remembered seeing the man near their room before he turned and oddly ran off. He had a- a bar thing in his hand." Sucking in a deep shaky breath, she clamped her lips together, pulling them in, and peered at Jesa.

Jesa nodded. "That's very good, Vanessa. Can you tell us what he looked like?"

Her gaze flicked to Tristano, his face remained stoic, his attention was now on the maid.

"Um," she said thoughtfully, her dark eyes shifted back and forth as she thought back. "Well, I did not really see his face. He was kinda medium height, thin, had big round glasses and crazy hair sticking out all over." Then she surprisingly laughed. "It was his clothes. He wore horrible things."

"Horrible like what?" Jesa prompted her, shifting to perch on the edge of her chair, roused at the significance of the familiar description.

"Oh…" Vanessa sobered right back up. "Like he wore a blue and green striped *camisa*, ah, that is shirt with these ugly brown plaid slacks. *Dios*," she made a face, "he was so mismatched it was awful, made my eyes go crazy." She paused, bumped one shoulder at Jesa. "That is it. I am sorry, he was running, I did not really see much."

Jesa glanced at Tristano who gave her a slight nod. "That's okay, Vanessa, you did really great. You've helped us so much. We want to thank you, right Agent Koffi?" A strawberry brow arched at him.

His lips twitched. "Ah, yes, yes. Thank you Ms. Chalia, you have, ah, been of great assistance to us." To the deputy who stood in the doorway, he said, "Have Ms. Chalia write down what she saw and get it to me at the station, then she's free to leave."

"Yessir," the deputy said. "What about those broads, uh," he blanched at the look Tristano shot him. "I mean, the- the models, what about them?"

Tristano told him, "Deputy Roarke will be by to ask them questions, if they might have a clue as to who was behind the break in." He turned to Jesa, said quietly, "I was informed on the phone on the way over that they weren't actually robbed, and the CSI confirmed that the only thing they could determine was missing was a notebook of Ms. Erikson's that she said only had first names of men she had...met... on the island, and numbers next to the names rating their...prowess.

"She said she has the same info on her phone and another list was lying on the coffee table in the living room that the burglar didn't take. It was almost as if the burglar was looking for something in particular. The chief wanted us to look into this since we had just questioned the models about the designer and the Westcotts and then this happened. A coincident or not?"

He pulled his phone out mumbling to himself, "I need to have Roarke ask the girls if they know what someone could be looking for." If he had to guess, it would be drugs since his preliminary report stated none of the jewelry was missing.

Tristano motioned for Jesa to get up. She stuffed her pad and pen in her pack and smiled brightly at the maid. "Again, thank you, Vanessa, you are so brave, we appreciate your help." She waited for Tristano to reiterate his thanks, but he just clasped Jesa's arm and walked her out to the hall.

They trod down the stairs silently and didn't speak until they were on their way to the station. As Koffi parked and shut off the ignition, he turned in his seat to face Jesa.

"Are you feeling any better?" he asked, bending his elbow and resting his arm on the back of the seat.

Her smile wan, a tad abashed, she said, "Yeah, I think the sandwich and coffee helped."

"Good." He managed to not appear smug. "You handled the witness just great," he sounded surprised yet proud. "You made her feel at ease, got the information, and praised her for helping. You have a way with people, Jesselin, you make even total strangers feel liked and appreciated." He smiled at the blush that blossomed across her face.

"Um, thanks, I guess." Fiddling with the zipper on her pack, drawing it up and down she focused on it. Then, crooking her head at him, somewhat perplexed she said, "You are confusing to me. You are…" her eyes flickered over him then lowered.

Curious, he prodded gently, "What? What am I Jesselin?"

The blush vivified, she altered her position to face him more. "Uh, you wear expensive, perfectly tailored suits like a high-powered executive, but," her gaze dabbled with his, her brow creased.

He nodded, said softly, "But what?"

Her head tilted more as she peered up at him. "You're so polished with your attire, but when you are dealing with people, interrogating them like Mr. Normandy, the Westcotts, Mrs. Chalia," she took a breath. "You are so- so harsh, ruthless even. It's just, it's so incongruent with the way you look." A small chuckle tinkled out with, "I mean, your face is kind of rugged but your clothes aren't, but your manner is…scary tough."

Under deeply hooded eyes, Tristano regarded her while he ruminated on her words. He moved so his body curved more towards her, so he was closer to her, and appeared pleased when she didn't shift away from him. "I am an FBI agent, Jesselin, but although I look it right now, I am not a desk worker. I don't work in an office, I work in the field. I," he considered how much to tell her.

"I am more of a- a soldier. I am not used to questioning people like the housekeeper and such. The people I normally deal with are more…like me, warriors where gentle interrogations would be laughed at. I wear a suit when I have to conduct more…diplomatic jobs, like this one."

"Hmm," she murmured, her lips pushed out but she didn't comment on what he told her.

Tristano waited for more but she sat quietly, just studiously watching him. He said, "So, what do you think about what she said? The maid."

Jesa grinned, then flattened her lips at the gravity of the situation. "It sure sounded just like that designer guy, Mr. Normandy."

"Ah." He lightly chucked her chin with his knuckles. "Beauty and brains. I'll have a couple of the guys go pick him up." Her blush at his praise made him smile, this time genuinely, the corners of his eyes crinkled. Then he remembered that she was telling him something last night in the car before she fell asleep. "You were saying something about Mrs. Westcott when we left the bistro yesterday, do you remember?"

Holding her pack in her lap she was quiet, brows knit in uncertainty.

He said, "Jesselin, any little thing could be important no matter how trivial you may think it is." Her gaze traveled over his rugged face, seeming taken aback at his gentleness. "Oh, okay." In a quiet voice she said, "I'm sure it's just nothing." He settled back against his door denoting he was interested in what she had to say regardless if it was worth anything.

Reassured, she said, "Well, at the press conference, I noticed, instead of being focused on the cameras, the conference, Mrs. Westcott kept looking off to the left side of the auditorium. I mean, she did it so often it caught my attention. It appeared to me that she was looking at this person in the crowd. It didn't seem all that important at the time but still, it was so peculiar I almost told Sheriff McKabe that day at the meeting. Then, when we were at the bistro," she lowered her eyes awkwardly recalling her getting so tipsy.

"Before she went to her table and before Mr. Westcott arrived, she was in that recessed alcove area in the back, and she was talking to this man. It was the same man that she was looking at so intently that day in the crowd."

"Uh huh." His head cocked as he listened to her. Tristano suggested, "They have no relatives on the island, maybe they're just good friends, or neighbors?"

"Hmm, maybe," Jesa concurred. "But, they were standing very close to each other. Her hand was on his chest, their faces were quite close, and they were, I guess you'd say smiling into each other's eyes. They seemed to me to be way more than just friends. They were only partially visible due to the alcove, I think they thought no one could see them. Mr. Westcott was still down the block at the police station." Shrugging mildly to dismiss her suspicious observations, she said, "I'm sure it was…nothing. But, as soon as I noticed Mr. Westcott come in the bistro, the man was gone."

Dark brows down in reflection, Tristano recalled how odd Stedman Westcott had acted after Roarke said he asked him if either of them was having an affair. The husband seemed to have been struggling to mask his antipathy, and he all but glowered at his wife until the models were brought up and the mood turned opposite with Elizabeth now the one shooting dagger glares at Stedman. "Hmm." He scratched at his chin while pondering what Jesa had said. "I'll tell McKabe we need more in-depth examination of the Westcotts, both of them."

"That's a good idea," Jesa replied. She was settled comfortably, leaning her back against the passenger door. Flickers of fear weren't fostering across her face as usual. The pigtails lay over the front of her jacket, they made Tristano smile.

"What about you, Jesselin?" At her questioning look, he said, "Family. Where do your folks live? Do you have any siblings?" He watched closely as her expression hardened, a wall came down over her face, blanking her eyes.

She said, "It's cold, can we get going inside?"

Neither moved for several heartbeats. Tristano's face impassive, Jesa's tightened, she fidgeted with the backpack and broke their connection turning to the door. *Interesting*, Tristano thought. He'd expected her to lie, make up a family story. Instead, she shut right down snubbing his questions. "Jesselin," he spoke, reaching out to touch her, force her to look at him, answer him, then Willie-Jean was at the window with her happy grin.

The older woman was trying to open Jesa's door. With both women pushing and pulling, they managed to pry it open enough for Jesa to scuttle out. She didn't wait for Tristano, just bolted up the walk and into the station.

Chapter Fourteen

At first Niels Normandy sat sheepishly as Tristano and Jesa entered the small interview room. When he found out they weren't arresting him for something, that he was only there for questions, he became belligerent.

"Mr. Normandy," Tristano said as Jesa sat in one of the plastic chairs with her pad and pen out. "You're staying in a different hotel than the models, right?"

The bony designer spat, "Yeah. So?"

"Last night, early this morning, tell me where you were. Precisely."

Jumping to his feet, his face red, Normandy sputtered, "What? I don't have to tell you jack shit. Am I under arrest? If not, I am leaving!" He'd tried that the last time and got the same effect.

"Sit- down." Tristano's frosted voice was a threat in itself.

Normandy stared wide-eyed with his wild hair sticking out all over, then plopped back down. Behind the big-framed glasses, his eyes nervously ran around the small area, from Tristano's iron face, to Jesa, to the door where a deputy stood just outside, then they dropped to the table.

He placed his wiry forearms covered with sparse hairs and freckles on the arms of the chair and dug his nails in clutching the ends. With false bravado, voice high-pitched in his nervousness, he bleated,

"You're just some kinda hired G-man, you can't push me around, I'm not telling you jack-"

Not appearing to have moved at all, Tristano was suddenly standing in front of the meek, pasty-faced man. The designer huddled back in his chair, unable to scoot away from the agent.

Koffi shoved his suit coat back and rigidly gripped his narrow hips like he was having a hard time keeping his fists from going after Normandy. Blistering fury fired from Tristano's cold eyes, the only sign he was struggling to hold back his wrath. Clearly, he wanted nothing more than to pound the little man into oblivion until he was nothing but a mess of blood and guts on the floor. And Normandy felt every iota of his fiercely held back rage.

"K- k- k-" Normandy stammered, "whatever you want, wha- what d'ya want?" He was so terrified of the hostile agent he couldn't remember the question.

Tristano wondered how much of Normandy's eccentricities were phony or if he really was a hundred percent sleazy douchebag. Today he wore a pink shirt with purple ameba-like designs, and black and blue checkered slacks with beige, lace-less tennis shoes. A plaid jacket lay over the back of one of the chairs.

Tristano moved his arms to cross them over his chest, glared down at the shaking designer, and repeated through his teeth, "Tell me where you were from 8 p.m. through to 6 a.m. I want to hear every second of your movements."

Normandy took his glasses off, wiped his eyes with his short sleeve and put them back on, his hands shaking so badly he almost dropped the specs. Clearing his throat several times, he let out a nervous breath and said, "I ate- ate, had dinner at the Shipwreck from, uh, around seven to- to maybe eight-thirty, then, I had a drink at the bar there. Maybe two, three, drinks."

He swiped the back of his hand across his nose then pinched the bridge. "Maybe more. You can check with the bartender, he'll vouch that I was there."

Tristano merely grunted and jutted his chin for the man to continue.

"Yeah, okay, so then I went home afterwards around midnight I think, and watched the game on Netflix until I fell asleep. I didn't leave the house again. I'm renting a cottage."

Koffi snapped, "What game?"

Jesa sat without moving anything but the pen on the pad and kept her head down. This militant Agent Koffi terrified her as much as he did the weasily designer.

"Last Friday's game of the- the- Pats and the Giants." He painfully swallowed the lump in his throat, his Adam's apple hopping like a rabbit bounding with a lion after it.

"What was the score at half-time?"

"Ahhh," frightened eyes bulging behind the lens blinked nonstop. His gulp distinct, he replied, "I- I fell asleep, I don't know what time, please-"

"You talk with anyone when you were home? Any phone calls? Any neighbors see you after you came home?"

His mouth flopping open and closed like a guppy gulping for air, Normandy's bug-eyes jumped frantically around the small room. "Ah- ah- ah- no, I don't know!"

Koffi smacked his palm on the table making Normandy and Jesa jump. Jesa sighed, she should be used to it by now.

Tongue slapping around his bobbing lips, Normandy lifted the hem of the pink shirt exposing a white belly and swiped at the sweat on his forehead dripping into his eyes. "I...I didn't talk to no one, I don't think my neighbors saw me or paid attention if they had." Shoving the glasses up his forehead to push back the whacky hair, he rubbed his eyes then squinted up at the agent. "Why are you asking? Why do you care?"

Ignoring his questions, the agent leaned over closer to Normandy who pulled his knees up trying to squirm back from him. "You're telling me you have no alibi for late last night, early this morning?"

Loud gulp. "A- alibi for-for what?"

Straightening and crossing his big arms again, Tristano said coolly, "The hotel room the models are staying in was burgled."

Normandy sat up, then slithered back against the chair under Tristano's steely glare. "Are- are you accusing me of robbing them? Because if you are-"

"Someone matching your description was witnessed near the room around 2 a.m. And, you're telling me you can't prove you were home at that time."

The designer's head flapped back and forth between Tristano and Jesa then stayed on Jesa. Tristano reached down, grabbed his chair and turned Normandy in one rough jerk so he was facing away from Jesa.

Normandy's jaw dropped, the color drained from his lean face, he ducked his head as if to block Tristano's expected blow. "It wasn't me!" he shrieked. "It wasn't me! I told you where I was, I wanna a lawyer, I wanna lawyer!" he pealed, shrieking hysterically.

Tristano stepped back and snapped at Jesa, "We're leaving."

Her eyes popped in surprise at his sudden retreat. Hurriedly shoving the pen and pad in her pack she leaped to her feet and followed Tristano as he stormed out the door.

The agent barked an acerbic, "Let him go," to the deputy, and stalked down the hall then shortened his steps so Jesa could keep up.

They reached the coffee room where hats and coats were stored. He took her backpack and shoved it in a locker then held out Jesa's jacket for her to slide into then shrugged on his own trench coat. "I gotta get outta here for a minute." He growled at her, "Put your hat and gloves on." He waited while she complied, one brow bent over a dark eye. "Mittens? No gloves?"

Jesa's cheeks flushed at the implied child remark. She wasn't about to tell him the red mittens were all she could afford when the cold weather first struck.

When she didn't reply, he grunted and said, "Come on, show me this Commons block." He ushered her to the door not saying a word to Willie-Jean or anyone working in the main room. People watched them leave, as soon as they left the gossip started.

The air outdoors, brisk as an icy popsicle was a shock after the warmth inside the station.

"Here." Tristano stopped, bent over and grabbed the bottom of Jesa's dark violet ski-jacket.

Her mouth opened in dismay as he grasped the zipper, hooked it and roughly zipped the jacket up to her neck. "You don't have a scarf?" He squinted an eye at the knit hat she wore.

She shook her head. The agent was in a foul mood and she was afraid she'd say something wrong and set him off. He treated her like a child and she felt like one. This had to stop.

Tristano started down the walk, glancing back at her when she hadn't moved. He waited until she caught up and they walked side-by-side along the cobblestone pathway passing the string of charming shops. He let out a long breath. "Sorry, Jesselin. I," he sucked back in a laborious inhale, "I know the bastard's guilty. It was Normandy that broke into their room."

"So why don't you arrest him?"

He replied, "Unless CSI comes up with evidence that he was there, or the maid can undeniably finger him and place him inside the room, there's nothing we can do. Describing his idiotic clothes and crazy hair isn't enough. Roarke said he showed the maid his picture but she couldn't say conclusively that it was Normandy. He's trying to get a warrant to search Normandy's place see if he stashed that pry bar there. Even so, proving it was the mode of entrance into the hotel room will be highly improbable. But, I'm not all that interested in the actual break-in."

Her forehead rose. "You're not? Why not? A crime was committed against those girls."

His derisive snort came with an unsmiling laugh. "That likely wasn't the first, nor going to be the last time those girls are targeted for crimes. They flaunt their bodies and jewelry; they're just looking for trouble with their snotty attitudes, disrespectful vulgar behavior, and parading strange men in and out of their places. Those three women are setting themselves up to be victims and I almost think it's deliberate."

Surprised at his declaration, she asked, "Why do you think they'd do such a thing?"

Under the trench coat the big shoulders shrugged. "Dunno, maybe attention. The more attention celebrities get, especially if it's negative, the more famous they become. How many display themselves more naked than not in magazines just to stay relevant?"

After considering his opinion on the models, Jesa said, "So what are you interested in if not the break-in? Don't you want to catch the culprit?"

They passed a café, when someone opened the door, delicious aromas of cinnamon and bread baking wafted out. A few more feet and they came to an opening between buildings. Beyond the shops lay an expanse of yellowing winter grass. Tristano clasped Jesa's arm and turned her, guiding her onto a paved path leading to the center of the Commons.

Strolling along the tar path, they observed scattered around the park, several colossal pieces of gaudy art sculptures that the county had paid a mint of money for, and children were darting in and around and climbing on top of.

The stores, police station, bistro, and other buildings surrounded the giant square. Still holding her arm, Tristano took a deep cleansing breath and let it out. "Yeah, that's better. Fresh cool air, open space, the sounds of goddamned nature instead of a pathetic whining guilty as sin little asshole."

Jesa made an exaggerated play of rummaging in her pockets.

"What are you looking for?" he asked her.

Grinning, she responded, "Soap."

"Soap?"

"Uh huh. To wash out someone's potty mouth." She squealed as he grabbed her just above the elbows and lifted her off her feet. She squealed again when he swung her around, twirling her until out-of-control gales of laughter gushed so much she couldn't breathe. She cried out, "Stop! I'm dizzy!"

His deep laughter blended with her lighter girlish shrieks, instead of setting her down as she begged through breathless giggles, Tristano held her up on the tips of her toes, their noses a fraction away from touching.

His long inky lashes stroked down, bringing his lids low. The enigmatic dark eyes slit, moving with sinuous slowness over her rosy cheeks, and the sparkly eyes wobbling as if she still spun, then lowered to her parted lips still open in laughter and catching her breath.

He knew he was looking at her as a man, not the agent that he should be. She was just so…soft, young, smattering of freckles over her tiny nose, the light shone from her with purity, sweetness, if only it were true.

Tristano knew he should pull back, set her down, step away, but, he couldn't. She held still, her wobbling eyes settled, gazing so damned innocently up at him. Like she'd never been with a man. Right now he didn't care if she'd been with a hundred, right now his brain had gone blank like an electrical outage had zapped it out. Not a thought in his head but opening his mouth and pressing it over hers and taking her-

"Your phone," she whispered against his lips, not exactly against, almost, almost.

"Huh?" his vague murmur breathed over her mouth, his mind a frazzled void containing only sheer desire. She pulled back, he tightened his strong fingers around her arms holding her immobilized, still on her toes, their bodies about to touch. He moved his head forward and down, his eyes on her lips.

There was a buzzing, yeah, it was his sizzling brain shorting out. She pulled back further, as he followed her, his chasing mouth open, preparing to take, she said, "Your phone, Agent, your phone is vibrating."

It was the 'Agent' that broke the spell. His face darkened as it hardened. What the fuck was he thinking, he set her down. Blinking, he just stared inanely at her. She said again, "Your phone."

Oh. He had been unaware he still held her. He released her and fumbled his phone out and somehow managed to turn it on. "Ah," he swallowed, blinked, stepped back further from the vixen looking at him in breathy confusion. He barked into the phone, "Koffi."

Chapter Fifteen

Tristano stopped at the aromatic café on the way back. They were just finishing their croissant turkey sandwiches when they reached the station. He took their empty wrappings and tossed them in a receptacle. They moved on to the lockers to grab her bag.

Willie-Jean looked up as they came in. She greeted them with her usual friendly smile, "Hi guys. The sheriff is in his office, you can go right in."

"All right." Tristano said to Jesa, "I need to wash up, I'll meet you there. What kind of soda do you want?"

Sharing a few amicable words with Willie-Jean, Jesa said nonchalantly, "None, thank you." She was getting more and more embarrassed his paying her way for her. She was feeling like a charity case. He regarded her quizzically, murmured, "Jesselin." At her determined expression, he nodded with a sigh then headed for the men's room.

Jesa hit the ladies room and stopped by the vending machine. Digging in her pack for her change purse she didn't notice Ronan in his uniform stopping beside her.

"Hey, Red Riding," his voice warm with a shade of sultry, "haven't seen you all day. You skipped out on me yesterday and so far you've spent all today with the big bad wolf. You survive okay?" He made a comical pretense of checking her over for wolf bites.

Giggling, she bumped her elbow at him. "Stop that. Someone will hear and it'll get back to him." She found her change purse and opened it. Masking her chagrin at the paltry pennies inside, she closed it and dropped it back in her pack.

"Hey, what, you need some money for a drink, Jesa?" He stuck his hand in his pants pocket.

"No, no, I'm fine, thanks." She smiled convincingly, but he pulled out a handful of bills anyway.

"What do you want babe, Pepsi, ginger ale, Red Bull?" He lifted a dollar to put in the machine.

"No, nothing, really, Ronan, thank you anyway." She tried to block his insertions of the bill but he only laughed at her, gave her a little nudge aside and pushed it in.

"I'm gonna get you a Diet Cola unless you say otherwise, Little Red, so choose." He chuckled at the peevish look she gave him. Then, turning her eyes up heavenward with a grin, he had already put the money in so she said, "Okay, cream soda, please."

"Good girl," he kidded with a smile and pushed the appropriate buttons. The soda fell with a clattered clunk and he bent before she could to retrieve it. "Here ya go, princess," he teased after cracking back the tab and handing it to her.

"Uh, thank you, Ronan." She smiled as she took it, then saw behind Ronan, down the hall Koffi was watching them. Jesa felt a flare of guilt. She had refused his offer of a drink and now it looked like she had accepted Ronan's. It didn't matter really, it was only a soda, but, gosh, it made it look like she had rejected Koffi's proffer choosing Ronan's over his.

She told herself she was being absurd; again, it was only a soda, but the two males could be so rivalrous. She was overthinking it, like either man would be jealous or anything over her was folly in her silly brain. Taking a sip, she didn't see Ronan's smirk at Tristano. The pair started down the hall to McKabe's office.

When they reached Tristano, the three of them continued on to the chief's office. Ronan said with incendiary guile, "Koffi, Tahni's been looking all over for you. After the meeting you can find her in the coffee room. The rumor is you two got it wicked hot and heavy goin' on for each other," he snorted a snide laugh. His hand on Jesa's back, he led her into the room grinning at the agent's stony face sharpen to a glare.

Inside the office there was a big cluttered desk and several brown leather chairs with gold studding, and a couple of tables, along with a filing cabinet and bookcase crowded with folders and law books. McKabe said as they entered, "Have seats, people."

Keeping his back to Koffi, Ronan drew a chair back for Jesa to sit. Smiling her thanks up to the tall sandy-haired rascal, she cupped her soda with both hands in her lap. He pulled another chair close to hers and flopped down on it.

His tough face expressionless, Tristano didn't sit. He wandered over to one of the bookcases and leaned a shoulder against it, crossed his arms and one foot casually over an ankle. Chief McKabe sat behind the desk. His burly hand rested on the landline on the desk as if he'd just hung it up.

His strong features official, the sheriff said to Tristano, "Agent, you were interviewing the suspect, Normandy. I was told," he glanced at Ronan who stared straight-faced back at him.

Then Ronan's gaze strayed placidly over to light on Koffi with the very barest of smirks. McKabe went on to Tristano, "That you suddenly up and charged out of the interview and out of the station hauling Jesa with you, without a word to anyone where you were goin'. You wanna explain that, son?"

Tristano gazed out the window behind and to the side of McKabe. With a negligible shrug, he said coolly, "I got everything I could out of the bast-" his eyes slid to Jesa then he turned his body towards the chief. "The ah, suspect. We have no evidence proving he was anywhere near the hotel and he knows it. The maid only caught a glimpse of him and couldn't give a solid ID. We were wasting our time." He kicked a cool glance at Roarke for his suspected tattling. Roarke grinned back unrepentantly.

"Maybe if you'd tried harder, stayed longer, asked the right questions, been a little more," Ronan said with not so subtle baiting, "professional, patient, smarter," the corner of his lip lifted in mockery.

Koffi turned a fully blank face to the deputy, paused, then turned back to the sheriff. "There was nothing else to get out of him, and he knew it, he was becoming an hysterical ninny. Staying there one more second would have been a waste of time and buying into his batshit crazy. Besides," his mouth quirked at Jesa's cough, "he lawyered up. You know that's it at that point."

136

"Hmm," McKabe hummed. Setting his elbows on his desk he studied the agent over his steepled fingertips then looked to Roarke. Roarke was grinning at Koffi, Koffi was back to staring out the window. Jesa's head bowed, her attention was on the soda in her hands. The sheriff eyed Koffi quizzically and asked him, "You think Normandy is guilty of the break-in and the kidnapping?"

Without turning from the window, Koffi replied, "Yeah. He's the one that broke into the suite, but I don't think he's the kidnapper."

"Oh?" McKabe's brows rose, he glanced at Roarke who shrugged at him. "Why not?"

Koffi turned slightly. "I just don't feel it. He's a coward and a bellyaching crybaby. He broke into the suite because he desperately needed something he thought might be there, but he doesn't have the balls to take the baby."

"What's he need from the hotel suite then?"

The agent bumped one shoulder. "Dunno. Drugs, jewelry, money. The girls denied all of that but, who knows."

"But you think we need to look in a different direction for the kidnapper?"

Nodding, Tristano leaned his hip on the windowsill. "Yes. But who, I have no idea. Yet."

McKabe pondered that, the room was quiet. He moved his hand to tap it lightly on the phone. "After you called and told me about what Jesa here noticed regarding Mrs. Westcott," he smiled warmly at her as her head popped up in surprise. "I spoke with Deputy Granger Wate. He just called back."

All three looked to McKabe with full attentiveness. "He got anything important, Chief?" Ronan asked.

The big man nodded sitting back in his chair with a thin grin. Clasping his hands behind his head, his elbows winging out, he said, "Yeah, bigger than Dallas, kids." Leaning forward, he dropped his arms down, twined his fingers together and set them on his desk. "Apparently, Elizabeth Westcott had bonded out a drug dealer from jail awhile back."

Unwrapping his thick fingers, he set his index finger on a piece of paper and pushed it in front of him. "Dude's name is Subie King."

A small chuckle came from Ronan as he looked down at the note. "Who the hell names their child Subie?"

McKabe responded, "Guy's a known drug dealer. One wonders what a blue-blooded, upper crust married woman is doing with a down and dirty street punk. Ronan, you take Jesa and head on over to the Westcotts' and talk with the missus. You," he spoke quickly with a stern frown at Tristano as he straightened and started to oppose his order, "I want you to go track down this dealer fella. I don't want Jesa involved in being near a dangerous thug or his element."

Tristano appeared to want to argue, but McKabe sat unmoving, eyes narrowed, his jaw set. Tristano growled anyway, "I can take Jesselin to the Westcotts, Roarke can go look for-"

"No. You do as I say. You are more experienced at tracking people. Now, that's it, go on then, shoo," he waved his fingers at them.

Ronan sprang up. "Okay, Little Red, let's hop to it," he held his hand out to Jesa. Snickering in overt triumph at Koffi's annoyance, and grinning at the agent's curious frown at the nickname of Little Red, Ronan helped Jesa up. She dropped her empty soda can in the trashbin by the door and didn't look at Tristano as they walked out the door.

Tristano called out, "Phone in your pocket, Jesselin."

Ronan helped Jesa into the cruiser. Driving to the Westcotts' they made small talk for a bit then he said, "So, you enjoying all the cop-stuff, Little Red?"

"Ronan, please stop with the Little Red, you're doing it to incite Tristano."

"Oh? It's Tristano now, is it? Last time I heard it was Agent Koffi." Canting a glance at her, his voice lowered, "You two aren't getting, ah, cozy now, are you?" He was unsuccessful at keeping the jealousy out of his voice.

Jesa glared up at the ceiling. "No." She turned so her body curved towards him. "You two guys need to stop this. Stop using me as a pawn in your- your macho competition. There are plenty of beautiful females on this island for you men to go after, you don't have to pretend interest in me for your tug-o-war of who is the most handsome or most popular or alpha or whatever it is. Please leave me out of your games."

"What? Come on Jesa, sweetheart, you can't really think that? That we are using you to one-up each other?" Shaking his head the sandy hair flopped over one blue eye, he shoved it back and looked at her quickly before putting his attention on the road. "Not at all on my part, sugar, but I don't know about Koffi. He's the kind that always has to be on top, show his dominance. So, yeah, he's probably using you to goad me."

He pulled into the Westcotts' driveway and parked. Turning to face her, Ronan reached for her hand. He gave it a little squeeze and told her, "Listen, honey, I don't give a wicked shit about that douchebag agent." Lifting his other hand he smoothed strawberry wisps off the side of her face. "Haven't I made myself clear that I am interested in you, Jesa? I'm not worried about him, when this is all over he'll be gone, outta here, back to whatever southern swamp he crawled out from."

She tugged at her hand to free it but he held on. "Ronan, listen," he didn't let her get it out. The deputy slipped his long fingers around and cradled the side of her head, he stated with an amorous smile, "I'd like...I want us to get together. Let me take you out for real, a real date, give me a chance for you to see me, learn about each other. After this interview I'll take you home and we can, you know, chat a little. What do you say pretty Jesa?" His thumb caressed her soft skin, he unbuckled his seatbelt and shuffled closer to her.

Behind her back, Jesa had her hand on the door handle. She lifted the handle and slid out. "We have work to do, Ronan." Lowering her head she hurriedly trekked up the walk.

Inside the mansion, Ronan was all business. He had his deputy hat on, his frustration with the way Jesa persisted in fleeing from him was not apparent in his official voice and authoritative bearing. Rolling his wide shoulders back in the brown uniform, he tucked his thumbs over the duty belt, and stared severely at Mrs. Westcott. At first the Westcotts clung to each other in apprehensive dread that there was news about their missing baby, bad news.

After Ronan declared calmly there was no word at all on little Brie, that they were there because they had further questions, he then had Deputy Gomez sequester Stedman in another room assuming Elizabeth would not speak freely in front of him.

Once Stedman was gone, planting his boots formidably akimbo, Ronan said, "I am not going to beat around the bush and try to trick information out of you, Mrs. Westcott. I'll get right to the point." Although Jesa's job was to take notes, Ronan tugged his own notebook out to jot things down. Later, Ronan would copy his pages and hand them to her. Using computers gave him the willies. Jesa would organize their notes on her iPad and forward them to Willie-Jean,

Elizabeth sat down on the couch as always, the queen holding court. She smoothed her short skirt over her thighs and crossed her legs at the ankles curving them with ladylike elegance to the side. Her regal pose wasn't strong enough to cover the tremor in her hands or the way she didn't look Ronan in the eye. Instead, she addressed Jesa.

Raising her chin with a noble snuff, she said with a touch of irritation, "You couldn't have just called to ask your questions? I mean, you come here and frighten us half to death, my God, we thought you had word of my daughter-" a catch in her voice. "And now you say you just want to ask a question? This is absurd, and why was it necessary to remove my husband from the room?"

Ronan replied calmly, "We thought this would be done better in person, and in private." He needed to watch her expression when he asked his question. Over the phone would give her time to react to it without being seen.

"Well, then," bristling she glared at him, "what could be so darned important?"

"Who is Subie King?"

It was like they were in a rapidly ascending airplane and the pressure in the room was suddenly unbearable. Dead silence. Elizabeth's stricken eyes looked about to pop out of her head, her mouth fell open and stayed there, an out of water fish gasping for breath. Her already fair skin turned ivory soap.

Ronan stood composed, and waited. Jesa didn't move or make a sound.

Elizabeth put a shaking hand to her head and plucked at a lock of blonde hair. Twisting it around her finger, she blinked and blinked at Ronan, she finally croaked out, "Who?"

His gaze never leaving her face, he repeated, "Subie King."

Fiddling with her hair, face white, she continued blinking at Ronan's sterile expression. The silence hollowed out the room cavern deep and earth-core cold. Finally, dropping the lock of hair, she got a grip, wriggled in her seat.

Pushing a stiff wave of thoroughly hair-sprayed tresses off her brow, she lifted her chin, cleared her throat, and looked down her nose at the deputy asserting piously, "I don't know this person. Am I supposed to?" Her lids lowered, she peered at Ronan. "Is he the one that took my baby?"

Ronan gave a short chuckle with a shake of his head. "We don't know, Mrs. Westcott." His tone sobered, "Subie King is the drug dealer you bonded out of jail eight months ago." Dropping the bomb, he crossed his arms and carefully scrutinized her expression.

Her lashes flickered, her head flit to the door as if making sure her husband wasn't in earshot, then she quickly dropped her eyes in deflection. Licking her suddenly dry lips, she swallowed urgently several times.

He waited, giving her time to formulate a response, when she didn't, he said, "Mr. King is not a relative or a neighbor, not here or when you lived in California. So, please stop wasting our time, Mrs. Westcott, what is Subie King to you?"

She raised her head, gaze flicking between Ronan and Jesa. Ronan stared unwavering at her; Jesa's head was lowered to her notepad.

"Ah," Elizabeth said, and smiled coyly at Ronan. Voice laced with innocence, with a vague shrug she said casually, "He's just an old friend from high school. He um, was down on his luck and reached out to me for help since he knew we were quite well off. So, you see, Deputy Roarke," she smiled with another delicate shrug.

"There is nothing sinister, nothing nefarious here. I never even saw Subie, I paid a bond company to bail him out. And that was it. I haven't seen Subie since our school days. Now, does that answer your question or have you more for me? If so, please get on with it, Stedman and I are expecting some people from our church to stop by."

A golden brow elevated in acquitted tolerance, she stood up. Pressing her skirt down with both palms, she clasped her hands calmly in front of her and smiled accommodatingly at Ronan.

Ronan's expression didn't alter from the official block it had been. "Just one other thing," he paused.

"Yes?" She didn't smile.

"Does Mr. Westcott know about this bail, that you bonded King out?"

Her fingers clenched, she said with a mild smile. "No. And I would prefer it stay that way. Subie is an old friend of mine and well," she chuckled, "you know how husbands can be when their wives have any sort of contact with other men. So, then, is that it?"

Ronan answered, "Yes, that's all. For now." He nodded at Jesa.

She closed her book tucked it and her pen in her bag, and the pair started for the door, Elizabeth followed them. He stopped and as he opened the door he said, "Thank you for your time and patience, Mrs. Westcott. In a dire situation such as this every rock must be overturned and looked under. You understand?" He gave her his boyish flirty smile in apology for having to have bothered her.

She mirrored his smile but hers had an edge to it. A deputy stood guard outside the door.

Ronan greeted him and walked Jesa to his cruiser and helped her in. Elizabeth Westcott still stood in the open doorway, the smile had turned into a troubled, taut line.

On the way to her house, Jesa asked Ronan, "She seemed really jumpy and distraught over your asking about Mr. King. Do you think she was telling the truth?"

His lips pulled in then pushed out and twisted. "I don't know. We'll have to dig deeper into her relationship with him. It could all be as innocent as she said, or," a shoulder lifted, "a tie-in to the baby's disappearance." They made small talk about some of the other deputies and staff at the station.

Ronan let out a little chuckle. "I wonder if Koffi met up with Tahni." Turning the wheel following the spiraling road from the lowland back up the hill, he grinned. "That girl's a pistol alright, he'll have his hands full with her. But, I think they'll really hit it off and become an item." His eyes on the road, his sandy lashes flipped up and down guilelessly. If he was hoping for a reaction from Jesa, he didn't get one.

Pulling into her driveway, before Ronan could stall her, Jesa said to him, "Okay, see you tomorrow." She sprang out of his truck before it barely came to a halt and dashed inside.

Chapter Sixteen

The next day Jesa rose way before dawn. Dressed, and her belly full of cereal, she tossed on her dark violet ski-jacket that she had been lucky to find at the thrift store in Oregon. Adding her mittens, hat, she grabbed the backpack and hurried out the door into the dark grey morning.

Trudging up the hill, she enjoyed the rush of icy air pushing the cobwebs out of her brain. She'd never been so...confused before. Running and hiding from town to town, cutting her hair, dying it, glasses, colored contacts, never letting anyone get too close to her, fleeing again as soon as the signs appeared, that he was getting near, and having to start all over again.

And now...she'd thought being on this soon to be isolated island she could finally let her guard down. When she'd come across a tiny obscure article about the Isle of Orainn, it'd seemed perfect. It would be near impossible to track her here to the relatively unknown peninsula, which thankfully became closed off from the rest of the world in the winter. She would be safe, no one could get to her, she could relax at least for the season.

She had thought that unlike a big city, she could better tell when new people arrived in the spring. Huh, she snorted, Orainn was larger and busier with their tourist season than the sleepy little resort town she'd expected.

Zipping her jacket up to her chin, the action brought the memory of Agent Koffi doing it, a show of caring. Then, how again when in the park he had seemed on the verge of kissing her. Ronan claimed interest in her as well, was she nothing more than a contest between the two men?

Shaking her head, she chewed at the inside of her cheek, sighed with resigned conviction. They didn't want her, they wanted to best the other and were using her for part of their one-man-upping. They had competed from the start to be the one in charge. Chuckling to herself, Jesa thought, sure, and Sheriff McKabe was the one that ultimately held the reins. Mostly. Koffi did, however, override him at times. Federal trumps County.

Sighing exasperated, Jesa was tired of being bossed around, she hadn't had a moment to herself since Agent Koffi blew into town. But even when she was home, she felt as if someone was there, watching her. Even now on the side of the mountain, she had the feeling that someone was following her, the hairs spiked up eerily on the back of her neck as if she felt a presence. A malevolent, menacing presence.

Glancing around in the damp dim morning, she saw nothing but a dense wall of bare trees sheathing the road on both sides, their branches bereft of leaves. The wind had stalled in the thick consuming fog. Ahead and behind her, the road disappeared into the twilight mist. She felt oddly cocooned, like grey cotton wool swaddling her, so silent, so still, like she was traipsing down a long dark tube.

Still, the eerie sensation of someone watching her, following her, persisted. Jesa stopped, stood motionless in the gloaming shroud and listened. Not a bird chirped, not a leaf rustled, no footsteps tromping purposefully behind her, just total dead silence. Shaking her head with a disparaging grin, she shook off her overworking imagination and trod on.

She needed to get to the station before Koffi came for her. She would call him when she got there so he wouldn't waste the drive coming to pick her up. A shiver of triumph rolled up and around her body, the agent was going to be livid when he discovers she rebelliously walked to the station.

A sneaky grin hovered around her chattering lips, then she shivered again but in unease. An enraged agent was not going to be a pleasant thing. Still, she frowned, he had no right to commandeer her car and order her around. She'd show him she didn't have to obey his dictates. She was not a child and refused to allow him to treat her as one.

Jesa snorted, "It's not like he could do anything to me. Right? Could he?" She recalled he had threatened her with punishment if she failed to obey him and went walking about alone and in the dark. Spanking. He had actually insinuated he would spank her! That would be battery! He wouldn't dare-

A picture came to her mind of her lying across the big agent's muscular thighs, a powerful hand holding her down while his other hard hand wailed on her bottom. Her bare bottom. No, she shook her head with a weak laugh, he couldn't. He wouldn't. The image of the ruthless Koffi's harsh cold face popped in her brain, oh heck, she should have waited for him, she strode faster.

Reaching the station without incident, Jesa pushed the door open. Entering the warm cozy building she gladly closed the door on the dank, looming fog. Sheriff McKabe was just setting his cowboy hat on a hook by the door, his bushy brows rose in surprise at her presence.

"Hey, little darlin'," he glanced around for Koffi, the brown brows lowered in confusion. "Where is Agent Koffi? He parking the car?"

Her shrug nonchalant, belying the nerves tingling at Koffi's name, and his potential wrath when he would arrive, Jesa smiled meekly, then coughed and straightened her shoulders. She wasn't afraid of some blowhard FBI agent for Pete's sake. "No, uh, I walked. Hey," she said quickly at his frown, "that reminds me. I need to call him." She pulled her phone out of her backpack, flinching at imagining Koffi's voice in her head berating her for not having it in her pocket, and entered her password.

"Uh," the chief dragged his hefty fingers through his thick mop of hair then said, "I thought Koffi said he was driving you everywhere?"

With a casual shrug of one shoulder Jesa pushed the number to Koffi's line, unnerved at the tremble in her hand. "Oh, no. I just needed a brisk morning walk, you know," she rattled on as Koffi's phone rang. "Clear my head, get some exercise, no biggie."

McKabe crossed his arms over his barrel chest and narrowed his eyes at her. "I don't think it's a good idea for you to be traipsing around alone in the dark on that treacherous hill, darlin'. Koffi and I discussed his keeping you safely close to him at all-"

She raised a hand at him as she heard the phone connecting. "Really, Chief, I'm a big girl, I can take care of my- oh, hello Agent

Koffi." She held the phone a little ways from her ear when the agent's rough voice admonished her for calling him Agent, framed in a colorful curse. "Yeah, okay, anyway," she spoke rapidly before he could get a word in, "listen, I'm at the station."

His voice barked harshly through the phone, wincing, she held it further from her ear. "I am fine, Agent, uh, Tristano. No, no one brought me, I walked. Everything is just fine, see you when you get here," and she quickly disconnected.

Panting like she'd run a mile, Jesa stared at the phone in her hand like it was about to sting her and shoved it in her pocket. Peeping up at the sheriff, her lips bunched at his admonitory expression, then his face lightened with a slight smile presuming the tongue-lashing he knew she was going to receive when Koffi got there.

Ducking her head from the sheriff's perceptive perusal, Jesa said feebly, "I'll wait in the conference room for our…uh, today's briefing." At least there would be a long table and a lot of people between her and Koffi, he couldn't do anything to her there.

She started heading for the meeting room, Sheriff McKabe called out cheerfully, "That'll be in my office, darlin', since it'll be just the three of us. I'll have Willie-Jean direct Koffi there when he comes in. She should arrive any minute. And," A grin pulled up his jowly face at the color rising up her neck, "I expect Koffi will be here lickety-split as well." The grin went full-fledged at her entire face blossoming with alarm. She scooted down the hall to his office with his belly-deep laughter in her ears.

Jesa removed her jacket and hung it on a coatrack, tugged down the sweatshirt she wore under it. Sitting stiffly in one of the big leather chairs, the more she waited, the more Jesa felt trickles of perspiration sliding down her spine. On the open road she hadn't worried, well not too much anyway at Tristano's likely wrath at her disobeying his orders.

But now, here, while waiting for the hard man to walk in the door, there wouldn't be anything or anyone between her and him in the closed in office. Except the chief, and he seemed inclined to let Koffi discipline her however he saw fit. Jesa had the uneasy feeling McKabe was going to leave them alone in there, deliberately. Sanctioning however Koffi desired to address her flaunting disobedience to his warnings.

Darn, she wished Ronan was coming, he would be a buffer between them. But, he had told her yesterday he was meeting with Deputy Granger Wate to delve deeper into the Westcotts' finances. They were going to take a microscope to every check they wrote, every cash withdrawal, every deposit. They'd tried to get a warrant to dump the Westcotts' emails, phone calls, texts, everything, but a judge denied them. They were the victims; there was no probable cause to snoop into their personal affairs.

Maybe she should just leave. It's not like anyone can force her to stay there and be- be punished. Her heart leaped and started hammering at the sound of deep rumbling male voices. He was here. Her palms grew clammy, she licked her suddenly dry lips, all the while reminding herself that he was just a man, he couldn't do anything to her. Still, if only Ronan was coming. He was such a nice man, protective, charming, gorgeous, treats her like she's an adult. He would never threaten, much less- punish her.

Suddenly, the forceful energy that surrounded the tough man radiated to her, he was in the room. Her back to the door, she kept her head down pretending to be reviewing her notes and jumped when a cup of coffee was set down beside her on a glass table. Two creamers and two sugars, a napkin and a swizzle stick joined it. Jesa's shoulders lifted as if to protect herself. A wrapped breakfast sandwich was set beside the coffee.

Jesa heard McKabe snigger, then harrumph, with the squish of leather and squeak of wheels rolling on the carpet as he took his place behind the huge messy desk.

Silent as a stalking wraith, Koffi made not a sound as he settled on one of the other leather chairs. He chose the closest one to Jesa, the chair was slightly behind her, keeping him out of her direct view. It felt like having a smoldering bull silently snarling at her back, nostrils snorting and flaring, its hooves scraping the ground in preparation for attack.

"Oh, how nice," McKabe said jauntily, "Agent Koffi brought us some hot java and breakfast. Wasn't that nice of him, little darlin'? Especially since I've heard you eat crap for breakfast." He twitched a grin at Koffi. Lifting the cap off his steaming coffee, he poured in one cream and stirred before taking a cautious sip.

147

Jesa sat unmoving, every muscle tense, taut, her heart blasting away at her ribs, waiting for Koffi to lash out at her. "Go on," his grin teasing, McKabe nodded at her coffee, said, "drink up, darlin'."

"Yes, do drink up, Bitty bit," Koffi's dark voice made the normal somewhat affectionate name he called her sound loaded with boding threat.

Keeping her head straight, looking forward, Jesa swallowed but then bolstered herself. She was not going to let the man intimidate her. She set her pad on the table, then, added the cream and sugar to her coffee, stirred it and set the swizzle stick on a napkin that miraculously appeared just as she removed the stick from the liquid. He was deliberately, without words letting her know he was there, behind her.

Lifting the cup with nervous hands, she put it to her lips when suddenly a hand grasped her wrist stopping her. She froze.

"Wait a minute, girl, if you forge ahead recklessly, defiantly, without thinking, you'll get hurt," his innuendo was plain as day. "The coffee is hot, you'll burn your tongue." Tristano kept his fingers wrapped tightly around her thin wrist, squeezing his point, then he released her. Her phone rang.

Thankfully, after she'd called him she'd stuffed the cell in her pocket, last thing she needed was more anger or sarcastic warnings from Agent Koffi. Setting the cup down she took out the phone and swiped to answer. "Hello? Hello?" At the silence, she looked at the phone, brows scrunched in puzzlement, then her complexion whitened. Quickly, Jesa shut the phone off and stuffed it in the pocket of her sweatshirt. Feeling warm suddenly, she pulled the sweatshirt off and laid it across her lap. The blouse she wore was pale yellow with a lacey collar.

McKabe watched her with wary curiosity. The two men shared a probing look. His low voice full of Texas twang he asked, "Who was that, darlin'?"

Jesa didn't move. Feeling the two male's eyes on her, she forced her lips to curve into a composed smile. Looking at the sheriff she said brightly, "Nothing. It was nothing, just a- a reminder."

"A reminder for what?" Koffi didn't disguise the alert interest, or the undertone of command for her to answer.

Jesa turned briefly towards him, saw the skepticism on his strong features. She picked up her coffee and made a big display of blowing on the brew to cool it. "Nothing," she repeated, "it was nothing." Hearing Koffi's swift intake of breath behind her indicating he was going to push her to answer, she said to McKabe, "Sir, what is on our agenda for today? I am ready to get to work."

"Jesselin-"

McKabe spoke over the agent, another look passing between them, telling him to drop it for now. "You are right, darlin'." He said to Koffi, "We spoke this morning, you worked late last night. Share with Jesa what you discovered."

Tristano sat stationary, his eyes fixed on Jesa's back, then they swept to McKabe where they sharpened keenly. At McKabe's nod, he took a deep, exasperated breath, let it out, said, "Yeah." He paused, raked long fingers through the waves in his short dark hair. "Jesselin," he paused again waiting for her to turn around and look at him. She did, but her eyes fell as soon as they made contact with his.

He said, "Mrs. Westcott lied about knowing Subie King in high school. She grew up in Santa Barbara, California and went to school there. She never moved until two years ago when she and Stedman relocated here. Subie King dropped out in tenth grade at Lawrence High in Harlem's lower south side.

"He was raised in the slums, and spent his life in and out of prisons in New York until a year ago when he found his way here. He had relatives that spent the summer seasons on Orainn. A couple of years ago when the season ended and they returned to the mainland, he stayed here."

McKabe nodded as Tristano spoke, then the chief said, "You reported that at no time did he leave New York, and you spoke surreptitiously with Stedman and he told you that his wife never went further east than Las Vegas." Folding his beefy hands together on his desk, bulky shoulders hunched, he said to the pair, "You need to go back and talk to her."

Jesa set her coffee cup on the table and bent to pick up her backpack on the floor. "Okay, how soon will Deputy Ronan get here and we can go? Should we call ahead first?" Chewing on the inside of her cheek, she said, "Mrs. Westcott was very put-out when we just showed up on her doorstep before. I don't want to upset her and Mr. Westcott again, they thought we were bringing bad news about Brie."

Tristano stood up, straightened his suit coat. "We, that is you and I, Jesselin," he said to her, "are going to the Westcotts' right now." He nodded intentionally at her unwrapped sandwich, "That is, we'll head right out after you eat."

Her churning stomach would never hold down food. Straightening her spine, she thought, *he cannot tell me what to do*. She mumbled, "I'll eat it on the way," stuffing the sandwich in her bag, Jesa got to her feet but charily stepped back several feet from the agent.

"But, Chief," she glanced at McKabe pleading with him with her eyes to agree with her, "that was Ronan's interview. We need to wait for him." She shoved the sweatshirt in the pack.

His chuckle muffled, McKabe pushed his chair back and stood up with a lean smile. He said to Tristano, "I, uh, have things to do. I will see you both later. Jesa darlin'," his face sobered, turned hard, bone serious.

Her green eyes rounded as he'd never looked upon her with anything but paternal warmth and kindness. Now...he looked as ruthless as Koffi. "I have turned your welfare over to Agent Koffi. Every ounce of your welfare. You understand?"

She blinked in bewilderment at him, Tristano stood silently at her back. He felt like an iron wall blocking her from leaving. "Sir, no, you can't, I-"

"Hush, darlin'." McKabe didn't look as cruel or as dangerous as Koffi, but, there was a stony uncompromising in his brown eyes. "We know there is something...gravely critical up with you. No," he held a hand up to stop her denial. "We will not dissect it now, just know, that I will not allow you, or anyone to jeopardize your safety. You are tugging on the tethers Agent Koffi has strung on you with his concern for your wellbeing, ignoring his security commands and recklessly doing as you please and risking your life. That's over, darlin'. Right now. You will do as he instructs and not disobey his orders. He has my blessing to do as he sees fit to keep you under his protective control."

His voice still strong, but the hardness in his eyes softened, he said, "You can't go anywhere to get aid, darlin', to prevent us from doing this, even from Ronan or anyone on the stateside. Until we verify what is really up with you, you are under our supervision. I am at the moment allowing you your freedom. Therefore, do as Koffi commands, or face his…consequences. If you won't care for your safety, then we will. That's all." He nodded to her and started to turn away.

Jesa's wide eyes flew to Tristano who stood immovable granite regarding her with his harsh inscrutable face. Taking a step towards the sheriff, she cried, "No, but sir, I am an adult! A free adult, not a criminal under your jurisdiction, you can't force me to- wait-"

"Later Agent," McKabe said, lifting his chin to Koffi, and he bowed to Jesa, "darlin'." And, with a twinkle in his eye, he left the couple alone, closing the door behind him.

Jesa stood staring at the door, panic rising, profoundly aware of Tristano at her back like a hunter about to strike and take down his quarry.

Chapter Seventeen

"Sit down, Jesselin," Tristano commanded quietly. So quietly, chilling fingers of terror ran up her spine, it was scarier than if he'd shouted. His deep voice jolting her, Jesa started for the door.

"I wouldn't," he said, silky dangerous, threat oozing softly. Her step faltered, then she took a breath and continued as if he hadn't spoken. "Last warning, Jesselin," his voice so quiet the air in the room stilled.

Her gulp could be heard in the next town, yet, she kept moving. The closed door was her oasis, her steps quickened, she reached the door, grasped the knob, went to turn it and wrench the door open, and it didn't budge. Panic strangling her throat, how could the sheriff leave her there alone with that- that tyrant-

Jesa twisted and yanked at the knob, it turned but the door seemed to be locked. Goose bumps prickling her arms, she looked up. Over her head Koffi's large hand rested against the wood.

"I said sit," the order was emitted softly yet heavy with warning.

Her legs like lead, Jesa couldn't believe he was ordering her about, preventing her from leaving. Facing the door, she said, "I want to leave. Right now," and she pulled futilely on the knob.

"You have one second, Jesselin." Deadly quiet voice coarse as a rough rug, he growled, "Or I will sit you down myself. Last warning."

The hardness of his baritone resonated frighteningly in her chest. Feeling his masculine heat on her back, he was so close his breath warmed the top of her head, Jesa felt his powerful body crowding her. He was the law, certainly he wouldn't dare manhandle her.

With a huff of irritation and fear, she jerked the doorknob as hard as she could. "You can't hold me prisoner! Move your hand!" she demanded. The words barely left her lips and she found herself lifted in the air. "Hey-" she yelped, "put me down!" Her bag fell from her hand in her surprise.

Carrying her as if she were a stuffed doll, Koffi walked to one of the chairs and deposited her on it, then stood in front of her.

Stunned, Jesa sunk back in the leather and gawked up at the agent. He didn't look angry, he looked…forceful. "Mr., uh, Agent, uh, Koffi, you can't treat me like this." She pushed herself to the edge of the chair expecting he'd back away. He didn't.

"Get out of my way," she ordered struggling to keep the tremor out of her voice. When he didn't move, she put her hands on his thighs and shoved. They were muscular iron posts, and did not budge a hair.

"Enough of this." Koffi bent over and set his hands on the arms of her chair fencing her in, causing her to skirt back.

"Agent Koffi," darn, her voice shook. Looking up at him, her heart stopped. His huge shoulders blocked her view of the rest of the room, the immense chest an immovable fort, his tie swung forward. Dark hair waved over his forehead and dark brows lanced over infuriated eyes. His mouth was a hard line of danger.

"You be quiet," he ordered, his voice etched steel. "We are done with your disobedience. Done. It appears no one cared enough when you were a child to discipline you for your own welfare. I am the law here, I don't make orders without strong reasons. You will obey me or suffer the penalties."

Dismayed at his high-handed dictatorship, Jesa angrily pulled her petite body up, straightened her shoulders and glared at him. Who does he think he is for Pete's sake! "You can't tell me what to do. I quit. I'm going back to the bistro, go find yourself some other pawn to order around. Now, move." He leaned over further; she put her small hands on his chest and pushed. It was like a fly batting at a wall.

"No, Bitty bit." He smiled sagely, harshly sculpted cheeks sharpened, glittering black eyes narrowed until to Jesa he personified the savage and fearsome devil himself. "It's too late for that. You have fucked up your life, and I will help you fix it. You are not leaving until I allow it, and from now on, you will do what I say."

"I will not and you can't make me." She pushed harder, well aware she couldn't move him.

"Okay, Jesselin." The smile gone, his features turned fierce with anger. "There is nowhere you can go, no one to help you. I will take your ID and you will be unable to leave Orainn. Your running away in terror stops here. From now on you will do as I say and stop recklessly endangering yourself."

"Huh." Flinging strawberry curls back, her nose turned up, lips pressed mulish, she queried coolly with a bravado she struggled to muster, "And if I don't?"

"Then you will go over my knee and I will beat you until you can't sit for a month of Sundays. And if you disobey me again, I'll use my belt the next time."

He lowered his head, face inches from hers. She could see each individual long black lash curl almost like a girl's around flinted ebony. She could smell the roasted coffee he'd drunk, the mild scent of his after-shave, virile testosterone poured off him in intoxicating, frightening waves.

"You- you can't," she stammered seeing the iron will, the promise in his obsidian eyes. "This is the 21st century. I have rights, you can't knock a woman around, it's against the law!"

"Ah, but as I said, little girl, I am the law on this rock, and as you heard I have the full backing of Sheriff McKabe. He knows you're hiding something, something that could hurt you, but he's letting it simmer for now. He could lock you up on suspicion alone, Jesselin, think about that. I have his permission to treat you as I deem appropriate, necessary. Young defenseless women do not belong traipsing around alone in the dark on a desolate, treacherous fucking mountain with a flux of veritable strangers entering and leaving this rock. You have done that for the last time. You hear me?"

"Oh, but it's okay for a man to do it!" she snapped in frustration.

Patience lacking, he countered derisively, "There's not as much call for raping and strangling men, Jesselin."

"Then- then I'll get a gun, a knife." She crossed her arms with an infuriated pout. "I am not defenseless."

His laugh snorted out fully disparaging her abilities to protect herself. "Sure. You are barely five feet tall and a hundred pounds, and obviously unskilled in any kind of self-defense. You pull a gun, not that you could purchase one here or afford one anyway," he smiled at her

154

scowl, "and the man you aim it, or wave a useless knife at, will take it from you without blinking an eye, and now he will have your weapon to use against you. No, we are done discussing this. You do as I say in regards to your safety or suffer the repercussions."

Wriggling in the leather chair, Jesa sought to slide off it and away from him. "No. I will not. No one made you boss over me. You are not my father, brother, or husband, and even if you were I still would not do as you say. Obey you?" she made a discourteous sound of ludicrous rejection. "Not on your life, Mr. Ancient living in the olden days when males thought they were masters over women. You have no right to hold me against my will, and try to tell me what to do with false threats, I am leaving."

One side of his mouth nicked up, he said with a laugh, "If I were your father, your brother, your...husband," his voice lowered, eyes low-lidded, "trust me, you would obey me. I would have taught you how to take care of yourself properly. Last chance, Jesselin, tell me you will comply and with no more trouble and I will let you go and we will get on with our job."

Giving up trying to get past him, he was a solid wall of brick and muscle, she sat back and crossed her arms with a harrumph. "No. Screw you and your commands. Go away, and let me up." He released the arms of her chair, stood up straight, and shrugged his jacket off. He draped it neatly over another chair. A few beats and Jesa made to spring up-

Tristano moved lightning fast before she could try to run, he grabbed her biceps, lifted her from the chair, carried her to the divan, sat down and laid her face down, her hips and stomach across his thighs. Her nightmare of him putting her over his knee had come to life.

"Let me go! What do you think you're- ow!" she shrieked as his hand came down on her jean-covered bottom. "Stop! Don't you dare hit me!" Her screams only spurred him to whack her harder and faster.

"Go ahead, Jesselin, scream, let everyone outside this room know what's going on in here," he sneered, and wailed on her ass.

That was enough for her to muffle her cries. She wanted rescue but not at the cost of her mortification of being seen in this position. But she grunted and huffed, kicked her feet, twisted her body trying to break loose, and pounded at his legs. He merely splayed a big hand over her slender back holding her immobile and continued.

She screamed into his calf, arms hanging down, flailing, tears flowing. Her hand flapped back trying to cover, protect her bottom, and he just grasped her wrist and held it against her back. When she ran out of fuel, her energy drained, she stopped struggling, he halted the smacks. Her chest billowed against his thighs with her sobs.

Koffi gripped her arms and lifted her to sit on his lap. He smoothed the hair damp from her tears off her flushed face and murmured, "Hush now, Bitty bit. I didn't hurt you that badly. This time. That was just a warning." He cupped her jaw, forcing her to look up at him. His hand so big it covered half her face was unbelievably hard and strong, yet he cradled her gently. The big green eyes shimmered with tears, plush lips quivered. "You are more humiliated than injured. So, have we come to an agreement?"

Hitching and sniffing, her lips pressed tightly, shuttering her eyes she refused to answer him.

"Ah, I see," humor was in his deep voice, "you need more of a lesson." He wrapped his fingers around her arms to lift her-

"No! No! Please," she cried then lowered her voice in a hush. "No. I…" her breath sucked in shaky with tears, "I will do as you say."

"Hmm," he murmured, keeping his strong fingers wound around her small arms. "I'm not sure I believe you. Maybe a few more, perhaps it'll be more effective on bare skin. Let's get these jeans off you," he reached for the button on her pants.

"No! Please!" she squealed. Her round childlike eyes widened in plea. "I mean it, I won't cross you, please Agent Koffi."

He lifted her up by one arm and smacked her on her ass with his other hand. At her wail he said softly, "Tristano. Don't make me remind you again, Jesselin. You do it on purpose to keep a wall up thinking you're protecting yourself, and to provoke me." He settled her back down on his lap, his heavy arm wrapped around her shoulders heaving with panting and sobs; he clinched her chin, raising it.

"Now, enough crying, girl. You do as I say and there needn't be a repeat of this. And, trust me," his eyes tapered with a swaggering smile, "next time will be ten times worse. This was just a light warning."

The humor was replaced by threat narrowing his dark eyes, fixing forcefully with hers. He instructed, "You will not run to Finn Barton, or Roarke, or anyone else with complaints or for help, I will simply take you from them and resume your punishment. Plus, someone could get hurt, or arrested in the tussle and I know you don't want that. Now, tell me you fully understand what I am saying, and you agree to comply. It's for the best, for your wellbeing." He waited, his dark gaze scanning her face, her trembling lips, tearful eyes. Finally she nodded.

"Out loud, baby, say it out loud, and mean it." He curbed his grin. "Remember, this is an island, I can find you anywhere you think you can hide from me." His hard fingers slid over her soft face to sift through the fine curls at the back of her head. Lowering his hand, he stroked her nape so delicately she was unaware of the caress.

Her inhale deep and ponderous, she exhaled with a shaky, "Yes, Agent," wincing at the squeeze around the back of her neck. "Uh, I mean, yes, Tristano."

"You better not be lying, Jesselin." His fingers brushed up her neck and down then spread over her nape.

Unaware she was bending her neck forward as he stroked her skin, she muttered, "I'll have you charged with battery, arrested, *ohh*," the groan etched out of her as he manipulated his fingers massaging her neck, her shoulders.

"Ah," his hard mouth curved up, he said, "I think you're looking at a 'he said she said.' You have no proof. You going to take a selfie of your little red ass and show it to the deputies so they can file a report?" Amusement rumbled from his heavy chest, his fingers continued stroking, rubbing, caressing.

"Oh, and I wouldn't run weeping with this to Roarke. It will only bring him and me into an altercation, huh," he half-grinned. "No, it'd be a knock-down drag out fight, and McKabe will banish him to the mainland, and I will still be here. And really pissed."

Jesa was stymied. No one had ever cared about her welfare before, not even her own mother. Her mother had never cared enough to discipline her, she let her come and go and do as she pleased even when she was still in diapers. Neighbors had brought her home from roaming the busy streets more than once. How she'd never been run over or snatched by a pedophile was a miracle.

Sniffing and blinking back tears, she didn't know what to do, how to handle it. Realizing she had no choice but to bow to his commands, for now, she relinquished a cleansing exhale purging the tension from her body, her taut muscles relaxed under his strong though gentle ministrations.

Sitting back in the chair Tristano pulled her gently to settle against his chest, tucked her head on his shoulder. They sat quietly, his arm around her, he sifted and stroked her hair while she calmed.

"I hate you," she murmured with a shuddering sigh into his shoulder. Rubbing her cheek against his shirt over a stalwart pec, she twiddled with his tie.

The edges of his mouth ticked up, he tightened his arms around her. "That's okay, pretty baby. I'd rather you are alive and hating me than dead and liking me."

Jesa snuggled into his embrace feeling oddly safe for the first time in a very long time, held against this brute of a man. Actually, she couldn't remember the last time she had truly felt safe. And it was weird, he had beaten her and yet she felt safe with him. They sat like that for a comfortable few minutes. Outside the closed door the sounds of more and more deputies arriving raised the noise level.

"Okay Bitty bit, we have work to do," there was a trace of reluctance in his voice. He helped her off his lap. "Why don't you stop off in the ladies room and I'll meet you out front."

Jesa slanted a ceding look up at him bound with mellow surprise. Clearly he was telling her to go wash the tears from her face and compose herself, but instead of swaggering arrogant and unkindly ordering her, he made it sound like an offhanded suggestion.

Gosh, she wanted to be so angry with him, to really feel hatred for the way he'd just abused her as a domineering male bully, using his strength on her to make her acquiesce, but, as she grabbed her jacket and bag, she peered at him through a few light curls.

He didn't look smug, or pompous, or gloating proud of what he'd done. His dark eyes were heavily hooded, a bare gleam eked out from under those long lashes, and the gleam stroked her from head to toe and back.

Still sitting, his hands were awkwardly clasped in front of his lower half as if he were uncomfortable. Wondering why he was posed so awkwardly, her strawberry brows drew down, she examined his face, dark red lanced his cheeks and the tips of his ears. Strange, why was he uncomfortable? She was the one who'd been paddled. "Agen-Tristano, are you okay?"

He cleared his throat, motioned with his head, his "Uh huh," affirmed in a gravelly rasp. He said softly, "Go on now, we're already running behind."

"Hmm, okay." Her smile a wobble of embarrassment and perplexity, and a sense of haven, Jesa went to the door. This time he didn't prevent her from leaving.

Chapter Eighteen

Jesa stared at her reflection in the mirror. The last time she'd taken the time to do that, she saw nothing but fear and misery reflecting back at her. Now, she combed the long curls off her face letting them dangle down her back, the fear and misery were replaced by ambiguity, and perplexity, and a true calmness she hadn't ever remembered feeling in her life. The ambiguity was her confusion, torn between anger at Koffi's treatment of her, and the odd feeling of security she felt because of it. And the uniqueness of feeling that for once in her life someone had acted like they truly cared about her wellbeing.

After cleaning up in the restroom, she went to the bullpen where deputies were milling about collecting orders, completing paperwork and chatting.

Near the front desk, Koffi stood with two female deputies, one of them, Tahni Genarino was hanging on his arm. Her yellowish butterscotch hair was down around her uniformed shoulders, not pinned up per policy. The deputy channeled a vamp with a heavy wave spiraled over one torrid sapphire eye, she flapped caterpillar-thick golden lashes over it at the agent she clutched.

Shrugging her jacket on and stowing her bag over her shoulder, Jesa felt her stomach tighten at the way Tahni clung on the agent with her huge breasts rubbing all over him. "Huh," Jesa grunted turning away. *Like to see him put her tall voluptuous body over his knee and try to spank her.*

Jesa lifted her long curls under the faux fur hooded collar of her jacket letting them tumble back and thought, the deputy would probably enjoy the spanking. Yeah, Tahni would like it, like his huge hard hand slapping her big bottom, making both of them hot. Then

160

Tahni and Tristano would strip each other's clothes off and fall on the sofa in a steamy jumble of naked arms and legs-

"Sugar, honey, I've been looking all over for you," the deep friendly voice of Ronan wrapped around her, easing the pit growing in the bottom of her stomach. Sandy hair and blue eyes came into her view, his grin expressing how happy he was to see her. He set a large hand on her delicate shoulder and gave it an affectionate press.

Jesa returned his welcoming smile. "Hi," she said shyly, "we've all been pretty busy."

He slid his hand under her hair lifting it then letting shiny curls spill off his fingers in a saffron stream. Bending slightly so their faces were closer, Ronan's voice tender, he brushed his thumb over her round cheek, "Yeah, but I can always make time for you."

"That's nice, Ronan, for you to say. But," she sighed, her gaze strayed over his handsome face, enjoying the sparkle in his baby blues, "we do have tasks to do today."

"Yeah." He drew the backs of his fingertips down the side of her face to her neck and further. "I heard Elizabeth Westcott lied about knowing the drug dealer. She needs to be re-interviewed. The dealer is penny-ante, it's a possibility that maybe he owes someone bigger than him a lot of money or something and snatched the baby to get the ransom to pay off his debt.

"We found ties to a big-time dealer that he keeps company with, that guy could have gotten the idea from King and taken her himself. Hell, maybe they're in on it together. We need to find out what Elizabeth's hiding. Come on, my cruiser's out front, let's go talk to her."

A frown pleated her light brows, her bottom still heated from the spanking Koffi had given her. She thought to tell Ronan, but the agent was right, Ronan would possibly go after Tristano in her honor. He was that kind of man, a gallant knight. Surely Koffi wouldn't care if she went off with Ronan to interview Mrs. Westcott. His complaint was that she wandered off alone, and in the dark. It was broad daylight and she would be with a deputy. Heck, she couldn't be any safer.

But… she caught a glimpse of Tristano and the two female deputies hanging on him. Tall enough, Tahni, if in heels and on tiptoe could almost look Koffi in the eye. Well, the neck. She wriggled as close as she could get to him, trying to wedge under his arm. With the pretty deputy pawing all over him he wouldn't even notice she was gone. Jesa said, "Okay, sure."

His delight written in the huge grin, Ronan rolled his arm around Jesa's shoulders. "Great, let's go before the big bad wolf scraps the idea." He maneuvered her towards the door and pulled his keys from his pocket. He wore a flannel shirt, jeans and a brown bomber jacket instead of his uniform today, his badge hung from a chain around his neck.

Just as Ronan's hand touched the door handle- "Jesselin," Koffi's cold voice stopped them.

Gritting his teeth, the deputy turned to address the agent that was now standing only a few feet from them. "Koffi, you have your own things to attend to, we're heading over to the Westcotts'."

Ignoring Ronan, Koffi held his hand out to Jesa. "Give me your phone." At her quirked brow, he said, "Deputy Saunders is going to run a trace on those hang-ups." His gaze followed Ronan's arm sliding from Jesa's shoulders down to her hip where he fondled it possessively.

"But," Jesa protested, "what if I need the phone? I-"

"You will be with me, you won't need your phone." Koffi's dark eyes leveled at Ronan.

Ronan shifted so Jesa was partially behind him, he said coldly, "Listen, Koffi, you had her all day yesterday, she can go with me to interview Mrs. Westcott. Now, if you don't mind," he set his hand on Jesa's waist to usher her out the door.

"I do mind," Koffi's voice artic ice. "Jesselin," he held his hand out.

Jesa's lips crimped at his flinty features setting harder by the second. She fished the phone out of her backpack, skin turning pink at the knowing way Tristano watched her, his brows punctuating down. She'd forgotten she had put her sweatshirt in the bag, and her phone was in the pocket. For some reason he must think that she would at some point be in trouble, break a leg or something, and not have her pack with her, ergo no phone to call for help.

But, darn, last thing she wanted was Koffi looking into her hang-ups, she didn't want him in her business. If he found out the truth about her, a spanking would be a gentle pat compared to what he'd do to her. Of course the hang-ups were probably just wrong numbers and when that's confirmed, she could set her fearful worries to rest.

Rolling her eyes, she slapped the phone in his open palm. His brows ruffled, then the corner of his mouth nicked up. Meaningfully gripping his belt, Tristano said quietly, "You're gonna pay for that, Jesselin, the phone not being in your pocket, and the disrespectful eye-roll."

"What the hell do you mean by that, Koffi?" Ronan stepped aggressively to him.

Koffi stood his ground, a hard smile hovering on the edge of his mouth. He said smoothly, "I mean that Jesselin will be going with me, Roarke. You have a problem with that, I suggest you bring it up with McKabe." He turned his head and called, "Deputy Saunders," and held the phone up. Ronan stood with his mouth open in angry umbrage, Jesa stared at the floor.

"Hey, Agent Koffi," Caitlin strode right over and took the phone from him. She greeted the others, "Roarke, Miss Jesa." Back to Tristano, she said, "I'll get this right to the tech guy and let you know what he comes up with. See you all later, my turn today trolling the docks for missing babies." She grinned at them all and trod through the small mingling crowd of deputies and CSA's.

"Tristy," Tahni cooed over Koffi's shoulder, "I need experience interrogating felons, how 'bout I tag along?"

Tristano said, "That's a good idea, Deputy Genarino,"

Tahni's face lifted, bright white teeth showed in her broad smile. "That's fabulous, Tristy, you can leave that shit-mobile with the half-pint," she tipped her head in disdain to Jesa. "I have a real car, we can take mine. I'll let you drive, I know what a dominant male you are." Setting her sharp nails on his sleeve she asked, "How soon can we go?"

Koffi grasped her wrist lifting her hand off his arm and pulled her forward. Tahni's smile widened, her lids pooched with sensual anticipation. "Ah, Agent, Tristy honey," she purred as she allowed him to draw her intimately closer, then she gasped as he gently pushed her at Ronan and set her talons on the deputy's arm.

"Sure, we can all head out, Deputy Genarino," Koffi said. "Jesselin and I are going to the Westcotts'. You can tail along with Roarke and listen and learn as he questions Subie King."

"What!" Penciled-in butterscotch brows shot up.

Ronan asked in surprise, "You found the dealer? The address he gave the bail bond and the court was bogus. He paid a fine and his whereabouts are unknown."

"I will as soon as I talk to Elizabeth Westcott." He said bluntly to Tahni, "Don't call me Tristy," and he clinched Jesa's upper arm and walked her to the door.

"Wait," Ronan said quickly, pacing to them.

His head tucking to the side with his impatient sigh, Tristano turned around, as did Jesa.

Grinning, Ronan said to Jesa, "Listen sugar, there's a concert tonight in the Commons Square under the stars. I'll bring a basket of food and wine. What'd'ya say I pick you up at seven?"

"Are you daft?" Tristano frowned at the deputy. "It's too cold to sit outside."

Directing a withering smile at Tristano, Ronan said smugly, "They have portable gas heaters surrounding the area." He turned to Jesa, the smile turned sensual. "It'll be romantic, babe, the cold dark night with flaming heat, wine, music, you, me."

Tristano grunted his objection. "Roarke, we don't know how late we'll be today. We-"

Ronan cut him off, "It's Saturday night, Koffi, I know an infant is at risk but you can't make everyone work 24/7. The deputies are all on rolling shifts. So what if you're late, I'll go get her-"

"What a great idea!" Tahni gushed. "We'll double-date. Ronan and the child, me and the hunky agent." Tristano opened his mouth but Tahni raced on, "Yeah, don't worry, honey, I'll prepare the basket. I'll give you my address. Oh," her lower lip pushed out in a coy pout, "please don't blow me off in front of everyone, Tristy, be a cool guy, okay?" She peered up at him through that wave of yellow hair, batting her lashes. Everyone stared at Tristano waiting for his response.

Tristano regarded the deputy, Tahni cocked her head and slyly flapped her lashes over the dark blue eyes in an unashamed plea, he shifted his flinty gaze to Ronan's supercilious grin. His sight pinned on Ronan's self-satisfied mug, Tristano said, "Jesselin hasn't agreed to go." Everyone looked at Jesa whose face pinked from the attention.

"Well, what do you say, Jesa? It's all worked out. Koffi and Tahni are going on their date, so it's cool. I'll pick you up at your house at seven." Ronan looked so hopeful, like a puppy about to get kicked. Tahni nuzzled Tristano's arm. The air slid out of Jesa's lungs. "Okay," she murmured.

"Great." Ronan grinned and bent over giving her a peck on the cheek. "I can't wait-" He didn't get to finish because Tristano snatched up Jesa's wrist and yanked her away and to the door.

Jesa said, "Agent-"

Tristano opened the door and they went outside, with Tahni and Ronan grinning ear-to-ear inside the station.

Tristano muttered, "Not a good start, Jesselin, I should think your butt would still be a stinging reminder how to address me." His mouth lifted in a small grin at the alarm that parted her lips. "We'll talk later about a refresher course," he whispered, "when there are no witnesses." At her swift intake of breath, his grin deepened. With a chuckle, he led her to the car.

At the Westcotts' mansion, Elizabeth threw a look over her shoulder to make sure her husband was out of earshot, then she covered her face with her hands, dropped her head and bawled.

A deputy by the door stood awkwardly, his gaze flittering all around the room, he wasn't sure what he should do, so he did nothing. Cloudy sunlight streamed in weakly from the floor to ceiling arched windows spreading faint stripes of yellow light across the ivory rug.

Uncomfortable as well, Jesa sat in the red-cushioned chair Koffi had directed her to with a prior caution that he didn't want her comforting the young mother, or speaking. Koffi stood staunchly in front of the weeping Elizabeth. Her shoulders shook with her sobs. Shoving his suit coattails back, he set his hands on his hips and waited patiently as Elizabeth cried.

"Agent," Jesa whispered, grimacing in anguish at the distraught mother. Koffi shot her a sharp look of warning and shook his head. Jesa bit back her objections at his stern treatment of the woman and sighed.

It seemed like hours by the time the tears slowed, her shoulders heaved less, and Elizabeth hiccupped into a wad of tissues Jesa had hurried and retrieved for her, ignoring Tristano's frown.

Tristano looked down at Elizabeth's blonde head and said with quiet command, "All right, then, Mrs. Westcott. I told you we know you lied to us. You didn't go to school with Subie King. You grew up in different states on opposite sides of the U.S. He's a well-known drug dealer that you bonded out of jail. Now, tell me precisely what your connection to this man is or I will have you arrested for obstruction of justice, and I mean right now." One thick shoulder ticked at Jesa's gasp of protest.

More tears came, Elizabeth dabbed the tissues at them. Koffi stood as a formidable statue; he would make the woman talk, even if he had to drag her down to the station. His gaze narrowed in warning at Jesa. He had precisely told her to keep quiet and not get involved, *shit*, he thought, *that little girl is just begging to feel his palm on her ass again.*

As before, when he was paddling her, his slacks grew tight. He could still feel her front squirming all over his lap, perfectly round little butt wriggling under his hand, wishing her squeals were of pleasure and not pain or humiliation. That he could teach her, bring her pain to pleasure where they sharply, exquisitely coalesce, tug off those jeans and panties- hell, he needed to get a grip, he wasn't a horndog schoolboy, and the girl was under suspect. The reason he had come to this damned rock.

Smothering a terse sigh, he flicked his attention back to Elizabeth. He could wait all night while she cried; a female's tears scarcely affected him, his gaze hopped back to Jesa. Well, maybe most females. Jesa was watching Elizabeth with tears of compassion welling in her own green orbs at the other woman's distress. Tristano felt a strange pinch in his gut. The urge to cuddle her on his lap and comfort her suddenly, inexplicably swamped him, he quickly quelled it.

Finally, Elizabeth sucked in deep breaths, her red eyes rolled up to the indomitable agent. A heavy sigh gushed from her, her shoulders slumped. "All right, Agent Koffi," she said, "I'll tell you. Just," she pleaded with her hands together under her wet eyes, mascara streaked like shoelaces down her face, "please don't tell my husband. I beg you, please."

Koffi crossed his arms over his big chest, his legs akimbo. He stared inscrutably at her with hard eyes for so long she dropped hers. Then he said, his voice grating, "I'll do the best I can. Now, I am this close," he held his thumb and index finger an inch apart, "from running you into the station and locking you up for hindering this investigation." He reminded her, "The investigation of the kidnapping of your daughter."

Wiping under her smudged eyes, her fingers smeared in black from her running makeup, Elizabeth sighed in resignation. "Okay." She glanced over her shoulder to make sure Stedman wasn't there, then sighed again. "It was a year ago or so when I met Subie at one of my friend's homes. There was a lunchtime fundraising soirée and he was part of the..." her eyes lowered in shame.

Koffi prompted, "Part of what?"

"Oh..." she scraped her nails over the black frame of the sofa she sat on, her face turning the color of a beet. "He was with the lawn maintenance crew. They were just finishing up before people started arriving, and I was on my way back to the pool patio when," a bawdy smile broke the embarrassment.

Koffi sighed and looked to the ceiling, his patience ominously ebbing. "Mrs. Westcott..."

She turned a flirty face up to him, "All right, Agent Koffi, don't get your boxers in a bunch." Her distress forgotten, she giggled at the impatient scowl on the agent's hard face.

"Anyway," she began, her face flushed darker with erotic memories, "it was a hot summer day, he had his shirt off, he was taking a drink from the garden hose. His...chest, was sweaty, tanned, toned," breathlessly she glanced at Jesa. "You understand, hon, he wasn't all that tall but he had a body that would make a movie star swoon."

Blushing, embarrassed for the mother, Jesa averted her gaze to the unlit, black marble fireplace with gold veining. It wasn't lit, Jesa wished it was if only for something to stare at.

His voice and face sharp as the edge of a knife, Koffi barked, "Mrs. Westcott, get on with it."

Elizabeth smiled at him. "Yes. Anyway, one thing led to another, he asked me my name and so forth, and well," her head lifted as she looked up at him through lids growing heavy with recalled lust. "So," she sighed, "yes, we had an affair. We made a date for later that night, but really," her gaze jumped to his and grew serious.

167

"The affair only went on a few months, then, well, he was a bit younger than me. A younger girl caught his eye and that was that," she clicked her fingers with a shrug. Her sigh was bittersweet. "Oh, you have no idea, his stamina, his virility, his size, he-"

Koffi's chest filled with a deep breath, he interjected, "All right. Can he be the one who took your child? If he did drugs heavily, or owed money, he would need the ransom."

Elizabeth sprang to her feet, expression indignant, she snapped, "Of course not. Subie would never do anything to harm me. Never. Besides," a small sad smile curved the side of her mouth, "I know for a fact he was on the mainland that day. He still kept in touch with me by text and Facebook. The girl he was seeing was in some sort of," her lips pushed out in slight jealous chagrin, "beauty pageant, and he texted me pictures of her, and of them together that day.

She rolled her eyes and sucked in the side of her cheek. "Honestly, like I would want to see that, but, like I said, he liked me, he wouldn't have hurt me. You can undoubtedly verify this with the pageant people. There would be records of tickets and videos of those present. Pictures on social media." She plunked back down on the red couch cushion like a balloon losing air.

One arm wrapped around his waist, Koffi rested his elbow on that arm and rubbed at the rough dark shadow on his chin. "I will check that out. King's own dealer, do you know where I can find him? His name?"

Elizabeth's eyes flashed startled. "Do think it could be him? He took my baby?"

Koffi bumped a shoulder. "Dunno. Do you know where he lives?"

Elizabeth got to her feet again albeit shakily, Jesa rose as well. "No. He lives part time on the mainland with his mother, in, uh, what did Subie say, oh, Sacramento. But, both boys like to spend the winter on the island so they should be back soon. I only know because," she shrugged sheepishly, "after...you know...sex, we chatted about our lives. Even about his," her cheeks tinted pink with abashment, "ah, drug business. It was actually kind of, you know, exciting. You need to ask Subie his dealer's name." She sighed with longing, "Subie was so sweet, so-"

"Yeah." Tristano moved to where Jesa was standing. "Okay." The full range of his abhorrence flared over his face, it was gone in an instant, but the disgust remained in the tightening of his jaw. Cheating spouses was something he could never abide, and when there are children involved, hell. Eyes flat hiding his loathing, he said icily, "Give Ms. Judan Subie King's phone and address."

Working to keep his repulsion for the young mother from showing, he watched the wind bending and shaking trees outside the window while she looked up King's address in her phone then repeated it to Jesa.

When they were done, he admonished Elizabeth sternly, "You think of anyone else...you might have been...involved with, you better contact me immediately. If I find out you're holding anything else back," he glowered his warning. He took Jesa's notebook, glanced at the address she'd written down and handed the book back to her.

Satisfied at the cowed Elizabeth plopping limbless back down on the sofa, he touched Jesa's shoulder. "Let's go." The pair turned and walked past the contemptuous face of the deputy who had stood off to the side listening as Elizabeth depicted her illicit affair.

"Wait, Agent Koffi," Elizabeth's suddenly weary voice called out. Tristano paused, turned towards her. "Please, you won't tell Stedman, you promised."

Wondering what explanation she was going to tell her husband of their private conversation as well as the first one that Roarke had conducted, Tristano stated coldly, "I said I would try to avoid it. Good day, Mrs. Westcott." His broad hand on Jesa's tiny waist, he ushered her down the hall and out the front door while unhooking his phone. He pushed contacts and then Roarke's number.

Ronan answered with sarcasm, "What now, Agent?"

Koffi told him what he'd just learned then told him to scoop up King and get the information on his drug dealer. He gave him the name and address then clicked off without saying goodbye.

Chapter Nineteen

Koffi drove down by the coast and parked in front of a shack. The parking lot was teeming with cars, an incredible tangy, smoky smell wafted in the air, the sign out front on a hand-painted sign said, *Sharky's*. He got out of the car and went around to wrench the rusted door open for Jesa.

She stared at the large hut-like building made up of pale sun-bleached wood. Different shades and sizes of boards were nailed mishmash like wooden potpourri on the structure, more than one shingle hung loose flapping slightly in the wind. It didn't look like it could survive the looming winter.

A grin lightening his harsh face, a rare affectation for Tristano, he grasped her hand helping her out. "Don't be afraid, you won't get food-poisoning, I promise. I grabbed a beer and a dog here the other day, food is amazing. Come on," he propelled her into the ramshackle restaurant.

It didn't look any better inside, but the place was packed. And loud. Laughter rang everywhere, beer mugs clinked in toast, and the aroma, again, was incredible, spicy, tangy, smoky.

A hostess in jeans, and a t-shirt with *Sharky's* and a big-toothed grinning shark on the front took them to a table. After sliding into the wooden booth, they were handed menus that were thin wooden planks. The redheaded server was there in a flash all smiles and freckles and jeans with the shark shirt asking what they'd like to drink. Her admiring, flirty eyes were all over the tough agent's hard countenance and broad shoulders.

Tristano barely glanced at her when he spoke, "Yeah, a draft and a cream soda, thanks," and lowered his head to scan the menu. When he heard Jesa draw a breath to speak undoubtedly about her lack of funds, he held a hand out without looking up. "Don't. I'm hungry, you gotta eat too, just relax and don't cause a fuss. Unless you want something other than the cream soda I don't want to hear it." A smile softened his face hidden by his menu when he heard her sputter, then sigh in submission.

They were halfway through and knuckle deep in barbeque sauce when Tristano's phone rang. Wiping his fingers, he answered it with a brusque, "Koffi." His head tipped as he listened, then murmured, "On our way," and clicked the phone back in its holder at his hip. Sucking on a bone, he said to Jesa, "Eat up, we have to go."

Jesa didn't ask until they were in the car. Tristano replied, "The models again. Now their rental car was broken into." At her faint, "Oh," he patted her knee. "Don't worry Bitty bit, we are really only making an appearance, a car break-in isn't that intense."

Glancing at her he caught her pensive look. The models were not nice people, and they were crassly mean to Jesa while blatantly hitting on him and any other male within radius. Commiserating her feelings, he said, "Really, Jesselin, I know they can be...difficult. But I promise we'll be in and out."

There was a gaggle of people, deputies and nosybodies crowded near the gaudy hotel's parking lot. Tristano drove right up and parked beside a police cruiser. He didn't get out of the car, one of the crime techs was already examining the burglarized vehicle.

Tristano rolled down a window and waved to Ronan. Spotting them, Ronan loped through the crowd but came up to Jesa's side of the car. She lowered the window and Ronan hunched down to be eye-level, with an elated grin.

"Hey, sugar, I didn't expect I'd see you at all today until tonight when we-"

"Roarke," Tristano's face stoic, his voice even, but a vein beat at his temple, "Give me a report."

Ronan rested his forearms in the window and raised the side of his mouth in a roguish grin. "Nice greeting, Koffi."

"We have a missing child to find, Deputy," Tristano reminded him coldly.

Ronan blinked like he was biting back a retort, then let his natural boyish smile come through. "Yeah, you're right." Lifting his head he looked to where the CSI was working, the models were nowhere in sight. "It's just a simple break-in, kinda like the hotel room. The passenger side glass was broken, good thing it's a rental, huh?" His twinkling blue eyes left the harsh face of the agent and lit with admiring charm on Jesa. Tristano's rough voice brought his reluctant attention back to him.

"Roarke, we don't have all fucking day." He threw Jesa a warning not to harp on his language.

Ronan grinned and winked at Jesa like they shared a joke. He said, "Anyway," it was obviously a chore for the deputy to keep his attention on the annoyed agent when it kept drifting back to Jesa who sat uncomfortably between the glaring men. "The only damage was the window. The girls said they didn't think anything was missing, but someone had rooted through the vehicle just throwing things on the floor. Like in the hotel room, it definitely looks like someone is looking for something.

"I can't figure how this invasion of the girls' things has anything to do with the baby. The models were only here for a shoot, and according to them, 'They've never been here before, don't know anyone who lives here, or who has been here, and they can't f***ing wait to get off this,' " he glanced at Jesa with a grin, " 'mother-blankety-blank anthill.' "

"They start the canvass yet, any witnesses?" Tristano asked.

"Ha," Ronan's laugh ironic. "Yeah, get this. Two little old ladies walking their poodles." He nodded towards the hotel. Still speaking with a deputy, the two tiny ladies looked enthralled and scared at the same time. "They said they basically saw a shadow. He was average or slightly shorter than average height, and he seemed to be dressed in black. He wore glasses because they saw one of the parking lot lights glint off the lenses. They said it was too dark to really make him out, but they said what stood out was his hair."

Both Tristano and Jesa sat up at that.

Chuckling, Ronan said, "Yes, they said it stuck up like a wild boar's around his head."

This time Tristano and Jesa shared a look. Tristano asked, "Anything else?"

Shaking his head he replied, "Nope, but it sounds like enough, huh?" Ronan grinned seeing they got his drift.

"Normandy strikes again," Tristano said wryly. "He's getting smarter, didn't wear the freaky clothes this time. I guess he never heard of a hat."

Ronan laughed. "I got the impression from the models that he's quite vain and doesn't want to hide his glorious mane even in the cold weather, much less in disguise. Unfortunately, just like the maid, the old ladies couldn't point him out of a photo lineup either."

Tristano's phone buzzed, he fished it out and put it to his ear. "Koffi," he said.

Ronan took the opportunity to poke his head in the window further and smile at Jesa. He whispered, "Hey sugar, I feel like Koffi is like the family that kept Romeo and Juliet apart."

Jesa covered the giggle that burbled out. "That's silly. You're saying we are Romeo and Juliet?"

Ronan laid his chin on his hands and winked at her. "You give me half a chance and I'll show you. Tonight-"

"We have to go, later Roarke." Tristano moved the shift out of park and into drive, biting back the impudent grin at Ronan having to jerk his head and arms out of the moving car. Ronan stumbled back cursing. By the time the deputy righted himself, Tristano had the car turned around and was heading back out. Ronan's face dark with anger, his curses muffled as they drove away.

"Agent Koffi," Jesa turned and said angrily to him, "that was uncalled for and just downright mean!"

Tristano forced his cocky smile into a grave line. His wintry voice stoked with condescension, "We are working, Jesa, trying to find a kidnapped baby, her life may depend on how quickly we can do this. We don't have time for frivolous romance games."

"Oh!" she huffed, her eyes narrowed at him in displeasure. "What a stuffed-shirt dispassionate man you are. You were on the phone, we were only passing the time while you…visited," her snip insinuating he had been goofing off.

Entering the address he'd been given into the GPS he'd purchased for the car, Tristano didn't comment. At least the GPS was actually working now on the island.

When they reached a main road that wound around to the other side of the big hill, he said, "The person on the phone that I was 'visiting' with, was McKabe. He said there's another break-in occurring right now. We're heading there."

Boy, he sure knew how to take the wind out of her sails, embarrassed at her snipe, Jesa turned and watched the scenery pass by out the side window. They didn't converse on the twenty-minute drive.

Tristano pulled up in front of a house that had two police cruisers in the drive, blue lights twirling. He got out and helped Jesa out of the car and they walked up the small stone path leading to the front door that was wide open. A deputy stood to the side of the open door.

"Deputy Alvino," Tristano read the tag on his uniform. "Special Agent Koffi with the FBI," he flashed his ID, his badge was hooked to his belt.

Alvino slightly inclined his head in greeting. "Sir." He looked at Jesa, and a smile curved his stiff face.

"Ms. Judan," Tristano offered gruffly enough the deputy's attention zapped back to him. "I was only given a bare briefing. Can you run it down?"

The deputy's gaze skipped back to Jesa until Tristano cleared his throat, and his brown eyes returned to the agent. Tristano's normal countenance of an abrasive rock had hardened to granite, his eyes narrowed impatiently at the deputy. *Hell*, he thought with a grunt, *is there a male on this island that didn't make goo-goo eyes at the girl?*

Alvino said quickly, "Uh, of course, sir. We received a call of a burglary in progress. When we got here there were two men engaged in a physical fight, we have them both secured in different rooms in the house. One of the guys claims the house is his aunt's and he was staying there."

Tristano asked, "Was this house searched for the Westcott baby?"

The deputy took a notebook from his pocket and flipped a page over. "Yes, this house was searched for the missing baby and at the time it was vacant and closed up, no one was living here. A neighbor provided a key to let searchers inside. We contacted a," he slipped a pair of reading glasses from his shirt pocket to his nose and squinted at his notes.

"Jesselin," Tristano said, "notes."

"Oh, yes," she uttered, forgetting again. She delved into her bag and took the notepad and pen out and flipped to an empty page.

Alvino read, then said, "Dispatch contacted a Mrs. Aileen Lloyd a few minutes ago and she said she owned the house, and confirmed that," he flipped a page, "a Dalvin Martin is her nephew but she had no idea that he was on Orainn and staying in her house. In fact, she sounded pretty riled that he was there, asked us to count the silver," he snickered.

"Could she identify this Martin over the phone?"

"Yes." Alvino nodded. "Deputy Grable took his picture and texted it to the aunt. She verified that he is her nephew."

"Okay." Tristano stuffed a hand in his trouser pocket and peered around the deputy into the house. "The intruder? I assume he was the one the nephew was grappling with, or is it the other way around?"

Alvino scratched the top of his short brown hair with a few fingers. "Ah," he reread several pages. "The aunt said she didn't know the other guy, so the nephew was not the burglar, per se. His story is that he was sleeping on the couch when something woke him. When he got up, he saw a man throwing things from the kitchen cupboards to the floor. He waited until the guy fumbled in the dark back to the window he'd broken to get in.

"On his way there he tripped over a table knocking things to the floor then he started to climb out, that's when the nephew jumped him. Martin managed to subdue the guy and called 911. While we were en route apparently the guy got loose and the two males tousled. We broke it up when we arrived on scene."

Watching Jesa taking notes, Tristano rubbed his chin, his lower lip pushed out slightly. "So, why did McKabe send us here? What does this incident have to do with the Brie Westcott case?"

Alvino moved to the side so Tristano could see better into the house. "Because of who the intruder was that the kid was tousling with."

175

One curious arched black brow prompted the deputy to continue.

"Ah," referring again to his notes, the deputy read, "the alleged burglar is a Niels Normandy." Shoving the glasses up pushed back some hair and made a few wisps quill up. "You know the fella?"

Tristano and Jesa made astonished eye contact at the same time. Tristano ordered tersely, "Take us to him."

"To Normandy?" Alvino asked.

Muscling past the deputy, Tristano forged impatiently into the house with a glance over his shoulder to Jesa to follow him. When she caught up, he said quietly, "Stay right by my side, Jesselin, I don't know if there is any danger here." He nodded to an officer who was standing beside a young man sitting on a couch.

The young man had a scratched face and arms, and was holding a bag of frozen broccoli to a bruise purpling on his jaw. Presuming the other detainee was being held in the kitchen, the agent strode through the living room, the house wasn't that big.

He came to a halt in the archway of the kitchen. Tristano's face remained passive when he saw Niels Normandy sitting at the kitchen table with his wrists handcuffed behind his back, and a huge shiner.

The dazed designer looked up with befuddled fright, the remaining color in his face fled when he saw Tristano in the doorway. Restrained by the cuffs, his narrow shoulders shook with fear hurtling towards hysteria. But the squirrely man went on the defensive instead of sniveling at the FBI agent's feet. "What the hell is this, Koffi? I've done nothing wrong!" The bluster quickly faded, "Tell these brain-dead fools that you know who I am. Tell them what a misunderstanding all this is, tell-"

Tristano walked calmly to him, jutting his chin at the deputy standing guard over him to leave. The guard, familiar with the agent, gave him an imperceptible questioning arch of his brows, but at Tristano's hard expression he left the kitchen. Tristano looked to Jesa and nodded to a chair on the other side of the kitchen, he didn't want her anywhere near Normandy.

When she sat down and took out her notebook, Tristano pulled a chair from the table and carried it to Normandy. He set it down facing backwards, straddled it with his forearms resting on the back, and clasped his hands. He was only a foot away from the designer, too close for comfort for Niels.

"Wha…" Normandy tried to recoil from him but with his arms restrained he couldn't move away.

"You have one chance to answer my questions, Normandy." The ruthless violence in his rough voice, threat impaling the designer from half-lidded, very dangerous eyes affirmed Tristano wasn't playing.

A steel edge to his voice, he said, "I am not the local police department hindered by their laws of no police brutality. I am FBI, we have our own set of rules which means," he leaned in close, Normandy cowered back in the chair stretching his skinny neck to get away from him, "that we do whatever it takes. The life of a child is at stake, Normandy, I swear to you if I have to beat it, break it out of you, cut it out," the dark eyes narrowed to slits, "I will." Leaning so they were inches apart, Tristano held his pose to let his words sink in.

Normandy's entire body shook like water roaring down steep falls, his flaccid mouth quivered with fright.

Tristano leaned back, clasped his hands together again and rested his wrists on the back of the chair. "Now, one chance, Normandy, I fucking mean it. Where is Brie Westcott?"

The designer's mouth opened as wide as his eyes behind the big glasses. "Ah- ah I don't know," he screamed, "*I don't know!*"

Tristano's gaze raked down the front of Normandy and back up. "What were you doing in this house? And," he reached out and grabbed a handful of the designer's black shirt fisting it in his hand, jerking him forward, he advised, "you evade, don't answer, lie to me, I swear to God, Normandy, I will cut that lying tongue right out of your mouth. No," his lids slid back down, "I will *rip* it out of your mouth with fucking pliers. You hear me?" He ignored the tiny sound Jesa made from her corner.

Tears flowing from his horrified eyes, Normandy couldn't speak, he nodded as much as Tristano's grasp would allow. The agent held him for a solid thirty seconds letting the man see the very real threat in his eyes. Then he slowly opened his fist, and shoved Normandy back in his chair. "Answer me."

Sprawling in his chair like a bag of wet washcloths, Normandy gagged, then coughed, blinked and blinked, licked his lips, and when

Tristano reached out for him again, he spat out, "I- I was here searching for my stuff!" His mouth flapped open and closed then stayed closed.

His face rigid with intimidation, Tristano hid his surprise at the answer and repeated, "Stuff? What stuff?"

Normandy's trembling wet eyes blinked at him a few times, then he lowered his head. His scrawny chest filled with air and then it rushed out of him leaving his body slack, lifeless. He looked up at Koffi, the tears making his blurry eyes huge in the big comic-sized glasses. "I have designs. My own designs, for red-carpet dresses," he sighed.

This was getting more and more screwy. "So what?" Tristano demanded with a bark that made Normandy flinch.

"Ah- ah, well, they are priceless, award-winning. I get them out there on the runway and I will become a hit overnight. A wunderkind, an artist, a genius, a-"

"Yeah, yeah, what the fuck, Normandy?" His patience was gone way before he had walked into the house, Tristano demanded, "What the fuck were you looking for when you ransacked the girls' hotel room and car, and now this house? You tell me right now, or so help me-" his face dark with brutal warning, he held his fist up to the designer's long nose dripping with snot.

"Okay, okay, back off, would ya?" Normandy whined. Sucking in another deep breath, he sniffed hard and explained, "I had my designs here, someone stole them, and I foolishly," he looked away, "stupidly did not make copies. I didn't photo them, or Xerox them, I just," his head fell back, he closed his eyes. "I had them in this small portfolio case." With a hard sigh he looked at Tristano then hastily lowered his eyes. "I had brought them with me to work on them, when, I...I realized they were missing. I don't know how long they were gone, just that...they were gone."

Tristano didn't move. "Go on."

"Okay, yeah, so I figured it had to be one of those bitches that took 'em. So," his face flushed, he said, "yeah, it was me that broke into their hotel room." He raised his fearful gaze to Tristano, then sniped dolefully, "You knew, you knew it was me all along. I could see it clear on your face, but you couldn't prove it."

"Go on, Normandy, spit it all out."

178

"Yeah, so, the case wasn't in their room so I tried their rental."

"And?"

Normandy shook his head miserably. "I couldn't find it anywhere."

"Why did you take Chantal's notebook?"

Turning scarlet, his breathing fluttered, he turned away from Tristano.

Tristano grabbed a handful of hair and jerked him back to face him. "Answer me, why did you take her notebook?"

Staring up at the ceiling, he mumbled, "She gave ratings to the guys she fucked. And, well, I wanted to maybe meet a few of them." At Tristano's confused expression, he explained, "I make passes at the models, but, I'm bi. I'm into dudes too. Chantal's such a skank, I figured some of them might also be bi." In the corner, Jesa clapped her hand over her mouth to keep in the sound that about leapt out.

Tristano didn't give a shit about the designer's love life. "When you were at the party at the Westcotts', you were found in their daughter's room. What were you really doing in there, and don't give me that poppycock shit about looking for the bathroom. You do and my fist will connect with your nose."

Normandy's eyes bee-lined to Tristano's huge fist not doubting in the least that the agent wouldn't follow through with his threat. His face scrunched as he tried to recall the night of the party. "Ah, hell, I didn't even know the people giving the party. The models were the ones invited, I came along as a package. Free food and drinks, who would pass that by?" he sniffed a sleazy smile, then winced from his bruised eye.

"The nursery," Tristano reminded him.

"Yeah, okay, yeah. It was the bitches," he hurried on at Tristano's nod. "The models. Like I said, I thought one of them had taken my portfolio. Chantal and Sierra were in the bathroom, giggling, doing drugs, going down on each other, whatever," he swallowed at the punishing look Tristano gave him.

"Anyway, I thought since they were high and drunk they might talk about stealing my design book. I mean, yeah, that was a real far-fetched idea. But I was desperate, and plastered, it seemed like a good idea at the time. I had my ear to the wall that separated the kid's room from the bathroom trying to eavesdrop, hear them, when some bitch maid comes in and sees me and has a fit, and next thing I know I'm being dragged out of the house. That's it. I swear." His concave chest heaved with his rushed dissertation.

Tristano pictured the Westcotts' house. There was a bathroom right next to the nursery. The day they first interviewed the Westcotts, when they were in the kitchen, Stedman had mentioned to Ronan in a turned on, man-to-man way that the models had spent a lot of time in the bathrooms together. Rumors were rampant and copious that while they snorted coke like it was air, they were banging everyone they could, male or female, each other.

Ronan was amused when he later relayed to Tristano that Stedman had gotten red and heated as he spoke about the imagined sex between the models. What Normandy said was likely plausible. Taking a few breaths, he asked, "So why this house? Why did you break in here?"

Normandy shrugged one thin shoulder. "This is where we stayed the first few nights when we got here. The uh, photographer knew the owner, Mrs. Lloyd. His wife and she were in the same book club or some-shit, and he knew she wouldn't be here. He managed to get the lock open, but he got scared after a couple of days and was afraid someone would catch us here and we'd get arrested, so we moved.

The models' hotel was booked up so me and the photog rented a tiny bungalow. He blew off the island the day after the party. The magazine, Flaunt This, was paying for our rooms. We all thought we could pocket that money, but," he shrugged again, "the jerk got scared. So I thought maybe my case had gotten stashed here so…" he raised a shoulder.

"Did you have time to search for it before the kid caught you?"

Sniffing hard with a gulp, he nodded woefully. "Yeah. The rooms are small they only took a quick search. The kid was a deep sleeper, snored like a damned freight train. I stumbled over a table in the dark and something crashed to floor and woke him." He sighed. "Alas, it isn't here either."

"The baby?" Koffi asked, "What do you know about the child?"

Normandy blinked in sheer stupefaction. "What baby?"

Tristano sat staring silently at the designer. Sweat poured off him in buckets, his crazy hair wet with sweat was awry liked he'd yanked vigorously on it in panic, eyes bugged out red and soaking wet behind the thick lenses, his nose ran like a faucet. His shoulder was snotty from rubbing his nose on it, and, Tristano sniffed, it smelled like the creep pissed himself at some point in his fright.

The agent's mouth twitched in disappointment, shoulders rounded, the discouragement deflating them. He was pretty sure the freak had nothing to do with Brie Westcott's disappearance. Twisting his neck, he peered over his shoulder at Jesa.

Gnawing her lower lip, the gloomy acceptance on her face told him she felt the same way. As soon as they heard it was Niels Normandy robbing the house they were positive they finally had a grasp on finding the baby. The realization they knew no more than they had before was horribly defeating.

Tristano pushed to his feet and shoved the chair against the table. He lifted his chin to Jesa. She put her notebook away and stood up keeping her eyes off the humiliated designer. Tristano started for the arched doorway, his hand out to Jesa to go with him.

"Hey! Wait!" Normandy squawked. "Where you going? What about me? What's gonna happen to me?" He squirmed in his chair jerking his arms back and forth to break out of the handcuffs.

His hand on Jesa's lower back, Tristano said, "You will be arrested for burglary and probably battery. You will not be allowed to leave the island until we find Brie Westcott. Even if you make bail, you are forbidden to leave."

Fluffy brows wild like his hair crunched over his glasses. "What? But I didn't steal anything or have anything to do with that- that- Westbrook- Westcock whatever baby. I have to get back to the mainland, I have pending jobs, you can't-"

His hand moving up under her hair to her nape, Tristano nudged Jesa through the doorway and into the hall to the living room.

Normandy's screams reverberated down the hall. "Wait! No! Don't let them keep me, Koffi! Help me! Help-"

The couple stepped outside, the guard shut the door silencing Normandy's shrieks.

When they were in the car and driving down the street, disappointment in her voice, Jesa asked, "What do we do now?"

One hand on the wheel the other dragged through his hair, Tristano said blandly, "I take you home so you can get ready for your big date tonight."

Her body softened with a little smile. "Yes. I think it'll be nice, outside under the stars listening to music."

Tristano snorted drily. "Except you'll have to suffer the insipid company of Roarke."

"Oh," Jesa smiled out the side window, replied, "I don't think being with Ronan will be quite so torturous."

"Huh," he grunted, "forced to spend the evening with an obnoxious twit."

Turning to him with a frown, Jesa claimed, "That's not nice." Then her smile resumed. "He's really very sweet," the strawberry brows angled down. "He doesn't spank me or abuse me or boss me around or take my car. If *he's* obnoxious then what, pray tell, are you?"

"In charge," he grinned.

Jesa playfully slapped his arm. "Oh you, you are incorrigible."

"Hmm." He glanced at her with a noncommittal grin. He pulled close to the side of the road and stopped the car, put it in park.

The smile dimmed, she turned her head to look at him. "Still, you had no right to...hold me against my will...hit me like you did. You think because you- you're a cop, sort of, that you think you are above the law. You-"

The planes of his face hardened, he cut in, "Care, Jesselin. I did it because I care about you. You are too reckless for a young female. You have no family here to watch out for you, support you, guide you. You never have." Before she could question that comment he lifted a long curl off her shoulder let it wind around his thick finger, rubbed its silky stands with his thumb.

Lowering his voice, his tone softened as did the flint in his dark eyes. "I will protect you from everyone, Jesselin," lips tightened, lashes lowered, "even from yourself."

Jesa's lips parted, her eyes flickered back and forth from one of his eyes to the other, and watched as they drifted down to her mouth. Slowly revolving his finger he wound more of the curl around it, and pulled her closer to him. His head lowered, his grip on her hair forced her head up, and she blinked with a harsh inhale, a shake of her head, she moved back forcing him to release her hair.

Lids heavy and low, a slight frown cooled the heat in his eyes. He moved the car from the side of the road and proceeded up the mountain.

Jesa forced her mouth into a shaky smile, choosing to lighten the mood, she said, "At least I have a date with a handsome dashing gentleman, unlike you who will be spending the evening with Deputy Genarino."

Tristano's frown converted to a scowl that he quickly vanquished. Then he beveled a sly smile at her. "Yeah, sure. A woman tall enough when in heels can almost look me in the eye, built like a brick- you know what- statuesque, not in the least bit delicate," his gaze intentionally rolled over Jesa's slight frame. "And mature, experienced, pretty, and she's obviously into me." Shaking his head. "Nah, I can't see anything to complain about there."

Her lips pushed out ruefully, Jesa didn't make a comeback.

After a mile of silence, Tristano shifted his gaze from the road to her. "What's up, Bitty bit? You should be happy, we both have a great evening ahead of us." She said nothing, his jibing grin turned grim, and they drove the rest of the way without speaking.

Chapter Twenty

Ronan laid out the blanket then set the cooler on it. "This is neat, huh, sugar?" He smiled up at Jesa. Both in jeans and jackets, she stood taking in the venue. They were on trimmed winter grass with a gathering crowd doing the same as them, setting down blankets and picnic baskets.

The people sat facing an outdoor stage, musicians were setting up as the sun was heading down casting long shadows. Laughter and conversation rippled around, noisy children skipped, weaving in and out of settling families.

"Yes, it's nice." Jesa gracefully lowered to the blanket and sat cross-legged, removing her ski-jacket. Gas heaters had been set up scattered around the crowd warming the entire area.

Ronan sat down almost in the middle of the blanket and reached for Jesa's wrist tugging her to sit closer to him. He rolled his arm around her shoulder. "C'mere, sugar, we need body warmth to stay warm."

Giggling, Jesa snuggled under his arm. "It's plenty warm with the heaters, Ronan, we don't need body heat."

"Uh huh," he curled a finger under her chin lifting it, said quietly, "maybe I just want an excuse so I can keep you close to me, and we can," he lightly set his lips on hers, smiled against them and said, "get to know each other better."

"No, Tristy, I don't wanna sit near them, let's go down further in front." Tahni Genarino's familiar whine grated through the serenity of the park causing Jesa to push awkwardly from Ronan's embrace. Ronan's groan was loud enough for everyone to hear.

"Huh, what? Near who?" Tristano's cool, puzzled baritone clashed with Tahni's stridency.

Keeping her head turned and slightly down, Jesa peeked up through a curtain of strawberry curls to see Tahni's pissed face, and Tristano, already tossing the blanket down on the grass doing a double take appearing as if he just noticed the couple.

"Ah, hey there, Roarke," the agent said, nodding briefly at Ronan while smothering his grin at the deputy's scowl, "and Jesselin. How unexpected is it that we just happened to stumble across you two where there's the last empty spot?" His placid face held pure surprise.

"Tristy," Tahni carped, pushing stiff yellowish waves off her shoulders, "we can see and hear better if we move down closer to the band, there's plenty of open spots there." She stood, her whining pulling down her abundant lips, spoiling her pretty face. The deputy wore high spiked heels, and a very short, quite low-cut floaty dress, the wind kicked up the skirt showing everyone the pink thong she wore under it. Over the top of the dress she had on a short leather jacket that she was peeling off.

On his haunches, Tristano opened and spread out the wool blanket then set the picnic basket he'd carried smack in the middle, then plopped down on one side of it. He looked up at Tahni patting the blanket. "Come on, they're almost ready to start. It's crowded, we'll step on people trying to find another spot, park it."

Her hands on her hips, Tahni tossed the stiff waves back out of her face with a snap of her head, and looked around. "No, Tristy, there's plenty of spots, let's-"

Tristano opened the basket and took out a container of chicken wings and macaroni salad placed them on the blanket. He added paper plates, cutlery, then retrieved wine glasses and a bottle of Beaujolais, set them down and reached in for the corkscrew. "We're already here and settled, Tahni, you called it a double-date, remember?"

He stuck the corkscrew in and twisted it then plucked the cork out. He poured some into the glasses then pushed the cork back in and put the bottle back in the basket. "Here." He held one of the glasses up to the fuming blonde.

With a snippy huff, Tahni flopped down on the blanket and snatched the glass out of his hand almost splashing it on her dress.

Tristano had placed the basket in the middle of the blanket forcing her to have to sit on the opposite of it from him. Without greeting Ronan and Jesa, she smoothed her skirt over her thighs with short piqued slaps, and then took a big gulp.

Tristano in black jeans and black leather jacket scooched down on his side and leaned back to brace on one elbow. Smiling innocuously at the scowling Ronan and pink-cheeked Jesa, he took a sip of his wine and said, "Funny running right into you two in this huge crowd, huh?"

"Yeah," Ronan sneered at him, "real funny." He tried to haul Jesa back next to him but she'd put distance between them. Frustrated at Tristano and Tahni disturbing them and causing Jesa to now sit nervously away from him with stiff limbs, Ronan said to Tahni, "Nice dress, Genarino."

That brought a vain smile to the deputy's face. "Thank you, Ronan, at least *some* men have gallant manners." Her reproving glance at Tristano's blank face told all.

"Yeah, pretty, but," Ronan said skeptically, "a little inappropriate for an outdoor, family, sit on your ass on the ground event, don't you think?"

Sticking her nose in the air, Tahni looked down it from Ronan to Jesa, taking in the younger girl's jeans and pale yellow sweater she sniffed. "At least some of us have taste and know how to dress with sophistication," sneering at Jesa, "and a modicum of sex appeal. Some just don't have it at all." She swung her head from Jesa and scowled at Ronan before looking away from the couple.

Jesa flushed at the insult while Ronan barked out a scoffing laugh.

Tristano leaned over and held his hand out to Jesa with his palm open. "Hear, Bitty bit," he handed her, her phone.

Taking it, Jesa smiled. "Thank you. Is everything...okay?" Surely if they'd found anything abnormal he would have already hauled her in for questioning.

"Bitty bit?" Ronan and Tahni said at the same time.

Ignoring them, Tristano looked only at Jesa. "They didn't find anything. The calls apparently came from burner phones, they were untraceable. You and I need to get together and discuss this. We need to figure out why you're getting these hang-ups." Nodding at her jeans, he reminded her, "In your pocket, Jesselin."

Rolling her eyes she did as he said.

Black brows like stakes lowered over his dark eyes, the side of his mouth curved up, "I think that eye-rolling thing, little girl, falls under the respectful thing we had a…" the lip curved higher with warning, "conversation about." A full-fledged grin broke out on his hard face as her cheeks warmed from his subtle reminder of the spanking he'd given her, and was obviously intimating another might occur. His voice rumbled low, "I think you need a refresher."

"Refresher for what? What the hell are you talking about?" Ronan said to Tristano, then turned to Jesa. "Hang-ups? What's that about? You should have told me."

Frowning at Tristano for blabbing her business about the calls, it didn't stop her face heating further in embarrassment from him mentioning, even in code about the spanking. Jesa shook her head at him, telling him she wasn't afraid of his threat of another spanking. Although her color and voice rose contradicting it, she said coolly, "The calls were nothing to talk about, they're just a few wrong numbers, not even worth mentioning. Agent Koffi was just being, uh, over involved in an insignificant thing."

Hearing a soft growl, Jesa could have bitten her tongue at calling him Agent. She could see a shifty smile on his rocky face and realized he was adding transgressions to her mounting infractions.

Before Ronan could respond, Tristano said, "Wait, how many is a few? Saunders said she only found two calls."

Her face darkening, Jesa said in a small voice, "It's nothing, really, four or five, uh, or so. Geez, can we please let this go?"

"What?" This time Ronan and Tristano blurted out together. "That many?"

"Really," Tahni drawled, bored. She lay back on her elbows, sticking her long legs out and crossing her ankles, unconcerned that the skirt shifted dangerously high up her thighs. "Who cares about some stupid hang-ups, wrong numbers, whatever. I get crank sex calls all the time you don't see me getting all upset and crying."

"Ha!" Ronan snorted. "That's because you deliberately instigate them when you're out bar slumming, handing your phone number out to every Tom, Dick and pervert in town."

Tossing her head back, Tahni's response to him was a sneered lip.

187

Jesa said, "I'm not upset-"

Tristano cut her off, "Shh, they're starting." The band struck up so loud the music was almost eardrum piercing.

Everyone settled down to listen to the music. Ronan moved to purposely position himself facing Tristano and Tahni, so Jesa would have her back to them thereby unable to see them. Pushing the basket off to a corner of the blanket, he rolled to lie down on his side, propped up on one elbow and shuffled closer to Jesa.

Jesa stayed sitting up, pulled her knees up, wrapped her arms around them, set her chin on her knees and immersed herself in the music.

Tahni had moved their basket out of the way as well. She worked her ample butt onto Tristano's lap and snuggled against him holding her wine.

The band played a variety of music from oldies to pop to rap to hip hop to even hard metal. At some points people sang along or clapped with the beat. The sun set bringing the park into darkness. Lanterns lit from trees, and the heaters glowed soft orange coronas, generating enough light that people didn't trip over others, but not bright enough to distract from the gloaming atmosphere. Down front the band was brightly lit up.

At the break, Tahni wriggled to cozy up to Tristano who had gone to the restroom awhile back and sat back down pulling his knees up mirroring Jesa so Tahni couldn't prop herself back on his lap. Slightly slurring, she purred, "Tristy babe, how about you open that second bottle of wine. We drank yours, I got a rosé."

Tristano's deep murmur carried to the other couple, "Tahni, you drank most of the bottle, I think you should slow it down, and I can't have more, I'm driving." They bickered as Tahni insisted on opening the other bottle.

Ronan pulled a bottle of tequila from their cooler and a couple of rock glasses. At his movement, Tristano glanced over with a disapproving frown. "Roarke, I don't think bringing hard liquor to a park is a good idea."

"It's a concert, Koffi, take a chill pill, stuffy, huh? You want some?" Ronan poured a few inches of the pungent tequila into the two glasses.

He handed one to Jesa. Shaking her head, Jesa said politely, "Um, I don't really care for any, thank you, Ronan."

Tristano said softly, "Good move, Jesselin. You aren't used to hard liquor. Remember the wine? The tequila is ten times more potent."

"Seriously, Koffi?" Ronan scowled at him. "Can you mind your own beeswax for more than a second? You don't need to stick your nose into our business. Take care of your own lush there," he motioned indecorously to Tahni who was trying to wind her body around Tristano's.

"Hey," Tahni blinked bleary eyes, slurred, "I think I'm offended," then giggled.

Tristano said, "Roarke, you-"

Jesa stood up, both men looked up at her. She said, "I'm going to the restroom, or that trailer thing."

Ronan threw back his tequila and said, "Wait, I'll walk you, sugar."

Jesa smiled back over her shoulder at him with a slight wave. "No, I'm good, I think I can manage." She took off, walking quickly from them with a deep breath. The competition between the two men, and the digs from Tahni as she laid on and rubbed all over Tristano was giving her a headache.

Jesa tread down the steps from the bathroom trailer and decided to take a small stroll around the park. Lights from the businesses stringing around the Commons shimmered in the dark, their illumination hazy in the cool night and slight wind. She had hoped she would run into some of her friends from the Divine Bistro but no such luck. Heading back to Ronan, she heard crying, sounded like a child, she followed the sound.

A little girl was crying. People were scattered around near her, some were watching her, but most were into their own space. The child started wailing, "Mommy, mommy," and wandered as if lost.

Jesa hurried over to her. When she reached her, she knelt down. "Honey," she asked the child, "are you lost?"

Dressed in a blue dress with tiny white flowers on it, the girl's skin was the color of cinnamon, she had dark springing curls wiggling around her head and huge chocolate brown eyes. Sniffing, she wiped at her eyes with both pudgy hands and nodded.

"Okay," Jesa said kindly, "give me your hand, let's see if we can find your mommy."

"You need some help there, Jesselin?"

She spun around at his voice. Tristano was by her side looking down at the child. He stood calmly in his black jeans and black shirt and motorcycle boots. If she didn't know he was a lawman she would be a little nervous, he looked like he had just stepped away from a motorcycle gang, and just as dangerous. "She's lost, we're going to try to find her parents," Jesa told him.

Tristano crouched in front of the girl. "What's your name, sweetie?" She looked warily at him. He pulled out his badge and showed it to her. "I'm a police officer, honey, your mommy probably told you that you can trust police officers to help you?"

The girl's lips pulled in as she stared at the badge, then a smile showed her baby teeth and she nodded. Taking a hiccupping breath, she said, "I'm Dani."

Tristano smiled a broad friendly smile at her. "Hi there, Dani. My name is Tristano, and this is Jesselin." The child looked from one to the other but didn't try to repeat their names.

"Okay, Dani, I'm going to pick you up and carry you way up high so your parents can see you, or you can find them. Is that all right with you?"

Dani nodded and held her arms up for him to lift her. His smile warmed at her trust. Tristano put his hands on her waist and lifted her then set his arm under her bottom to hold her secure. "There ya go, Dani," he pushed a tangled curl off her damp cheek. "You okay?" She nodded shyly, the tears gone.

They had walked around for at least five minutes when they heard, "Dani! There you are!" A frantic woman with a man at her heels ran up to them. Giving Tristano a cold look, she held her arms out for her child. "You were stealing my daughter?" she accused.

Jesa said, "No, Dani was crying for you and said she was lost. This is Agent Tristano Koffi with the FBI."

The man reached them and both parents encircled the girl in their arms.

Tristano flashed his badge again. Both parents looked embarrassingly chastised.

"Sorry, sir," the man apologized, "we were sitting on our blanket talking to the people next to us, we looked up and she had just disappeared. After that other missing baby, well."

His wife picked up, "We were so scared. Thank you so much, Agent and Miss," the mother smiled her appreciation at the pair.

"Happy to help," Tristano said, wrapping his fingers around Jesa's arm.

The couple said thanks again and little Dani waved at them as they went back to their blankets.

As Tristano and Jesa reached their own blankets, both ignored the huffy looks from Tahni and Ronan at them being together.

The music started up again loud and boisterous making conversation impossible. By the time the concert was over, everyone was bushed and half deaf. They packed up, Ronan held a hand to Jesa to help her to her feet.

They mumbled good nights and both couples went in opposite directions.

Tristano half-carried an inebriated, horny Tahni to her car and poured her in, clicking her seatbelt before climbing behind the wheel. Across the lot, Ronan and Jesa drove off in his cruiser.

At Jesa's house, Ronan caught her arm before he put the car in park. "Before you scurry off, Jesa, can we talk just a sec?"

Leveling a leery eye on him, she said, "I guess. But just for a minute, it's really late and I'm tired."

Ronan moved his hand down her arm to twine their fingers together. "Okay. I just, hell Jesa, I'd like to date you, you know, for real. I mean, I would like to have a relationship with you."

Her mouth tightened, body stiffened. "No, I mean, listen Ronan, it's not you. I just don't want to get involved with anyone, I told you that before. Can't we just be friends?"

"Honey," he protested, trying to pull her closer but she resisted. "I want more than friendship with you." His eyes narrowed. "It's not someone else is it, are you seeing someone else? Is it that asshole Koffi?"

Quickly shaking her head, she tugged her hand from his and reached for the door handle. "No, I told you, it's just...me. Please respect what I say. I can't…uh, don't want…" growing agitated, her hands started shaking.

Seeing her distress, Ronan said gently, "Okay, don't get upset, Jesa. I do respect you, but I think we can have something real here, with you and me. You have to admit there's amazing chemistry between us." His voice lowered, "I'm thinking something traumatic happened to you to make you so…so fearful. I can help, Jesa, just let me in, tell me."

"Ronan, please, there's nothing, nothing happened. I just don't…" she trailed off in a sigh.

"Honey, let me help you. I can- all right," at her shaking head, he held a hand up with an acceding smile. "I'll let you go for now, but," he sifted his fingers down her arm. "I won't give up, I think we can really have something here. Just…like I said before, think about it. How about I give you a call and we can plan something, oh, a little romantic?"

Frustrated, and exhausted that he just wouldn't take no for an answer, she said quietly, "Okay, Ronan, that's fine, but not romantic, just friends." She lifted the door handle and pushed the door open. "I'll talk to you, or see you at the station, good night, Ronan." She slipped out and hurried up to her door and slid inside.

Peeking behind the drapes, she saw that this time he didn't pause in the driveway as if pondering whether or not to go knocking on her door. He took off, his tail lights red streaks into the night.

Hours later, long after Jesa's lights went out in the little bungalow, a man stepped from the shadows. Staying near a tree to blend into the darkness, he stared at the house, whispered, "Yeah, sweetheart, I want to go in right now and get you." He chuckled. "You thought you could hide from me? Fuck, I've tracked you from shelter to shelter."

A profane sound grunted from his chest, "Those damned people were quite tight-mouthed about you and where you fled to, even when I beat the mother loving fuck out of them. You will be devastated to know I had to terminate a few of them, after all, they saw my face."

Keeping close to the tree, he studied the window, looking for any sign that she might still be up. His head shook side-to-side with a longsuffering sigh. "Yeah, the trail finally went cold, hell, I couldn't find a trace of you. Then," chuckling again, his nasty smile evil in the dark, "there you were my sweet, on goddamned national television. Sure, you tried to stay tucked in a corner and hide behind that veil of hair, I'm glad you let it go back to your natural color by the way, so pretty. But, you can't hide from me. You forget, I've spent a few years tracking you. I know you so well, like a lover, I'd know your silhouette in the pure black of night."

Feeling emboldened by the dark, he moved to lean his back against the tree and tucked his hands in his pockets. Amused at his own good luck he chattered on, "Imagine, sweetheart, to my great surprise, seeing you on that television, finding out you were on this island. I've pretty much checked out the entire rock and learned that very soon the island will be closed off from the rest of the world. So I need to get a move on, take you out and get the hell off this rock while I can."

He looked yearning at the cottage. "I just can't yet take the chance of your cop friends coming by. Just a little more time, sweetheart, and you will be mine. Mine to fuck and mine to kill."

Car lights came down the road startling him. Bowing his head, he ducked into the bushes and headed for his car parked down the street.

Chapter Twenty-One

Jesa pulled her jacket on, grabbed her hat and mittens, purse, keys and went to the door with a tight glimmer of angsty victory. It was Sunday and she was going to church. She didn't tell Tristano because she thought he'd make fun of her, and maybe be perturbed that she would expect him to come and drive her there. The church was only a couple miles away, she wouldn't have driven even if she had her car because of the gas.

Smiling, she patted her purse. Willie-Jean had told her they direct-deposited money into her account and she could access it with an ATM. Sheriff McKabe hadn't lied, they had paid her much more than she could have dreamed of earning. She felt guilty, she didn't think she'd really done anything to earn it. But McKabe had been liberal with his praise of the way she had handled the maid with compassion which elicited the maid's comfort and trust thereby giving her description of the designer skulking about in the hotel.

And, McKabe told Jesa how pleased he was with her perspicacity in noticing Elizabeth Westcott's interest in the man at the conference as well as her suspicions of Elizabeth's dubious behavior with the man at the Bistro.

Her hand on the knob she hesitated. If Tristano caught her, no, she turned the doorknob, she would go and come back and he'd never even know she'd left the house.

She opened her door and stopped dead. Her car was in her driveway and Tristano was leaning against it, ankles and arms calmly crossed, a wolfish smile on his dangerous face. Under his trench coat, he wore a dark blue suit jacket, black slacks, and white shirt but no tie.

Jesa closed her door and leaned back against it. She was wearing one of her few dresses, ankle boots and regular dark violet, ski-puffer coat with fur lined hood.

A light frost crystalized the grass, puffs of white vapor from Tristano's breaths illustrated how cold it was. *Oh God, she did not want to go down the steps.* But, heck, it was light out, she wouldn't have been traipsing around in the dark, he had no reason to be mad at her…but still…

Tristano cocked his head, his expression clearly asking why she was dragging it out.

Expelling her held breath, Jesa moved her feet, she had to beard the lion, or wolf as Ronan would say, last thing she needed to do was make him angrier. She studied him carefully, his expression was tranquil, but she could read the fury burning under the hooded lids. He moved to open the passenger door. Watching her approach, his gaze roved around the small yard, it halted at the big bare-limbed tree near the house. "You were out earlier, Jesselin?"

"No, why do you ask?" Seeing where he pointed, Jesa's eyes rounded. Footprints were imbedded into the frost all around the tree and through the brush separating the yard from her distant neighbors. They went up near to her house but not all the way.

Tristano moved to look at the prints, squatting to see them better. Straightening, he said to her, "They are large, a man's prints, Jesselin. Whose are they?"

Her mouth dropped, she muttered, "Uh- uh, I don't know, Tristano, I…" her skin pinched as she paled, her eyes skittered away guiltily from his. He stared at her for a long time until she shivered, from the cold, or him, or the footprints. "Let's go." He touched her arm to move to the car.

Wordless, Jesa climbed in, gripping her purse on her lap, her mouth set in grim consternation, eyes blank with thought. When Tristano got in and turned the ignition on, he reminded her calmly, "Seatbelt, Jesselin."

She buckled up and he drove to the main road. Clearing her throat, Jesa said, "Why are you here? Where are we going?"

He flashed her an approving glance that quickly ran down her figure and back up, said matter-of-factly, "Why, to church of course. You look nice."

Her head snapped to him. "How did you know I planned on going to church?"

Tipping his head towards her with a patronizing smile. "Really, Jesselin? You don't think I don't know everything about you?" He watched her face crease with confusion, and worry. His voice lowered, "Everything." Her breath caught, she blinked, then quickly looked away.

Tristano told her, "In one of our chats, Finn Barton told me you asked for Sunday mornings off when you were working for him." He cranked the wheel around a pin curve in the road, jolting their bodies back and forth. "Why didn't you tell me you wanted to go? I would have made arrangements last night to pick you up."

His jaw flexed. "I thought maybe you had made plans with Roarke to bring you. I called him, it went to voice mail, I thought he might be…" he didn't finish the sentence. The thought had come to him that perhaps Roarke had stayed overnight at Jesa's. Tristano took the chance and came anyway knowing if Roarke wasn't there the pigheaded girl would hoof it.

Jesa nervously combed her fingers through her hair. "I…didn't want to bother you, I mean it's Sunday after all. And, I thought," her mouth pulled in sheepishly, "that you might…make fun of me for wanting to go."

His lips clinched, he glanced at her then back to the road. "Seriously, Jesselin? You really think that badly of me?" The side of his mouth tugged in. "That kind of hurts my feelings." His mouth drooped dejectedly.

"Oh my gosh!" Jesa scooted as close to him as she could get with the seatbelt on and put her hand on his arm. "Tristano, I am so sorry, you know I would never want to hurt your feelings on purpose or by accident. Please, I'm sorry, please don't feel bad. I just, it's happened before, I…" she watched his lips edge up. She smacked his arm and threw herself back in her seat. "You're teasing me, that's not very nice, I felt bad I hurt you."

His chest rumbled with his chuckle. "I did feel bad, Jesselin, really I did. But," he paused the car at a stop sign and moved the shift into park. Reaching over he cupped her chin forcing her to turn and face him. Her long lashes swooped down to cover her eyes. He said, "Jesselin," and waited until she raised them. "I know you would never deliberately hurt someone's feelings, even my feelings. You are too soft hearted for that."

"Huh." Her mouth curved up under his hold with a snicker. "Who knew you had feelings?"

This time his hard mouth twitched in dismay, then he laughed. "You're a doll, Bitty bit, a smart-assed doll that's just adding to her punishments." And he lowered his head capturing her lips before either of them realized his intent. Almost as quickly he released her and jerked back from her with a stunned expression so fast, her lips were still parted, her confused green eyes half closed.

"I-" He lurched back behind the wheel. Shooting her a regretful frown, he put the car in drive and sped down the street.

She fumbled with her purse strap waiting for him to apologize, to say that it was a mistake, that it would never happen again, but he didn't. Apparently he hadn't liked it and had no intentions of kissing her again. She didn't know whether she felt relieved or disappointed.

When they arrived at the small chapel overlooking the ocean, Jesa thought Tristano would drop her off, and come back and pick her up when the service was over. But, he parked, got out, wrenched the door open and waited for her to climb out.

Jesa had to clutch her skirt as the wind swept their clothes and ruffled their hair while they made their way up the walk to the wide-open double doors. Music poured out of the doors and into the street. Tristano set his hand, big, warm, solid on her back keeping her close as they accepted their bulletins and friendly greetings, and made their way down the aisle, both nodding to fellow officers and patrons and a few employees of the bistro.

Nothing could have surprised Jesa more when Tristano stood beside her holding the prayer book at her level so they could both see it, and he chanted the familiar words she had learned from the churches she'd attended even while on the run. She'd needed a friend to be with her as she ran and hid from death, and she'd learned she could depend on God, Jesus, to be there. They didn't fix her problems for her, but they gave her support and buffed up the strength and intuition she needed to keep going.

She sang the hymns along with the congregation, Tristano held the hymnal but he didn't sing. When she peered up at him, he gave her a wink that said, 'you really don't want to hear me sing.' It made her smile.

They visited briefly on their way out after the service, shook the minister's hand as he welcomed Tristano, and smiled broadly at Jesa whom he knew. Then they headed to the parking lot. Once inside the car, Jesa said politely, "Well, thank you, Agen- uh, Tristano for taking me, that was nice of you. Are we going on any interviews or anything today?"

His evil grin teased her, he rubbed his palms together as if warming them up for a swat. "Ah, nice save, Bitty bit. But it's too late to protect your behind now, you already have a ton of infractions piled up."

She swung her head at him, strawberry curls jostled over her shoulder to ripple down her front. "What? You can't be serious, I mean, you don't really intend to, you know," she was too embarrassed, and scared to say it. Slamming her arms over her chest she crossed them tightly and scowled. "Well, I won't let you touch me, do that to me again. I am not a child to be punished and spanked, and this is a free country, and-"

Laughter rolled out. "Feisty little thing, you are, Jesselin. Right now we're going to have Thanksgiving Sunday brunch at the bistro. Finn Barton called me and said he was doing a dinner for those of us that have no family here. He wanted to make sure I brought you."

Her mouth opened. "You-" He was grinning at her. She couldn't help but laugh at him.

The bistro was warm and bright and cheerful. Turkey cutouts decked the walls, and thanksgiving themed tableware bearing gravy, buns, pies and extras decorated the white cloths. Tables laden with heated chafing dishes were set up along the walls containing turkey, stuffing, potatoes, corn, the works, and hungry people lined up loading the plates in their hands.

Brunch was delicious and boisterous, everyone in a gay mood. Between employees, customers and deputies, so many people stopped to greet them, Tristano and Jesa barely said a word to each other.

As they were finishing, a deputy came up to their table. "Uh, Agent Koffi, sir." His eyes jetted to Jesa and back to Tristano.

Tristano's imposing brows rose with a cool, "Yes?"

"Yes, sir. Ah, Deputy William Estes, sir, I have a report for you. Sheriff McKabe says Willie-Jean told him you weren't answering your phone."

Tristano set his coffee cup down, then reached down and pulled his phone out, looked at it, and frowned. "Oh, I silenced it while we were in church, I see the missed calls. What's the report?"

"Sir," Estes bowed then said, "it's been determined that the dealer Mrs. Westcott was…involved with, Subie King, has an airtight alibi, he only just returned to Orainn two days ago. Deputy Roarke verified the travel records of the ferry and King's ID he had to show to get on and off the ferry. He'd left months ago and hadn't been back until Friday. Roarke got the low down on King's dealer's name and location. So next we checked on the guy he buys from, ah," hands clasped behind his back, he lowered his head trying to recall the name without reviewing his notes. "Yes, a Dev Irons, he goes by Ironman."

He waited for Tristano to laugh, his eyes slid to Jesa who was patting her lips before folding the napkin and setting it beside her plate. She looked up at him, her mouth curved up friendly yet shy. The deputy was young and attractive with dark hair and a sunny smile that he shared with her.

"And? Deputy?" Tristano pressed gruffly.

"Uh, yes," he continued, smiling at Jesa, "it seems that this Ironman has been doing a two-year mini in the Colorado State pen. We had a detective question him and she was pretty confident the guy had nothing to do with the kidnapping. He was more interested in bargaining conjugal visits with his girlfriend and getting nickel-dime money for smokes." Estes said nothing else, just smiled at Jesa. He rocked back and forth on his heels with his hands still clasped behind his back.

Tristano's acrid sigh was loud enough to draw the deputy's attention from Jesa and back to him. "Anything else, Estes?"

Estes' eyes hopped back to Jesa like she was a magnet. A testy growl from Tristano and the deputy faced him directly, and he shook his head. "No, sir. We fully checked out that blond dude, Subie King that Mrs. Westcott had relations with, and the convict Irons, his dealer, and found nada ties to anyone here. The kids buying their drugs had floated away with family back to the mainland even before the season fully ended. There's just no connection to any of them and the missing Westcott baby. So..." he gave his solicitude to the agent but snuck sidelong glances at Jesa.

"That will be all, Deputy," Tristano said dismissively and raised his hand to a server indicating he wanted the check.

Estes stood awkwardly for a few seconds. Jesa offered him an apologetic smile. Bright red spots on his cheeks, the deputy bowed once firmly then pivoted on his heel and strode off.

Laverne toddled to their table with a huge grin. "Hey kids, how's it going?"

"We need the check," Tristano said curtly.

"No checks today, kids, the dinner is on Mr. Barton. He likes to do these things to treat people." Laverne looked up with a frown when a number lit up on a board on the wall by the kitchen. "Hey, gotta go, good to see you guys, come back soon," she popped a kiss on Jesa's cheek and bustled away.

"Um, Tristano," Jesa said softly as he set some bills on the table for a tip. His brows rose blandly with his normal stoic expression. Her voice soft so no one else could hear, "You, uh, were kind of short with that deputy. I mean, he was doing his job bringing you information, you could have been, you know, a little more civil and appreciative."

A curl of his lip wound up one side of his face pulling in a dimple that normally was invisible. "Ah, Bitty bit, are you trying to tell me how to deal with a trained, sworn officer?"

"Well, um, no, I mean..." she pushed her napkin around on the table next to her plate.

He leaned towards her over the table with one droll brow arched, said glibly, "Was I to invite him to tea and crumpets and kiss his hand in deep gratitude as he lingered long after delivering his message while making moon-eyes at you instead of being at appropriate professional stance and departing immediately once he imparted the message as he is trained to do?"

"I…well, no, I mean yes." Her forehead bristled in irritation. "You could have been a bit more polite, it wouldn't have hurt your image of the rough tough FBI agent."

Tristano sat back with a cock-eyed grin. He watched her as her face swept with pink and lashes fluttered self-consciously making feathery shadows on her round cheeks. He said, "My initial conception of you was so far off, Bitty bit, you are truly sweet, and caring, aren't you?"

Face reddening further, Jesa glanced anxiously around, why when she wanted someone around everyone was busy elsewhere?

Chuckling, Tristano set his napkin on the table and told her, "You did good, Jesselin, noticing Mrs. Westcott's interest in the young man. It could have led to something, and because of her secret, it makes us delve deeper into the Westcotts' finances and livelihood. We may still find something that leads to why the child was taken."

Shaking her head with a frown she said, "No, it turned out to be a big waste of time. I should have just minded my own-" Suddenly something struck Jesa, her face screwed up in concentration, lips pressed, eyes squeezed as she tried to pull from her head something…

Elbows on the table, Tristano clasped his hands together and regarded her actions quizzically. "What? What is it, Jesselin?"

She blinked at him. "The deputy, did he say the 'blond dude?'"

Tristano started to confute the importance of her question, then he folded his mouth, brow lifted as he recalled the conversation. "Yes, he did use the term, 'blond dude' for the paramour, Subie King. Why does that capture your interest?"

Jesa rested an elbow on the table and propped her chin on it as she considered how important was what she was thinking.

"Jesselin? Tell me whatever is on your mind."

She looked up at him judging his sincerity. He wasn't gazing in mock at her, he watched her with an open expression of interest. "Well, the young man I saw Mrs. Westcott staring at during the conference, and then later she was so…cozy with, he had dark hair. How tall is Mr. King?"

It was Tristano's turn to blink at her. "Ah, if I recall from the interrogation video, he came to Roarke's collarbone, that'd make him about 5'8 maybe 5'9. Why?"

Her forehead crinkled drawing her brows down, she said carefully, "Besides having very dark hair, I mean it could in no way be described as blond or light, the man was at least six feet tall. His head almost brushed the lowest point of the alcove and I remember Mr. Sloan, the bistro's manager, was always complaining it should be raised as he's hit his head a couple of times on it, and Velvet says he's around 6'3"."

Tristano stared mutely at Jesa as her words rolled around in his head. "So, you're saying that we know she had an affair with King, that she was, is, possibly also involved with another man, a different man, with dark hair?"

She bumped one shoulder. "I don't know. I just know both times I saw them together, if I hadn't know any better I would have thought they were boyfriend and girlfriend, or married. They were half hidden in the corner of the alcove beneath the loft. They, um, were gazing into each other's eyes, and," her cheeks brightened, "his hand was on her back holding her close, her palm was on his…chest. They seemed to be quite…intimate."

He pawed his chin regarding her thoughtfully. "That's interesting. What do you say we pop on over to the Westcott house?" She answered him with a game smile.

After thanking the Bartons for their generosity and hospitality, they stepped outside and felt the steep drop in temperature. Sleet struck like ice bullets, the biting wind slapped their skin red and raw by the time they reached the sanctuary of the car. Tristano cranked the heat on high and they were on their way chugging down the winding craggy hill.

On the way to the Westcotts', Tristano handed his phone to Jesa. "I texted Roarke to send a picture of Subie King, take a look."

It took less than a second for her to say, "That wasn't the guy I saw Mrs. Westcott with." She handed the phone back to him, he clipped it to his belt.

"Okay," he said, "let's go stir the pot."

Chapter Twenty-Two

Deputy Granger Wate called Tristano before they were a hundred yards down the hill. Answering the phone, he put it on speaker so Jesa could hear what he said.

"Agent Koffi," Wate told him, "I've got some info for you," his voice faded as if he'd turned his head from the phone. "Info on Mrs. Westcott. I'm just getting some more figures in, you might want to come and see what I found." A small chuckle, "In fact, I know you'll want to see it."

Tristano turned the car around and they headed back up.

The station was warm but Tristano and Jesa left their coats on as they strode quickly through the main ingress and down the hall to the conference room where Willie-Jean told them the deputy was waiting.

Granger was seated at the big table. In front of him was his open laptop, and on both sides of the computer spread loose papers as well as a notebook. Nibbling at the end of a pencil, the deputy's attention was on the computer. He looked up when he heard them come in.

"Deputy," Tristano said as they entered the room. He didn't smile in greeting, but nodded to the deputy as he pulled out Jesa's chair for her and then took his own seat.

"Hey, Agent." Granger dipped his head politely to Jesa, said, "Miss." The dark whiskers were a tad longer than they had been a few days ago, his brown hair needed a trim. He pulled his long legs in, tucking them under his chair. A slight canary chewing smile curved his mouth as he looked at Tristano.

"Okay," Tristano steepled his fingertips on the table and asked, "whatcha got?" Beside him Jesa already had her notebook out and open and pen in hand.

Granger's mouth turned up at one corner in a half grin and he pushed his computer towards Tristano so he could see the information. "I couldn't find anything that stood out as wrong in the Westcotts' bank accounts. They each had a separate one and a joint account. But," a gloating smile increased the grin, "it took some doing but I met with the branch manager of their bank, Chase Federal. He mentioned there might be something to investigate at another bank.

"Apparently one of the Chase tellers was in Pacific Savings and Loan and heard one of the tellers there call Mrs. Westcott by a different name. The teller told the manager how odd it was. It was enough for the chief to get a court order to compel the records."

"Hmm." Tristano scrolled through the page.

"Here." Granger plunked a key with a long knobby finger and a graph appeared on the screen. "We assayed the account at Pacific. Mrs. Westcott had a secret one under her sister's name, Lauren. It looked like Lauren was writing checks to a guy named Jackson Burl, a relatively large amount of money."

Tristano leaned in closer to view the monitor.

Granger said, "We understood Mrs. Westcott's family was broke, but there were trust funds for both sisters, under their maiden name, Pierce. Lauren had transferred her trust to her married account of Radcliff. Money had been transferred from Elizabeth's trust to a Lauren Pierce account. When we showed the bank employees a picture of Elizabeth, they identified her as the one utilizing the account. Apparently she used her sister's identification to open the account. There is very little left in the balance, less than a hundred dollars, just enough to keep it open and active. I'm pretty sure the signatures on the checks of Elizabeth Westcott and Lauren Pierce are a match. The sister Lauren resides in California."

Tristano merely grunted as he perused the figures and scans of checks. When he reached the end he looked up quizzically at Granger. "That it?"

A lazy nod and smug smile, Granger's shoulder lifted. "Yeah, Agent. I found the flames, you go seek the fire." He laughed at

Tristano's tilted head and corner of his mouth nicking up. He said, "This has made me curious to rummage around Stedman Westcott's money. See if he's done the same thing, kept money hidden from his wife. Some people do that in case of divorce, keep hidden assets."

A few minutes later Tristano and Jesa were back in the car heading again to the Westcotts' with the heater on full blast. The weather had roughened, wind blasted the small car back and forth on the twisty road.

Tristano called Ronan. At his "Yeah?" Tristano informed him, "Elizabeth Westcott has a bank account under her sister's maiden name of Lauren Pierce. Her sister keeps her own accounts under Lauren Radcliff, her married name. Contact Mrs. Radcliff to confirm this. A small threat of fraud should get her to speak freely."

"Okay," Ronan muttered, "repeat those names so I can write them down." Tristano did and both men clicked off without salutations.

Needle spikes of sleet mixed with snow blew in the Westcott house as Deputy Gomez opened the door. The wind roared and whipped around the couple as they braced against the violent onslaught until the deputy fought the door closed.

Tristano and Jesa stomped the fresh snow from their boots on the mat then Gomez escorted them to the now familiar red and black living room. A fire now danced in the fireplace helping the heater take the edge off the freezing air outside, and warming the outraged yet apprehensive, ashen-faced Elizabeth Westcott.

She stood as they entered the room, their hair and shoulders dusted with melting snowflakes. Elizabeth's tall body vibrated with rigid anger, her arms straight down, fists clenched at her side. She wore blue wool slacks and a cream-colored cashmere sweater that luxuriously embraced her figure. The blonde hair was twisted in a chignon at the back of her head. Stedman was nowhere in sight.

She snapped, "What is it now, Agent Koffi that you are here to harass me about? You could have said over the phone when you spoke with Deputy Gomez and spared me the indignity and aggravation of you showing up again on my doorstep."

Jesa struggled to keep her back straight and head high at the offensive verbiage the demeaning woman spewed. Elizabeth didn't deign to even glance in Jesa's direction. Her fury was centered on the indomitable agent standing calmly, unflinching at her rage. His hair was short but still mussed from the wicked weather. He briefly ran his palms over it neatening the locks.

To their left, the lashing wind beat at the arched windows, the snow diminished, but the sheets of sleet crackled as they hit the glass. Shivering at the sight, Jesa looked to the orange flaming fireplace, then raised her eyes to the red abstract painting over the mantel.

Tristano asked quietly, "Where is Mr. Westcott?"

Elizabeth suddenly looked panicked. Her hand went to her throat. "You- you said you only needed to speak to me, he's at his office."

"On Sunday?" Tristano asked.

Calming down some, she crossed her arms over the cream sweater, shrugged. "It's nothing new." Her sigh heavy with exasperation, Elizabeth dropped down on a red cushion on the black-framed sofa, and crossed her lithe legs. Jesa watched her, wondering how she didn't catch those four-inch heels in the dusky ivory carpet. Filaments of beige and red threaded through giving the rug even more depth than the natural plushness.

The anger flowing away, Elizabeth draped her arms across the back of the sofa like a queen and sighed again, wearily, as if she found all this tedious. "All right then, Agent, what is this about this time?" She didn't offer either of them to have a seat or refreshment.

His fingers laced casually behind his back, boots planted firmly, his face blank as usual, the dark dangerous eyes studied Elizabeth callously, she chafed under his dogged scrutiny. He waited until her face flushed and she squirmed on the cushion then he asked, "Who is the tall man with the dark hair that you have been keeping company with?"

She pretended noninterest, but the color drained leaving her skin grey, and she moved her hands, sitting on them to still their sudden betraying shaking. "Uh," ahem, "who?"

Tristano turned from her, he said to Deputy Gomez, "Please get Mrs. Westcott's coat for her, we're going to the station." And, shoving his coat aside he blatantly removed handcuffs from the back of his belt.

Elizabeth's eyes popped, her mouth dropped open. "No, wait, wait," she protested, standing up as if she could stop him.

He hesitated, brows arched.

"Ahh," the air whooshed from her lungs, she thumped back down on the sofa, hands up in surrender. "His name is Jackson Burl."

They already presumed that, but wanted to hear her confirm it, see if she'd lie again. Tristano glanced at Jesa to see if she had her notebook out. She did, and she wrote in it.

Tristano took a few steps closer to Elizabeth standing a few feet from the glass coffee table that still had wires hooked up to their phones and a monitor awaiting the expected ransom call. At the police station a computer also monitored incoming and outgoing calls, messages, emails.

Her plum-colored eyes fell to the phones, every feature on her pretty face sagged bleakly, the ransom call still hadn't come. Everyone knew the longer the time passed from Brie's disappearance the less chance of the baby returning safely home.

"All right, Mrs. Westcott, who is Jackson Burl to you? And-" he held a palm up before she could speak. "I want it straight this time. If I have to waste time researching this guy and finding people who will tell us who he is and what's between you two, my sympathy and patience with you will be gone and you will find yourself behind bars."

Jesa's expression was appalled at his ruthlessness, but she contemplated the young mother. Her child was taken, and yet she had been terribly evasive with the police, wasting their time and manpower having to search out information she could have easily given them in moments.

Tristano's tone sharp, voice hard, he said "Mrs. Westcott," prevailing upon her to speak.

"Jackson Burl," a harsh abashed laugh rung from her along with the name, the color rushed back to flush her face, her eyes deflected to the fireplace. "Well, he is, was, another...lover of mine."

To her credit, Jesa kept her face blank, stifling her flabbergast. She looked to Tristano; he appeared as stoically grim as always. Clearly he had assumed that's what the man was to Elizabeth. Jesa sighed, she would never get used to all this subterfuge and cheating. Her life had always sucked, but that didn't mean she didn't keep her naïve ideals of happily ever after. For some people, obviously not for her.

When Elizabeth faltered, Tristano commanded, "When and where did you meet, how long has it been going on, where does he live and what does he do for a living?" He gestured for Jesa to sit so she could write more easily.

Elizabeth shifted to sit sideways on one hip and rested a forearm on the back of the couch; she crossed one leg over the other. Her heavy sigh resigned, she said, "I met Jackson on a cruise Stedman and I took. We were in the casino, Stedman was obsessed with his blackjack and I was bored. I sat on a stool sticking coins in a slot machine when this, handsome, no, *gorgeous* man engaged me in conversation. He bought me a drink, next thing I knew," she demurred, fiddling with her wedding band. "Well, when we returned to Orainn the affair carried on."

"What does he do for a living?"

"Harrumph," she snorted, "he gambles. He doesn't have a steady job."

"Are you still seeing him?"

"No. I was…" Her gaze downcast with shame, she murmured, "I was giving him money. He'd lose a string of times and owed some big debts. He came to me one night, his eye," she touched under her own plum eye. "It was so horrible, swollen, black and blue," she cringed at the memory. "He said if he didn't pay they'd break his legs, and then…it would get worse, until…" Tears filled her eyes blurring the purplish color she leaned forward in an anguished plea, set her hand on her knee. "Don't you see? I had to help him, they would have killed him."

His expression untouched at her distress, Tristano stared unwavering at her. "When is the last time you saw Burl?" He issued a warning glare at Jesa as she moved to retrieve tissues for Elizabeth. As predictable, Jesa ignored him. She ran into the closest bathroom, returned and stuffed the tissues in Elizabeth's hands. Elizabeth didn't say a word to her, Jesa returned to her seat steering her face from Tristano's glare.

Ungraciously wiping her nose with the wad of tissues, Elizabeth replied, "A few nights ago at the Divine Bistro, Stedman and I were having dinner. Jackson had called me earlier, said he wanted to see me. I…I had broken it off, weeks ago. He kept asking for more and more money. I couldn't hide the cash withdrawals any longer, Stedman was getting suspicious, he said my shopping had to slow down."

"Yet your trust fund was still flush?"

Her head jerked, startled. Blinking several times she studied Tristano, gaging how much he knew. His expression remained enigmatic in his hard face. The burdensome sigh took the last bit of starch from her shoulders. She muttered redundantly, "You know about the account, don't you?"

His eyes icy coals froze the breath in her lungs, expelling what air was left in them. She said wryly, "Of course you do. Well," her lips pinched, "there's not all that much left anyway."

"So why did you agree to see him at the restaurant?"

First glancing at the door to the living room, Gomez was not there, tipping her head to the side, her mouth puckered. Her exhale rough and loud, with a flailed hand she explained, "I was...crazy about him. I hated breaking it off. After seeing him at Brie's press conference, I thought he was there to support me, I," she looked away, staring sightless at the flames in the fireplace. "I guess I was fantasizing that he had gotten lucky, maybe won a lot or," she snorted, "actually gotten a job and wanted to continue to see me."

"You were going to ask Stedman for a divorce?"

Her mouth parted, she coughed out aghast, surprised, "Of course not. What a stupid thing to say." Tristano and Jesa couldn't help but look at each other, both trying to suppress their reactions.

Taking a breath, cynicism inflecting in his tone, Tristan asked, "What did he want, then?"

Sighing her heartbreak, Elizabeth turned her wan face to Tristano. "Money of course. He thought we had been apart long enough for me to miss him and that I would give in. But," she shook her head regretfully, "I couldn't. Stedman put the reins on my spending. He had the bank block my credit cards, ATM card, and checking account. He told me I was spending too much, that I had to give up shopping for a while. I was to go to him if I really wanted something." She grunted her dissatisfaction at him controlling her spending. "The trust account was about depleted."

"What did Burl say when you refused him?"

"Nothing really. He just looked sadly at me, said if I changed my mind to call him; otherwise he was heading for the mainland, to Vegas. Said he has friends there that would help him."

"Did he say anything about Brie? Any hint he had her? Any threat if you didn't give him money?"

Elizabeth shook her head again. "No. Jackson was an even bigger wuss than Subie King. Jackson even hated getting a speeding ticket, terrified he'd get thrown into jail. Said he was way too pretty to be locked in with barbarians." The laugh was short.

She said sincerely, "He was right. Jackson is an incredibly good-looking man, hot as hell. In bed and out. Anyway, he not only didn't have the balls to take a baby, he had no way to take care of her while he had her, he had no family or friends here on Orainn, and," she smoothed her skirt then skimmed a palm over her hair, "he would never hurt me. He understood Stedman froze my money and I couldn't help it. He knew although Stedman had a great income, at the moment we had no liquid cash. No, Jackson would never kidnap Brie."

Tristano's expression gave no indication of his thoughts about what she told them. He let a few silent moments go by to raise her level of discomfort before saying, "Any more boyfriends going to slither onto the radar? You'd better tell me now, or-"

Shaking her head miserably, she replied roughly, "No, no, no one else in the past, ah, year."

His eyes beaded unmercifully at her, she shuddered under his glare. Deciding she was telling the truth, he said with a motion to Jesa, "Give Ms. Judan Burl's address and a full, explicit description of him. A picture texted from your phone would be even better." He didn't doubt for a second that Elizabeth's lovers, however many there were, were pictured in her phone.

Jesa quickly left her chair and sat gingerly beside Elizabeth on the couch.

While the women conversed, Tristano stuck his hands in his pockets and wandered over to look out the window. The wind bashed past the house swiping at trees, brutal and savage, the sleet had turned to icy snow and was piling up without the heat of the sun to melt it.

A few minutes, and Jesa came to stand beside him, her notebook tucked in her backpack. He said to her, "You got everything?" She nodded. "Okay, let's go." His hand on her back, by the time they reached the archway to the hall, Gomez appeared.

Tristano said to Elizabeth who had traipsed sullenly behind them, "You think of anything else, you call. If I have to come out here again because we get word of another boyfriend or fraudulent bank account or anything else, hell woman, I'm done. You understand? Done. I will take you to jail." At Elizabeth's teary nod, he ushered Jesa to the front door.

"Pull your hood up and zip your jacket," he instructed Jesa. He was buttoning his own coat, saw her scornful expression. "What?"

Lips pushed out and eyes sparking ire, Jesa pulled herself up as tall as she could, still, she had to look up at him. "Why do you treat me like such a child? I've lived on my own for a very long time with no one to help me, look out for me, barely had a childhood and you act like I can't take care of myself."

Tugging the hood over her head, Tristano tied the strings with fuzzy pom-poms on the ends under her chin. He smiled kindly and spoke softly, "Then isn't it time, Bitty bit, that someone looks out for you? Cares about your wellbeing? Carries some of your burdens on his strong shoulders?"

She didn't know what to say, he patted her cheek. "Let's hit it, Jesselin. A bad storm is settling in, let me get you home."

Chapter Twenty-Three

After a hot bath, Jesa made a cup of tea and settled on the sofa with a book. She was about fifty pages in when there was a knock at the door. She couldn't believe someone was out in this weather. Setting the book down, she got up and as she passed the window, she noted the weather had quieted a little. Peeking through a pane of glass near the door, she sighed and stepped back. It was Ronan.

His voice carried through the door, "Jesa, honey, I know you're home, the lights are on. Come on, open the door, it's frickin' freezing out here." She heard him stamp his feet trying to warm them. Reluctantly, she opened the door. His grin huge, he ducked his head shyly, "You gonna let me in?"

"Ronan, no." She kept her hand on the door, about to refuse him entrance. But he grinned so boyishly, his blue eyes filled with harmless hope. His tall muscular body filled her doorway and he was coming in regardless. "Okay," she stepped aside, "But really, just for a minute. It's late."

"Sure," he agreed and trod inside unbuttoning his heavy pea-coat. Jesa kept a wide distance making him frown.

"Hell, Jesa, I just stopped by to see you. It's been a couple of days and I heard about the messy shade on Elizabeth Westcott. Geesh." He combed his fingers through his sandy locks shaking the snow off them. Removing his coat, he laid it neatly on a chair. "Not the nice, grieving mother she portrays, huh?" He made his way to the old plaid sofa and nimbly sat down.

"Um, well, she may be an adulteress, that doesn't necessary negate her being a loving, terrified mother, worried about her missing baby."

Jesa stood watching him, undecided, unsure what to do. She couldn't bodily force him to leave, and she really didn't want to make him angry or hurt his feelings by insisting he go. That made her think of when she was driving with Tristano and he pretended she'd hurt his feelings by insinuating he didn't have feelings. A tiny smile curved at the remembrance.

"Yeah, you're right. What?" Ronan smiled with her. "What's so funny? Share with me." He patted the cushion beside him. "Come, stop hovering, I don't bite, tell me what just amused that cute little brain of yours."

She shook her head, lifting her curls she pushed them off her shoulders to wave down her back. "It was nothing."

"Okay." He leaned back making himself comfortable. "You have anything to drink? I'm kind of parched." The boyish grin teased at her.

"Um, sure. I have tea?" At his tongue sticking out of contorted lips, she laughed. She'd used the last of the milk on her cereal yesterday. "Okay, the only other thing I have to offer is the water." At his nod, she scooted out of the room to the kitchen.

Reaching in the cupboard for a glass, she held it under the tap. She didn't have a fancy ice-making fridge and didn't do bottled water. Now, as much as she liked the handsome deputy and was really attracted to him, she pondered how to get him to leave.

When she returned to the living room, Ronan was sitting comfortably, his legs sprawled out. She handed him the water. "Thanks, babe." He took a sip and set it on the end table. "Come on, Jesa, don't be timid, I'm not going to pounce on you, come over here and sit so we can talk. Get to know one another."

She stood awkwardly shifting from one foot to the other. She wore thin pink sweatpants and an even thinner sweatshirt with buttons. Her hands were tucked nervously in the pockets of the sweatshirt making it stretch out a little. "Well, a...it's kind of late, Ronan...I don't think-"

"Come on," he said gently holding out his hand to her, "tell me about your visit with Elizabeth Westcott. Heck," he shook his head in disbelief saying, "the lady is full of surprises, eh?"

Taking a deep breath, Jesa looked at his hand outstretched in friendly coaxing, and let the breath drain out slowly. She moved to the couch but didn't take his hand and made sure there was a foot between them as she sat down.

"Ah, sugar, that's better. Now, tell me about this new gigolo of hers?" He settled back again, laying his arm across the back of the couch, his fingers were barely an inch from her shoulders.

Jesa wriggled back to sit more comfortably, sinking into the old cushions. She explained about her and Tristano's meeting with Elizabeth. She said, "It's so crazy, Ronan. Mrs. Westcott has a hardworking husband, an incredibly beautiful home, servants, and a darling baby girl. Why would she jeopardize all that with affairs? Why isn't she content with what she has been blessed with?"

Letting out a low chuckle, Ronan leaned to the side and picked up the glass of water. He took a sip and lifted slightly off the sofa to set it on the coffee table in front of them. When he settled back again he was several inches closer to Jesa.

His arm slung back over the couch cushion, he curved one knee on the couch with his other foot on the floor so he was facing her. "I guess people get bored. Fall out of love. Maybe Stedman isn't holding up his manly duties, you know what I mean? Not keeping the wife satisfied at home will cause her to stray and look for someone who does."

Jesa thought about this. "But they made vows. If she fell out of love with him and needed to have something more fulfilling, she should have divorced him, that's only fair."

Ronan lifted his arms and stretched them behind his back then subtly shifted closer to her. When he set his arms down, he did like the cliché maneuvers of a movie teenager, he laid his arm along the back of the couch again, but this time he was close enough he was able to curl his arm around behind Jesa.

"A lot of people don't get divorced, Jesa, even when they fall out of love or get the itch for another person. Stedman could lose a bundle in alimony and child support, so maybe he looks the other way when his wife strays. Or some people truly love their spouse and just want a little strange outside of the marriage but don't want to leave them. Who knows what the Westcotts' story is."

Her brow wrinkled. "But-"

214

"Forget about them, sugar, let's concentrate on us." He lowered his arm draping around her shoulders and pulled her to him. She stiffened instantly and put her hands against his chest. "Ronan," she warned.

"You're just shy, Jesa, nervous. I won't hurt you, I promise. Give me a little kiss and I'll leave happy, okay?"

"No, Ronan," she insisted, pressing against his chest but his arms like steel bars pulled her to him.

Keeping an arm around her to hold her close, he cupped her chin in the V of his hand and said gently, "Sweet Jesa. I won't hurt you, just a kiss. I've been dying to kiss you since I first laid eyes on you. Give me one kiss and I'll get right up and leave. Please?"

"Ronan, I-" she pushed at him but he held her chin taut and at first gently set his lips on hers. Angling his head, he nudged her lips apart, a low moan rumbled in his throat as he intensified the kiss. She let him ravage her mouth for a moment, hoping he would get his fill and then leave.

But, his breathing deepened, building rough and fast, with a growl he besieged her lips, sinking his tongue in her mouth to chase and capture hers before shoving it halfway down her throat. Her palms were still pressed against his chest as he moved, lifting his body to push her back, forcing her to lie back on the couch.

She tried to break off the kiss, turning her head, she cried against his mouth, "Stop, Ronan, please, I- I'm not ready for this!" She could feel his chest puffing up with his heat and excitement, his breath harsh and hot on her face, in her mouth.

He lowered his heavy body over hers, restraining her with his weight, and pushed his legs between hers forcing hers to spread for him to press his erection flush against her sex. Feeling the hard evidence of his growing lust pressing at her core, panic flooded through her. "Ronan, please stop," she cajoled, her hands rolled to fists she struggled under him hitting at his big arms.

"Jesa, just relax," he gasped in her ear, and grasped her wrists stilling them. Licking her neck, he nipped down to her collar bone then pushed at her shirt with his chin, shoving at it roughly, he bit at buttons until he tore off a few. Kissing and nibbling down to the upper swell of her breast, he latched onto her flesh and sucked so hard she cried out in pain bucking her hips to push him off.

Holding her wrists, Ronan pushed them up above her head, pinning them to the cushion with one hand, shoved her thighs further apart and thrust his erection at her, humping and rubbing over her sex with ravening moans of a hungry animal.

Splayed out under his bulk, Jesa squirmed and bucked, twisting her head and body to avoid his mouth, then he moved his hand between them and started tugging at her pants, and she screamed. And screamed, until he stopped sucking on her flesh and thrusting at her pelvis, and released her hands.

He moved to prop his weight on his elbows on the sofa, leaning over her, panting from his exertions and his enflamed arousal, he smoothed hair from her face. "Shh, sugar, Jesa, calm down, don't freak out, I'm stopping." Seeing her eyes wide with fright, a gleam of tears shredding the green, her arms rigid as she tried to push him off her, he stalled. A hunk of sandy hair flopped over his brow, the sideburns at his temples were dark with perspiration, he groaned out a long hefty sigh.

Ronan rolled to sit up and pulled her with him. He adjusted her shirt he'd nudged down but the mark he put on her upper breast was visible under the torn buttons. A grin of possessiveness hovered around his handsome face at the mark, but his eyes reflected worry and sadness that he'd scared her. "Shit, Jesa, I- I just get carried away when I'm near you. You," he shoved the flop of hair back with his palm, exhaled and adjusted his jeans. "You just turn me on, I...I guess I lost control. Hell, those pouty pink lips," he cupped her jaw, his eyes on her mouth, his head lowered and her hands came back up to press at his chest.

Twisting her head from him, she said, "No, please Ronan." He held her for a moment to calculate the seriousness of her objections. Her jaw was taut, mouth clenched, eyes rounded with panic, her body trembled under his touch. He released her with a ragged exhale. "Okay, okay," he moved a few inches from her. "Listen, Jesa-"

Clutching her torn shirt in one hand she rasped, "I want you to leave, Ronan. Now."

"Wait, listen to me, Jesa, just relax, wait a second." He dragged his fingers raggedly through his hair.

216

She jumped up and backed away from him, crossed her arms protectively over her chest. "No, now. I want you to go, leave *now.*" She walked over to the door, her shoulders hunched and opened it. A wail of violent wind burst in shaking her curtains and lampshades, her hair flew back, sweatpants flapped on her legs.

Ronan leaned over with his forearms on his knees and folded his hands together, his harsh breathing slowing. His head hanging, looking up at her through rumpled strands of hair, he beseeched her, "Honey, I swear, I won't hurt you, don't make me go."

"Please, Ronan." She turned to the door, her arms crossed, shivering.

"Ah," he groaned, raked his fingers through his hair again and reluctantly stood up. He grabbed his coat off the chair and tossed it on. Tramping to the door, he stopped in front of her. Jerking the collar up around his ears, he shoved his hands in his coat pockets. "Jesa, I'm sorry, I didn't mean to scare you. Hell, we're adults there's nothing wrong with making out a little, you know, getting to know each other like I keep saying. You're just so damned," he reached a hand to her, she turned away to avoid it, he dropped it to his side.

"You're so beautiful, sexy, you heat a man's blood." He stood still watching her, her head was down, he let out a frustrated sigh. "Okay, I'm going. Jesa," he waited for her to look at him. When she did, he said softly, "Don't let this ruin things between us. I got a little out-of-control; I won't let it happen again. Can we still be…friends?"

He said it so shyly with that boyish charming grin of his, her body relaxed a tad. She smiled but it didn't reach her eyes. "Sure, we can be friends. I, uh, it's late, Ronan." She stepped back from him.

"Okay, you got it, sugar. I hope I'll see you tomorrow. If not I'll give you a call, all right?" He chucked her chin gently with the pad of his finger then stepped out the door. "Goodnight, Jesa," he said quietly.

Her soft, "Goodnight," was barely audible as she closed the door. She pressed her back against the door as she waited to hear his car go down the street. When it did, she sighed with strained relief, pushed her tangled hair off her face and went to pick up her teacup.

Taking the cup and his glass into the kitchen she chastised herself. "Ronan is such a good looking, nice man, a brave policeman, what is wrong with me that I can't just…make out a little with him like he said?"

She padded to the sink and set the cup in it. Reaching up she pulled the yellow curtains closed over the window and muttered to herself, "I'm safe here. He can't find me. Ronan doesn't have to know, doesn't have to discover who I really am. I can have a relationship with him and still hide my identity from him."

Her fingers trailed over the mark he'd left on her breast. It still hurt, there were slight bruises on her wrists, she hadn't expected him to be so rough. She chuckled, the man doesn't know his own strength. A frown brought her brows down, maybe he did. She thought about Tristano. Both men, extraordinarily strong had manhandled her professing they cared for her. Well, Ronan said he cared for her, Tristano said he'd cared *about* her.

Did she want the agent to care for her too? No, he probably only viewed her from a parental point. He wanted to keep her out of danger, that's all. But, she pondered, Tristano had kissed her too. Sure, he instantly broke it off, but he had kissed her. Why?

She went back to the living room to shut off the lights when a knock at the door about made her jump out of her skin. Her heart hammering at her ribs, she crept to the front window and peeked through the drapes. She saw blue jeans, and with a groan, jerked the door open and said, "Really Ronan, I said to leave, can't you-" She was gently pushed aside as Tristano muscled his way past her to come inside the house. "Tristano," she gasped.

The wind howled as he closed the door and looked at her. "What the hell is going on here, Jesselin? I happened to drive by and I see Roarke's truck hightailing it down the road. You look troubled, did he hurt you?"

He slipped his big hand along her jaw to cradle the side of her head, growled, "If he hurt you, I'll fucking take him apart." The top of his black hair was dusted with snow; the locks were tousled from the wind. Snowflakes wet his long black lashes; he blinked the moisture off them.

She moved back from the angry, powerful agent shaking her head. "No, no, he- he, it's okay, Tristano." But she was trembling, obviously upset. His eyes lowered, then narrowed when they landed on her torn shirt.

His nostrils flared with a snarl, Tristano gripped her top and pushed it apart to see the hickey Ronan had left. "He fucking marked you, Jesselin." His enraged eyes rose to hers damp with unshed tears. "Did you want him to, did you let him do that?" He gripped her upper arms. When she didn't answer, turned her head from his scrutiny, he shook her, her breasts wriggled with his assault drawing his gaze to her full flesh and the brutal looking hickey.

Skin darkening with his rising temper he growled gruffly, "Answer me, Jesselin. Did you want him to do that to you?" She trembled in his grip. Her silence answered his question. Tristano grit his teeth and brought her to the couch.

She froze and tried to back away from the sofa with a shake of her head. He frowned, "What's the matter, baby, why are you afraid of the-" His eyes widened then slit in fury, he yelled, "Did he...did he rape you, Jesselin?' His barking voice as taut as a piano wire, the skin stretched across the fierce severe features, his irises ground black.

She didn't say anything, just tried to pull the halves of her torn shirt closed.

Tristano forced himself to calm down. Lightening his grip he spoke softly, "It's okay, Jesselin, tell me what happened. I'll take you to the hospital," *then I'll go murder the motherfucker.*

Comprehending the extent of his rage, Jesa gathered her scattered wits and said quickly, "No, no, he didn't rape me. He didn't really...hurt me. I- I mean, he just kind of got...a little carried away. I made him leave." She looked down at his hands wrapped like vices around her arms. "You're hurting me, Tristano."

He blinked, swallowed hard then made himself let go of her, stepped back to give her space. Taking a deep breath, the hard edge rough in his voice grated as he struggled for calm, he said quietly, "Just tell me, Jesselin, did you want him to do what he did?"

Instead of answering his question, she asked, "Why are you here? Why were you driving by?"

Raking his agitated fingers through his short damp hair, he appeared slightly embarrassed. "Ah, I wasn't going to bother you. It's just, the hang-ups then the footprints in the frost; I'm worried someone is maybe...watching you. I just had to make sure there was no one lurking around your house in the dark."

"Oh." She smiled wanly.

"Now, you tell me, answer my question. You're very upset, anxious; the deputy did something to frighten you. Did you want Roarke to...assault you like he clearly did?" His body calmed, he smoothed the fury from his face making it blank again, but he studied her intently.

"He didn't really hurt me, Tristano, and he basically stopped when I asked him to." She looked away guiltily, unconsciously rubbing her throat that was hoarse from screaming at Ronan to get off her.

An experienced lawman, Tristano read her reticence to tell him how frightened she'd been of the deputy, and Roarke obviously hadn't backed off right when she told him to. But, he had left when she'd requested, and hadn't completely forced himself on her, at least not for long. He and Roarke needed to have a conversation.

A line creased between his dark brows, he lectured her, "Baby, you have to be really sure, really careful when you invite a man inside your home. Unless you're really clear, most men will take that invitation as a yes to sex. You-"

Throwing her head back, Jesa crossed her arms wrapping them tightly around her body, then looked at him with short laugh. "I didn't invite him in, Tristano, any more than I did you. And look where you are."

"But I-" he closed his mouth with a rueful grunt. "You're right. I kind of pushed my way inside."

"Kind of?" Her stern grin came with a hooked brow.

Tristano stuffed his hands in his jacket pockets, his nod solemn. He said with a contrite crooked grin, "I saw Roarke driving away like a bat out of hell, and those hang-ups and footprints, and shit, I just had a flash of you lying beaten and bloody, or worse. I guess I," he sheepishly raised and lowered his shoulder, "I panicked when you opened the door so quickly."

His grin flattened in temper. "So quickly you didn't look out to see who was there. And, if you just had...trouble with Roarke, it would be dangerous to just throw the door open to him again, don't you think?" Scowling his displeasure, he shook his head, "Hell, Jesselin, I wasn't Roarke, but you didn't know that. You recklessly opened your door to what could have been a stranger, some freak that could-"

"Please, stop." Holding a hand up, a shiver rolled through Jesa, she was standing in thin clothes, the top torn, in her socks. "Tristano, I'm tired, I just want to go to bed."

He didn't move, his gaze strayed from her weary eyes down to her half exposed cleavage. Watching him, she snapped the shirt closed again and held the top with her fist, and took a step back from him.

"Yeah." He zipped up his jacket and walked to the door, she slowly followed him. "Lock up tight, okay Bitty bit?" He opened it, and caressed the side of her face holding his fingers there for a second.

"You know, you can always call me in situations like this. You know I'll come straight here, don't ever be afraid to call me. I mean," he angled her head up, "unless you want Ronan…in a…" he couldn't say it so he shut up.

"Anyway, keep your phone with you at all times with my number ready to push." That was an order, the heavy tone of his voice insinuating she'd have trouble from him if she didn't obey.

"I'll pick you up at seven. Don't bother with that sugar crap you have for breakfast, there'll be eggs and croissants at the station. Now, promise me you will call me if anything, *anything* at all isn't right."

He stepped over the threshold. "Promise me, Jesselin. This is no joke. It's either all very coincidental the calls and the prints, but LEO's don't believe in coincidences. If I find out something happened and you didn't call me, I will first tan your hide then haul you to my place and you'll stay there the duration until every single thing is resolved. Now, promise me." He almost smiled at her skin paling when he said he'd smack her ass, but he thought what really scared her was his threatening to force her to stay with him.

"I will wait until I hear your door lock." He stifled a grin at first her look of exasperation at being treated again as a brainless child, then a ripple of anxiousness as his eyes hardened implying punishment for the rude retort she snorted. But he was smiling a minute later as he heard the lock latch- loudly.

Chapter Twenty-Four

Early the next morning, they talked casually about the case on their way to the station. Tristano drove the car up as close to the front door as he could, put it in park, then jogged around to wrench open the rusted door. The weather had grown increasing rougher overnight. Tristano got out, and threw his arm around Jesa as soon as she was out of the car.

He held her in his iron embrace striding quickly from the car, their heads bowed to the voracious wind lashing tears from their eyes. The wind howled and socked at them as they fought their way to the station.

Tristano opened the door, as soon as Jesa stepped inside he hustled back to park the car in the lot. When he trudged back up the drive he ran into the sheriff. "McKabe," Tristano murmured with a nod, his breath white vapor blew away with the wind.

"Koffi." McKabe had a hand on his Stetson to keep the railing wind from taking it. Canting his head to the side, he smiled at Tristano. "I heard you got little Jesa's heater fixed in that thing she calls a car."

His mouth twitched in a half-grin, Tristano said, "Yeah. And took a load of shit for it too. She was furious and didn't even know about the oil change, tune-up, new windshield wipers." He shot a side glance at McKabe. "Let me give you a head's up, I don't think she cares to be called *little*."

The sheriff chuckled, "Uh huh. She might be shy and delicate but that little girl has a spine of steel and is stubborn to the bone. She doesn't like what she considers charity. Finn Barton said they all tried to make excuses to give her rides but she sees through them. They tried to loan her money, she declines saying she's fine. Finn paid her what he could but it's really barely enough to survive on, and now that's winter's upon us no one will be hiring again until season starts next year, and the customers as well as the income will decrease til then."

Tristano's collar was up around his neck, his hands in his pockets, he could still feel the wind knifing stings at his face. "Mmm, she's a tough one. This investigation is bad for the Westcotts but kind of beneficial to Jesselin since she's making more money now."

McKabe stopped walking and touched Tristano's arm so he would halt too.

Turning his back to the wind, Tristano arched his brows at the sheriff.

"So let me ask you this," McKabe said with a sly grin. Tristano lifted his chin for the sheriff to go ahead. "That passenger door can easily be fixed. She's never used it, or Finn or someone else at the bistro would have done it long ago. So, why haven't you fixed that for her?"

With a furtive smile, Tristano said, "What, and have her jump all over me again for helping her?"

McKabe smirked. "No son, I'm figurin' you don't fix it because it's a control thing. It keeps her dependent on you. She can't get out of the car until you let her. Forces her to stay put when you take her home so she can't keep you from safely walking her to her door, and also holds her from dashing about before you can check for danger."

He tapped a few fingers against the side of his head, grinned. "See, I listen when folks talk, especially you, Agent." His voice lowered, he tipped his head closer to Tristano so no one passing by could hear. "Anything on those phone calls or footprints around her house?"

"No. If we had enough deputies to spare I'd request a detail on her home. I'd like to make her stay with me for now then I wouldn't have to worry and drive around checking on her house. But," his grin wry, "she would refuse before I finished my sentence."

McKabe smiled with him. "No doubt. So, it appears you've changed your position on what you think of her? The real reason you came to Orainn?" When Tristano remained silent, the chief asked, "You get the lab report back on the hair you sent?"

His hands deep in his pockets, lips pressed in a line, Tristano nodded.

Crossing his arms over his barrel chest, McKabe said quietly yet loud enough to hear over the wind, "It's verified then. You've confirmed it's her." It was a statement, not a question. Tristano didn't respond. McKabe shoved his hat down further on his head to keep the wind from stealing it.

"Yeah, well son, the picture from the saloon, it was a few years old but we were pretty sure that it was her. At least it's verified." He watched the agent for any emotional reaction to his words, but Koffi's face remained implacable, although a vein at his temple, under a white scar beat faster. "Carlo DeFranco's sister kept after the police to find her brother's killer, she kept the case active."

A loud truck rumbled by drawing both men's attention. Grey exhaust followed it, fouling the air. Tristano brushed snow from his shoulders, looked to the station. "Yes." He scrunched his eyes and turned his face up to the sky. "I need more…information. Something…" he took a breath lowered his head to look at McKabe. "I think she might have had an accomplice. She's a tiny thing, only 17 at the time, DeFranco was a big man, she wouldn't have been able to get him into the dumpster by herself."

Nodding, McKabe shrugged his large shoulders. "No, but, stranger things have happened. There're records of occasions when people have achieved a kind of weird strength in times of great stress. As in the stress of getting caught, getting away. Still, maybe a homeless drunk helped her, maybe a boyfriend."

Tristano squinted at him through soaring snowflakes catching on his lashes. "The police could never locate anyone that may have been involved. The reports stated that she worked almost nonstop 24/7 at several jobs, illegally, and no one could dig up any friends or relatives much less a boyfriend. There is a mother somewhere but appears to be completely out of the picture. The girl was left to fend for herself." The side of his mouth grit in anger at the irresponsible, uncaring mother.

"When the police traced the girl to a shelter in another state they called in the FBI. I followed her from state to state, shelter to shelter. She obtained fake ID's and managed to skip when I would get close. It was like she had a 6th sense that someone was honing in on her."

McKabe said, "You interviewed the manager of the club, he had told you of her strange and sudden disappearance that night. The body was found in the dumpster the next morning when trash was picked up. She left in such a hurry she left her purse, and never came back for her pay. She never returned to her apartment and her car was found in another state abandoned and shot up. That could have been done by local delinquents."

"Hmm, there's more."

Bushy brows arched. "More?"

Tristano looked at him then away. "I went back to re-interview people at the shelters and shithole apartments she hopscotched to across the country." His complexion darkened, his forehead furrowed as his black brows drew together over grimly narrowed eyes. "There were murders at two of them. Unsolved murders."

McKabe's eyes widened. "Coincidence?"

The agent shrugged with a grunt.

The men fell quiet, watching officers pulling in and out of the station. McKabe sucked in a deep breath and exhaled hard. "So, then, what are you going to do? I surely do not believe that darling young lady could harm anyone or anything. Something else was going on I think. However, are you going to take her now?"

"Ah," Tristano muttered, "we have a case to solve. She has been…helpful as you had predicted. I've been able to keep an eye on her. And," his mouth quirked, "the storms have heightened, the ferry made its last tour yesterday. It will be too dangerous to leave the island now."

"Hell, son, you're not thinking of locking that little girl up in a cell until winter's over?" He shook his head, stomped his cold feet. "I know she looks guilty as sin, but, shit Agent, like I said, I really don't believe she is a killer. You need to-"

Tristano's eyes darted around the area. The wind and snow kept most everyone from wandering around outside, but still, he needed to be cautious. "We'll talk about it later, McKabe, not where there might be ears."

McKabe bowed his head with agreement. "Let's head inside." He started walking and Tristano fell in beside him on the path to the building.

225

They bustled inside wrestling the door away from the wind and entered the warmth of the station.

The smell of fresh brewing coffee and bacon mouth-wateringly permeated the main room kicking their taste buds into high gear. McKabe dropped his hat on the hook by the door and peeled off his leather jacket, shook the snow off it onto the mat and hung it on the coatrack. Both men wiped their boots on the wide mat. Tristano removed his trench coat and hung it on the rack. A small group of deputies wandered through the room speaking with early morning quietness.

Willie-Jean stood in a doorway and greeted both men with a wide smile. "Come on in, boys, the vittles are in the big training room." She didn't have to tell them twice. They followed her down a hall into a large room.

Tables and chairs were scattered for seating, and a long table was set across the front of the room containing bowls and pans of food. Heat and aroma pouring off them had people filling plates of eggs, bacon, grits, biscuits, gravy, pancakes, fruit, and on and on.

McKabe and Willie-Jean went straight to the buffet line. Tristano hung back scanning the room, and finding Jesa his eyes cooled. She was off to the side with a plate of pancakes, sausage links, biscuits. His hands empty, Ronan had a palm on the wall next to her and was hunched over her. Both looked upset.

Tristano started across the room heading straight for them. Jesa looked up and saw him and discretely shook her head at him. He stopped, briefly, then Ronan looked over his shoulder at him, his blue eyes tapered in irritation clearly warding Tristano off.

It took everything the agent had to keep himself from going over there and slamming his fist into Roarke's jaw. But, Jesa was obviously asking him to back off. If he went over there, there would likely be a brawl, and this certainly was not the time or the place. *Hell*, Tristano swerved and made tracks to the buffet table. Piling his plate sky-high with eggs, grits and gravy and stacks of toast, Tristano found a place near McKabe. They dug into their food while reviewing the latest bits of data in the case.

Across the room, Ronan gingerly led Jesa to a table and they book seats with Caitlin Saunders and Jerry Osborne and two other deputies.

Ronan leaned in close to Jesa, said quietly, "Listen, Jesa, I think we should talk about last night. I," his mouth pulled in at a corner in chagrin, "I was out of line." He turned so his body curved towards her blocking the others out. "Can we, uh, start over?"

Jesa sipped at a glass of milk, cut pieces of pancakes swimming in maple syrup on the plate in front of her. She gazed up at the dashing deputy smiling abashed at her, blue eyes warm and begging for forgiveness. In the light of day, she ran last night through her mind. She was still acting like a child, getting all freaked out because Ronan had stolen a few kisses. A few rough, forceful kisses, but, yeah, he had stopped and left when she resisted his advances. Her eyes slid to the side, over to where Tristano was sitting with McKabe. The two men appeared in a serious conversation.

"Jesa? Honey?" Ronan slipped his hand over hers on the table. "You're not really angry with me," a lopsided grin creased his handsome face, the blues twinkled, "are you?" He squeezed her hand. "I can't help it if I find you irresistible, wildly sexy. Heck, hon, I'm a red-blooded male, it's only natural I'd...want to...kiss you," he squeezed her hand harder. "Hug you," he bent to gently buss the side of her head, whispered, "maybe do more."

He said quickly, "When you're ready." He lifted his head to see her expression. "Okay? What do you say, sugar?"

But Jesa was still staring at Tristano, who had gotten up and was heading their way. She turned to Ronan and her heart melted. What a sweet, hot, hunk of a strong, brave man. Probably the most attractive man she's ever seen, really. Her gaze flit to Tristano and her body tingled with a shiver of arousal. But Ronan didn't fire up her emotions, set her...womanhood to burning, ignite her deep down, awakening craving like the dark, dangerous, grim agent did.

She sighed. Leave it to her to desire the man that could have less than zip interest in a gawky, childish, small woman. Girl, he called her. He had been quite clear that he preferred the lusty, stronger, bigger, full-figured Deputy Tahni Genarino. Jesa tried not to, but she couldn't stop herself from looking up at the agent as he approached their table. But he wasn't looking at her, his eyes were on Ronan.

"Roarke," Tristano's deep voice made Ronan's shoulders tic.

Ronan grimaced at Jesa then sat back in his chair and smiled dourly up at the agent. "Koffi."

"Tristano-" Afraid he was going to confront Ronan about last night Jesa tried to cut him off.

The agent spoke over her, "We have a new person of interest to interview," he said. Everyone at the table stopped talking and turned their attention to the agent.

"Yeah?" Ronan covered a faux yawn, he was more interested in the girl next to him than the investigation.

"Elizabeth Westcott had a second lover. Jackson Burl. She said he's a heavy gambler and is in deep debt, may have a loan shark after him."

Surprise reflected on the deputy's face. "Oh yeah?" He sat up straighter, fully facing Koffi. "Woman gets around, eh? Likes 'em shady."

Unclipping his phone, Tristano tapped on it, said, "I'm sending you his last known addresses. He has had apartments here, Mrs. Westcott told us she believes he may be in Vegas hunting up friends for money to save his legs from being broken."

Ronan's phone buzzed, he fished it out and read it. "Why did you send me Burl's info?" His gaze flicked from his phone to Tristano.

Tristano replied, "You are going to track him down. Him and any others he deals with."

A brow cocked, Ronan's lips pursed. "And you? What are you going to do?"

Tristano didn't say anything for a minute. His eyes landed briefly on Jesa before returning to the deputy. "Not that I have to tell you my plans," his mouth tugged up at the frown creasing Ronan's face. "But," he allowed a cold smile to appear briefly, "I don't want you wasting your time tracking down the guy's loan shark. I've already had feelers out for him. I'm going to go talk to him when I leave here."

Ronan sat back and glanced at Jesa. "What about Jesa? I'll take her with-"

"No," Tristano said curtly. He allowed a swift glance at her then back to the deputy. "It's too dangerous for her to go with either of us. She'll stay here and put her notes together. There is more information coming in from officers in the field that she can cross-reference and circulate."

Everyone sat quietly for a moment. Caitlin stood up. "I guess breakfast is over." McKabe was now at their table. Caitlin said to him, "Give my happy belly gratitude to Finn Barton for sending over this great food for us today." She grinned at the chief. The others got up, more officers came over and conversations struck up as they made their way to the door.

McKabe asked Tristano to come with him to his office before he left for his interview. Tristano gave Jesa a cool, hard look, said, "Jesselin, you are not to leave this station until I return."

Her mouth dropped. "But, I thought I would hop over to the bistro at lunchtime-"

"No." His jaw set, dark eyes narrowed at her. "You do not leave this station. Chief McKabe will be checking on you, and Willie-Jean will call me if you attempt to leave." Jesa opened her mouth to argue, he said very quietly, "No." He glared his warning at her, shifted his gaze to Ronan, then he and McKabe left them and exited the room.

"Well then," Ronan expelled with a snorted grin. "The Emperor has spoken, eh? And all we peasants obey and do as he says." He reached out and took Jesa's hand.

Jerry Osborne harrumphed said, "Yeah well, he trumps McKabe, and even if he didn't," a shudder rippled his shoulders, "I sure as hell wouldn't cross the man." As he left he mumbled with a shake of his head, "No fuckin' way."

Ronan rolled his eyes. "Ah, he's got them all running scared. Everyone but you and me, huh, Jesa?"

She smiled at him. She was already considering how she could sneak out and run to the Bistro and back before anyone returned. She happened to look over and saw Willie-Jean near the doorway. A kind smile on her face and a firm shake of her head. *Nuts*, Jesa scowled, she had a babysitter.

Chapter Twenty-Five

Ronan held the directions he'd taken off his phone in his hand that rested on the steering wheel. "Hell," he groused, scrutinizing the area. One of the older, rundown streets on the island, it was at the bottom and on the furthest side of the mountain, away from most of the stores, restaurants and fancy houses. The street sign on the corner read Brinkle Ave.

Ronan swung the wheel and turned down it. Each house he passed was seedier and more dilapidated than the last. Most of the homes were cheap clapboards. The street ended at woodlands. Rusted, beat-up cars and trucks littered the street and yards. No one seemed to care how they parked. There were more vehicles on lawns than there was grass.

The last house, peeling yellow paint, grass overgrown so high the first step of the front porch was hidden by tall brown grass and weeds. Ronan parked the cruiser in the dirt driveway and climbed out. His hand on the gun at his hip, he cautiously approached the residence.

An old truck with four flat tires squatted in front of the porch; he had to walk around it to get to the house. Glancing around, he scanned for anyone in the area that could be a danger. The grubby street was dead quiet. He trod up the steps and knocked on the door.

And waited. He knocked again, louder, more rapidly, was about to try the knob when the door slowly opened. A wan face appeared in the thin strip of doorway.

"Hey, there, I'm Deputy Roarke," he said, pointing at his badge. "I'm looking for Jackson Burl." He was pretty sure Burl was inside. They'd had police in Vegas confirm the guy wasn't there, and his name wasn't on any of the ferry's manifests. Of course he could have gone on another boat, but, Ronan took in the corroded truck, peeling paint, trash scattered over the yard, and presumed the guy wouldn't have had the money to buy or rent a boat.

It was unlikely the destitute gambler had any friends wealthy enough to afford a boat big enough to cross to the mainland as the root of land between Orainn and the mainland was already washing out so he couldn't leave by vehicle, and the ocean was now too hazardous to traverse even by a big ship.

The door opened slightly wider. A young Asian woman with stringy greasy dark hair blinked bloodshot brown eyes at him. Through a yawn, she muttered, "What d'ya want with him?"

"Uh, just need a chat. How long has he been here?" Ronan eased the door open and stepped inside. The tiny girl moved back, not objecting to his coming in the house.

"Huh," she grunted and started to walk through the dingy living room, Ronan followed her. She would have been very pretty if she wasn't so skinny her elbow bones and kneecaps jutted out sharply, and her sallow skin was grimy. She wore loose shorts and a stained tank top, clearly braless, her filthy bare feet slapped on the floor then quieted as she crossed onto the rug.

"He's been shacked up here for almost a week. "Huh," she sniffed and traipsed down a hall. "He ain't paid me a dime. He ain't got a dime. I gotta make do with my welfare checks."

Ronan followed her into a small cruddy room. She moved to the side of a double bed. A man was propped against soiled pillows clutching a half empty bottle of bourbon. Scraggly dark hair half covered his face, but Ronan could see he was the guy in the picture Koffi had forwarded to him. Jesa had confirmed he was the man she'd seen with Elizabeth Westcott by his DMV picture, and Elizabeth admitted her affair with him and also identified his photo. Still, he asked, "You Jackson Burl?"

The man pushed the scraggly hair off his face and thinned his eyes at the deputy. "What do ya wanna know for?" Firing a glare at the girl for letting Ronan in, he lay in shorts and a tank undershirt on top of the worn blanket with his back against the pillows. Ronan could see both his legs were in casts.

Normally the deputy could see why Elizabeth Westcott found him good looking, but now he was dirty, excruciating pain pinched and ground his sweating features, deforming him into a sickened weak monstrosity.

Ronan moved closer to the bed, saw the pain quiver through the guy's body. "Whoa, bro, what the hell happened?"

Tears filled Burl's red eyes, his chest heaved. The woman leaned against the wall, she pushed off. "I'll git you water for the meds the doc gave you, be back. Remember what the doc said about drinkin' and meds," and she shuffled out of the room.

Swallowing a sob of pain, Burl groaned, "I owed a guy some big money and couldn't pay him. He, ah," Burl grimaced as a wave of agony strangled his words. "Ah, he took his payment out in my legs, and the rest of my body."

He lifted the bottle to his cracked lips and chugged a few mouthfuls, didn't bother to wipe away the booze that dribbled down his chin. The bottle bounced on the thin mattress as he weakly dropped his arm.

Ronan asked, "A loan shark?"

Burl nodded glumly.

"What's his name?"

"Pablo Greka, they call him 'the Greek.' Ha." His face bunched up with a scornful laugh. "I don't know why 'cause he ain't no Greek."

Ronan eyed him to see if he really was that dumb he didn't get the connection between the man's name, Greka and Greek. But Burl just stared blankly, painfully at his legs. Yeah, he was that dumb. Apparently a lover, not a fighter, definitely not an intellect. "When did this happen?"

Burl's eyes clamped closed. "Ah, I guess three or four days or so ago. The meds make time fuzzy."

Ronan typed notes on his phone. "Does this Greka guy know your..." he glanced around for the woman, "girlfriend, Elizabeth Westcott?"

Brows knit. "Huh?" He shifted in the bed and cried out at the pain. "Why would Greka know Elizabeth?"

"Maybe he knows she has money, maybe he snatched their baby for ransom. Get some big money, right?"

Pain lancing his red eyeballs, Burl cringed. "Na, no one knows about my affair with Lizzy." He gingerly turned to check the doorway for the Asian woman. "No one. Why would I even mention her to some scum-sucking loan shark? Besides," he wiped at his eyes with the back of his hand. "The money had run out. I bled Lizzy for all I could. She showed me their bank papers, the balances were just barely in the black. Even if someone is after ransom they ain't gettin' nuthin', ya know? That well is dry." He clutched his stomach and yelled, "Kaiko! Where's my fucking medicine!"

The girl rustled into the room with a pill bottle and glass of water. "Gimmie two," he snarled. Shaking her head, she shook out two pills and handed them and the water to Burl. When he shoved the glass of water away and tossed in the pills washing them down with a slug of liquor, the two started arguing and Ronan made his exit. He'd gotten everything they needed.

He called Tristano when he got in his car. "Koffi," he said when the agent answered. "The dude's got two broken legs, looks like he got a helluva beat down. If he'd taken the baby he would have tried to get the ransom and avoid the beating. He said everyone knew the Westcotts were low on dough. I glanced in the few rooms in the house on my way out and verified there's no baby being stashed there."

Tristano said, "Okay. Just in case, I have a deputy searching the Dark Web sites in case someone is trying to sell the baby through the net. I found the loan shark." He muttered sourly, "I was surprised to see such a putrid part of town, mostly blacked out shitty alleys, he works out of a scummy pool hall. It was weird seeing that crud on this lush resort isle."

"After being on Brinkle Ave," Ronan grunted, "I can easily picture it. There are two or three tiny pockets of crappy areas where the criminals and indigents hang. I guess I've never taken any of the crime calls in those areas. Lucky me."

"Yeah. Anyway, Greka is a fat slovenly pig, but I'm convinced he does not know the Westcotts. And, trust me, if that fucker or any of his enforcers had been around their neighborhood, those thugs would have been noticed, those big ugly thumbs would have stuck out."

Ronan breathed a sigh of relief when he drove out of the area and towards a main road. "So, we can cross another of Elizabeth's lovers and their thug-buddies off our kidnap list."

"It-" Tristano's phone pinged. "I have to go, Granger Wate is on the other line." He cut off without saying goodbye, smiling, he knew that irritated the deputy.

"Wate?" he said as he switched lines.

"Hey, Agent Koffi," Granger Wate's voice came through. "I have something, you wanna come by?"

Chapter Twenty-Six

Tristano hurried back to the station. First thing he did was seek out Jesa. He found her in a small office, her notebook open, several pieces of paper were spread out on the desk, she was tapping on the iPad Willie-Jean had given her.

"Jesselin."

Her head came up, cheeks instantly pinked. "Tristano, you're back," she said redundantly. "Find out anything?"

A brief shake of his head, he moved inside the room. "No. Unless Mrs. Westcott has more lovers, that lead is done. I'll give you the particulars later for your reports; Roarke has a bit to add too." He neared the desk. "Granger Wate has something to show me, come along?"

A bright smile puffed her round cheekbones. "Yeah, sure. I'm done, I was just reviewing my notes in case I missed anything. Tried to memorize maps and graphs and stuff to more fully fill out the information as the deputies forward it to me." She closed her notebook, shut down the iPad, then paused. "Oh, listen, Deputy Morgan Martschmidt called me." She bowed her head to her phone, pushed some buttons.

"Yeah?" Tristano stood closer, looked down at her. He captured a few locks of her shiny hair, drew them back so he could see her face, and smiled at the habitual soft blush that brightened her cheeks. So shy, it was amusing, and stirring, the way she was so easily embarrassed. He brushed his knuckles along her cheek, feeling the delicate richness of her skin as it heated further under his intimate caress. He let her hair sift from his fingers as she raised her head.

Keeping her face aimed at the notes she'd made on her phone, Jesa blinked out the rousing sensation he evoked from her guarded green eyes. She appeared as surprised at his intimate touch as she did at the feelings it seemingly induced. "Uh, y-yes," scrolled down, "here. Deputy Martschmidt said Deputy Genarino advised him that the, um, photographer, Mr.," her eyes on the phone, "Rupert James. You know, the one that worked with Mr. Normandy and the models?"

At Tristano's nod she went on, "Deputy Carl Johnson tracked him to his home in L.A. Johnson called the L.A. police station and asked an officer to go talk to him."

"What'd he have to say?"

Jesa shut off her phone, clutched it in her hand. She grinned. "He admitted he was the one who stole Mr. Normandy's designs. Dev Martin, the man Mr. Normandy tangled with at that house isn't pressing charges against Mr. Normandy. Apparently Dev wasn't supposed to be at the house at all. His aunt is furious. She had told him to stay away because he stole things and sold them, and he made bad messes, smoking and burning holes in furniture, stuff like that.

"He had broken in and he thought when the aunt returned in the spring she'd think it was just vandals. So, when, if, you release Mr. Normandy and he eventually returns home, Rupert James will return the designs to him and Normandy in return won't press charges for the theft. Mr. Normandy agreed to pay for the car window he broke as well as whatever damage he had caused while burglarizing the Lloyd house." She grinned at her phone. "The models left on the last ferry."

"Goodbye to disgusting rubbish. All's well that ends well, for them anyway," Tristano said. He looked at the phone then frowned at her. "Why did Martschmidt tell you and not Tahni, or Johnson for that matter? All info was to be sent directly to you."

She bumped one shoulder. "I understand Deputy Johnson had told Tahni about the photographer in conversation, and Tahni mentioned it to Deputy Martschmidt. Deputy Johnson was going to contact me but Tahni told him she'd forward the information to me. I guess when Deputy Martschmidt realized she wasn't going to, he felt he should." She paused as Tristano's face darkened.

Slight embarrassment tinged her girlish voice. "Deputy Martschmidt called me after he sent a text. He said...well, that Tahni thought I was insignificant and had no business being involved in the investigation. That I'd gotten a…a swelled head, thought I felt I was real important, indispensable. That I didn't need the information anyway, as it had no bearing on the kidnapping." Her eyes turned down, Tahni's words hurt her, Tristano could see the sting flickering over her soft face.

He pulled a chair next to her, sat down and slid his arm around her small shoulders, brought her against his chest and wrapped his other arm around her in an embrace. Her face tucked in his shoulder. At first she was stiff in his arms, then, the tenseness lessened, her body relaxed, pooling like warm supple liquid against his concrete chest. His mouth in her hair, he murmured, "You are worth 1,000 Tahnis, Jesselin. You're courageous and strong, smart, compassionate, and sexy as hell."

She drew back at that, he tightened his arms.

"You're the cog of this investigation, you're the one keeping everything and everyone moving smoothly. You gathered and organized and prioritized all the information the deputies garnered and made sure it was disseminated properly like McKabe tasked you to do.

"You got valuable information out of that maid using your compassionate questioning, and you were the only one that noticed Mrs. Westcott and her boy toy. Tahni is a malicious, jealous bitch, baby, she's hasn't a tenth of your integrity or your grit."

He was quiet a moment letting her digest his words. "And, maybe, when you accept that, you can open up, see your own self-worth, and then realize you can trust me, with all your secrets." Petting her head, he stroked his big hand down her slender back enjoying the soft warmth of her under his hard hand.

He murmured, "Let me help you, Jesselin, trust me to understand and to help you." Her body turned rigid, she lifted her head. He smiled against her hair. "For now, pack up your stuff and let's go see what Wate has for us."

He squeezed her shoulders, pressed her harder to his chest, then unwound his arms, pushed his chair aside and rose to his feet. And grinned widely at her bright pink cheeks and moist eyes.

Jesa awkwardly stood up, without looking at him she pushed her papers together, and put them and her phone, iPad and notebook in her bag and slung it over her shoulder. But Tristano's lips pursed.

"What?" she asked. He stared pointedly at her bag. "Oh." Her mouth made a little moue as she reached in the bag and took out her phone. Sheepishly stuffing it in her jean's pocket, she smiled meekly at him.

"I just don't know about you," Tristano admonished as he led her out of the room. "You have to be careful, Bitty bit, use the tools we give you to look out for yourself."

They trod down a few halls until they reached another office. Granger Wate was inside. They greeted each other, Koffi pulled a chair out on one side of Granger for Jesa, and like before, he sat on the other side of him.

"Whacha got, Deputy?" Tristan asked.

Wate sat back in his chair and clasped his hands behind his head, his grin smug. "I'm good, Agent, I have to tell you, damn good."

A concurring grin laced Tristano's harsh face. "Okay, I'll agree with that. Now, what did you find?"

Granger sobered, he pushed his computer towards Tristano. "When I found that secret account of Mrs. Westcott's, I figured if she did, maybe he did too. I executed an intense, scrape the dirt off the ground diligent search of Stedman Westcott, like panning for gold," his bragging expertise shameless in his voice.

Tristano smiled. "And you found something I take it?"

When Granger turned the computer so Jesa could see it, the page on the screen flipped to copies of rows of checks displayed, but Jesa saw the name of the bank and it was the Pacific Savings and Loan. The checks were from Mr. Westcott's personal account, and a few of the Westcotts' joint account, nothing new there.

Grinning triumphantly, the deputy leaned forward and rested his forearms on the desk. "Stedman Westcott does indeed have a hidden account. I found it searching through his company's financial records."

Dubious dark brows arched. "You got a court order to go through them?"

His grin sneaky, Granger said, "Well, I kind of found myself inexplicably fishing around in the accounts."

Jesa fumbled out, "You hacked?"

Granger hushed her with a frown. "I didn't say that," he mumbled, "exactly."

One side of Tristano's mouth quirked showing he didn't care how the man got the info, just that he got it. "Go on, Deputy."

With a conspiratorial wink and a short nod of thanks, Granger relayed, "Once I'd analyzed the data and figured out what was going on, I told McKabe what I found. He didn't ask any questions he didn't want to hear the answers to, but he went and had a chat with the corporate heads. When they heard what I'd discovered, and with the kidnapped baby and all, they gave up their confidential records without a fight. It's a toss-up if we could have gotten a subpoena, but McKabe took a chance with his threats and the corporation coughed up."

"More worried about looking like bad guys when a missing baby is involved then giving up their client's confidential info," Tristano remarked.

Granger agreed grimly. "If any of the clients catch on that I surfed through their personal account records," he shrugged with a grin, "they might be looking at lawsuits, and my potential arrest. But I presume no one's telling them, they'll just out themselves that they blabbed and were cheated. If it gets out that an exchange company was basically robbed, it will lose all credibility and security. Clients will jump the sinking ship in droves."

"Ah ha. Well, what was Westcott up to?" Tristano asked, interest gleaming in his dark eyes.

Sitting back, setting his palms on the table, Granger answered, "Westcott had the personal account under a phony business name, Alden Enterprises. He withdrew cash. No checks. The withdrawals were for the same exact amount every time, $5,000."

Tristano and Jesa gave him their rapt attention at the fascinating news.

"Thing is," Granger said, "I couldn't find any corresponding connections to where he is putting it. No IRA's, mutual funds, no savings accounts, the money doesn't come up anywhere. I matched all the Westcotts' expenses and purchases for the past year and the money doesn't show anywhere. McKabe called Westcott himself. Westcott said the money was from and for gambling. He didn't want his wife to know."

Tristano turned the monitor back to him and flipped back to the other page and scrolled through the numbers. Granger went on,

"Yeah, thing is, we had deputies scour the two casinos on the island as well as any other gambling locations. They checked with bookies. Any big or constant wins are carefully recorded and the IRS noted. Stedman Westcott was not a regular gambler. He went on one cruise. The ship's records show he broke even. Other than that trip he hasn't left the island for years so he isn't gambling on the mainland."

Jesa said quietly, "It would be extremely coincidental that he would and lose and win $5,000 over and over again. That exact amount. That's not possible."

His smile warm at her, Tristano murmured, "You're right." To Wate he said, "But he could prevaricate and claim he rounds the cash off, doesn't deposit it until he has the exact $5,000 because he has OCD and has to keep the money the same. Or profess it's a superstitious good luck thing."

Nodding, Wate said, "Anyway, I hunted with a fine tooth comb his computer and phones, reviewed his emails and texts, corresponded them with phone and internet records that I..." he grinned, "just happened to come across. He wasn't gambling by phone or online, unless he has a burner but I doubt that. And he surely wasn't mailing cash anywhere, and getting bank checks to mail or the like, again, would draw attention, there'd be records."

"So, where did the money go?" Jesa asked. "Actually, where did it come from? You told us before that they lived within their means, barely, but still..."

Granger's mouth pulled in. "Uh, yes, well, they were, kind of. I searched his business accounts for unusual activity, as well as I dug into his company's accounts. That's when I located his fake account and followed the paper trail as it were and discovered he was moving money from the company's accounts into his. He funneled it around and around from here to there, moved it in and out through various customer accounts until a normal audit wouldn't have captured the activity, the theft."

"Whoa, embezzlement?" Tristano blurted.

"Looks like it."

After a pregnant silence, Jesa said, "Okay, so you know where it came from, where did it go?"

The men looked at her, then the computer, they shrugged. "That's the million dollar question."

"Ha, more like the $5,000 question." Jesa laughed lightly.

The edge of Tristano's lip curled up in amusement. "Yeah, whatever it is, it's what we need to find out."

Jesa pushed off her chair to her feet and grabbed up her bag. Tristano raised a brow at her. She said, "I assume we're going to the Westcotts'?"

He smiled at her astuteness, she was thinking as an investigator, not as just a scribe he was dragging along, she grinned back. Tristano patted Granger on the back. "Good job, bro, real good."

They met briefly with McKabe then drove right out to the Westcotts'.

Chapter Twenty-Seven

Snow and wind pummeled the little car, tossing it around like a giant batting a soccer ball, Tristano had to work to keep it on the road. Visibility was almost nil, it wasn't night but it seemed like it. He had to drive slowly in case another car was coming around a tight bend in the dark. The heater was on full blast; he rubbed his gloved fist over the condensation on the window. They hadn't called ahead, Tristano didn't want them prepared. Although they would have had a head's up from McKabe's call earlier.

Tristano parked the car as close to the house as he could and shut it off. His hand on the door handle, he said, "Wait for me, Jesselin to come around and get you, it's vicious out there, I don't want you blown away from me."

Jesa canted her head at him with a teasing smile, she ribbed, "Really, Tristano, it's not like I can get the door open on my own, you've seen to that."

His brow lifted, he said with a short laugh, "That door was dented and rusted like that when you came and retrieved me from the wharf, little girl."

"Uh huh." She smiled. "But after opening it a few times it was getting looser, easier. But now it's harder than ever to get open."

"You accusing me of something, Bitty bit?" he said, the side of his mouth curved up in a pretend affronted smile.

She tugged her hood up and tied it under her chin. "Oh, nothing I can prove, but," she grinned, "you are a control freak, especially around me. I wouldn't put it past you to have, well, *adjusted*, the door keeping it hard for me to get out."

He shoved his own door open; the wind swooped in blowing his hair. As he stepped out, he said with a laugh, "It's science, baby, the cold air, it tends to swell metal, make it fit tighter." He hurried to her side and when he wrenched her door open a big grin filled his face at her droll expression of disbelief of his theory. He bundled her out and into his arms and kept a secure hold of her until they were inside.

A deputy ushered them into the now well-familiar living room, and they sat themselves on red cushioned chairs, and waited. It was fifteen minutes before Elizabeth came into the room. The stress was showing on the young woman. Her hair was less perfect, makeup less pristine, she wore flats instead of heels. Her eyes were puffy and red rimmed. As she entered, she avoided Tristano's eyes, for the first time she looked directly at Jesa as if hoping Jesa would be on her side against whatever the agent planned to throw at her this time.

Tristano moved off the chair to his feet, he said brusquely, "Where is Mr. Westcott?"

"Ah," Elizabeth murmured as she settled onto the sofa. "He had to return to work. We have bills to pay. I am here if," her gaze flit to the phone on the table. In sleek slacks, she crossed her legs, sat stiffly back against the cushions. She wrung a wad of tissues in her shaking hands. "You have more questions of me? I swear, Agent Koffi," her voice trembled, "there are no more boyfriends, no men, that I'm seeing. Subie and Jackson were the only ones in the last year." The way her eyes slid away, obviously there had been more lovers in her history.

Tristano let it go. It explained why when they'd first interviewed the Westcotts that Stedman had turned surly, shooting nasty glares at his wife. Roarke told them later that he had asked him about any extra marital affairs. It was obvious now that Stedman knew, or suspected that his wife was running around on him, and didn't like it pushed in his face.

"We wanted to speak with Mr. Westcott," Tristano told Elizabeth.

She turned to him, making eye contact, a hitch in her voice when she asked, "About what?"

Tristano contemplated whether or not to tell her. "You husband has a secret account, like you do. Only, his has a hefty balance in it."

Her brows flew to her hairline, she leaped to her feet. "What?"

Tristano glanced at Jesa, then back to Elizabeth. The wife was shocked as he figured she would be. "He withdraws a standard amount of money about every four months."

"L-large?"

"Five thousand dollars." He was watching her surreptitiously, yet very carefully. And he saw it. No shock.

Elizabeth stood, smoothed her hair back off the sides of her face and said nonchalantly, "Oh? Who was he giving it to?" She glanced at Tristano then quickly away, her complexion paled.

"That's what I expect," Tristano was going to say Stedman, but instead he said, "*you* to tell us." And got the reaction he was looking for. Her eyes shifted then fell to the floor.

She kept her gaze averted from him, said in a high-pitched voice, "Me? How would I know?"

Tristano's already tough face hardened into glacial granite. He took a few steps towards her, his voice callous he said with chill in his voice, "You do know, Mrs. Westcott, and you will tell me, now. Right now. You balk or lie or stall, and the three of us are off to the station." He pushed the side of his trench coat back and moved his handcuffs to the front of his belt.

Elizabeth's eyes rounded at them, her lips parted, she licked them. She stuttered, "I- I-"

"Right. Now."

Jesa had been sitting, she rose. Elizabeth's face was white as a sheet, her eyes huge in consternation. She twined her fingers and held them clasped to her chest. "I- I, uh, I have to go get something, to show you." She stared back at Tristano's hard glare. He nodded sharply. She turned and quickly rushed out of the room. Tristano looked at the guard. The officer bowed and followed her.

They heard some banging around, then, in several minutes she returned with the deputy at her heels. She carried a folded leather case. She brought it to the coffee table and set it down. Her hands shook so hard she had difficulty opening it. She unwound a string that wrapped around the brown case, then she opened it and pulled out pieces of paper. She set them on the table. "There, I found these a while ago. I was scared to ask Stedman about them. I didn't want him to be...angry with me for snooping." She stood back, her unsteady gaze on Tristano, then Jesa, then she lowered her head.

Questioning curiosity on Jesa's face, Tristano's was his customary blank as he picked up a paper carefully by a tiny part of an end and unfolded it using his pen. He read it silently then passed it to Jesa warning her to hold it like he had, and picked up another.

Her eyes widened at what she read, mouth parted. She set the handwritten note down and took the next from Tristano, and he picked up another one. There were dozens. They all basically said the same thing:

"Put the money in the sack and leave it at the regular drop off by tomorrow at 9:30. I don't get my money and everyone will know what you did."

There were no dates on the notes, but Tristano assumed they were delivered at the same time of the withdrawals, right after the banks opened at 9. He set the last one down. Elizabeth had moved away to stare unseeing out one of the arched window. He slowly went to stand next to her. She held her body rigid, her fingers twined and twisted expressing her agitation.

"What do you know about the notes, Mrs. Westcott?"

She cocked her head, mouth tightened, she parroted, "What do I know?"

"Yes. Tell me about the notes. Do you know who they're from? Do you recognize the handwriting? Is Stedman the writer? What are they relating to? They are clearly blackmail. What did your husband do that he was being blackmailed for?"

Before Elizabeth could respond Jesa said, "Mr. Westcott didn't write them. I saw his handwriting on the checks in his and your joint accounts on Deputy Wate's computer and there isn't the slightest match. Plus," she hesitated, Tristano nodded to her to continue. "Why handwrite them? Why not just print one on a computer then make copies of it? There are a few differences in the notes, but not big enough to change the gist of the message."

Tristano gave her a surprised but proud look for her discerning observations. He turned back to Elizabeth. "Tell me about the notes, Mrs. Westcott."

She was tall but she still had to look up at him. Wringing her fingers, her head still angled at him, she huffed a labored sigh. "Agent, I swear, I don't know anything about them. Zero, zilch, zip. I don't know what he did, when he might have done...the...deed they refer to. I don't know when they arrived, I came upon them accidentally one day. He kept them locked in his desk drawer. One day I needed the key to our safe, it was kept in the drawer. I knew where that key was. I mean," she shrugged with a wry smile.

"This is my house. I'm home all day, I know where everything is. Except," her lips twisted with irony, "I didn't know about the letters until I inadvertently found them. Obviously they came over a period of time and Stedman has managed to keep them hidden from me. There were no envelopes, just the notes."

Tristano carefully scooped the papers up and stuffed them back in the leather folder. He closed the flap and wrapped the string around it, tucked it under his arm. "I'll take them to your husband and ask him."

"Huh," Elizabeth made a sound of derision in her throat. She released her fingers and combed them through her hair. She was regaining her composure. It showed in the raising of her chin, the haughty look in her plum eyes, the squaring of her shoulders. "He won't tell you, Agent. He didn't make a great living at not being a good salesman, spin a tall tale and convince you to buy this or that stock. No," she smiled wearily up at Tristano. "You won't get the truth. He'll say they weren't his, that maybe he found them after his daddy died. He can even say they weren't written to him. He'll have an excuse for the money."

Tristano agreed with her, Stedman had already told McKabe the money was from gambling. Wate proved that it wasn't, and Tristano believed him one hundred percent. But, Stedman was slick, and he could say he gambled off shore either with someone's help or using a burner, which would likely be impossible to disprove, especially if he said he destroyed his records.

Wate had checked into the cruise the Westcotts went on, if he'd won any kind of large amounts there would have been documentation for tax purposes. But lesser amounts, no. And Stedman could say the smaller amounts just added up. Elizabeth was also right that Stedman can deny the notes are even his, there's nothing denoting that they were written specifically to him.

Tristano said to Jesa, "Jesselin, call Mr. Westcott, tell him I want to talk to him."

Jesa took her phone out and looked up the contacts. Willie-Jean had entered all the deputies' and everyone they had spoken with like Niels Normandy and the models, and all of the Westcotts' phone numbers.

He stared unblinking at Elizabeth, thinking. Yes, she was right. The notes were damned important, may tie in with the kidnapping, but there was no way Stedman would admit to embezzling if there wasn't any proof, and certainly not to being blackmailed because he'd hang himself. What the hell did he do?

"Uh," Elizabeth's voice wavered between fright, anger and relief of getting the burden of the notes off her chest, she said, "how, um, much, you know, is in that account? I mean, I only know about the notes, I don't know anything about the money."

Tristano considered her thoughtfully, then shrugged. "About a hundred grand."

Her brows jumped, mouth parted, she actually licked her lips. "Oh yeah, wow, really?"

He shook his head wryly, "The money is likely stolen, it will be returned. Stedman might go to prison and even have to pay restitution."

Emotions rifled over her pretty face, greed, worry for her husband, greed. There was even a flicker that Tristano deciphered as her brain cells synapsing on how to keep the money. "Mrs. Westcott." Her eyes glazed as shopping danced in her head. He said louder, "Your daughter, Mrs. Westcott."

She blinked. "Huh?"

"Brie," his tone chilled, "remember her?"

Blink, blink. "My daughter?"

"Yeah, you know, the child that's been kidnapped?"

She frowned at him, struggling to transfer her brain from money to her missing baby. "What about her?"

He had to make the effort to not roll his eyes, especially in front of Jesa. "These blackmail notes, they might have something to do with her kidnapping."

Her lashes flapped more rapidly. "What? What do they have to do with Brie?" Finally, tears blossomed in her eyes.

"If I knew that, Mrs. Westcott, I wouldn't be standing here wasting my damned time. Are you sure you have no clue about these notes? Anything. It could be direly important."

Elizabeth looked down at the case in his hand, wiped at the tears then looked up at him, the greed had turned to desperation for her baby. "No," she whispered, her hand at her throat. "No, I would tell you, I swear to God." Her face hardened. "If Stedman has done something that hurt our child, I'll-"

Jesa said, "Tristano?" She held her phone on her lap, waiting until he turned from Elizabeth's terrified, conflicted face to her. "Mr. Westcott doesn't answer, I left him a message. I called his secretary and she said he was out for lunch."

"She say where?"

"Yes, the Wispy Wave. She said it's around two miles from his office."

When Tristano buttoned his trench coat, Jesa put her things away and zipped up her own jacket to prepare to battle the weather outside. He strode to the archway leading out of the living room. Jesa followed him, tugged on his sleeve. He hesitated, looked down at her with a quirked brow.

"Tristano." She jerked her head subtly to Elizabeth. The bewildered young mother stood with her back to the window watching them with a grief-filled expression dimming her prettiness. Jesa whispered, "Don't be cruel." Insinuating his rudely leaving Elizabeth without a word, as if she was nothing.

Keeping his head straight his eyes lowered to Jesa. She was so earnest, kind. Tristano had a one-track mind, work. He generally didn't care about the people involved in his investigations. He had a job to do and that was the only thing that was important. Jesa smiled wistfully, as if she believed he would always do the right thing. Huh, innocent little girl.

He faced Elizabeth, said gruffly, "Mrs., ah, Westcott, thank you for showing us the…notes. We'll be in touch." Turning his heel he strode to the hall. Jesa smiled gently at the woman and hurried after him.

Chapter Twenty-Eight

Tristano parked in front of the restaurant, Wispy Waves. It was painted pale blue with white trim carved into ocean waves. The place was elegant and upscale. "Okay, Bitty bit, I'm up for some chow, two birds one stone as they say. Food and Westcott."

Jesa peered out the window at the restaurant. "Here? No, Tristano, it's very expensive. Mr. Westcott's secretary told me the executives lunch here to do business with only their wealthiest clients."

He opened his door, grinned over at her. "Then the food must be really good, let's go." He pulled his collar up to protect his neck from the biting wind and went around to get Jesa. Yanking her door open he reached in for her. She leaned back from him shaking her head. "What's wrong, Jesselin? Breakfast was a long time ago, you have to be starving."

Clutching the bag on her lap with both hands, she said, "We may have to work together, Tristano, but that doesn't mean you have to feed me, take me with you when you need to eat. You go ahead inside and speak with Mr. Westcott, get your lunch, I have soup at the station I can eat. I'll wait here for you."

"Ah, Bitty bit, you are so smart but sometimes you can be so dumb. Come on, quit fooling around, I am too hungry to argue with you." He grabbed her bag off her lap and tossed it on the floor then quickly grasped her wrist and easily pulled her from the car. Ignoring her protests, he ushered her through the squalling wind to the warmth inside the fancy restaurant.

The maître d' nodded stiffly at Tristano, but his lip curled when he took in Jesa's worn jeans and purple jacket. His gaze shifted back to

Tristano and he blanched at the fierce look the agent speared him with. A slight cough and he said quickly, "Ah, two sir? Right this way." He moved efficiently with an arrow straight spine through the throng of elegant burgundy clothed tables. Crystalline vases held candles that flickered sunset halos on the tablecloths.

At their table, Tristano helped Jesa out of her jacket and draped it over one of the four chairs. He pulled out her chair, then when she sat he removed his coat but remained standing. "Sir," he said to the maître d'.

The man arched an inquiring brow as he handed Jesa her menu and laid the other at the other place setting for Tristano.

"We were told Stedman Westcott was here." He glanced around. "I don't see him."

The man nodded stiffly. "Mr. Westcott and his associates only had cocktails, they went elsewhere to dine, I don't know where."

Tristano's suspicious gaze leveled at Jesa, he said, "I wonder if the Missus called and warned him." He saw the same idea was echoed in her bunched lips. He turned to the waiter and asked, "Do you have cream soda?" At the man's horrified look Tristano said, "Bring the lady a cola and I'll have a Heineken," he sat down, dismissing the man.

The maître d' sniffed in lofty arrogance at being treated as a server.

"No, but Tristano," Jesa objected, setting the menu down. "Mr. Westcott isn't here. We can go to a- a cheaper place or better yet, back to the station to eat." She made to push her chair back.

Tristano clasped her wrist, holding her. He gave her a cheerful smile. "Nah, I saw a plate of blackened salmon go by that looked plump and crispy. Here, see what you want," and he picked up her menu, opened it and handed it to her.

She opened her mouth, he said, "Jesselin, every time you give me shit about money or argue about my feeding you, I'm going to keep track and add to your…punishment." He wiggled his brows at her with a crooked grin, then laughed out loud at her heavy swallow and alarmed wide eyes.

He turned to address the waiter who stood at the table that announced, "I am Kirk and I will be taking care of you today." He smiled politely. "Your drinks are being prepared, do you know what you would like to order?"

Their food was brought to them surprisingly quickly. While Tristano cut his flaky salmon, Jesa chewed on a morsel of penne fragiole. "Where are you from, Jesselin?" he asked casually, washing the salmon down with a slug of beer.

Jesa's hand froze with another piece of pasta on the tines of her fork. She slid the bite into her mouth, swallowed it without chewing. "I, uh, have been all over, you know? Never stayed in one place too long, what about you? It's faint, but I hear the south in your accent and you come out with some southern sayings that I don't think you are even aware of."

He scooped up rice, said flatly, "Georgia," and covertly watched her expression. Her features grew taut and eyes flung big. And scared. "Ever been there?" He stuffed a pile of saffron rice in his mouth and observed her rising panic.

She shook her head turbulently, her voice cracked, "N- no, never." Dropping her fork, she grabbed her soda and chugged, her eyes dashed everywhere but at Tristano, color vacuumed from her cheeks leaving her face pale as lambskin.

Tristano calmly studied her while he ate. She was gobbling, swallowing half without chewing, or tasting. "Jesselin," his voice steady, low, he told her, "we need to talk, baby."

She kept shoveling in her food, croaked out around the pasta in her mouth. "There's nothing to talk about."

"Jesselin-"

"No." Tears gathered making her eyes shiny, she turned her head from him as she painfully swallowed chunks of food.

"Jesselin, just listen to me, please-"

She dropped her fork and put her hands against the table to push her chair back. "I- I have to go, I'll wait in the car, no, I can catch the trolley. It goes up a portion of the mountain."

Her panic was twisting his gut, he caught her hand, held her from leaving. "It doesn't go anywhere near the mountain, come on now, calm down, you don't need to be so afraid." Now he worried that he'd spooked her and she'd go try to find some way off the island, and kill her damned self trying.

"Tristano, leave it alone, please." She tugged at her hand.

His jaw softened at her distress. "Okay, Bitty bit, for now, I'll let it go. Just…sit, chill." He sighed. She was probably scared to death he would arrest her, and at this point, he couldn't relieve her of that fear. There was too much he didn't know. But once he had the facts, then he could jump on it.

Her chest heaved and hitched with her fright, she pulled so hard to get free of him he was worried she'd hurt herself. He said softly, "Tell me what your thoughts on the blackmail notes are."

At the blatant change of subject, Jesa looked warily at him. He had a slight smile, the normal hardness was not present in his dark eyes, he let go of her hand, patted it gently then sat back to appear less threatening. She still clutched then end of the table, but the panicked flight eased from her clenched jaw. Her long curry lashes fluttered as she calmed. She didn't look around to see if she'd attracted attention at her outburst.

"I, uh, don't really have a clue about the- the letters. Do you think maybe bringing Mr. Westcott into the station and seriously questioning him will get him to spill?" She twiddled with her fork but didn't pick it back up.

Tristano plucked a warm roll from the bread basket and set it on her bread plate and took one for himself. He cut some butter and added pats to both their plates. When she just silently watched him without moving, he picked up her roll, slathered it with butter and pushed it into her hand. She stared down at it, swallowed the rest of her nerves and took a small bite. He smiled when she settled back in her chair and finished her lunch.

He kept the conversation light after that, told her a few war stories of when he was in the military. But he only told her the adventurous or funny things that happened, he had buried the shit, the bad, wretchedly bad things to himself. Like his last sniper mission that had ended everything. His friend, his comrades, his career, his pride, and his soul.

He'd had to construct a thick wall around his heart, his feelings, he'd never let anyone in since. His feelings were dead, murdered, destroyed, along with that kid. He made no new friends, no serious relationships. He had sex, of course, but that's all it was, sex. And that was only because women dropped on him, he couldn't be bothered to make the effort to hit on them. He didn't give a shit about anyone or anything except his job, until…

"Jesselin, tonight why don't we-"

"Oh?" She blinked those big greens up at him. "Are we working? I have a date with Ronan, but I can cancel it of course, who are we going to go talk to?"

The prospect of doing more interviews seemed to enliven her. Tristano had to struggle to smother the scowl her words brought him. "Uh, no, I was just going to tell you there's nothing going on tonight, that you can unwind. Enjoy a night off." With fucking Roarke. Shit. He finished his beer asked if she wanted dessert, at her decline he motioned for the check.

They went back to the station to meet with McKabe then Tristano drove Jesa to her cottage. He helped her out of the rusted car and huddled her out and to her door. The wind had built up to ferocious gale gusts, the snow was shooting wildly, blinding them if they stood still for a second. Jesa put her key in the lock, Tristano hovered at her back, a bulwark against the rough elements.

"Jesselin," he said, as she turned the key.

He reached around her and pushed the door open. "Promise me you'll be careful. Don't let anyone inside, including Roarke. Don't leave the house until Roarke comes and then meet him on this step."

Her brows linked, confused. "Tristano, Ronan and I are friends, he would never hurt me. I told you, he got a little excited that night, he backed off when I said to."

His voice ugly, he snapped, "Friends don't kiss you with their tongues shoved down your throat, forcefully hold you down, tear your blouse and suck ugly painful hickies on your tits, unless you want it, Bitty bit."

"Tristano-"

He set a palm on the doorframe over her head. A sigh roughed out, he said, "Just promise me that you'll be careful and keep your phone on you at all times, bab- ah Jesselin, okay?"

She slipped past him with a quick, "All right." Standing in the doorway, she said, "I don't understand why you worry about me. I'm nobody. I'm just a nobody." Her attempt at a smile failed, it curved down despondently.

He cupped her face with both hands, held her gently and connected their eyes. "Ah, Bitty bit, I hate when you do that. You are as important as anyone else on God's green earth. Give me some time, and some trust and I'll prove it to you. For now," he stroked her skin with his thumbs, "just be careful. Do me a favor and call me when you get home. Even if," his face stiffened, "Roarke is…with you." It's not like he had the right to tell her whom she could date, or screw. She was, as she was always telling him, an adult; she was allowed to make her own decisions, even if they sucked. For him.

"Tristano." The smile swerved up at his foolishness.

"Just do it. If I don't hear from you by, say, midnight, I'll be by. Got it?"

She laughed self-consciously, puzzled at his caring about her wellbeing. "Okay, if you really want me to. Now, you should go before you turn into the abominable snowman."

Still cradling her face, he leaned in and covered her mouth with his. Her lips didn't move until he pressed at them, when they responded he slanted his head and seduced them apart. Once he had access, he sent his exploring tongue in and was instantly dazzled at the sensation of sweet Jesselin.

His body hardened in a split second and he escalated his sensual exploration of her exquisite gifts, imbibing her unique flavor. A harsh groan rattled from deep in his chest, damn, beyond heavenly, she was tasty as hell. Purity, all soft honey, tender and savory, fresh and hot as sin on a stick, and a suspected murderess.

Tristano realized his brain was quickly shorting out, it didn't care what she might be, his loins sure as hell didn't give a fuck. And she wasn't rigid, or fighting him. To his delight and doming arousal, those plush lips clearly inexperienced were giving back heat and breathy interest.

As he leaned into her, her back arched and she was pushed up onto her toes, her little fingers clutched at his big arms.

When his tongue sought hers to suck and stroke and lust, her tiny tongue tried to follow his movements and duplicate them. "Ahh," he moaned into her mouth, one hand cupped her head, the other moved to her back to pull her closer, haul her petite curves as hard as he could get them against him, fighting the bulk of their coats. His throat captured her panted whimper, using the weight of his body he pushed her against the doorframe and dug deeper, shot fire into the kiss.

Her hands moved to his chest, and she pushed at him, not hard, not in a panic, but he felt her stiffen, she broke the kiss, turned her head. Her chest rose and fell rapidly from both the heady kiss and her burgeoning nerves. "Tristano, please," she whispered.

Now he knew how Roarke had felt. Her hot little body in his hands, he had an erection that could knock down a building, her fresh taste, damn, the kiss had blown him away and he wanted more. More of her mouth, more of her taste, he wanted her clothes off immediately, the urge to rip them away struck him like a fevered arrow. Shit.

Before he kicked her legs out from under her and dropped her to the floor and fell on top of her, shoved her thighs apart, he forced himself to open his clenched hands, sucked in a heavy breath, and stepped back from her.

Jesa's head was down, her cheeks pink and glowing, face red roughened in places from his evening scruff. She peeked up at him through messy, wind-tossed strawberry curls; those huge luminous eyes shimmered with arousal, fear, and innocence. Hell.

"Listen, Jesselin," he paused, took a breath, palmed his hair off his forehead, lifted his hand to touch her again, and dropped it. "Listen, call Roarke, cancel your date. When I was pursuing the loan shark before I found him at the pool hall I traced him to this tiny, quaint restaurant, all candles and smoky duskiness, blues band, dance floor. Let me take you there and we-"

She stepped back with a soft shake of her head and a befuddled expression. He could see she was confused with her feelings, the sensations he'd triggered that went roaring through her newly awakened feminine body, zinging it alive with blazing heat that scorched parts of her she had kept shut down, blocked off.

He reckoned that always hiding and on the run, Jesa could never let herself become interested in a man long enough, let him get close enough, for her body to experience the natural sensuality that Tristano had awakened. The thought of him being the one to rouse her, to cherish her, and her body the way she should be, thrilled the hell out of him. Unless she fell under Roarke's spell, and it was to him she gave her innocence to. Fuck, he spat the idea out of his head; it made his gut pinch and twist.

There was the fact that the young deputy was a much better man for Jesa than him. Roarke, other than that brief assault on her, was gentle, a gentleman, a nicer guy with softer edges. Not the ruthless, brutal, hard-hearted cynical agent with jagged edges that Tristano was. Tristano had seen war, blood, vicious, deadly violence and torture, it certainly molded a man.

Yeah, he was too old, too hard, too cold, too rough for the beautiful, dainty, sweet, likely virgin. That should stop him in his tracks. Not even counting that he was an FBI agent sent to arrest and return her to Georgia to face murder charges.

He could tell himself all day long that he was wrong for her, no good for her, but, it made no difference. His body took over, and for the first time in his life it did what the hell it wanted, and it wanted that soft little bundle of delicate purity. It wanted her in his bed, those strawberry curls on his pillow, and by his side, where he could breathe in her freshness, feast his eyes on her gentle beauty, and protect her from the shit dangers of the world that she was so woefully ignorant of.

Roarke may be the better man for her, but Tristano had an uneasy feeling about him. He was unable to determine if that was a real gut instinct, or he just didn't want the deputy anywhere near Jesselin.

She turned from him; now he did reach out, catch her arm to hold her from leaving. It was so wrong, and he had no right but he still blurted, "Cancel it, Jesselin. Come with me-"

"No," she said firmly with a polite smile pinned awkwardly to her very confused face. "It wouldn't be right, I told him I would go."

He squeezed her arm. "So what. Break it, call him. You gonna tell me you'd rather go out with him tonight than me? And I'm not talking a business date." One black brow rose, not in narcissism but in seeking her honesty, with him and herself. There was no denying the vibrant spark that ignited between them. They both felt it. He'd kissed her twice now, and he knew when a woman was turned on with him. That curvy little body had oozed heat all over him, her lips wet and open and accepting. He pushed aside pictures of what else he wanted to do with her mouth.

His stomach unclenched when she looked away from him and gently shook her head. Relief flooded his heated brain. "Good, okay, so call him-"

Jesa pulled her arm from his clutch, said again, "No, Tristano. It doesn't matter. I said I would go; I don't go back on my word. Please, understand that." The big green eyes pleaded with him to not be hurt, angry, even though she clearly still couldn't comprehend that he would be interested in her.

"Jesselin-" he wanted to argue with her, but, her integrity was one of the things he appreciated about her. His shoulders twitched as he gave in. "Okay, I hate it but you're right. Just, promise me you won't let him inside, and if anything happens, anyone knocks on your door, hangs up when you answer your cell, that you won't hesitate a second and you'll call me. Okay?"

He couldn't believe this stunning young woman had wormed her way into his brain, under his skin, in his...no, he wasn't going back there. But, for the first time in a very long time he cared about someone else other than himself. And he didn't really think much of himself.

Her smile grew. "All right. But, please don't worry, I'll be fine. Ronan is a gentleman, he won't harm me. He apologized for his actions that night, said he wouldn't pounce on me again, that he'd slow down, let us get to know one another."

"Ah," Tristano's teeth ground, "that's not what I really want to hear."

Jesa grinned. "As friends, Tristano, just as friends." She brushed snowflakes off his shoulder; the wind just blew more back on, and spiked his black hair.

"Uh huh," he murmured, moved in closer to her again, his lids lowered heavily over the glittering black pupils. He had zero business getting involved with her but he couldn't stop his mouth. "And what about us? Are we just...friends? Only colleagues? Or, are we...more, Jesselin?" He lifted a long curl off her shoulder, let it slip through his fingers. "I'd like us to be more. Can we be...more?"

The confusion flooded back into her eyes, she moved away from him, her hand on the door to close it. "I...I don't know, Tristano. There's so much, you're an FBI agent and I'm a..." what could she say? She shut her eyes, then opened them, her head tilted up to him.

"I don't understand, what are you asking me? Why would you be interested in…me? I mean, Tahni-"

He grabbed her upper arms hauling her to him, snapped fiercely, "Stop with her, I don't give two fucks about her, or any other woman. This is about us, you and me. I want you to give us a chance." Tristano was surprised by his own words. He hadn't dated since high school, hadn't had the inclination to hang around any longer than the time it took to get off with a female. In the service then the FBI, there wasn't much time for relationships.

After the shit that went down in Iraq, hell, a shudder ran through him, last thing he wanted or felt like, was getting close with someone. But Jesselin, he couldn't imagine not being with her, never seeing her again, let some other man have her. What if the guy hurt her? No, he couldn't bear it, he needed to have her, protect her.

He was older, more experienced, he could bring her around. Might take time, deliberate seduction, a lot of patience, but she was worth it. He'd only known her a short time but already he couldn't imagine even one day of not seeing her. How he'd reconcile the terrible conflict of his job and whatever was true about her actions he had no idea. He just knew he couldn't let her go.

Her body shivered in his grasp. "A- a chance? A chance at what?"

Squeezing her arms over the puffy jacket, a growl rumbled in his chest, but a lopsided smile smeared away his natural toughness. "Damn, woman, I forget how innocent, how naïve you are."

He drew her closer, lowered his head, his lips hovered over hers, their breaths mingled. "A chance at us. In a relationship. Can you give us a shot at that?" Mentally he pushed aside the murder charge, they'd deal with it, he'd deal with it. Every second more he spent with her he knew the fragile young woman with the big heart did not kill a man, and he'd prove it.

Her eyes widened incredulous. "You mean, like- like boyfriend girlfriend?"

He laughed into her mouth as he captured a kiss, long, slow, teasingly mind-boggling. With his lips and tongue, nibbling, sucking at her mouth, he murmured, "Yeah, something like that. You and me, exclusive." He bussed her lips, leaned back, smiled down at her. "I could never share you with another man, Jesselin." His skin darkened at the thought of her in another male's arms. "Never."

Shock overrode the confusion. Saffron lashes lowered over her eyes hiding them from him, hiding her thoughts. She gently pushed at him and he reluctantly released her.

"Jesselin?" he questioned softly. "Tell me, tell me what you're thinking."

She was quiet, the wind wound and slapped and whaled at them with occasional gusting shrieks. "I…don't know. I…no, we can't," she moved deeper into the house. "I, there are…issues, Tristano, big issues. Insurmountable." Sadness crept over, shading her loveliness.

He set a hand on the doorframe as the wind howled at his back, blew his hair forward. "Okay, Bitty bit. We'll let it go again for now. For tonight, just, have fun, relax," his mouth flattened into a frown, "but not too much. We'll talk tomorrow."

Her face closed off and he said firmly, "Yeah, we're talking tomorrow. You're going to tell me everything, and you're going to trust me to take care of things, take care of you. I won't let anything happen to you. So, for tonight, you aren't mine, but tomorrow," he bent, kissed her gently, then he gripped the back of her head, slanted his head for a tighter fit and the burning kiss raged hard and hungry.

Rapidly on his way to devouring her, he caught his breath, dropped his hand and took several steps back, smiled. The green in her dazed eyes glimmered, her breath raced, she lifted the back of her hand and pressed it against her trembling mouth.

Tristano said, "Think about what I said, baby. Be careful tonight, tomorrow we talk. About everything. Your troubles, and about you and me. Okay?"

Her smile was watery, shaky, but she nodded in shy acquiescence. At that, he grinned and said, "Lock it," and closed the door.

Chapter Twenty-Nine

Jesa stood by the window, the parted drape held aside by her hand as she watched him back down the driveway then disappear into the swirling grey snow-globe. For the first time since she could ever remember, she felt faint optimism, hope. And excitement, the thought of having more with Tristano bubbled through her, nestled in her heart, and she had to admit, heated every atom of her lady parts.

When he had asked her to cancel her date with Ronan, the aching desire to do that, and go out with Tristano instead bit at her, hard. A big bite. She had to swallow the bite. She wanted to do it, so badly she couldn't believe the strength of passionate hunger the harsh agent wrought in her. She wanted dearly to cancel Ronan and enjoy an evening of dancing in the misty lowlights to the steamy blues in Tristano's powerful arms.

But, she sighed, she'd agreed to Ronan's date and it would have been wrong to cancel. Besides, Ronan had said that he only wanted to develop their friendship. That's all she wanted with him. As gorgeous and hunky and sweet as the deputy was, Ronan didn't make her body burn and boil and tremble like Tristano did. Just a hooded look from the agent's dark dangerous eyes made her body tingle with want, desire, lust, and all sorts of other feelings she was not familiar with.

She'd do as Tristano said, go out, have a good time with Ronan, then tomorrow…her chest tightened. Tristano wanted her to bare her secrets to him. He said he would, could help her. But, she stared blankly out at the dark, twinkling foggy storm, would he still say that when she told him the truth? Would he believe her, help her…or would he arrest her? And forget her.

Jesa set her bag on the small kitchen table. She freshened up, changed her clothes into her best slacks and frilly green blouse that matched her eyes and nicely foiled her curry colored hair.

She could hear Ronan's rumbling engine coming down the street, she grabbed her jacket to do as Tristano had asked, meet Ronan on the porch, not let him inside. She certainly didn't want the messy uncomfortable situation of refusing his advances if he pursued them.

She headed to the door, then stopped. Swiveling on her heel she hurried back to the table, took her phone out of her backpack and slid it into her pocket. There was no reason for her to need it, but, a tremble rolled up her spine, if Tristano found out she didn't have it in her pocket, well, a naughty grin lifted the edges of her mouth, he'd surely punish her.

As she hurried to the door, a warm tingle spiraled through her and she realized she wasn't afraid of his…punishment, no, it kinda made her hot. The agent thrusting her over his muscled thighs, his big hard hand pressing on her back to hold her immobile, his other hand-

Slam. Ronan had exited the car and was making his way to her door. *Oh no*, she rushed to the door, flung it open and stepped outside. She closed the door and locked it just as he reached the porch.

Snow sprinkled his head and shoulders, the wind whipped his blond hair, his boyish grin was cheeky and impish, it made her smile back at him. Yes, he was a nice guy and they'd have a nice, friendly evening. Was that a licentious spark that flashed in his blue eyes as they roamed over her head to toe and back? Her stomach grew unsettled. It was gone in a heartbeat as he held his hand out to her.

"Hey, sugar, I thought about seeing you tonight all damned day. You sure are a treat for sore eyes." His gaze went to her hair swirling around in the wind. "You need your hat, let's go inside and get it," he started up the steps.

"No, I'm good." Jesa hurried down the porch and hastened past him to the cruiser.

Shaking his head in amusement, Ronan went after her, got to the cruiser first and opened the passenger door. When they were both tucked inside out of the elements, he headed to the main road.

"So, Jesa," he said, grinning at her, reached over and patted her knee, he kept his hand there. "You ready for a fun night?"

Her eyes on his hand, she stiffened under it, but said with forced cheerfulness, "Uh, yeah, sure, of course. Where are we going?" She didn't want to hurt his feelings and make him move his hand. It made her uncomfortable but it only seemed to be a just friendly gesture, she tried to relax her leg.

One hand on the wheel, he turned down the longer twisty road that led down the mountain, and squeezed her knee. The car whipped to the side with the help of the blasting wind, Ronan gripped the wheel to keep control and stay on the road, at the same time his hand slipped up her thigh.

"Um, Ronan, it's pretty blustery out here, I think you need to have both hands on the wheel." She grasped his wrist and tried to lift his hand off her.

He gave her thigh a slow, firmer squeeze, said cheerfully, "I'm good, sugar. I have strong hands, see?" He gripped her harder and threw a quick grin at her before facing the windshield.

Jesa tugged harder. "Yes, I know you're quite competent and strong, Ronan, but it's making me really nervous, in fact," she flinched as a branch hurled with a bang into the side of the car. The storm made the road pitch black, only the car's headlights gave any illumination and the wind jerked and tossed them so much she was getting dizzy watching the beams lurch and hop over the blacktop.

She had to speak louder to be heard over the wailing wind, "I think this storm is getting worse, I think I should go back home. We should just call it a night."

Ronan's lower lip pushed out in a pout. "Awe come on, Jesa. It's taken me forever to talk you into going out with me. Don't shut me down now, honey. It'll be okay, you're safe with me, I promise."

She was staring anxiously out the window watching the storm pound the cruiser, his hand on her thigh forgotten in her apprehension. The trees along the dark road were bent over from the fierce wind, their branches whipped, howled, leaves thrashed around the car, visibility was like being in a dark spinning tornado.

He patted her leg, then clasped it again, he kept the cruiser on the road but just barely. "So, Jesa, there's this club down by the wharf. They have great bands playing all the time and the food is superb. I thought we could have a few drinks, work up our appetites with some dancing and then pig out. Sound good to you?"

She turned and looked out her side window. Tristano had wanted to take her dancing. Would he consider her…cheating on him if she danced with Ronan? Regardless, she really had no desire to dance with the handsome deputy. There was only one man's arms she wanted around her, and it wasn't the man sitting next to her.

While trying to figure out what to say, she watched the evening pass, the forest blacked out from the dark clouds hanging heavy and low, and the gale force wind and thick blowing snow. Thick gelatinous fog clotted the view in front of the rocking car.

Ronan veered the cruiser off to a secondary road barely visible in the riotous storm. It wasn't the way to the wharf. "You turned off the road to the wrong way, Ronan, this isn't the road that goes to the docks. You need to turn around."

"No worries, sugar." He squeezed her thigh and shifted his hand a hair higher. "I forgot my wallet, we need to stop at my place and get it. No big deal."

Apprehension tightened her throat, her head swung towards him, he looked calm and confident, his big hand spanning the wheel. He glanced at her, grinned. "I just need to grab my wallet and we'll be at the club having a good time after."

Jesa stared at his profile. He'd been driving around all day without his wallet? Without his license? What did he mean by 'after?' She was unnervingly aware her protests would fall on deaf ears.

Tristano had almost reached his hotel. The howling wind slammed at the car, the sky darkened to rough black ink, the storm had worsened into a violent blizzard. His heart clenched at the thought of Jesa driving around with that idiot in this tempest. He pulled over and took out his phone. He dialed her number. He was going to order her to stay at home, or go back if she was already on the road.

If she balked, he'd call Roarke and give him a direct order to take her back. He would threaten him with going to McKabe if he didn't comply. His heart clamped harder at the thought of Roarke alone with Jesa in her home. Sure, compared to Tristano he thought of Roarke as softer, but, he had attacked her. Fuck. Her phone rang, it went to voice mail.

He barked into his phone, "Jesselin, I am ordering you to stay home if you haven't left, if you're already out, you're to turn right around and go back. I mean this, you don't follow my instruction and not only will I blister your hide I'll toss Roarke to McKabe's wrath. You hear me? You call me right back."

He didn't wait for her to call back; he turned around and headed back up to her cottage. No way could he sit home and be calm knowing she was out in this storm, or in her cottage and trapped with the deputy. He didn't trust the bastard. Jesa was so innocent of men, their desires, the way they looked at her with their mouths watering and dicks hardening. She thought the blond deputy was all nice and harmless. Bullshit.

The image of her that night he saw her blouse torn, ugly hickey on her breast, her hands were shaking, she was obviously distraught. Roarke had forced himself on her, and next time he wasn't going to stop, Tristano could feel it in his bones.

He figured Roarke had backed off that night only because he thought Tristano might come by. As it turned out, it was true. But, tonight, she was completely at Roarke's mercy. He would force her, and she probably wouldn't tell anyone, wouldn't make a complaint, she was so afraid of her past being revealed she wouldn't want any kind of an investigation into her.

If she did cry rape, Roarke would claim a he said-she said, and if he was careful to keep the bruising and other shit at a minimum, he might be believed. McKabe wouldn't believe him, but without evidence he might not have a choice in what to do about it. Tristano pressed his foot on the gas pedal all the way to the floor and fishtailed savagely up the mountain.

Jesa's phone rang; she started to slide her hand into her pocket to get it.

"Aw, come on, sugar, please give me the respect of not having your phone glued to your ear. It's selfish and inconsiderate." Ronan cocked his head at her with a crestfallen boyish smile.

She pulled her hand out, he was right, it was rude. Yet, if it was Tristano and she didn't respond to his call, well, she knew what he'd do, he would be angry with her. She'd check the phone when they got to the club.

Ronan parked in front of a structure, more a house than a cottage. It was too dark to clearly make out the color or size of it. He hopped out of the car and ran around to Jesa's side and opened her door, a rush of wind and thick flakes blustered in. "Come on, I'll just be a minute but I don't want to leave you out here in this squall." He held his hand out to her to take.

Jesa cringed from him. Gripping her seatbelt with one hand, the other on the dashboard, she nudged her butt in the seat a few inches away from him. "No, I'll be fine. Go ahead, I'll wait here."

"Don't be ridiculous." He scowled at her refusing his request. "Come on now, there's nothing to be afraid of. Come inside with me, I'll be quick-"

"It'll take you half a second to grab your wallet," she insisted, squirming from his reach.

His face darkened, jaw worked, he growled, "I need to take a piss, too. Now, stop being difficult and get out."

The big man loomed large and angry over her, the pleasant boyish charm gone. There was nowhere for her to go. If she stayed in the truck, he had the keys, she'd freeze, and he would probably drag her out anyway with his brute force. If she made a run for it, she surveyed the land around his house.

The building was so far from any neighbors there wasn't another house visible, the wind was so slicing it hurt, the sleeting snow stung her eyes. It was twilight dark from the thunderous black clouds, and it was cold. Really cold. Already shivering, she rubbed her arms.

He was right. She was being silly, he wasn't going to hurt her. He'd backed off right away before, well almost, each time he'd tried to kiss her, and that night at her house. Yeah, she was being over the wall, no reason to be scared of him.

Chapter Thirty

Jesa unbuckled her belt, let him grasp her hand and help her out. Ronan quickly shut the door, tossed his arm around her and hustled her to the house. In moments they were inside, dry and warm. He went right to the thermostat and pushed it up higher.

She remonstrated him, "Oh, Ronan, don't waste the electric, we'll be going right back out." She stayed by the door. Her eyes widened when he took his jacket off and tossed it on a chair, set his hands on his jean clad hips and regarded her with humor. The thought was capricious of course, but he looked at her every bit the vicious wolf he'd accused Tristano of being.

That reminded her, her phone. She pulled it out, said, "You go ahead and use the bathroom, Ronan and I'll check my messages," she lowered her head to the cell.

He moved so fast she never saw him coming, he slapped the phone out of her hand, it went flying, slamming into the wall, it shattered. Her mouth popped open in shock, he'd hit her hand so hard it hurt. Her head fell back, she staggered backwards and looked up at him dumbfounded.

His voice low, with an unusual darkness, he said calmly, "I told you, no phone. I want every molecule of your attention focused on me." His smile cold, he combed his fair hair back with both hands, he said, "Now, take off your jacket, have a seat on the couch," he gestured to the large sofa in front of the brick fireplace. "Let's get comfortable. I have a nice bottle of Patrón for us."

Ignoring her stunned expression, he trod to a bar at one side of the room and grabbed up the bottle of tequila and two rock glasses. He

266

went to the couch, bent and set the bottle and glasses on the mahogany coffee table. The room was rather stark with just a few pieces of heavy dark furniture, a large flat-screen but there were no pictures decorating the walls or personal photos on the tables.

Straightening, he rolled up one blue flannel sleeve then the other to his elbows. A half smile curving his handsome face, he said with a little more friendliness, "Why are so resistant to my charms, Jesa? I know you find me attractive, and there's no question," he took a few steps towards her, lids lowered over fervor-heated blue eyes.

"I find you hot as shit, sugar. Now, c'mere." He held his hand out to her. "You know we'll be good together. I can tell you aren't very experienced with men." He shrugged, his smile curdled with a carnal kink, eyes sharpened wickedly. "I am more than happy to be the one that pops that ripe little cherry, initiate you into real womanhood. It'll be good, great, sugar, you'll see."

Jesa inched backwards to the door, her hand on the doorknob; she strained to keep the tremor of fear out of her voice. "No ah, really, Ronan, just get your wallet and let's go." Her frightened eyes beseeched him to be the decent man she thought he was.

Instead, a devilish grin puckered his gorgeous face, drawing sharp wantonness over it. He slowly shook his head, patted his back jean's pocket. His wallet bulged in it. "Damn, girl, you really are naïve like Koffi always says. Hell, you can't tell when a guy's hitting on you? When he's made plans for the evening? Not the 'let's go out and dance plans,' no," he grinned with cold humor, "the plans were for us to dance here. On my bed, or that couch," he nodded to the brown and green sofa. "Or the floor, kitchen table, anywhere, I'm easy.

"It would have been easier to stay at your place, but, speaking of Koffi, the asshole would undoubtedly drop by and ruin our evening. The fucker has it bad for you too. He thinks that icy hard face and enigmatic dark eyes cloak his interest in you, but everyone jokes about it." He sniggered. "Yeah, the harsh brutal agent and the shy sweet little girl, you guys should be in a Lifetime chick-flick movie. But you're mine, sugar, and he ain't here, so," he motioned to the couch with his head. "Let's do the horizontal dance and then we'll hit the club then come back for round two."

Trying to hide the panic in her voice she said cheerfully, "Ronan, please, wait, slow down, can't we talk, get to know each other, like you said, friends." She firmed her hand over the doorknob behind her back.

His snort jolted out, grin went broader with disbelief. "Seriously, Jesa, you think I really meant it when I said I just wanted to be friends with you? With that smokin' hot body, shit," he moved closer, eyes gleaming in avarice.

"Honey," he reveled, "your body was made for sin, for sex, for me. Now, don't make me come and get you, just get that fine little ass over here on the couch, we can start there before hitting the bedroom," his voice deepened, tone darkening when she struggled with the door behind her and didn't do as he commanded.

She held a hand up to ward him off. "Wait, Ronan, you- you know I'm…green, I'm nervous. Why don't we have those drinks you talked about and relax a bit first, okay?" Her voice was as calm and seductive as she could make it. "Why don't you go ahead and pour us some drinks? It'll help me loosen up a little, you know?"

His hard glare pinned her as he studied her for trickery. His ego told him she wanted him, she was just playing hard to get. "All right, you get that jacket off and I'll pour the tequila." When her fingers went to the zipper on her jacket, he smiled and turned slightly to pick up the bottle. Jesa spun around, gripped the doorknob and twisted, jerked the door open and started to run out- but he grabbed a fistful of her hair and yanked her back inside.

Slamming the door, he twisted her hair in his fist, cruelly forcing her head back, her face up, snarled furiously, "Goddammit, Jesa, you're not going anywhere until I'm done with you. And I don't plan on that being until the dawn fucking breaks. Now," he released her hair and shoved her at the wall.

The breath knocked out of her she couldn't stop him from unzipping her jacket and wrenching it off her. It fell heedless to the floor and he grabbed her by the hair again. Winding locks around his fist, he dragged her to the sofa and shoved her. She stumbled backwards, her legs hit the couch and she fell on it. He strode back to the door, jammed his key in it, locked it and shoved the keys in his jeans.

Scrambling to get back to her feet, Jesa cried, "Wait, please Ronan, don't do this. You're a nice guy, you can't-"

His head fell back with a short bark of laughter. His fingers went to the first closed button at the top of his shirt, and he unbuttoned it. "You're the first bitch to call me nice, Jesa. You fell for the soft blond hair and pretty blue eyes, the strong, brave deputy bullshit, damn girl," he huffed out another smug laugh.

"Yeah, you're green, but you won't be after tonight. Take off your blouse." He unbuttoned a second button and moved in closer to the sofa, Jesa wriggled across the cushions to hop off the other end.

"Uh, uh," he admonished her, "there's nowhere for you to run, honey, except to my bedroom. Don't make me tell you again unless you want me to destroy it when I rip it off you," he sneered, "and you know I have no problem tearing your clothes. Now, take off the blouse." He shifted to block her way off the sofa.

Jesa struggled to her knees on the cushions, her hands up, palms out she pleaded, "Please Ronan, don't do this- I- I'll tell Chief McKabe, Agent Koffi, I'll-"

"You won't say shit, sugar. I ran your papers, you didn't exist beyond the last six months." His mouth curved sardonically at her stunned expression. "Whether it's an abusive boyfriend, or the law you're hiding from, I'm leaning towards you're wanted for some serious crime."

The pure anguish splintering her face, her body shriveling in as if to disappear, told him he was on the right track. Jesa's chest rose and fell with panicking breaths, her pulse raced, beat at her neck. "No, Ronan, you can't-"

The side of his grin hiked up. "Babe, I don't give a shit what you're hiding, what I do know is you don't want it exposed, if you blab about this, that secret is sure to come out. I'm gonna use that fear to my advantage, in that I can take advantage of you because you're ensnared by your past. It's my good fortune that you're helpless to stop me."

Her entire body trembled, she bit her lip, wrapped her arms around herself but she couldn't stop the shaking. "L- listen, Ronan, you're a good guy, a policeman, I don't believe you would-"

"Jesa, think about it. You're going to want me on your side. If I know you're hiding something and you aren't really Jesselin Judan, then

Koffi and McKabe a hundred percent know it too. Why they haven't done anything about it yet," he shrugged a shoulder, "who the hell knows. Koffi has an agenda, no doubt. He didn't come here to help look for that missing baby. No," he shook his head with a smile, "he's here for something else. You need me to help you, Jesa," he lurched at her.

With a scream, she jumped up and scrambled to climb off the back of the couch. He snagged her ankle and jerked her hard enough she flew off her feet and fell on her back with a snap, breath expelled harshly from her lungs.

Laughing, Ronan tossed a leg over her, straddling her, he sat on her legs so she was imprisoned. Leaning back, he snickered at her accelerating hysteria, unbuttoned another button then reached over his back and pulled the shirt over his head and dropped it on the floor. "I wanted to make your first time, nice, gentle, take our time, but you're pissing me off and I'm afraid," he reached for the front of her blouse, said with a smiling snarl, "our first time is gonna be rough and fast. You piss me off even more and honey, I can be quite violent. Just ask that bitch model, Chantal."

Her eyes bugged out. "You- you slept with her?"

He barked out a sarcastic laugh. "Duh, hon. All three were throwing themselves under anything with a dick. Who would I be to turn down freely offered pussy? Sierra was actually the best of the bunch. Girl had some moves, she was up for absolutely anything no matter how kinky, or," he winked at her, "painful. Bitch liked pain. I can teach you to like it too, sugar."

Wincing at his mounting dirty vocabulary, she asked, "What about Agent Koffi? Did he sleep with them all too?"

"Huh," he snorted, "fuck no. The man's too picky, too good for down and dirty sex with immoral sluts that do drugs and have slept with half the town. Besides," he forked his fingers through the hair that was hanging over his eyes. "That prick is too besotted with you to give any other bitch the time of day."

At her look of surprise, he chuckled, "Really, sugar? You're the only one that didn't see his moon eyes on you every time you're in his vicinity. You couldn't tell by the way he kept you with him wherever he went except when he decided it would be too dangerous for you?

"You think he couldn't have gotten another vehicle to use by now? Nah, he wanted to keep you dependent on him, and safe under his muscle-bound wing. He about lost his mind with rage when you trotted around the mountain in the dark by yourself. Yeah," he grunted, bent and fisted the front of her blouse.

"You were the only clueless one that couldn't see he was smitten the second he laid eyes on you. Well, screw him, sugar, he lost out. I tried to get you to be with me willingly, but you kept shutting me down. Now, you have no choice. You're mine, for tonight, and any other time I tell you. You will not go out with Koffi, or spread your legs for him, only for me. You won't balk when I call you and tell you to strip, get on your back with those pretty legs wide open, waiting for me to get there."

His eyes narrowed in menace at her he threatened, "Don't even try and tell him about this, he'll never see me coming at him. I'll take him right out, sweetheart; I won't give him the chance to get to me first. So, if you don't want to see loverboy agent dead as a doornail with a bullet hole between his black eyes, you'll keep your trap shut, and do as I say. Now, you're gonna take off your damned clothes and open those legs." He wrenched at her blouse and the top buttons flew off- she screamed and hit at him.

Bending over her, he wrapped his hand around her throat and squeezed until she was gasping for air and her eyes bulged. Unable to scream she clawed at his hands but he squeezed harder. "Stop fighting me, you're only gonna get hurt worse. Submit and it'll be better for you. Spread those beautiful legs for me, sugar, let me in."

He grasped the edges of her blouse to tear it off her. The material rent, with a shriek, Jesa slammed her knee up as hard as she could into his groin.

The air caught in his throat, he froze, his mouth open in a silent scream. He folded in half, clutched his manhood, and rolled off the couch to crash to the floor. His gagging and choking filled the room.

Jesa paused, she hated harming anyone, ever, but she only had this one chance, she leaped off the couch and bolted down the hall. He'd locked the front door, she needed to find another exit. She ran into the first room she got to, raced into the darkness and slammed the door

271

shut. Frantically searching for the lock, she pushed it in and secured the door.

Huffing with panic, she felt all over the wall until she found a light switch and flipped it on. A desk and an easy chair, a couple of old tables and a bookcase packed the room. It must be his study. There was a window, she could get out. She ran over to it, struggled to turn the lock on it and tried to shove it up so she could climb out. Just like everything else on the island, like her darn car, she couldn't budge it. She hadn't the strength, it was probably painted closed.

She needed something to break it. Hurrying to the desk, maybe there was a stapler or something she could throw at the glass. Pushing things around, she shoved papers off the desk so she could see more, when, something caught her eye. Something weirdly familiar.

Her forehead furrowing in prickling recognition, she picked up one of the papers. It was identical to the blackmail notes at the Westcotts'. *It couldn't be*, she swallowed, shaking her head. Picking up another, this one was only half-written.

"*What on earth*," she threw pens and papers aside and found a notebook. She recognized it as the one Ronan used for his interviews. She held a page up next to one of the notes, a cry of denial eased out. They were both in Ronan's handwriting. She set them down on the desk, her face embroiled in confused amazement.

There was another notebook on the desk, she gingerly opened it, peered anxiously at the pages, afraid of what she'd read. It was a journal, like a diary. She flipped through, page after page, most were about his sexual encounters, then, she read something that chilled her to the bone.

He had written in his neat penmanship, the name and address of a Jay Egan. Under it he'd written, "On July 8th, I was cruising the streets on patrol and was coming down the rural Range Road, ahead appeared to be an accident. Two cars, a Mercedes and a Ford were crushed up against each other.

"By the time I got there, a man I recognized stumbled out of the Mercedes, staggered around to the front of his car, examined the damage, then climbed back inside and took off. It wasn't as damaged as the Ford. The Ford was practically folded in half and smashed all to hell. I ran to the crumpled car and looked inside.

"God it was awful. Blood and glass all over, no seatbelt on the occupant inside. He had smashed his head on the windshield; his bloodied nose and forehead were split wide open. He lay back against the seat, must have bashed into the glass then bounced back. Blood streamed down his face, glass stuck out all over the torn up skin. I felt for his pulse. He was dead.

I hit my radio and called for a bus. Should have called for a hearse instead of an ambulance. Standing in the middle of the street, I stared off to where Stedman Westcott had disappeared. I didn't record that I'd seen the Mercedes. I made no mention in my report of Westcott leaving the scene of the accident, a hit and run with serious bodily injuries.

"I made sure I was the one that conducted the following investigation of the accident. My reports were that the perpetrator had ditched the other car which had been a stolen vehicle. I listed an old heap someone had dumped years ago out in a vacant field, and that the suspect couldn't be identified, and closed the case as unsolvable.

"I waited a few months, letting Stedman settle down, thinking he'd gotten away scott-free. Then I made my first blackmail phone call. Sure, he denied it, fought it, he soon learned he had no choice. To keep his job, his wife, the lifestyle he enjoyed, no, he wasn't about to give it up for a dank prison cell. I had his nuts in my hand, and I twisted until he gave in. Yeah, man, it was great. Every four or five months I sent my letters, instructing him when and where to leave the money.

"I kept it at an even $5,000, it seemed easier. If I got too greedy Stedman would panic and make a mistake and get caught embezzling and I'd lose my golden goose. We all have our secrets. His was guilt and mine was knowledge and greed, being in the right place at the right time. I don't even give a shit if he discovers it's me blackmailing him. What's he going to do? He can't turn me in, and I carry a badge and a gun.

"He threatened me once and I charged him double that time for it. He backed off after that, resigned to it. Didn't stall or threaten or plead, just put the bread in a bag and left it where I told him. Oh yeah, life is good. Easy money, and with the badge, free sex. It's the best when I stop the speeder, catch the shoplifter, the DUI offender, and make the bitches do things they don't want to. Their tears, anger, begging only make it hot- hot- hotter-"

Jesa set the book down, her stomach revolted, she couldn't read any more. She leaned over setting her hands on the desk to take a breath, and feeling something sharp, drew back. She'd pressed her palm on a spare set of keys. Something crashed into the bedroom door, she jumped with a yelp.

Ronan banged his fists on the door and bellowed, "You let me in you bitch or I'll really put a fucking hurting on you!" He banged the wood with his fist, the door shifted slightly.

Scooping up the keys, Jesa fret frightfully, "I need to get out of here!" She spun around, spotted a marble bookend on the bookcase. She snatched it up and hit the window with it. Again and again until the glass was mostly gone.

Covering her hand with her sleeve, she brushed the broken glass out of the way. She hurried back to the desk, grabbed up two of the notes, stuffed them in the notebook, and shoved it in the back of her pants and climbed out.

Chapter Thirty-One

Ronan's punching and kicking the door, his foul curses stinging her ears Jesa dropped to the hard ground, landing in six inches of hard-packed snow. Her ankles stabbed with sudden pain of hitting the frozen earth but she couldn't take a moment to let it ease. She could still hear Ronan banging and slamming into the door, he would break it down any second.

The bitter wind struck her, she'd left her jacket inside. Desperate to escape the madman, Jesa ran around the house to the front. The deputy's truck was covered with a layer of snow. While racing to it, she flipped through the keys in her hand. There was no key fob. Frantically, she wrestled the first one her hands were shaking so badly, and it didn't fit, nor the second, her lungs were tight with fright and the icy air.

White vapor expulsed in frenzied puffs from her heaving lips. Her hands shook from fear and cold, she was terrified she'd drop the keys in the snow and lose them. Forcing herself to focus on the keys, she saw the biggest one, a vehicle key, it fit.

She opened the door and hopped in. Not taking the time to move the seat up, she shoved the key in and turned on the ignition just as Ronan came barreling around the side of the house. His face was lived, beet red with fury. Seeing her in the truck, he ran towards her.

Ronan was almost to the driveway. His face promised horrible retribution when he got his hands on her.

She grabbed the wheel and wrenched it to the side as hard as she could and pressed the gas, the car skidded on the snow covered driveway. Ronan reached her and slammed his hand on the side of the cruiser yelling for her to stop. Jesa jumped at the bang, her heart in her throat, she floored the gas, spun in a doughnut on the snow-covered grass.

Then the tires found purchase and she managed to straighten the car out and headed for the end of the driveway, aiming between the two posts, Ronan ran cursing after her bellowing threats. Déjà vu all over again, the night that caused her to flee her home swarmed over her, flooding her with the renewed terror of running for her life.

The car speared through the posts and spun, see-sawing onto the street. Perched to the edge of the seat so she could reach the pedals, Jesa tried to search blindly to turn the heater on but she couldn't take her eyes off the road, what if Ronan had another vehicle in his garage and he could be right on her tail? In his office she had memorized the name of street she wanted to go to. The problem was, she didn't know where the street was located.

She did know where the police station was, she headed there.

By the time she reached the station, her body was shivering, shaking uncontrollably. Someone had decorated the station in Christmas lights. A Santa Claus and reindeer pranced across the roof. Everything was blanketed in snow.

Jesa parked the truck and raced through frosted air to inside. It was late, the place was almost empty. A deputy she didn't know sat at a desk. He looked up at her abrupt entrance.

"Can I help you?" he asked, tone bored, but his eyes fixed at her torn blouse.

She hurried over to him. "Please, is Chief McKabe or Agent Koffi here?"

He studied her with a laconic gaze, sniffed. "Nah, all gone home. I'm manning the dispatch. What can I do for you?"

Panting, Jesa tried to think. She was so scared, so cold, her thoughts jumbled around her head. "A- a phone, can I use a phone?"

Lips pushed out, he nodded to a phone on the desk beside him. "Sure, hon, go ahead." He looked back down at the newspaper he'd been reading.

Jesa grabbed up the phone, tried to remember Tristano's number. "245, no, 254, yeah, that's it." She dialed on the landline as fast as her trembling fingers could go. A safety pin was in a bowl of paper clips, she fished it out.

He answered on the third ring. "Koffi," he gruffed.

"Tri-" she couldn't suck in a breath, her throat was clenched in fright, she almost dropped the phone with her numb quivering fingers.

He barked at her, "Fuck, Jesselin, is that you?"

Struggling for breath, Jesa glanced over at the deputy but he was into his paper. Pressing her palm against her forehead, she willed herself to calm. Taking a deep quivering breath, she sputtered through chattering teeth, "*Tristano*," then faltered.

"Baby, Jesselin, what the hell is going on? Why aren't you using your phone?"

"I- I- I-"

His voice came through dark, deep, commanding, "Okay, Jesselin, take a few long deep breaths, talk to me."

His voice calmed her, she did as he said. Her heart was beating out of her chest. She gushed the words out, "It was Ronan, Ronan's the blackmailer!"

"What? Where are you, I'm coming to you."

She felt the strength in his voice shudder up her spine. She blurted, "I think I know where Brie might be! I have to go there, before she gets hurt!"

He was quiet for a half a second, then said, "Calm down, Jesselin, tell me what the hell is going on. Don't move, where are you?"

Shaking her head she said, "No, no, I have to go. Listen, I have proof Ronan is the blackmailer, he might be after me. I need to get to the baby. I have Ronan's truck, he- he-" she gasped, "he tried to rape me. I had to steal his truck to get away."

"Jesselin," he barked, "where are you?"

She knew she wasn't making any sense, but she couldn't calm her brain to straighten her thoughts. "Listen, Tristano, I- have to go, get the baby-" she sucked in a tight breath. "I'm going there-"

"No fucking way, Jesselin. I'll have deputies go, give me the address, you go home. Straight home. I'll meet you there-"

"No, Tristano, I have to get to that baby! There might be no time! I'll- I'll let you know if she's there." She hung up before he could respond. She didn't want to waste his time and make a fool out of herself if she told him where she was going and she was wrong, that

Brie Westcott wasn't there. She'd check it out first and then let him know if she found Brie.

Heading to the door, she glanced around for a jacket, hat, anything, but there was nothing there for her to put on. Spying a map on a desk, she grabbed it and rushed out the door and back into the truck. It was so cold, the seat, the wheel, she had to use her hand to wipe the windshield so she could see out.

Huddling over the wheel, body shivering so hard her bones were banging against each other, she had the map open over the wheel. She found the location she wanted, and poked at the heater until she got it on. Then she burned rubber down the street.

The road was so dark, the forest and falling snow blocked any ambient light from houses, her eyes strained to see the blacktop and stay on the road and not vault off it and over a cliff. Concentrating on the road, she was unaware someone had followed her from the station. Down and around she went descending the mountain black in the night. The wind rattled the car, the snow picked up, thickening, making it almost impossible to see the road.

At the bottom of the mountain, she turned right onto Bridge Street. Thankfully it was better lit from some shops and residences, and would turn into another street that she hoped would lead to her destination. Most of the shops were strung with colorful Christmas lights.

Suddenly, a car sped past her, the loud roar of the engine surprising, shocking her, she almost hurtled off the side of the road. "Gosh," she huffed in fright, steadied the car, muttered, "reckless fool with a death wish," she managed to stay on the road. Her fingers clutching the wheel cramped from her tight hold, her back hurt from leaning forward to see out the window.

Finally, she read the street sign, Blackstone Way and was relieved that the street she wanted was off this one. Just as her body started to relax that she'd found the right neighborhood, it tightened back up when she remembered why she was there.

Someone had kidnapped Brie Westcott and Jesa was positive they were holding her captive here. This could be dangerous, she needed a plan. The car slowed as it moved down the street, the houses were very sparse and quite far apart, the twilight was consumed with black angry clouds that the wind shoved roughly across the night sky. Even the twinkling Christmas lights on a few houses didn't illuminate much.

She turned onto Wood Road and drove so slowly the car was barely moving. Peering into the dark, her fingers curled over the wheel struggled to keep the car rolling straight and not get blown off onto the grass. Her mind had been in such a frantic jumble, the realization that she really should have told Tristano or the deputy at the station where she was going, they could have sent officers, too late now. She should have just chanced wasting their time. Then again, the images in her mind at the time were of a swat team barging in the house, and the occupants, or the police, shooting Brie. She just had to take this chance!

There, at the end, a small house tucked away, just caught it in her headlights. She quickly turned off the lights and pulled over a few hundred yards from the house and parked. Shutting off the truck, she pushed out the door, no easy feat, the wind was a monster.

How she was going to prove they had Brie was going to be difficult. Jesa had studied every bit of information the police had on the investigation. They had a map of Orainn on the wall and had circled all the houses that had children in them but were gone to the mainland for the season. Every single family had been checked out. Jesa had spent her time staring at the map while she waited for meetings to begin or for Tristano.

The island had been divided on a graph. Each section denoted residence, business area, hotels, etc. The residences were color coded where there were children that stayed the winter. She had taken copies of the graph and map home to study on her off-time. She clearly remembered this house contained no children year round.

The owners of the house, if she recalled correctly were an older couple. Since all information had funneled through Jesa, she had reviewed, organized, and dispersed the information out to all the deputies, McKabe and Tristano. Through repetition a lot had stuck in her brain. She didn't know why this house stuck there, but for some reason it did.

Pinning her blouse with the safety pin while she searched her memory, she thought there was also a younger woman, a widow, yes, the couple's daughter had lost her husband a few years ago. In a car accident. There had been a notation to tread carefully when questioning them about Brie Westcott. The recollection of the memo regarding the accident roiled shivers through Jesa popping goose bumps along her arms.

There had been very few fatal car accidents on Orainn so it totally stood out. Jesa was impressed with herself that she remembered all that. The thing she knew for sure, there were no children living there.

Her arms wound around her body, her head bowed against the gale, her blouse and jeans were no protection against the frosted chill and biting wind. She made her way to the little white house with green trim. Several cars were parked in the driveway. Before she could lose her nerve, she hurried up the steps, took a deep breath, and knocked on the door. It was a couple of minutes wait, and the door swung open.

Her arms wrapped around herself, her body shivering knocking her knees together, her teeth clattered like skeletons in the wind. A man stood in the doorway, both brows up in question.

Jesa said through the screen door, "Uh, hello, sir, I... my car broke down, my cell died, could I perhaps, can I borrow your phone to call a tow truck?" She held her breath thinking he might leave her standing there to freeze to death and tell her he would make the call for her.

His gaze rolled down her shivering body, lips pursed then he pulled them in and pushed the door open. "Sure honey, come on in. You've gotta be freezing out there. Where's your jacket for Pete's sake?" Standing back, he let her in.

"I, uh, I needed something from the store and was in such a hurry I- I forgot it. Silly, huh?" She gave a girlish grin, one shoulder curved up in a coy, dumb blonde look.

"Huh," he grunted. "You girls. Come on in."

Chapter Thirty-Two

The man looked to be about 60 or so, grey temples with dark hair. A beefy build, big hands, Jesa tried to keep an arm's length from him in case he went to grab her. He led her through the small living room to the kitchen. "You can use the phone in here."

A woman sauntered in, then stopped when she saw Jesa. Her eyes hopped to the man and back to Jesa. The man said, "Oh, honey, this young lady's car broke down, she's going to borrow our phone to call for assistance."

The woman who also appeared to also be in her 60's started at first, then she smiled kindly. "I see. It's a terrible night for a young woman to be out and about by yourself, and," her disapproving gaze took in Jesa's clothes slightly damp from the snow and not wearing a jacket. She scolded, "You aren't dressed for the weather, dear."

"Yeah, uh," Jesa stammered, she tried to discretely scan the area for signs of a baby. "I," she shrugged with a foolish grin and said, "my mother always said I was so flighty, leave my head if it wasn't attached. I was in such a hurry, I just," she shrugged, "kinda forgot."

The couple shared a paternal 'kids will be kids' look then smiled at Jesa. The older woman said, "I'm Patty, Patty Mesina and this is my husband, Kevin." The couple stood waiting with friendly smiles for Jesa to introduce herself.

"Um, it's very nice to meet you," she replied with a wavering smile. "I'm, uh, Jesa Judan."

The pair beamed kindly at her. She waited, they smiled.

Kevin chuckled, he said, "Oh yes," "the phone. It's right over there. Do you need me to get on the net and find a number for you?"

Jesa turned to the phone that was on the wall near the refrigerator. The kitchen was white with stainless steel appliances, beige tiled floor, stools with blue seats lined a small island. "Thank you, but," she pretended to wince. "The car breaks down all the time. I've memorized the number."

Kevin nodded. "Okay, sure."

Patty said, "Can I get you something to drink, dear? Hot tea maybe?"

As much as she would love some tea to warm her up, Jesa figured she should try to learn something quick and get out as soon as possible. "No, um, thank you. I'll just call and then go wait and meet the tow truck." She reached for the phone.

"All right, sure," Kevin said, tugging his pants up over his plump belly. Patty hit his arm with a smile, told him, "Let's give her a bit of privacy, Kev, come on."

Kevin grin. "Okay. When you're done, Jesa was it?" At her nod, he said, "We'll be in the living room, come on in when you're done."

As soon as they left, Jesa lifted the phone and dialed Tristano's number. Tucking the phone between her ear and shoulder, she started quietly opening and closing cupboards. When he answered, his hello was suspicious as he didn't recognize the number.

"Tristano," she whispered, "it's me."

"Motherfucker-"

Jesa held the phone back from her ear as he bellowed and cursed at her. When he quieted, he said, "For God's sake, please, Jesselin, tell me where the hell you are."

She bent and opened a low cupboard, closed it silently, whispered, "I'm at the house. I'm looking for-" and had to hold the phone away from her ear again. "Tristano, hush now, I'm looking for evidence of a baby." His shout blasted her ear, more curses, he ordered her to leave immediately.

"What house? Get out of there, Jesselin, get out right now!"

She'd looked in all the cupboards, her face fell, there was no baby food anywhere. Could she be wrong? She held the phone as Tristano yelled, telling her he was going to blister her ass when he got his hands on her- she opened the fridge. "Tristano," she cut him off. "Bottles, Tristano," she whispered triumphantly.

"Bottles?"

"Yes," she grinned into the phone, said with glee, "baby bottles. And formula. Tiny jars of baby food. She's here, Tristano, I know it, Brie is here!"

He growled at her, "If you don't get the fuck out of there right now, Jesselin, I swear to God you won't be sitting for a month of Sundays. Do you hear me? Get. Out. Now."

"Okay, I'm leaving, I-"

"Were you able to reach the tow truck people?" Patty asked from the doorway.

Jesa jumped guiltily. "Oh! Hi, um, ye- yes. They're on their way. I called my- my dad so he won't worry. I hope you don't mind." She smiled weakly.

Patty Mesina dyed her hair auburn to cover the grey. It curled to below her chin. She wore glasses and flowered slacks with a yellow sweater. She looked homey, comfy, not quite grandmotherly but on the cusp. "Of course not dear. I know I would be worried to death if any of my family was out in that storm. You can wait in here until the truck comes."

Jesa hung the phone up, Tristano's voice was still coming from it. "That's kind of you, Mrs. Mesina, but they said I have to be with the vehicle. It's okay, they said they would be here in about ten minutes."

Patty's brows furrowed in concern. "Oh, I don't know, dear, it's frightful out there. The storm is raging, it's fearsome. I'm afraid a tiny thing like you will get blown right away. You really should wait in here. We can call them back and have them come to the house when they arrive."

A tingled gripped the back of Jesa' neck. What if they figured out why she was there? What if they didn't let her leave? She forced her shoulders to loosen, she was being silly. The Mesinas thought the truck was coming, they wouldn't try anything. "I'll be fine, Mrs. Mesina, really. I just want to get my car taken care of and go home. Get warm, dry, have a mug of hot chocolate." She ambled across the floor and past Patty. Patty followed her to the living room.

"Please call me Patty," she said kindly with a nice smile.

When they reached the living room, Kevin, two young men and a woman were sitting inside. "These are my sons Billy." Patty pointed at one of the men slouched in a chair. Twenty-something, he looked like his father but without the bulk that he'd inherit as he grew older. He nodded politely, then when he looked up at Jesa, his eyes widened in appreciation, mouth kicked up in a quick leer.

Patty said, "This is my other son, Duncan." Billy had dark hair and a square-ish head like his father, Duncan's hair was a light brown, his face a little longer, they both had Patty's hazel eyes. They both ogled Jesa like she was a mouthwatering dish they wanted served to them. Sprawled on a couch, Duncan sat up when his eyes lit on Jesa.

Jesa's gaze travelled to a woman sitting at the end of the couch, and the hairs on the back of her neck rose.

The woman looked in her thirties, brown hair in a long bob, clamped lips and a pinched face. She looked bitter and angry, her regard of Jesa was clearly suspicious, and unwelcoming. Patty rushed on awkwardly seeing the woman's anger at Jesa, "Um, this is our daughter, Virginia. Ginny honey, this is Jesa…uh, Judan. Her car broke down and she borrowed our phone to call for a tow."

Patty's explanation did nothing to remove the cutting distrust Virginia narrowed at Jesa. Jesa stammered, "Um, yes, well, it's so nice to meet you all. And, and thank you for letting me use your phone, I'll be on my way now." She headed for the door. Kevin stood up.

"Jesa, it's nasty out there, you can wait right here until the tow arrives," he said firmly and moved towards her.

She inched to the door. "Thanks, really, but they said wait by the vehicle, I'll just-"

A baby wailed. The room froze. All eyes turned up to the stairs, then moved in unison to Jesa. Her skin paled, the boys stood up and trod to stand by their father.

Jesa mumbled, "Yes, I'll be on my way-" the baby cried again. Virginia stood up, and the entire family advanced on Jesa.

Kevin sighed, "I'm sorry, honey, we can't let you leave."

Patty said with regret, "The truck will come, maybe see your car down the street, or not. When you're not there, he'll leave. By the time the police get around to looking for you, one of the boys," she gestured to her sons, "will have moved the truck, far from here."

Kevin took a step closer to Jesa, he looked regretful too. "If the police ever track you to this neighborhood, by that time we'll have shuffled the baby around like we did during the search for her, right, hon?" He smiled sadly at his wife.

The boys stared with anger, and lust, at Jesa, Virginia was seething. Her face pinched more, lips pulled in fiercely. They all inched closer to Jesa, penning her in.

"Wait." She held up her hand. "Please, at least tell me why, why did you take little Brie Westcott?"

Kevin sighed again, glanced at his daughter, nodded.

Virginia moved in front of Jesa, dark red spots stained her gaunt cheeks. She was thin, too thin. Her body shook with fury. "You want to know why? You nosy little shit. You want to know why I, yes, it was me who snuck in the Westcotts' unlocked house and took their baby."

Jesa's eyes darted from each family member then landed back on the furious woman in front of her. Not just furious, Jesa could see pain in her eyes, grief in the twist of her hard lips. "Miss Mesina-"

Virginia spat, "That's Mrs. Egan. Mrs. Jay Egan." Tears brimmed her eyes, hazel like her brothers', she sniffed them back, grit her jaw. "Stedman Westcott killed my husband."

Jesa knew from reading Ronan's notes yet she still gasped. "It- I understand it was an accident."

Virginia snorted, her face contorted with a ghastly sneer. "No, he didn't take a gun and shoot him," her eyes lowered to the floor as tragic memories flooded her thin face. "No, he was drunk. Stedman Westcott was drunk and he hit my husband's car. According to the coroner Jay lingered for a few minutes then died. Stedman," her teeth clenched with fury and regret, "the coward left my beloved husband there to die, alone. He didn't call for help. He didn't try to help him, or comfort him, he ran like the coward that he is."

The room was quiet, so quiet only their breaths were heard.

Jesa's heart broke for the grieving woman. She asked, "But, if your husband died, and Mr. Westcott fled the scene, how did you know what happened?"

Virginia shrugged, crossed her skinny arms over her thin chest. "My girlfriend, Lindsey, she's kind of a..."

"Tramp," Billy filled in for her.

Virginia scowled at him, then said, "Anyway, Lindsey does get a little, loose, when she drinks. One night she got wasted along with

Stedman Westcott. They went to a hotel, because they were both married. "During their...evening," her arms tightened around her body as if she needed to hold herself together, keep her heart and soul intact. "They were both trashed, they were trading stories, laughing, trying to one-up the other with the worst thing that had ever happened to them. Stedman told Lindsey what he'd done. He confessed to her."

It was still quiet, no one moved. Jesa said, "So, was he arrested? Charged with the death of your...uh, husband?"

A darkness surged over Virginia's pale face, sharpening her already acidic features. "Huh," she grunted her helpless fury, hands clenched into fists. "They were both drunk, Stedman recanted, there was no proof. He told Lindsey if she pursued it he'd tell her husband of their fling. She'd lose her house, her children. No," her gaze stroked morosely to the front window.

The sleet and snow hammered the glass. It was too dark to see outside, but the wind shrilled, they could hear things banging against the house, branches whipping.

"Not a word was said. No proof, Lindsey backed down, I went to a deputy and tried to make a report, but," she sighed, "he said there wasn't enough evidence to prosecute him."

Kevin crossed his arms over his barrel chest, said, "Our family has a...bit of criminal history." Jesa looked at him, confused. He said, "We're, ah, grifters, ya know, we con people. We generally do not talk to cops, and they don't believe a word that comes out of our mouths anyway. So, the officer that took the report wasn't going to give us the time of day."

Virginia said, "The deputy jotted a few things down in his notebook then left. We never heard another word about it. He blew off our calls."

Thoughtfully, Jesa said softly, "Is that deputy's name Ronan Roarke by any chance?"

Virginia's brows lifted, she wiped at her eyes. "Well, yes, as a matter of fact. How did you know?"

"Ah, just a wild guess. But, why take their baby?"

Creases wrapped around Virginia's aggrieved eyes and gouged her bitter lips. She said coldly, "I wanted to hurt the cowardly bastard, he deserved punishment and the law didn't even seriously investigate the crime." A snort of pain, lip curled in derision, she told her, "My

286

husband was murdered and the police blew it off, Westcott's baby is taken and they pull out all the stops because he's wealthy. Well, they dead-ended finding the missing baby just like when they investigated Jay's death."

Jesa backed up to the door. These people were criminals, they would never let her leave alive, they knew she'd run straight to the police. "I…see. That makes some sense, sort of. So, I've gotta go-" she seized the knob, twisted it, pushed the door open, the wind took it.

"No!" Virginia shrieked. "Don't let her go!"

The three men stormed at Jesa- Duncan caught her shirt, already torn it shredded further in his grasp. Jesa cried out as Billy ran to them and scrambled to grab her arm. Patty stood back, Kevin plodded over to help his boys. Virginia stood in front of Jesa screeching her agony.

Jesa flailed her arms, ripping them out of Billy's grasp. Billy cursed her and tried to grab her hurling limbs- Jesa kicked at Duncan, catching his shin. He roared, gripped her blouse and pulled her, trying to hold her immobile.

With a shriek, Jesa threw out both hands and shoved Virginia square in the chest. Jesa was tiny, but Virginia was almost emaciated in her grief, just a bag of bones, she stumbled backwards falling into both her brothers. They caught her, throwing themselves off balance, and they knocked into Kevin. Jesa turned and flew out the door.

She heard them shouting behind her, pounding footsteps, again, déjà vu of the day she'd witnessed that man get murdered in that alley. Her feet pedaled, carrying her into the dark woods behind their house. She ran and ran, then darted into an evergreen bush and tucked herself down behind it. She heard the Mesinas calling to one another, shouting for them to split up and find her. Jesa's frightened breath huffing so loud in her ears she feared the whole world could hear it.

Footsteps came her way; she huddled down, burrowed into the bush and held her breath. It was pitch black, unless he stumbled over her or heard her heart pounding, he wouldn't be able to see her. The falling snow quickly piled over her footprints.

He paused; she bit her lips to still her quaking body, holding her breath back. Her feet were covered with snow, the wind sliced right through her thin clothes. She grabbed her hair to keep it from billowing and giving away her hiding spot.

Whoever was there, stood still, obviously trying to listen for her. The other Mesinas' voices echoed through the dark woods. The footsteps started, they moved away from her. When she heard them move out of the trees, she let out her breath. A shaking hand on her roiling stomach, Jesa stayed where she was, she didn't know how long.

When she was sure they had returned to the house, she stood up, pushed her tossing hair back and tried to get her bearings. She shuffled slowly, quietly through the woods along the grassy perimeter until she reached the street. Her nose frozen she couldn't feel her fingers. When she hit the pavement, she ran like a wild hunted animal.

She sped down the street, a sob of relief gutted out as she spotted Ronan's truck. It had an inch of snow on it. She sprinted faster, the heater, she needed the heater, her brain started jumbling from the cold, the fear, get away- get away it chanted. Her poor freezing feet spat on the wet road, shudders wrung through her, her lungs constricted with iced air she almost couldn't inhale.

Tears slipped out, turning to ice on her red cheeks. Praying the Mesinas couldn't see the truck at the end of the street in the dark, she reached for the door-

Someone grabbed her shoulder, pulled her up against a hard chest. She screamed, he put his gloved hand over her mouth. His grip like iron, he whispered in her ear, "Finally, my little travelling witness, finally I have you. All that running, changing identities, slipping away just as I found you. Ah, fuck, life is good again."

Growling his pleasure of triumph, he wrapped his arm around her, holding her arms down, he crushed her brutally against him. His hand pressed so hard on her mouth her head was shoved back, painfully arching her neck to the breaking point.

He lifted her off her feet, she kicked violently. He hustled her to a vehicle that was parked behind Ronan's truck so she hadn't seen it. Opening the door, he bodily threw her inside and slammed the door.

Horrified, Jesa jammed her fingers all over the door handle trying to get it open. The man climbed in the driver's side, he reached out and grabbed a handful of her hair, twined it around his fist and held her taut. With his other hand, he pulled a length of rope from his pocket and viciously shoved her to face the passenger window. Her forehead banged on the glass hard enough she saw stars. He tied her wrists behind her, then grasped her shoulder to turn her back to face him.

He seized her jaw, gripping it ruthlessly between his fingers, grinned at her pain. "Ah, yeah, that's the beautiful face that has haunted me for four fucking endless years. Indiana Kolbi. Finally, it's been a long race, sweetheart, but it's over. I got ya." He released her with a callous shove, her back bashed against the door.

Her breaths rushed, petrified, Jesa's chest pumped with terror. She stared at the blond man, her eyes as huge as beach balls. "You- you, you're the one I saw shoot that poor man in the alley." Jesa slumped, he'd caught her. Her run, her life, was at an end. She had to stall, find a way out. Fearfully she spurted, "Apollo, the other guy called you Apollo."

A big man in his thirties, extremely light blue, lethal eyes, long face, the tuft of yellow hair below his lower lip joggled with his discordant laugh. "Yeah, we were afraid you'd heard that. That's Apollo Cross, just for the record. I might have gotten by if you'd only just seen me, but," his head bobbed back and forth. "With my name and description, the cops could have eventually found me. After all, the town was small and I lived there, I had a rap sheet, I had nowhere to go, to hide away. Like you."

His depraved eyes were so light they were creepy. Not light like the sky or baby blue, no, so light they were almost ghostly white. They regarded her pompously, smug, without a shred of pity. "Of course, because you made a run for it, I had to track you across the entire damned country." His voice lost the levity of victory and lowered dark with fury, the spooky eyes convulsed with hate. "I lost my job and had to fucking rob convenience stores and shit to pay my way."

Struggling with the rope tied around her wrists, Jesa thrust her shoulders up and down, her torso wriggled back and forth as she tugged at the binds. Almost blind with horror of her dire situation, yet she still said brashly, "Job?" A slight jeer to her voice although it shook with fear, taking a shot in the dark she scoffed, "Working for the mafia? You call that an occupation?"

Scowling at her, his noxious snarl vindictive, "Yeah, bitch, that was my job. I was an enforcer, got paid good bucks for it."

Turning her head from him she murmured, "Murderer you mean."

His teeth ground together at her scorn. "Whatever, it paid the bills and I liked it. I like beating people up, terrorizing them, torturing before killing them. What do you think of that?" He shifted so he was in her line of view. "You ruined it for me. My buddy snitched to the don there was a witness, and he told me I had to eliminate you." Snorting with ironic humor he said angrily, "Never thought it'd take so goddamned long."

She turned back to face him, saw the sadistic desire in his twisted face to hurt people, her. She wanted to tell him what she thought of his assassinating people but wisely held her tongue. Instead she said, "It was your footprints in my yard, the hang-ups, they were you."

A sneer raised his cruel lips. "Of course. I did the phone calls to track you, put you on edge so you'd maybe try to run and I could easily catch you on this rock. I was at your house numerous times, waiting for my chance to get to you. But there were goddamned cops continuously at your door, driving around your block, I couldn't take the chance and get caught. I followed you relentlessly, but you were never alone. The big bruiser, the FBI agent, fucker wouldn't let you out of his sight. Well, he lost, I won and you're screwed."

It was apparent by his leering grin he enjoyed watching her struggle knowing she couldn't get loose, couldn't get away from him. "I followed you today," he sneered arrogantly, "parked down the street from that cop's house you were at. Hell, you came flying out from the back of the house, drove like a madwoman, took me by surprise, it was a bitch to catch up with you."

The ropes burning her wrists, Jesa fought to keep the tears back, she'd never give him the satisfaction of knowing how horribly scared she was. Repulsed by the man and his story of how he stalked her, she turned her head away from him again in rebuff.

Ghostly eyes dipped to her shredded blouse, the pupils dilated, his tongue came out, slathered around his lips. "Wow. Nice. I was going to just do you, plug you," he patted a gun at his hip, "drop your body in the sea. They'd never find you." Sharp canines glistening in rapacious excitement, he crowed, "But shit, girl, you're fucking hot. Look at those titties. I bet you got it going on down there," he reached between her legs, laughed when she clamped them together and swiveled away from him.

"I think I'll get me some before I do ya. No one will be at the beach. I'm gonna take you there right now, I can fuck you and shoot you without anyone seeing. It'll give me time to figure out what piece of you I'll cut out to bring back to my boss, the proof that you're dead." He lifted a curl off her shoulder, twisted it around his fingers and tugged hard, forcing her to face him.

With a shriek, Jesa jerked her head leaving strands in his clutch. "Don't you touch me, let me go! I've never told, I won't tell now. Please, just let me go!" Blinking hard, she crunched her eyes to keep the frightened tears at bay.

A laugh barked out, he tossed his head back with a shake of it. "Yeah, sure, I've chased you for four years and now I'm just going to let you go. Run free. Fly away little birdie. Damn, you're kind of dumb for being so crafty in dodging me all this time. No," he grasped her upper arm, pulled her towards him. "No, I'm gonna fuck you then put a bullet in that cunning little brain of yours."

Laughing at her hysterical fighting to get away, he hissed, "C'mere." He grabbed her other arm and dragged her across the bench seat to him. His vulgar eyes dipped to her open blouse. Licking his lips again like he planned to take a big bite out of her, he let go of her arms and gripped the torn sides of the frilly material.

"This has to go first, I wanna see these naked jugs bouncing free while I drive to the beach," he laughed unpleasantly, and tugged the blouse off her shoulders. "Nice bra, girl," he admired her peach lace. "It goes next."

"Don't' do this," she begged, thrashing her body to get away from his hands. Ignoring her pleas, he strung a hand around her neck to hold her still, his other hand fisted the back of her blouse to rip it off. He lowered his head to suck at her lips. "I want me a little kiss before we go." Jesa screamed at his mouth, he chuckled. "Yeah, I like that wild terror girl, do it some more."

He held her too tightly, her hands bound behind her, she was helpless. Still, she tossed her body and screamed, and screamed.

Then, instead of trying to get away from him, Jesa suddenly flung herself at him. Taken by surprise he was knocked back- and- the door flew open- and the man swooped out like a tornado had grabbed him and sucked him right out-

Jesa scrabbled to her knees, hustled to the door and looked out.

Chapter Thirty-Three

All the way down the mountain Tristano cursed a blue streak. He prayed no one else was out in this blizzard; he'd never see them in time to swerve to avoid them. Dragging a furious hand through his thick hair he growled, "What the hell is that little girl thinking? I damned told her to go home, I told her to not go to that fucking house, but no. She has to forge head on into danger that reckless, foolish woman."

He cursed some more as he jerked the wheel just in time to miss a huge tree limb broken off and lying in the road. He should stop and move it so no one could get hurt, but, he had to get to Jesa before she was injured. Or worse.

Pushing on through the raging storm, he thought about what she'd said, it was all insane, crazy shit. She said Roarke was the blackmailer, and she believed she knew where the baby was. Seriously, how in the hell did she figure all that out? And was she right? He'd heard other voices through the phone, she'd had to hang up before she could tell him where she was. He raked his fingers through his hair again unconcerned what he made his mop look like.

Why couldn't she do what he says? Why does she have to run about heedless of her own safety? Huh, he grunted knowing the answer. Because she cares. She cared about other people more than about herself. She was brave and rushed into peril if she thought she could save someone from harm.

When he got to the bottom of the mountain, the GPS told him to turn right onto Bridge Street. He cranked the wheel, the tires slid in the snow, he skidded a few feet before he was able to straighten the car. He knew he should slow down, but he couldn't. Picturing someone hurting Jesa kept his foot pressed hard on the gas pedal.

The GPS led him down street after street until he reached Wood Road. He turned onto the street peering out the icy window trying to read the house numbers of the few cottages that sparingly lined the street. None of them had lights on or smoke spiraling from chimneys, they must be mainlanders, gone for the winter.

Deputy Jerry Osborne had been damned quick tracing the number Jesa had called him from, and locating the address. Dammit, when gets his hands on that woman, he's going to-

In the snow sleeted gloom, he just could make out dark figures at the far end of the street. More like silhouettes it was so hard to see, a large person and a much smaller- her long curls whipped in the fierce wind. The larger figure grabbed her up off the ground and literally threw her inside the truck and shut her in.

It took an eternity to get down that damned street, Tristano kept his boot hard on the gas, his heart banging against the inside of his chest heaving with dread.

When he got close, he slammed on the brakes and skidded to a stop within a few feet of the truck. Through the truck's back window, Tristano could see the bigger male with his hand around the smaller person's throat.

By the time he hurtled out of his car and raced to the truck, and looked in the window, a male was tearing Jesa's blouse off her. She was screaming and trying to fight, but shit, she's so small, and- ah hell her hands were tied behind her back.

Tristano was the tornado, he didn't even remember wrenching that door open, reaching in and grabbing the bastard. He dragged him out- before the guy landed on his feet, Tristano thundered a brutal punch to his jaw. The man flew backwards, staggered then arms whirling he gained his balance.

Tristano leaped at the male and took him down to the ground. They both landed hard with grunts and Tristano started wailing on the guy, punch after punch, the man's head snapped back, cracked to one side then the other. He smashed an uppercut and the man's head jerked back so hard Tristano thought he might have broken his neck.

No such luck. The guy threw his own wild swings. He was a big guy, a street fighter, but Tristano had been in combat, the guy didn't stand a chance. He slashed one glancing blow off Tristano's jaw, and that was the only connecting hit he made. An image of the bastard pulling Jesa's blouse off her, his hand around her neck, he went nuts and pounded and pounded the man into the frozen ground- blood spattered, the man's screams faded, Tristano kept punching then, he heard her.

"Tristano, stop, please, you'll kill him, you can't kill him, stop!" Her voice trickled in through the buzz of the blood roaring through his head. Fearing he'd hurt her with an errant punch, he sat back on his heels, his hands on his thighs, his chest pumped with heavy panting breaths.

He looked up at her through a lock of black hair that had fallen over one eye. Sweat dripped down his temples even in the freezing cold. She looked so scared, so breathtakingly beautiful, his heart clenched. "Bitty bit," he held his arms out. Her hands still bound behind her back she stumbled into his embrace.

He pulled her down to sit on his bent knees and cradled the back of her head, held it to his shoulder, her own shoulders shook with her sobs. His other hand wrapped around her waist pressing her so tightly against him he feared she couldn't breathe.

"Shh, my little baby girl, everything is okay now. You're safe now. He can't hurt you, he can't chase you anymore." He stroked her while he calmed her. Tristano didn't know who the bastard was, but he had a feeling he was the reason Jesa had run, hiding in shelter after shelter across the country like a tiger had her tail. It was time she spilled her shit to him, everything.

Her body vibrated with shivers of cold, terror, and amazing relief. He clasped her arms and held her so he could drink her in, then frowned, his fury rising again. "What happened to your blouse?" His gaze stroked over her exposed bosom.

He snatched the ends of her blouse and jerked them together. "Was it that fucker, Roarke? I'll kill him. As soon as I get you home I'm going to hunt him down like the animal he is and tear the bastard apart." He ripped at the ropes binding her wrists, tossed them angrily to the ground and rubbed her burnt skin.

Her teeth clattered together, chest hitched with her subsiding sobs. "It doesn't matter, Tristano. I'm okay now, and we can rescue the baby."

His response was a primitive grunt of promised reckoning when he found the deputy. He rubbed her freezing arms, then drew off his jacket and helped her into it. "Get in the truck, baby, I'll secure that fucker. When everything is settled down, you can tell me all about it."

She warned him, "He has a gun, Tristano, on his hip."

He glanced at the prone man, blood pooling around his head. He wasn't going to be moving for a while. His face was pulverized pulp.

Tristano helped Jesa up the high seat in the truck. Leaning in, he cranked up the heater, then grabbed her arm and the back of her head and jammed his mouth on hers. The kiss was rough, brutal, he had been so scared he'd never see her again.

At her whimper he moved back a hair, breathed at her lips, "Thank God you're okay, Bitty bit." He kissed her gently then stepped back and closed the door.

The man on the ground didn't even groan when Tristano rolled him over on his stomach. He removed the thug's gun, sticking it in the back of his own belt and frisked him for any other weapons. Finding a knife in his boot, Tristano confiscated it then cuffed his hands behind him.

Unmoving, blood leaked from the man's nose, his mouth, his ears, cuts on his body. Tristano put two fingers to his throat, there was a pulse, it was barely detectable but the asshole was alive.

Tristano gave him a hard kick to the ribs, hearing satisfying cracks, he muttered, "That's for terrorizing my girl, you son of a bitch." He opened the door to the truck and slid inside.

Jesa huddled, shivering in his jacket. Her face was red with cold and wet from tears. The strawberry curls draped around her like a protective web. She sniffed and wiped her nose with the back of her hand. Tristano smiled tenderly, "Here." He pulled a handkerchief from his pocket and handed it to her. She took it gratefully, her fingers hadn't calmed, they still quivered.

Tristano slid his phone out and called Chief McKabe. "Chief. Yes, I have her." His ebony gaze filled with relief, and the heat that he always felt when near her, and yes, rare caring and tenderness flickered over her sweet face. "She's pretty shaken up, but she's unharmed," his heart flinched, he hadn't asked her if- his stomach pitched. He asked with a guttural rasp in his voice, "Baby, did they hurt you? Did Ronan or this guy-" he couldn't say it. "I'll take you right to the hospital."

She smiled softly at his concern, tears still clung to her curly lashes. "I'm fine, Tristano. No one hurt me." She lifted her hand and gently caressed the side of his tough face. His eyes dropped to the torn blouse under his open jacket, angry red spread across his etched cheeks.

"Your blouse, who tore it?" He turned to look at the man lying outside on the ground. Was probably getting hypothermia but Tristano didn't give a shit. To Jesa, he said incensed, "Was it him? I'm gonna-" his hand on the door handle he was going back out and finish the job.

Jesa caught his arm. "No, it wasn't him, it was..." she stopped at the murderous spawning in his dark eyes. Trying to diffuse his rage, she mumbled, "I...I fell, it was-"

His phone still in his hand, Tristano cupped her jaw, lifted it, her eyes canted to the side, clearly she was lying. Not wanting to upset her more than she was, he said quietly, "Okay, baby." His kissed her lightly and put the phone back to his ear.

"McKabe, you need to send deputies to arrest Ronan Roarke, Stedman Westcott, and I need a dozen to come here." At the booming questions bursting from the phone, he waited for them to stop, then he took a breath. "We will explain everything when we get to the station." He glanced at Jesa. "Jesselin has a lot to tell us." He fastened his warm gaze on her, murmured, "A lot." He clicked off while McKabe was still throwing questions at him.

Drawing Jesa into his arms, he pressed her against his chest and smiled at her released sigh of relief, and at the feel of her in his arms. Safe, his.

He hugged her for a few moments, then put her from him, his brows down in a glower. "Jesselin, don't you ever do anything like that again to me. The hell you put me through not knowing what you walked into. I drove like a goddamned maniac scared to death you were hurt, killed. I was helpless, baby, to help you. God, girl, what you do to me," he cradled the side of her delicate face with his big rough hand.

"Well, little miss," he said, "your ass is going to hurt so bad. What if I hadn't been able to trace the phone or get here in time? That guy was about to leave with you- I never would have been able to find you. What if-"

She turned her head and kissed his palm, smiled serenely. "But you did, Tristano, and I knew you would. I never doubted you wouldn't get to me in time." Her fingers brushed through the lock of hair over his eyes, she pushed it back. "Yes, there were a few shaky moments. The guy and the people in the house all made it clear they were planning on…disposing of me, but I knew you'd find me, save me."

He stroked her face with his thick fingers, lowered his head to capture her lips- she put her fingers against his mouth. "No, not now, Tristano, the baby, we have to get Brie."

His eyes had warmed to black licorice, they shone with affection for her. "It's okay, the cavalry will be on the way. Thirty or so minutes and they should be here, time for us to," he looked down at her open blouse, trailed the pad of one finger over the swells of her exposed breasts.

She leaned back. "No, the Mesinas will have time to run!"

His massive shoulders shrugged. "So what? They can't get off the island, there's nowhere we won't be able to find them." His lids heavy, low with lust radiating at Jesa, he flattened his palm across the top of her bosom.

Shaking her head vehemently, she shuffled back from him. "No, they can hurt Brie. We have to-" Suddenly she pointed, screamed, "They're leaving the house!"

Tristano swung around and saw the Mesinas tearing out of the house carrying bags. They tossed the bags into the SUV in the driveway and hopped in after them. Virginia carried a bundle close to her chest as she climbed into a back seat.

"Fuck," he barked, grappled at the door handle. "Stay here," he ordered, and bolted out of the truck and ran to the driveway.

The Mesinas were already jumbled inside the SUV and with his face stricken white at the sight of the agent coming after them, Kevin put the weight of his beefy body into his hands cranking the steering wheel as hard as he could. The car made a wide circle over the snow-covered grass but there was a thick wooden fence around the yard trapping them, they could only run down the driveway, right at Tristano.

Tristano stood stalwart, his stance firm, boots wide apart, facing the car barreling towards him, his gun in both hands, he held it up. Arms stretched out, he aimed the weapon at the approaching car. Realizing that he couldn't shoot into the car and endanger the baby, he lowered the gun slightly to aim at the tires. The car wasn't going to stop- suddenly a branch smashed into the driver's side window.

Tristano snapped his head to the right; Jesa was running towards the escaping car, another branch in her other hand. The car swerved and crashed into the fence, the fence didn't stop the car but it caused it to spin, Kevin struggled to stabilize the out-of-control car.

"Goddammit, Jesa, get the hell back!" Tristano shouted as he sprinted after the car. He shot both front tires, the car skidded into a tree and came to a rocking stop. The driver's door opened and Kevin leaped out and ran.

Tristano raced after him, tackled him to the ground. The big man landed hard with a pained grunt. Tristano lifted the back of Kevin's head by his hair, and punched him- Kevin was out before his head landed back on the ground. Tristano leapt up and rushed to the car.

No one else left the vehicle, the other doors remained closed. Tristano stood a few yards from the SUV, his gun back out and aimed at the vehicle. "Okay," his voice loud, commanding, "everyone get out, one at a time, your hands in the air."

No one moved. "If I have to go in there and drag you people out you will not like it, trust me. Now, come out." A moment passed then the passenger door opened slowly and Patty Mesina slid out, her shaking hands raised.

"Don't shoot! Don't shoot!" she cried. "It wasn't me, I didn't take the baby!"

Tristano motioned with his gun. "Go over there, lay down on your stomach, hands stretched straight out in front of you."

"But- but, there's snow, it's cold-" she whined, walking towards where he gestured.

"Thoughts of the horror you put the Westcotts through should keep you warm until we get you to the jail. Now," he waved the gun at the SUV, instructed, "the rest of you." The other doors opened and Billy and Duncan slithered out, they slunk slowly across to where their mother lay in the freezing snow.

Tristano said coolly, "Take your time. The longer it takes you to comply the colder your poor mother will get." When he turned, Jesa was nearing the car.

"Jesselin, no, get away from the car!" Tristano started for the SUV.

"The baby, Tristano," Jesa cried as she reached the car, "we have to get Brie!"

"No!" Tristano broke into a run as Jesa reached the vehicle.

In the blink of an eye Virginia popped out with a knife in her hand. She grabbed a startled Jesa, threw her arm around the front of the smaller girl and put the knife to her throat. "Stop!" she yelled at Tristano. "Don't come any closer or I'll cut her, I swear to God I'll slice her head right off!"

The air paralyzing cold, he slowed but kept moving towards them with his gun raised. "You can't get away, Miss. Your car is damaged and you won't get anywhere on foot. The land is too vast, your house too far away from the town, the police are on their way."

The savage wind howled by flapping their clothes and hair, forcing tears from their eyes. Snow stormed down in sheets, everyone was swabbed with snow that blew off as soon as it landed, and more took its place. Tristano was in his black pants and shirtsleeves, the material damp from the snow, his black head powdered with white.

Virginia snarled, holding the knife so close to Jesa's neck a bead of blood formed. Jesa bit her lip to keep from crying out in pain. "Get back," Virginia ordered Tristano. "Give me the keys to the truck. I'm taking this girl with me. When I get on a boat and reach the mainland, I'll let her go."

Shaking his head, Tristano said, his tone as icy as the air, "I can't let you go, you know that. The island is surrounded by violent water and weather, there's not a person on this rock foolish enough that would take you on their boat. Put down the knife and release Miss Judan or I swear I will shoot you."

Her arm tightened around Jesa, her panicked eyes darted back and forth, searching for an escape. Her chest rose, expanded with her desperate breath as she realized how trapped she was. Then she smiled, her confidence returning. "I'll take my chances at the wharf, money buys anything, even dangerous crossings. Put the damned gun down or I will decapitate this girl."

Tristano took in Jesa's bearing. Her body was rigid, head arched back from the knife, but her eyes leveled calmly at Tristano. She trusted him to save her. His gaze switched back to Virginia. "Okay, before you go, can you tell me why you took the baby?"

Virginia's lips quivered, grief struck her eyes, the color bled from her thin face. The brunette hair swung around her head in the wind. "He, her father, Stedman Westcott had his three martini lunch and then hit a bar for more cocktails. I know this because my brothers Billy and Duncan went afterwards and discretely questioned people at his business and traced his steps to the bar. After a few hours of drinking and partying, Stedman hopped in his Mercedes and drove happily home. Except," tears tumbled out, rolled down her gaunt cheeks and plopped in the snow, her voice broke on a sob.

Tristano kept his gun up, his eyes trained on her, they wavered to Jesa, she smiled bleakly at him. "Except," he prompted the woman.

Virginia moved the arm that was across Jesa and she wiped at her eyes with her jacket sleeve. One side of her mouth nicked up in pained remembrance, "Except," she inhaled deeply. "On his way home he smashed into my husband. His car crashed into Jay's car so hard my husband's head broke through the damned windshield, and- and Jay was- was killed," her voice hitched, sobs twitched her chest.

"He killed my Jay. He didn't try to help him, call 911, no," she shook her head ruefully, her voice breaking, "just drove off in his expensive car and went home to his beautiful wife and rich mansion. Huh," she snorted, another sob broke out.

"The baby?" he asked. "Why did you take the baby?"

Virginia stared vacantly at him, her lashes fluttered blinking back her grief. Without a flicker of emotion in her voice, she shrugged, her eyes had gone blank, said coolly, "He took what I loved, so I took what he loved. I don't consider us even, but," her brows daggered down in renewed fury, "at least he will suffer, the conscienceless bastard."

"What had you planned on doing with Brie Westcott? Were you going to keep her, raise her as your own, or eventually return her to her parents?" Tristano asked.

The aggrieved face hardened with fury. "Why would I keep a remembrance around of what that piece of shit did to my husband? And I wasn't about to sell her on EBay and get myself caught."

Struggling under the bigger woman's hold, Virginia's arm was holding Jesa's arms restrained to her sides, aghast at the coldblooded, heartless woman, Jesa choked, "You planned to- to *kill* the baby?" They could hear Brie's cries from inside the car carrying on the wind.

Completely remorseless, Virginia shrugged as if the child was a scrap of lint to be plucked off her sweater and tossed without a second thought. "She's nothing to me but a source of revenge. Why give her back and end his anguish, when mine will never be relieved, huh? When the hunt for her died down, I'd planned on mailing him little pieces of her." Sniffing back her infinite suffering, she shook Jesa with her arm, her voice like steel she demanded, "Give me the damned keys or so help me God in one second I cut her."

Tristano held one arm out, palm up, gun still raised in his other hand. "Okay, okay, don't hurt her. Here," he stuffed his hand in his pants' pocket and pulled out the keys. He didn't glance in Jesa's direction, knowing he'd see the look on her face. She knew the keys to the truck were still in the ignition. If they were closer to it and the wind wasn't so loud and vicious they would be able to hear the engine running. He held his own keys out in his palm. "Come and get them."

Confusion seesawed to panic, Virginia faltered. She couldn't hold Jesa and get the keys at the same time. "All- right, just, toss them over here, near my feet."

"Okay, just stay calm, here you go." Tristano lobbed the keys so they landed a few feet from the women. His body braced for action, but his stance, his expression remained relaxed, and calm.

Virginia stared at the keys, then raised her eyes suspiciously to Tristano. But he stayed where he was, he hadn't moved any closer. He was a couple of car lengths away. She judged the distance and determined that he couldn't possibly get to her before she could get the keys.

"You," she said to Jesa, "you get the keys. If you try anything funny I'll kill you." She gave Jesa a push. Jesa stumbled forward. When she crouched to get the keys, Virginia grabbed a handful of her hair so she couldn't run off, and stood behind her.

Blam! Tristano didn't hesitate, he pulled the trigger. The bullet slammed into Virginia's shoulder. The woman dropped the knife and slapped her hand to her shoulder with a cry, her face stark with shock, she staggered backwards, then fell on her butt. Jesa jumped up and lurched to the car.

"Dammit, Jesa, get away-"

Jesa leaned in for a few seconds, then she stepped back from the car with a wriggling bundle in her hands. She looked down at the shrieking baby, then beamed at Tristano. Sirens wailed in the distance.

The street was swarming with police, the area rampant with shouts and chattering as they went about their business. Some deputies were inside the house with search warrants, two were checking out the Mesinas' car, others wandered the yard clearing the area. More deputies arrested the Mesinas and took them to the jail.

McKabe climbed out of his car, his grin spread ear-to-ear. "Good job, kids," he praised Tristano and Jesa when he reached them. "Damned good job." He clapped Tristano on the shoulder and hugged Jesa. He pressed his Stetson down tight on his head as the wind tried to steal it. "After the hospital checks the baby out, do you want the honors of returning Brie to her parents?"

He leaned over and patted the baby that Jesa still held. Brie grabbed his thick finger and held on, gurgling and cooing. McKabe smiled down at her.

Tristano and Jesa shared a tender gaze. "No," his eyes on Jesa, Tristano said, "you go ahead and bring her home." He didn't dampen the emotional moment of rescuing the kidnapped baby by mentioning Stedman was going to be arrested for embezzlement.

McKabe looked from one to the other, they only had eyes for each other. Chuckling, his hands on his hips, snow covered his hat and shoulders. "All right. I get to play the big man. I'll see you two tomorrow at the debriefing. It's late and it'll take a while to arraign the Mesinas and tie up loose ends."

Another ambulance pulled up. The other two were transporting the unconscious Apollo Cross and Virginia to the hospital, with armed guards. As soon as McKabe handed the baby to a paramedic and climbed in the back of the ambulance, Tristano took Jesa's hand and led her to her little rusted heap.

Inside the warm vehicle, with big smiles they watched McKabe two-finger salute them as a paramedic shut the door and the ambulance took off, sirens wailing. Tristano rolled his arm around Jesa and nudged her to hook her seatbelt, then stretched across and crushed her against his chest. He bent and bumped her nose with his. "Jesselin, what the hell am I going to do with you? The danger you put yourself in, damn, you're going to give me a damned heart attack, girl."

Nestling against him, Jesa yawned. "What did you expect me to do, Tristano, that baby's life was in jeopardy. I couldn't let anything happen to her." She snuggled down with another yawn, "I just couldn't."

Turning the wheel with one hand, hugging her tenderly, Tristano smiled out the window where the night was dark and turbulent, the blizzard wild as a stampede of buffalo, just as treacherous as the people they'd just dealt with. His sigh resigned, but happy, "I know, Bitty bit, I know. Let's go home."

Chapter Thirty-Four

Tristano pulled into Jesa's driveway, the tires rolling over hard-packed scrunching snow instead of gravel. He parked and helped her out of the car. Holding her arm, he didn't move, just tipped his head back to look up at the sky. In the time that they had driven up the mountain, now only a sprinkling of snowflakes pelted his face.

A slight smile, he blinked at the flakes and said thoughtfully, "The blizzard, it's lessened, wind's not so biting and wicked, and I think it might be a couple of degrees warmer than it was a few hours ago."

"Thank God." Jesa shivered. "I hate to admit it but the storm and snow have had me on edge. I thought I would like it once Orainn was cut off from the mainland, feel safer, but, now, I feel kind of boxed in, like a little claustrophobic." She caught Tristano's brows rise and an imperceptible lift to his mouth, as if he was happy about that?

She was going to ask him about it when she realized she was wearing his jacket and he was in just his shirt. She took his hand, pleased when he twined their fingers, and they hurried up the steps to the cottage.

Inside, Jesa peeled his jacket off and handed it to him. He stared at it, his lower lip pushed out in almost a pout. He took it, sighed. "Jesselin, listen, ah," for once in his life he seemed unsure of what he wanted to say. His eyes lowered to the womanly flesh exposed under the ruined blouse. Feeling his loins heat and harden, he jerked his gaze back up to her face.

The big strong tough agent with a pout on his dark stubbly face was too adorable for her to resist. With a soft smile, Jesa offered, "Would you like something to drink?" Then she blushed slightly. "I mean I have tea or water, not much of a choice."

His forehead creased with a quirked brow. "You asking me to stay, Bitty bit?" She'd run him and Roarke off whenever they tried to hang with her in her home. Plus, she was careful, except for today, to not find herself alone with either of them at their domiciles.

Wanting some private time to get her more comfortable with him, Tristano had tried a few times to persuade her to go to his hotel under pretense of he needed to retrieve something, but like with Roarke, she'd always insisted that he take her where she needed to be then go back and get whatever he'd forgotten. Tristano had abided by her wishes, Roarke had not. Today Roarke had basically forced her to go inside his home where he'd planned to restrain her and take what he wanted, with or without her permission.

She had been right to keep both men away, look what happened when she hadn't. Jesa had told Tristano on the way home about Ronan, his attack, the blackmail, how she determined where Brie Westcott was.

Recalling Jesa's account of Roarke's attack, Tristano felt rage heat from his tensed gut and spread to his chest. He knew she'd sugarcoated it, made it sound like it wasn't that big of a deal. But, hell, her blouse was in shreds and she'd had to break a window to get away. She had turned his diary and the notes she managed to swipe over to McKabe.

Jesa watched his vengeful face darken with anger, eyes slitting to ruthless coals, she said quickly, "Don't dwell on things, Tristano. It's done. Just," she ducked her head shyly, "be with me."

"Ah," he opened his mouth, he wanted to just dash out the door and go hunt that bastard down. They had the fucker, Apollo Cross who'd chased her across the country. Cross had told Jesa he'd killed some of the people she'd stayed with. The murders had come up under the NCIC search Tristano had done on her when investigating her.

He had called the local police departments and learned Jesa had been the suspect in those cases since she'd disappeared from each location shortly before the murders occurred. The police didn't have her true name, but Tristano recognized her description. If they'd caught her, they would have matched prints she'd left at the homes.

Tristano would have to ascertain if there was DNA or prints left at the scenes, or witnesses, and research if Cross was in the vicinity at the times of the homicides, but he didn't doubt it. Anyone who would kill a guy, toss his body in a dumpster, then chase after a young woman to assassinate her so she couldn't be a witness, for years- wouldn't hesitate to slay someone else.

With everything Tristano knew from Georgia and now here, he believed he had most things figured out. Yeah, thank God they had Cross in custody, but Roarke, Deputy Caitlin had called and said when they went to arrest Roarke he was gone. There's nowhere he could hide on the island, but Tristano hated it that he was still out there and therefore a danger to Jesa.

"Stop it, Tristano," Jesa said softly.

He blinked at her. "Huh? What?"

"Stop thinking about Ronan and going after him." She could read him like a book. "Just, be with me," she repeated.

The tension eased from his broad shoulders, a small smile softened the harsh edges of his face, the lower part covered with evening black scruff. "Okay, Bitty bit. But, I'm going to need a distraction. A big distraction." He wiggled his eyebrows at her signaling his intentions, and grinned at the color blooming on her cheeks.

"Distraction?" She asked gawkily, "Uh, like you mean you want some tea?"

"Ah, Bitty bit, you know what I want." He stepped around her and locked the front door then turned to face her. "I want this," he slid his big hand around her jaw and the side of her head, and lowered his mouth slowly, barely touched her lips with his, giving her a chance to push him away. She didn't.

His other hand slipped around her to splay on her lower back, he pulled her tight against him, and seized her mouth with a full-on assault of her lips, her tongue, he sucked the very breath, her energy out of her. She clung to his shirt sleeves as if her legs were too shattered to hold her up.

Relishing the feel of her slender delicate body in his strong hands, Tristano browsed his mouth across her lips to her cheek, licked the apple roundness of it, then kissed down her jaw, to her throat. Growling with bites at the soft skin of her neck, he moved lower to where her breasts swelled out of the torn blouse.

Jesa's panting breaths rushed in his ear, instead of pushing him away; her gripping fingers clutched him more tightly to her. His hand on her jaw slid to web the back of her neck, he moved the hand at her back to her chest. His fingers spread across her breasts. Their heat meshed, his hard hand, her soft bosom.

When her eyes rolled up to his, her heavy lids slid low over the entranced greens, shining with her arousal. Her tongue wetted her lips as if searching for his since he'd taken them away.

"Jesselin," his voice husky with erotic hunger. If his impassioned eyes were his mouth she'd already be eaten up. He shifted his hips, pressing his erection against her making no mistaking what he wanted. He held his breath, her response was to stroke her palms up his chest and twine around his neck. "Baby," he rasped, "you know what I want, tell me if you're ready."

Jesa tugged on his thick neck to pull his mouth back down, her head tilted and she kissed him like he'd kissed her.

Smiling, *a fast learner, his Bitty bit*. He drew back slightly, asked, "Are you ready, Jesselin? If you're not, we can wait. As long as you need, whatever you want, baby."

Jesa lowered her head, pink crept up her neck, she fiddled with a button on his shirt.

"It's okay," he said gently, stroking his hand down the back of her hair. "Do you want to talk about it? Or, are you just not interested in me…" Tristano had felt her response, saw the way her eyes torched when he kissed her. His hand half covering the upper swells of her breasts, she'd shivered and pressed her body closer to his.

She wanted him, he was sure of it. He needed to get her to talk to him. "Jesselin," he said softly, moving his hand from her chest and curled a finger under her chin and lifted it, "tell me what you're thinking, feeling."

Her big eyes blinked up at him with a hint of embarrassment, then lowered. "I…Tristano…"

"Tell me, baby, what? Are you afraid of me? You don't want me?"

Shaking her head, a small shy smile bowed her pretty face. "No, I mean, yes, I'm not afraid of you, and…" she peered coyly up at him, "I want you, very much. It's just," she trailed off, shielding her lowering eyes with a turn of her head.

He pondered her half giving, half pulling away. "Baby, are you a virgin? Is that what's stopping you?" He had suspected she was, it wouldn't be a surprise. "That's all right. I told you if this isn't right that it's okay, no pressure." It was difficult for him to back off, his entire body hard as a rock hummed, surrounded her curvy form in throbbing hunger.

"It's not that, Tristano." She bit her lower lip. "I'm afraid if you know I'm a virgin that you won't want me, being so horribly inexperienced. I mean, I know you like women like Tahni-"

With a groan, he dropped his head back, then bent forward and kissed her, kissed her long and hard proving there was no question he wanted her. Taking a breath, he cupped her chin, "Baby, if I hear that woman's name out of your mouth again I swear I'll-" at her sad look, he sighed, then smiled.

"Jesselin, Tahni made my damn skin crawl, she'd practically hump my leg, it was like trying to pry a squid off. Slimy and sticky. I've wanted *you* from the moment you picked me up at the wharf. You had me at 'excuse me if my limo's in the shop.'"

He licked her puffy lips. "I was pretty sure right from the start that you were a virgin, an essence of innocence freaking glows from you. Baby," he looked in her eyes and stated, "it doesn't matter to me what you are, hooker, virgin, whatever, I want you. Only you. Only *ever* you, from this day on."

Her brows peaked together. "What does that mean?" She seemed completely unaware that she snuggled against him.

He put his hands on her shoulders so she'd know he was serious. "Jesselin, I'm not looking for a one night stand or a quick fling with you. I'm in this for the long haul. I want you with me every day, every night, in my bed, by my side."

"But," she bit her lip, her voice husky she asked, "why me? All those glamorous women-"

"Lord, Jesselin, stop it. Forget about other women, other men, it's just you and me. Just you," he kissed her, "and me."

"But," she argued, so insecure after all her years of having a mother who didn't care, and then unable to stay in one place and make friends. She could never trust anyone. She was socially stunted. Jesa said in a small voice, "Why me? I have no confidence, I don't trust anyone, I'm not even decent looking. My mom and a barmaid at the saloon I worked in and others told me all the time how sad it was that I was so homely."

His eyes rolled, he squeezed her shoulders. "You are shy and sweet and self-conscious. You've been on the run for four years looking over your shoulder in terror of a killer stalking you across country. You couldn't make friends in case he used them against you, you couldn't put down permanent roots, gain any kind of stability. You *should* be wary, on edge, lacking in self-confidence. But," he gripped her upper arms.

"Jesselin, Bitty bit," he said with a crooked smile, "you are the strongest person I know, and the bravest, and," he grinned, "the sharpest. You were able to discern instinctually when Cross was getting near, and you were brilliant in your continuing to evade the bastard. And me."

Her face brightened at his compliments. Then her brows lowered in a confused frown. "Wait, how did you know that?" She started to pull away, worry etching her face. "How," a gulp shook her throat, "how long have you known who I was?"

Gently drawing her back into his embrace, he wanted to keep her in the moment, not sink into her past, he said, "We'll talk about all that later, right now, I want to talk about us."

"But-"

Diverting her from the conversation of who she really is, he kissed the tip of her nose and smiled. "Besides smart and brave, you're the most compassionate person I have ever known." He said wryly, "And the most reckless and foolhardy," he laughed at her frown. Combing his fingers through her silky curls he said, "You're beautiful, Jesselin. Your mother, that barmaid, they were mean and jealous. Your beauty shines from the inside out, baby. I've never seen anything more breathtaking in my life, than you." He stopped talking; they stared into each other's eyes.

"Now," his deep voice sultry, he plucked at the safety pin on her blouse. "What do you have to say? Will you trust me to take care of you, in all things?"

Her smile brilliant, she nodded. "Yes, Tristano. I trust you," she blushed, "and I want you too. Now. Right now. Can we-"

He bent and slid his hands under her butt, lifting her so her legs could wrap around his hips, a squeal eeked out with a giggle, she linked her ankles behind his back. Tristano kissed her, smiled with relief and fiery lust. An arm rolled under her bottom to brace her, he caught the hem of her blouse and pulled it over her head and tossed it behind them as he carried her down the hall to her bedroom.

In the doorway, his kiss charged vigorous, demanding and determined, his body so hot for her he feared he would rocket to the moon before he got her on the bed. With a gruff groan, he broke from her lips, leaving them wet and parted and panting, her half-lidded eyes gleamed with her own heat. His dark eyes delving into hers, the green windows of her beautiful soul, husky with emotion and arousal, he rasped, "I love you, Jesselin."

Her eyes popped, brows flew up. "You- you do?"

He nodded with a casual bump of his shoulder. "Yeah. Have for a long time now. I know we've only known each other a relatively short time," he shrugged, "but I feel what I feel. It started with the picture your saloon owner in Georgia gave me. I was struck with…" how could he describe the damned arrow that had struck him when he saw her picture? Pierced his heart, his manhood, set him aflame before he even met her. And when they did come face to face? He'd been blown clear away. "I just, I love you, Jesselin, plain and simple. I can't imagine my life without you."

She grinned, happiness sparkled. "Me too, Tristano, I- I love you too. I don't know when it happened, but when I was so positive you would rescue me today, that's when I knew for sure."

She took a deep breath, brushed her palm tenderly down his stubbly cheek. "When you found the footprints, then the hang-ups, I'd have feelings of being watched, followed, I feared he'd found me, which," she sighed wryly. "As it turned out I wasn't just being paranoid. Anyway, my thoughts turned increasingly to fleeing, trying to figure out how to get off Orainn and, then," there was pain in her voice grown small with sorrowful reluctance, "start a new life all over again, somewhere…else."

"Baby." He hugged her, shaking his head.

She looked up at him. "Thing was, Tristano, all I could think about was you. Never seeing you again, well, it hurt, physically. It was literally a physical sharp pain in my heart."

His arm under her bottom he lifted her for his kiss. "Yeah," he murmured. "I was afraid too. Afraid you'd figure out why I was here and flee before I could convince you everything would be okay. I'd make sure of it. I couldn't tell you in the beginning, you would never have believed me that I wasn't there to arrest you. You would have run. I've always believed you were innocent."

Stroking her small fingers through his short hair, she said miserably, "I knew when Ronan kissed me that I had no interest or desire to have any other man's mouth on mine, other than yours. Nonetheless, I needed to go. But every time I'd try to still my brain to make a plan to leave, you would float into my mind, and I couldn't think. I didn't want to never see you again. It was...agonizing, Tristano."

Kissing the top of her head, his lips against her hair he said, "And now it's over. You don't have to run anymore, Jesselin, and now, we can be us, right?"

The sad smile broke into an effervescent grin. "Yes, yes, Tristano. Make us an us!"

Sighing with a growl of delight at her acquiescence, and a chuckle at the way she phrased things, Tristano moved them through the threshold. Entering the darkened bedroom, he said, "I only have one question, sweetheart."

Jesa peppered his face with kisses as his fingers deftly unclasped her bra. "Hmmm, what is that?"

His smile pressed against her lips. "Do you want your spanking before we make love, or after?"

"What? My- my spanking? You can't-"

One arm supporting her butt, still carrying her, he slid her bra off her arms and let it drop to the floor. His eyes lowered, pupils enlarged with sizzling heat at the exquisite sight of her bare, plump flesh.

Caressing her soft flesh with his big hand, grinning, he said, "Yeah, I warned you and warned you and still you threw yourself right into the pit of danger, you could have been killed. I can't live through that again, Bitty bit, I'll have a damned heart attack. I need to do something to dissuade you from putting your life in peril again. I'm going to redden that little ass so bad you'll think twice before being so reckless again. So, before, or after?" He walked them into the room, his hand on the button of her jeans.

Stringing her arms around his neck, Jesa sighed. "After."

Grinning broadly, just as he let her slide to her feet to the floor, he smacked her on her bottom.

"Owe! Hey!"

His deep laugh teasing, he kicked the door closed.

Chapter Thirty-Five

The dawn was just breaking, poking fingers of faint light around the plaid curtain at her drowsy eyelids, pushing them up. Jesa sat up in bed. Yawning, she lifted her long curls off her shoulders, and felt the locks slide over her skin. Her bare skin. "Oh my gosh!" She looked down, she was naked! Then, last night came gushing back to her, and a blush rose up her neck to color her face, her skin flushed with heat as the memories flowed.

Images of Tristano, peeling off the rest of her clothes, teaching her what a man's hands, and mouth, and other appendages, the blush deepened, could do to her body. She was certainly no longer a virgin!

A joyful smile lit her face, he'd made a woman out of her. Not once, or twice, her body quivered with the remembrance of their time in the shower before he curled around her in bed and cuddled her tight until they fell asleep. A sated sigh rolled through her spent body. Spent, sore, including her bottom from the spanking, but, darn she felt wonderful, and she couldn't wait to do it again-

She looked to the other side of the bed and he wasn't there. A sudden prick of fear riveted up her spine. Had everything he'd said been a lie? Was he spoofing her when he'd told her he loved her? Was it just to get her into bed?

An angry scowl was replacing the deep pang of hurt the thought gave her. Pushing the sheet aside, she padded to her dresser, dragged out a long sleeved t-shirt, jeans and panties and got dressed. A noise rattled down the hall, her bedroom door was open. After everything that had happened yesterday, a shiver of fright tickled the hairs on the back of her neck. Cautiously, she tiptoed down the hall and to the kitchen where the noise emanated from.

Tristano was there. Dressed in different clothes than last night, black jeans and a black button down. In bare feet he was setting plates on the table.

Jesa stood staring with awe. He was pulling things out of a white paper bag and setting them on the table. Her gaze flit to the counter, brows rose, there was a coffee maker percolating away. She didn't own one. The smell of fresh coffee wafted through the small room to her nose.

"Tristano?" her voice bewildered, uncertain.

He turned around, a big smile sheathing his hard face, his dark eyes rolled down her body and back up. The smile widened. "You're not wearing a bra, are you, Bitty bit?" He chuckled when her face reddened and she wrapped her arms across her chest. "How are you feeling," he asked her. "I mean about what we did last night, make that all night, are you okay?"

Not answering his question, she asked, "What are you doing? You weren't in bed, I thought you left…"

The hurt evident in her small voice tugged his smile down. He quickly stepped to her, gathered her in his arms, bent and kissed her growling like a tiger devouring its mate. Hard, hot, heavy, breathless. When she was melted butter in his arms, he leaned back and peered down at her, his smile soft and serious.

He tucked a strawberry curl behind an ear. "Jesselin, I meant every word I said last night. I'm hoping you and I," he paused, considered his words. "When this whole business is over with, I think we should talk about how we're going to have our…relationship. Like where we're going to live."

Tilting her head, she said with some bewilderment, "Where we're going to live? Like, you mean to- together?"

Straight white teeth gleamed in his smile. "Yeah, together." A hint of doubt flashed in his ardent eyes. "That is, if you want to. Do you want there to be an…us, as in together?"

He was so handsome in a rough, rugged way, black hair flopping in his gorgeous dark eyes. How could she have ever thought Ronan's eyes were gorgeous? If you looked up gorgeous in the dictionary it would say: Tristano Koffi. Powerful heroic man, strong body, muscled and masculine and daring.

And an insane lover, rough and gentle, slow and hard, he did it all. He brought her to so many intense peaks and had made her hurl off them in a blaze of mind-blinding, body launching sensations of incinerating heat and screaming, pleasure-bursting agony.

A blush hinted again, her nether parts tingled and heated as she recalled his initiating her into the wonders of love-making. She pictured his brawny naked body. Pure granite, dark hair over his strapping chest, and down below- she blinked and swallowed the thoughts away. "Yes, I would like there to be an us," her lashes batted shyly.

His smile grew big again with alleviated elation. "Good. That's settled then." Hugging her, he smiled placidly down at her, "So, what did you think about last night? Was it as you thought it would be?" Her face reddened, he loved her blush. She was so sweet, so young. Too young. But he was greedy and selfish, he wasn't giving her up.

"Uh..." Her eyes turned down in shyness, then rolled back up to see him grinning at her. "Yes. It was...amazing. A hundred times better than I had dreamed. I...liked it, a lot. I can't wait to do it again, except," her cheeks burnt red.

"You're sore?" He smiled with indulgent pride at her embarrassed nod. "It would be abnormal if you weren't," he caressed her cheek with a thick calloused finger. "I'll draw you a warm bath after breakfast, after a soaking you'll feel better. There's other things we can do for now, while you recuperate," his leer a promise of more eroticism to come.

Puzzled, her strawberry brows inverted in question. "Like what?"

An endearing laugh at her innocence, he had so much to teach her. Damn, he couldn't wait. "Here," he said, nodding to the table, "sit down. I ran out and changed my clothes and got us some breakfast. I know you have nothing edible or nutritional here."

Grinning at her affronted harrumph, he turned and poured them coffee, set the two steaming mugs on the table. "Go on, eat now," he prodded when she hadn't moved, "it's better if I show you than tell you." If he shared some of things he wanted to do to her she'd likely freak out and run for the hills.

Warily, Jesa pulled out a chair and sat down, then immediately hitched her behind up off the chair with a whine. Rubbing her bottom, a reminder what happens when she doesn't heed his warnings for her safety, she scowled at his laughter as he set the coffee pot back on the counter.

Her stomach grumbled at the platter of pancakes and sausages, bowls of biscuits and gravy. She reached for a glass of orange juice he'd set at both plate settings. Taking a small sip, she said, "But, I don't see how we can have a- a relationship. I live here and you live," her brow knit, "where do you live?"

Tristano sat down and forked a few pancakes on his plate and motioned for her to do the same. Dropping a glob of butter, then half a cup of syrup on his cakes, he cut off a chunk. "Well, that's something we need to talk about. You said you were feeling claustrophobic here on Orainn, and I know you have friends, but no family here. Would it be hard for you to...pull up roots and move to Georgia?" He popped a forkful of syrup laden pancake in his mouth.

Reaching for the butter, she froze. Remembered he'd told her before. "Georgia? You're from Georgia?"

He chewed with relish and nodded. "Yes." Setting his fork down, he crossed his forearms laying them on the table in front of his plate. His face serious, he said carefully, "I wasn't sent here, Jesselin, to find the missing baby. I had tracked you here. We used the kidnapping as a cover for my initial investigation."

At her stricken expression he hurried on. "There was a man, a mobster, Carlo DeFranco, found in a dumpster behind a tavern called the Noir Den Saloon in Savannah." Ignoring the white that replaced the color in her skin he went on.

"Local police investigated and they learned a singer, a very young singer," he gave her a look of disapproval, "had been singing in that bar that night. Patrons had seen her suddenly rush off the stage and disappear out the back door. She never returned, just inexplicably disappeared. She left her purse at the saloon, never went back there or to her apartment. Left everything she owned and just, poof," he snapped his fingers in the air.

Clutching her suddenly trembling hands in her lap, Jesa lowered her eyes to stare at her plate, she didn't move, her skin was white as the snow outside.

"The man in the dumpster had been murdered, and the girl became a person of interest since she was seen fleeing out the back door where the dumpster was. Police didn't know if maybe she'd been killed too, or she was the killer. They issued a no bond warrant for her." His eyes narrowed at her tiny gasp, her gaze raised to him. Gnawing on her inside cheek, terrible fear radiated so intensely from her it was palpable. He had talked about Apollo Cross chasing after her, but she hadn't known Tristano had been after her too. To apprehend her.

It pained him to see her distress, but he needed to tell her that he knew everything. "The police searched for the singer but couldn't find her. Then, one day quite some time after, in Oklahoma there was a murder. The description of the young woman who had again, mysteriously vanished, was entered into the NCIC system. That's an electronic clearing house of crime data that any criminal justice agency in the U.S. can access. The description of the young woman matched the bolo for the girl from the Noir Den. That's when they contacted the FBI."

Her body rigid as a metal pole, Jesa set her fingertips on the edge of the table as if preparing to bolt. Tristano reached over and gently laid his large hand over her trembling one.

"She started changing her hair color, length, and wore colored contacts. They were unable to trace her until there was another murder, this one in Ohio. That's when I was brought in. I am a lead investigator, I get assigned the unsolvable cases.

"Using facial recognition from surveillance videos around each location such as from convenience stores, banks, the shelters and apartments where you had been recognized, as well as at bus stations and the like, I was able to track you, Jesselin, or, I should say, Indiana Kolbi. I had a computer program to pick up your photo at any public transportation in the country, including the ferry you took to Orainn. Matching fingerprints and DNA were left at the identified locations, I sent yours from here out to a lab and-"

Blanching, her eyes swung in a panic up to him.

He gently squeezed her hand. "Yes, I know who you are. Actually," he chuckled, "the second you took your hat off the day you brought me to the station, and I saw that glorious hair and those amazing green eyes, I knew it was you. Pictures from the saloon did not do you justice. And," his grin lopsided, he said, "I was hot for you the minute you stood on the dock and told me you were my ride."

Staring at his hand covering hers, she was quiet a moment, processing his words. "Why didn't you," her voice croaked through her constricted throat, "arrest me then?"

"I had to confirm it. Then, since I knew you couldn't get off the island without my being made aware," at her questioning look he said, "we had a lot of deputies posted at the wharf looking for that baby. Anyway, since I knew you weren't going anywhere, and the more I got to know you, I was sure you weren't a murderer, and I planned to get down to the bottom of the mystery."

A wounded pout pushed her lips out. "So, you only kept me with you so you could keep an eye on me."

"Hmm," he shrugged a shoulder, "part of it. McKabe knew I was after you," a chuckle huffed out with a shake of his head. "He planned that scheme of you being the disseminator of all the information so we could have eyes on you at all times. But really," he leaned closer to her, "I wanted you to be with me because I...hell girl, I had the hots for you, bad. I didn't want Roarke getting his horny paws on you, and, well, I truly enjoyed your company. I missed the hell out of you the times we were apart. Plus, I wanted you by my side so I could protect you."

He grumbled, "We see how well that turned out, Miss I Gotta Dive Headfirst Into Danger." He squeezed her hand again, observing her facial features loosen somewhat; a meek smile appeared briefly.

"So," she said very quietly, "you don't think I'm guilty of...killing that man?"

Ludicrous, his snort said. "Please. You're barely over 5 feet and 100 pounds. The body in the dumpster was 6'2" and weighed 250, and the dumpster was over your head. Unless you had help, and I really doubt that, no way could you have tossed him in there. You were singing one second and gone the next, how could you have killed such a big man, tossed him in the dumpster and fled in such a short period of time?

319

Plus, no motive could be determined. Police found no connection between you and Carlo DeFranco."

She nodded emphatically as he spoke, budding relief breathed color back in her pale skin.

He told her, "The cops canvassed the area, found a couple of homeless men that said they'd seen a car parked next to the alley and the shadows of two men in the dark emerge from it and slink into the alley. They also said they saw a small person, female they figured, with long light hair, hard to tell in the dark. The girl was running like the devil was after her, and they thought the shadows chased after her. Then," his mouth tipped up at a corner, "they smoked their joint, drank their whiskey and passed out."

Jesa sat up, the first signs of hopefulness on her face. "There were witnesses? They know those two men killed that guy, they can prove it wasn't me, oh Tristano-"

He patted her hand. "Calm your liver, Bitty bit. They aren't the most credible witnesses. They were drunk and high, both had warrants out for them. I read the police report. Their story had changed a few times. Once it was the males chasing the girl, then it was the girl chasing the men, then there were zombies stealing bodies."

Smiling at her head jerking at their nonsensical stories, he said, "Also, it was dark and all they could see were shadows, silhouettes, they couldn't describe any of the suspects. You remained the main suspect since you'd unaccountably disappeared."

Big green eyes rounded in wonder up at him. "But you believe me, you know it was those men that killed the man. I was the witness. But they saw me. I was working illegally, I was underage working in a bar, my mother had run out on me. There's no way the police would have believed me. I would have been arrested. Since the one guy saw me, I was afraid he'd go in the saloon and ask about me. Maybe find my purse, learn my name, know where I lived. I was between a rock and a hard place." Panic escalated, tremors rattled in her voice, he could hear her breaths start racing.

Tristano picked up her hand and held it in his larger one. "Everything will be okay, Jesselin. We have Apollo Cross. He had a 92 Beretta on him. The gun can take 9mm bullets, and I found a silencer in his cargo pants' deep pocket. The guy in the dumpster was shot with a 9mm bullet.

"There's a very good chance that he was too stupid or too cheap to toss the murder weapon, and when Ballistics tests it, they'll find it a match. He'll likely snitch his partner out to throw the blame on, and the cops can pick that thug up as well. My feeling is that it was a mob hit. The important point though, is that your name will be cleared."

The breath Jesa felt like she'd been holding for four long years oozed out, the tight coil in her stomach slowly unwound, the tension she bore in her back, her shoulders, finally purged. She felt light as a feather, lighter than air. She was free, free to be with Tristano, free to live her life as she pleased, where she pleased without having to look over her shoulder and keep her things packed for quick escape.

A slight pall lingered. "Did Chief McKabe know about me? What about Ronan?" Her stomach re-clenched. "Mr. Barton, Clarie? Oh, Tristano, I couldn't bear it if they all knew, thought I was a- a murderer- a criminal!" She pulled her hand from under his and pushed her chair back. Mortification sorely marking her face, she stood up.

Tristano got up and quickly gathered her in his arms. "Okay, Bitty bit, don't jump to conclusions. No one but McKabe and I knew. Just as I'd traced you to Orainn, the news of the kidnapping hit nationwide. McKabe didn't know completely about you in the beginning. I had my headquarters call him to have me link up, told him since it was a kidnapping the FBI needed to be involved, giving me an excuse to be on the island."

A wry chuckle, he told her, "He was suspicious from the start. He questioned me and I told him I couldn't divulge everything, but hinted there was something involving you. The guy didn't think you could ever be up to no good, so his concern was that you were in danger. When you mentioned the hang-ups and I saw those footprints in your yard, I fully informed him. He already had a clue, one reason why he wanted to have you included in the investigation. That way we'd know where you were most of the time, and you'd be protected."

Listening to him, Jesa calmed down, burrowed into his chest. "Okay, I'd hate for anyone to think that I was…a bad person."

"Uh, huh." He petted her hair, kissed her head, then drew her back so he could look at her. "Now, about what I was talking about before,

321

you and me. Would it be a terrible hardship for you to leave Orainn and move back to Georgia? I work out of Atlanta. I have an apartment on the outskirts of the city, but, we could build a house…"

"A…house? You and me?"

"Yeah," he laughed. "You and me living in a house together. I plan on asking you to marry me, Jesselin, but after some time. I know I'm sure what I want, but I need for you to be absolutely sure. You're so young, and you haven't lived what anyone would call a normal life. You may want to put your feet in the water, test different things out. Well?"

Her gaze wandered his face, the dark enigmatic eyes; his mouth was harsh yet so very kissable, sturdy jaw, strong nose. Brawny, strapping body, and unbelievable in the bedroom, and elsewhere as she'd learned last night. "I have made friends here, at the bistro. We could always come here for holiday?"

Nodding happily, he grinned. "Yes, of course. I love you, Jesselin; I can't wait for us to settle. When we're alone, and can take our time learning about each other," a sensual snicker chipped out.

"What?"

"We need a really big house, Bitty, bit, so we can christen every room and then some," his mouth curved in a promising leer, eyes heavy-lidded with plans for them.

She pretended to hit his arm. "You are insatiable!"

He wrapped his arms around her and lifted her off her feet. "Only for you, baby, always for you." Swooping his head down he claimed her lips, took ownership of his Jesselin.

Tristano was carrying her off to the bedroom to show her what other things they could do, when his phone buzzed. Setting her on her feet, he slipped his phone from his pocket and answered it.

Jesa slid an arm around his waist, looking up at him as he spoke. Her body tingled with desire, waiting for him to get off the phone so they could-

Tristano's half-smile when he'd heard Chief McKabe's voice faltered, then flattened to a grimace. His eyes flicked to Jesa. She felt the anger in the sudden rigidness of his body.

He argued with the chief, "McKabe, come on, you know she isn't guilty. There is no way I'm gonna fucking-" McKabe cut him off. Tristano lowered his head, scraped his fingers through his hair in frustration. "Yeah, yeah, I hear you. We'll be there shortly." His lips clamped as he angrily shoved his phone in his pocket.

Feeling his anger, Jesa stepped back from him. "What is it, Tristano? Did Apollo Cross get away?"

He set his hands on his narrow hips, face had darkened with ire, then his gaze flickered to her and he saw her fear. "Ah, Bitty bit, it's not really, ah," how was he going to do this to her? His tiny, delicate, tormented Jesselin?

Chapter Thirty-Six

"Baby," his voice with rare gentleness held angry regret. He stifled the anger. "That was McKabe." At her nod, he sighed. "McKabe had notified the authorities in Georgia that he has Cross, and you, in custody. We knew we'd have to deal with the charges against you, but," he dragged his hand up his face, pushed his hair back. "Hell, Jesselin, McKabe and I thought I could get you cleared before going back to Georgia."

First confusion clouded her green eyes, then they flared with horror. "What are you saying, Tristano, what do you have to do to me?" A few stumbled feet backwards and she would have fallen if Tristano hadn't grabbed her arm.

"Steady, baby, steady. Stay calm. We'll get through this, I promise. I have to- now keep cool, I won't let anyone hurt you. Right now I need you put on your jacket, hat and mittens." When she just stood staring at him, he commanded softly, "Do it."

Her lips pushed out in consternation, but she did as he said. When she had her outerwear on, eyebrows wrinkled in dread, she said, "Now, what-"

He caught one of her wrists, and gently turned her so her back was facing him. He tugged his handcuffs off the back of his belt and snapped one over her tiny wrist.

She tried to swing around. "Tristano! What are you doing? Stop it!"

He grasped her other arm and pulled it carefully behind her and snapped the other one on. It pained him worse than her to have to do this. Make her so defenseless, the humiliation she'll have to suffer, the fear. He held her small, fragile wrists in his large hands and his stomach

324

pitched. Putting his hands on her shoulders he slowly turned her to face him. The fear and betrayal in her eyes killed him. "Ah, little one, I have to arrest you. This is only until we're, ah at the station."

Her whimper wailed, "But I don't understand?" She struggled to get free of the cuffs.

He squeezed her shoulders. "Don't fight it, you'll only hurt yourself. As soon as we get to the station I can take them off."

"But, why? Tristano? Why are you doing this to me?"

Bending towards her, he zipped her jacket up, touched her face in a soft caress, but she jerked her head from his hand, turning it quickly to hide the burgeoning tears.

He grabbed his coat and hat and grasped her upper arm. "Come on, the sooner we do this the sooner it'll be over." He ushered her to the car, helped her into the backseat, buckled her seatbelt. The whole time she kept her head averted from him, her lower lip trembling. Her worst fear was being realized.

Tristano climbed in behind the wheel, reached back and petted her knee, ignoring her moving her leg to shift his hand off her. Starting down the road, he told her, "McKabe said I have to arrest you, bring you in this way or the Savannah Chatham Metropolitan Police Department, SCMPD, will come and appropriate you. They'll come by helicopter, they'll take you from us, from me. I have to do it this way for it to be a legal arrest, then we can deal with bail here and then take care of the charges."

"I- I'm going to- to jail?" Her chattering teeth broke up her words.

He knew her teeth chattering was fear, but he turned up the heater. "No, baby, this is to avoid that. We have to do this by the book. If the SCMPD thinks we have arrested you and have you in custody they won't come racing here to get you. Trust me, they'll accept any excuse to not have to chopper in to Orainn in this hellish weather."

Her head turned away from him, tears rolling down her cheeks, she sniffed, swallowed with a choke, closed her eyes hard, the tears leaked out the corners.

His hard hand on her small knee, he clinched it gently. "Bitty bit, Jesselin, look at me." She refused to do as he said. Insisting, he repeated, "Baby, please, look at me."

She slowly turned, blinking back the tears. Her eyes speared him full of hurt and betrayal.

"You need to trust me, Jesselin. Have I taken care of you so far?" He waited. She nodded with a chuff in her chest, shivering with fright. "I won't let anything happen to you, you know that, right?" He waited until she nodded with a shade of calm.

They drove silently up the mountain; the snow had decreased to a few flutterers spooling around the car. He parked right in front of the police station under the 'no parking sign,' and helped her out. She listed awkwardly with her hands cuffed behind her back.

Standing in front of her, he clasped her arms. "Honey, I know this will be tough on you, humiliating. It'll be over soon, quickly, trust me, okay?" He cupped her chin, she whispered, "Okay."

Tristano held the door open for her to pass through, and the occupants of the lobby all looked up. Their gazes funneled in at her. Willie-Jean hurried from behind her desk, went right over to Jesa.

"Jesa, honey, we're all on your side, please don't worry. We all know you aren't guilty, right?" She glanced around at the group there. All but one nodded, smiled, called out their support of her.

"Jesa!" Caitlin, Jerry, Granger and a few more cheered, "we're with you, be strong!"

Her heart melted at their trust, their kindness. She ducked her head shyly, smiled bleakly at them as Tristano led her through the room. Just as they reached a doorway, someone snarled from the side, "I knew there was something shady about you, you convict whore."

Tahni moved from the corner to step up to Jesa. The deputy was a head taller than Jesa, but Jesa pulled her spine up, straightened her shoulders. She didn't deign to respond to the snarky woman.

Tristano kept Jesa moving, but Tahni followed them spitting nastiness, "A criminal, a killer, yeah, and you were near us, you could have murdered us at our desks! Tristy," she implored Tristano, "how could you let that filth-"

Tristano swung around and snapped at her, "One more word you bitch and I'll make you regret it. You think you'll be able to speak without a tongue?"

Her eyes popped, face paled, stamping a hand over her blowsy chest in fear, Tahni backed away from them. Tristano wrapped his burly arm possessively around Jesa's slender shoulders and led her away from the shrew.

He brought her to a room where he removed the cuffs, his stomach gripping at the red rings around her thin wrists. The handcuffs had been as loose as he could make them, but she rubbed at the marks they'd left. He stood with her while a deputy fingerprinted her. Her face boiled red in mortification. All the while Tristano softly murmured reassuring words of comfort.

The deputy squirted her blackened fingers with alcohol then gave her paper towels to clean them. Next the deputy took her picture. When they completed the booking process, Tristano brought her to McKabe's office.

Inside, the chief was waiting, seated behind his big desk. Another man sat off to the side in one of the brown leather chairs, his legs crossed neatly in starched slacks. They both rose as Tristano and Jesa entered. Jesa shrank back against Tristano. Keeping a supportive arm around her, he whispered in her ear, "Chin up, my brave girl, everything will be just fine, trust me." He felt her relax slightly under his arm.

"Hey there, little darlin'." McKabe moved from behind his desk to stand in front of her. He wore the brown and tan uniform shirt but had on blue jeans. "This is all just a process to protect you, keep you out of jail." He gestured to the other man. "This is Judge Meyer Coleman. Judge Coleman is here to set your bail."

Jesa's eyebrows punched up, "Bail? I read online there was no bond. That if I was ever arrested I couldn't bond out. How can-"

Judge Coleman moved near her, he smiled kindly. He was tall like McKabe and Tristano, but much older and more on the thinner side. His neatly combed hair was almost all grey; his face was paunchy compared to his thin body. He wore a dark grey suit and blue tie. "Jesselin Judan, ah, that is Indiana Kolbi, right?"

Lips tight, her eyes darted to McKabe, then back to the judge, she gave him a small nod.

Coleman advised her, "Chief McKabe asked me to come here to give you a bond."

"But how can you supersede Georgia's no bond?"

He had nice blue eyes that twinkled mischievously at her. "I am a judge, I can do that. Now, that said," he looked to McKabe.

The chief lifted a paper off his desk and handed it to the Judge. Coleman set it back down and took a pen from his pocket. With a flourish he signed the paper, picked it up and handed it back to McKabe. "There you go, Chief." He smiled at Jesa, "I have ordered you released on your own recognizance. That means you don't have to post bond. It will take only a matter of a few days to clear all this up and the charges will be dropped."

McKabe said, "We had to arrest you, Jesselin, so that the judge could post bond and thereby release you. The warrant has been served and you can't get arrested on it again. You understand?"

Her head lowered, she glanced from one man to the next. "I, I think so. Thank you, Chief McKabe, I appreciate all you've done for me. You didn't need to-"

A hand raised to cut her off. "None of that darlin', none of this was your fault. You are the victim in all this. You shouldn't have suffered for the police's lazy investigation. It will all be over in a couple of days. Now, Judge," he said to Coleman, "we mighty appreciate you comin' out here and doin' this an all. We'll see you and Lillian next Sunday at service?"

"Yep, yep." The judge gave smiles all around. Swinging his long trench coat on, he said, "Well, I'll be on my way, thank goodness the weather has lightened," he appeared a serious yet gentle man. To Jesa he said kindly, "Good luck to you, young woman. From what I hear, you've earned it. Chief went on and on how brave you've been, how valuable you have been to the department.

"It was you that found and rescued that missing child. You, Indiana Kolbi are an extraordinary person and Orainn should be grateful you are one of them." He bowed, covering his grin at her blush at the compliments. He shook Tristano's hand. "I also heard what a stupendous job you did, Special Agent Koffi." Plopping a fedora on his grey head, he nodded to them and made his exit.

"Alrighty then, folks," McKabe said with jaunty cheer, "let's go on into the conference room, Willie-Jean has made us some hot chocolate and brought in pastries. We'll review what we've learned." The three of them trod down the hall, then he said, "Oh, wait, I need something from Willie-Jean's desk." He herded them back to the lobby area.

Jesa tried to protest, dragged her feet, "Listen, I'll wait in the conference room, Chief."

Tristano deliberately twined their fingers, showing the people that not only was she un-cuffed and free, that he believed in her innocence, as well as silently announcing they were an item. When they entered the room, everyone present started clapping. Thank goodness Tahni was no longer present.

Eyes wide, mouth open in awe, Jesa glanced around at the deputies and Willie-Jean who wore a proud, big-toothed smile. Tristano leaned over, whispered in her ear, "See baby, no one thinks you were guilty of murder. You rescued Brie Westcott, you're a hero, Jesselin." He led her around the room and each person shook her hand and praising her ingenuity and courage.

Seeing her face grow brighter and brighter crimson with her embarrassment, Jesa was so used to hiding, avoiding attention, it was all overwhelming for her, Tristano ushered her from the room and with Chief McKabe they traipsed back down the hall to the conference room.

They took seats at the big table. McKabe filled them in. "After getting checked out at the hospital, Deputy Carl Johnson and Deputy Caitlin Saunders brought Brie home. Needless to say, the parents were overjoyed, weeping with gratitude. Unfortunately," he plucked a bear claw off a plate filled with pastries and took a huge bite. "Mmm, darn that's good." He licked his lips. "Yeah, after the big reunion, Stedman Westcott was arrested for embezzlement."

Stirring her hot chocolate, watching the steam spiral from the mug, Jesa tsked. "That is so sad. I hope he doesn't get a lot of prison time, little Brie needs her daddy home. They've all suffered enough trauma."

"It'll be up to the District Attorney what kind of a plea they offer him," Tristano told her. "He still has to answer for the tragic car accident," he picked a chocolate filled donut. When he took a big bite, chocolate oozed out the sides. He leisurely licked the escaping dollops of chocolate.

Munching on his bear claw, getting powdered sugar all over his mouth, McKabe said, "Deputy Howard questioned Apollo Cross at the hospital." He slew a look at Koffi who just shrugged and helped himself to a second donut.

Jesa commented, "I'm surprised he could speak, or was even conscious." She also leveled her gaze on Tristano.

McKabe chuckled. "Yeah, well, apparently his jaw was wired shut and his broken nose was taped up so he was having a hard time breathing. And yes, he wasn't conscious for very long. But Howard was able to get some answers from him. One of which was how had he planned on getting off the island since all transportation on and off had been halted. Howard gave him a pen and his notebook and Cross wrote 'helicopter.'"

Tristano's head came up. "I was informed when I got here that there was no aircraft on the island. He didn't fly in, he would have been spotted right away."

"Yes, there's a record of when he arrived on the island. He came in on one of the last ferries. He used an alias, but there are cameras all over the ferries and at the wharf. ICE keeps alert to illegals entering Orainn. When he realized he was having a hard time getting to Jesa, and he would be landlocked, he told Howard he did a minute surveillance of the island, spent hours upon hours searching and studying the land.

"He stole an old motorbike rusting away in someone's backyard. Daggone lucky son of a gun the key was in the ignition. He came upon an ancient bunker way out in some heavy scrub. There was a chopper hidden in the brush. It was actually, we now determined that it was one of ours, Orainn Police's. I guess he could fly a copter, or hoped he could, which is probably more like it. He's all kinds of stupid as far as I'm concerned."

Tristano frowned, pulled at his lower lip. "That's kind of shoddy police work, Chief. We had search parties that were supposed to scour the island looking for the baby. That bunker and chopper should have been found."

Lifting a mug to his mouth, McKabe nodded, slurped noisily. "True that. I'm disappointed in our people. When I find out who had that grid to search, they'll pay hell. I'm putting my money on Roarke. Anyway, Cross stays locked up until Georgia comes and picks him up, gonna be a long winter for that boy." He sipped more of the hot brew, sighed out his pleasure of the cocoa.

Wiping his fingers on a paper napkin, Tristano reached for yet another pastry. Sitting back with it in his hand, he said, "Speaking of, I want to know about Roarke." Jesa stiffened and McKabe's face at first rocked his fury at the mention of his deputy, then his ridged features slackened into profound sorrow.

"Ah," he grunted. Weaving his sausage thick fingers together he set them on the table, his heavy shoulders slumped in shame of one of his well-known and well-liked officers. "The boy," he said somberly with heavy remorse, "he had us all fooled, especially me. When I read his journal, damn," he scrubbed a beefy hand down his grim face, then folded his hands together again.

"I had Deputy Wate review complaints issued against him over the years. Wate discovered many of them had been…deleted or altered. Roarke must have had help, everyone knows how incompetent he is with computers."

Jesa nodded in agreement. "Yes, that was why he hand-wrote the blackmail notes."

"Huh," Tristano grunted again, "and one of the pieces of evidence that will help to hang him at his trial."

McKabe's head hung, bobbed slightly, then he sat back. "Well, that may take a long time to come to fruition." Tristano and Jesa regarded him in dual query.

When Tristano's expression grew thunderous and he started to speak, McKabe stopped him, "I'd sent deputies to pick him up, and as you were informed, he'd fled his home. I dispatched several officers to scatter all over Orainn and hunt him down. They were still looking when a report came in, from one of the men stationed at the wharf."

Jesa and Tristano leaned forward as he peaked their curiosity. Tristano's anger heightened, he barked, "What are you saying, Chief, spit it the fuck out." At Jesa's scolding huff, he absently patted her hand. He knew the news wasn't going to be good.

His lips bunched, stocky face shook with his own rising anger, McKabe responded, "Yes, well, that helicopter we were talking about, the hidden one that Cross was going to use to escape. Apparently it had originally been stolen and stashed by Roarke. Wate uncovered that he'd entered on the manifest that it had been transported along with the others to the mainland.

"He falsified the report and took the copter for himself. I think originally he just wanted it so he could travel freely around the island. When it was time for the chopper to return to Orainn it would look like it had gotten stolen on the mainland."

Tristano rose half out of his seat, his hand fisted on the table, "Are you saying that son-of-a-bitch got to that chopper and flew the hell off the island?"

The chief sat back, rubbed his chin in vexation. "Yeah. As I said, any aircraft leaving Orainn would have been seen. The only safe way, actually there is no safe way off the island this time of year with the lethal winds and blizzards, treacherous seas and all, but the least dangerous would be going over the wharf side following the washed out road. Still," he repeated gravely, "there really is no safe way out of here."

Shoving his chair back, Tristano slammed his fist on the table and stood up. "Goddammit, Chief, you're telling me that bastard got away?"

McKabe raised and lowered his palms in a calm down fashion. "As far as we know, yes. But, I have a bolo out on him to the mainland. He'd have to go in undetected and have a concealed place to land to get away. That usually means in the wild where he can't be observed. It's winter everywhere, he'd have to travel by foot to the nearest town.

"And it's for sure that either the storm will take the chopper down, or if he makes it, he'll die of hypothermia trying to get to civilization, or at best, he gets out but the law will catch him. Regardless, he'll pay for his crimes."

In aggravation, Tristano dug his frustrated fingers into his scalp and held his head. "Yeah, sure, if he doesn't crash, if he makes it out, if the cops don't capture him, then he's out there, McKabe. A deadly danger to Jesselin, as well as to any other unsuspecting person. Hell, you read the journal, he raped women, forcing or coercing them into having sex with him. He's a treacherous monster, Chief, a goddamned ticking time bomb."

Jesa reached up and circled his wrist with her dainty hand, he looked down at her fingers, they didn't make it all the way around his wrist.

His gaze fell to her upraised face, and his heart raced with desire for her, and dread for her life still being in danger. He let her tug him back down to his seat. He twined their fingers, and the three of them sat in morose silence.

Chapter Thirty-Seven

Three weeks later

"You going to be warm enough?" Tristano handed the knit hat to Jesa. Her dazzling smile as always illuminated her beautiful face and his heart. Stuffing her hair up in the hat, she reproached him without anger, "You worry too excessively about me, Tristano. I've told you repeatedly, I'm a big girl, I can take care of myself."

He bent to her and cradled her small pointed chin in his huge hand, and covered her mouth with his. Using his tongue to part her lips, he tasted her sugar and spice, her sultry sweetness and valiant, sexy heat. Her palms skimmed up his chiseled chest, encircled his neck to hold him closer, cinch them tighter together.

Breathless, he ended the kiss, his rough mouth pulsed against her softness. "Bitty bit," he said, "when will you realize I want to take care of you? I love to take care of you. You're the most precious thing in the world to me, and I want to protect you and cherish you." He had moved out of his hotel and into her cottage.

"Sometimes, I'd like to take care of you, Tristano." She traced the pads of her fingertips along his bristly jaw, across the stern lips, over rugged cheekbones, the intimate stroke loving and sensual at the same time.

His lips brushed the tip of her nose. He slipped his hand under her hair, splaying his fingers around the back of her neck he held her dominantly yet gently, a shiver rippled through Jesa's body.

He murmured softly, "Baby, every time you let me kiss those plush lips, allow me to sink into that heavenly body," a hand strolled around to grip her hip, hold her pelvis against his. "Even when you just allow me to hold you, touch you," he grinned against her mouth, "you're taking care of me."

She giggled, slid her palms down to fondle his muscular pecs. "That's silly, Tristano. Maybe when we get settled I can cook for you, massage your back, do something to make you feel as good as you make me feel."

"I just told you, Jesselin, you make me feel good just being with you." His arms wrapped around her, he cuddled her to his chest. "I have to remember you're Indiana, Indiana Kolbi. I forget to call you Indiana."

Jesa trickled her fingers through his thick hair. "I don't want that, Indiana is…gone. I'm Jesselin Judan now. That's who I want to be. That's who I was when we met. Besides," the edges of her mouth curved up prettily, she said, "our names are too alike. Koffi and Kolbi, it's kind of funny, huh?"

"Hmmm, yeah, funny. Listen," he said, grinning down at her, he cupped her bottom, squeezed her round flesh. "What do you say we go back to the bedroom, I have something to show you."

Jesa pushed from his arms, waggled a finger at him. "Uh huh, no Tristano, I don't want to be late for the lighting of the tree. You've hardly let me out of bed these past weeks. I'm eager see my friends."

Reluctantly, Tristano let his hands drop. He grabbed up the car keys and shrugged into his jacket. "Okay, my little temptress, you know I'll never get enough of you. Let's hit it." They strolled outside and headed for her bucket of bolts.

Up at the Commons, Tristano parked the car then went around to open her door. After he wrenched open the rusted door and she climbed out, Jesa instructed him, "I know you can fix that door, I insist you do that, tomorrow. You can't keep holding me prisoner, Tristano, you're always trying to control me."

"I only try to control your safety, because you aren't great at it." His hand at her waist, he chuckled. "It's a habit I'll work on." They made their way on the pedestrian walks past businesses to the central park where most of the town was gathered.

"Oh, Tristano," she gushed, "isn't it beautiful?"

He squeezed her hand in agreement. The buildings that surrounded the Commons were all decorated and strung with fairy lights, colorful lanterns hung in trees, the entire park was twinkling and glittering. The holiday arena was overflowing with boisterous partyers.

They enjoyed the sight of the glitzy park under the starry sky for a few moments, then Jesa pulled off her hat, stuffed it in her pocket and spoke over the loud throng, "I want to find Velvet and the others."

He nodded, tucked her hand in the crook of his arm and they lumbered through the thick, excited crowd. Halfway across the park, Jesa shrieked, "There they are!"

A foot taller than most of the people there, the Divine Bistro's manager, Benoit Sloan lifted a hand for the couple to follow through the mob.

Breathless with the hearty walk and exhilaration of the party atmosphere, Jesa laughed as the bistro gang surrounded them with cheerful greetings and hard hugs. Tristano shook hands with Benoit, Finn Barton, Cook, Hayes the bartender and numerous other staff.

Watching Jesa so happy to be with her friends, and they clearly loved her, brought a somber smile to Tristano's rugged face. Would she choose to stay here because of them? His gut churned, but he smiled pleasantly at everyone. Well, as pleasantly as he was capable of.

Velvet clung to Jesa in a colossal bear hug while Laverne pet her long strawberry curls that sifted in the breeze. Velvet trilled, "God-doggit girlfriend, have we missed you!"

Jesa laughed happily. "Oh Velvet, it's so good to see you guys!"

Finn hugged her then his wife Clarie grabbed her. Finn said, "We all heard what you did, Jesa. Rescuing Brie Westcott, so smart, so brave."

Clarie frowned her concern. "We were so worried when we heard about that horrible business in Georgia, and that terrible man stalking you. He almost-"

336

"But he didn't," Jesa assured her. "Tristano saw to that. He had my back the whole time." As she said that, he moved to her and rolled his arm around her shoulders in a clear proprietary manner, establishing that she was his.

When she nestled into his side, Velvet and Laverne cooed. "Ah, I knew you'd get one of those fine men, honey," Velvet praised her with amiable envy. "I think you choose the best one. He's so hot." She winked at Tristano.

Pink swam up her face as usual, Jesa ducked her head shyly, murmured, "Yes, I did."

"Considering her other choice was a murdering, rapist bastard," Laverne affirmed, "I'd say you were right."

"Laverne!" Clarie chided the ex-exotic dancer at her language.

Laverne shrugged and huffed, "Well, it's true. There had been rumors for a long time about that scoundrel. We never believed them because he was so good looking, that angelic blond hair and pretty blue eyes, the badge he wore. As they say, you can't judge a book by its cover."

Finn grinned at Jesa then Tristano. "This town owes you both a great deal. You rescued a kidnapped child, captured a very bad man, caught the family that stole the baby, and brought to light the wicked person that Deputy Roarke was."

"It wasn't just us, Mr. Barton," Tristano said, "the entire police department had a part in it. We certainly couldn't have done it on our own."

Clarie offered her corny two cents, "What you're saying is that it takes a village!" Everyone laughed, agreeing with her.

"Hey." Deputy Jerry Osborn joined the group. "I have news, about Ronan Roarke."

That got everyone's attention. Tristano asked tersely, "What about him?" His arm tightened around Jesa's shoulders.

Jerry tucked his hands in his jacket pockets, glanced around at the group waiting for his announcement. "We got word from the Coast Guard. The helicopter that Roarke had commandeered was spotted tumbling and rocketing in the storm. They followed after it by boat, but they couldn't keep up with the chopper's speed, and they lost sight of it. Half an hour later they heard a tremendous boom. By the time they got to it, the chopper had gone down inland and was just a burning mess." Aghast at his dreadful news, everyone just gawked at the deputy.

Tristano dipped his head, kissed the top of Jesa's soft hair, said solemnly, "That's not what I would have liked to hear. But, at least he won't be a danger to you," he kissed Jesa's cheek, "or anyone else, ever again. "

Jerry nodded soberly. "We can all sleep feeling safe and secure in our beds at night now."

Seeing the tears slipping from Jesa's eyes, Jerry said quietly, "He was a bad man, Jesa. He had nasty plans for you, and besides the other terrible things he did to women, a few of us have been suspicious that he may have been involved in some unsolved murders. The victims were as unsavory as he turned out to be, so investigating their deaths hadn't been a top priority."

Tristano dabbed at Jesa's tears with his thumbs, then lowered and gently kissed her trembling lips. He whispered, "It'll be okay, Bitty bit, it's all over." Still, the young woman with the soft heart was going to mourn the handsome deputy's death.

"So." Velvet tugged one of Jesa's long curls. "What's next on the menu?" Her light brown eyes hopped from Jesa to Tristano with a wink, then back to Jesa. "What are your plans? I'm pretty sure the way he looks at you that he isn't just leaving you here as he resumes his life in Georgia. Right?" She nudged Laverne, the two servers grinned. "So, give us the goods, girlfriend, what's happening?"

"Yes, what's the next rung in your ladder?" Chief McKabe approached with Deputies Caitlin, Granger Wate, Tom Christianson and others. All eyes were on the couple beaming at each other.

Shy as always, Jesa smiled at Tristano then said to their friends, "We haven't really worked things out. I guess," her big green eyes shimmered up at Tristano, "we'll try to figure something out. A long distance rela-"

"Ah, I think not, Bitty bit, we discussed this. Not in depth, but..." Tristano suddenly sank to one knee. When he pulled a tiny black box out of his pocket, the group around them gasped. Velvet slapped a hand over her mouth to keep in her excited squeal.

"Tristano-" Jesa's forehead creased in confusion, she gasped, "What are you-"

"Jesselin Judan, Indiana Kolbi, love of my life," Tristano's baritone as hard as usual, dark eyes harsh, but now they contained a hint of warmth, only for Jesa. "Baby, will you marry me?" He opened the box and now Velvet and Laverne both let out squeals at the brilliant diamond glinting in the Christmas lights.

Dumbfounded, Jesa stood speechless with her mouth open, eyes like green moons. The gang twittered. Velvet gave her a nudge with her hand. "I think he's waiting for a response, honey."

His grin slightly crooked, Tristano said, "I'm looking for a yes, Bitty bit. We talked about you coming with me to Georgia. We'll build a home, for our family," the grin widened at her cheeks staining pink. "I can't bear to think of us not living together. We can come here for visits any time you want. Make me the happiest man in the world, baby, say yes."

He took the ring out of the box, grasped Jesa's left hand, and slipped the ring on her finger. "Marry me," he urged at her frozen silence.

Velvet gave Jesa a sharp poke with her elbow.

Jesa blinked, looked at the ring on her finger, then at Tristano's dark, earnest gaze. She could see the desire and love for her gleaming in the black depths. "I," she swallowed, started again, "Yes, Tristano, I will marry you."

The crowd whooped and hollered, Tristano bent and lifted Jesa in his arms, twirling her around and aground, her giggles and happiness his delight. All he needed in his life was this sweet bundle of delicate, courageous, femininity. Just a glance at her made his blood boil and his heart sing.

He'd never been so happy, felt so complete as he did when he had her in his arms, in his life. She calmed the deep rage that simmered just below the surface. Especially now that he'd gotten word that someone in the village where he had been in the military overseas, where the slaughter had taken place that he had taken the blame for, was speaking out.

It's a possibility his name might be cleared. But, he wasn't getting his hopes up, yet. Still, if he could marry Jesselin as a Marine with his honor restored, that would be the icing on the wedding cake.

As he set her down, in the center of the hubbub the thirty-foot tall Christmas tree decorated with tinsel and shiny ornaments suddenly lit up. The winking colored lights popped on and the huge gold star at the top sparkled brightly. The crowd ooed and ahhed, roared their delight.

"Oh Tristano," Jesa exclaimed, "it's stunning," she smiled up at him, her hands on his chest as his wound around her, "this is the happiest day of my life!"

"Yeah." Tristano bent his head down to the petite woman. "Mine too. I love you, Bitty bit." He slashed at the pink ribbon of her plush lips with his tongue, then covered her mouth and drowned them both in ecstatic joy.

Epilogue

Spring

Half the town showed for Jesa and Tristano's wedding. Congratulations abounded, confetti tossed like colorful butterflies, well wishes rang aloud. Every color of tulips sprouted bordering the deck.

Pinkish white, apple tree blossoms bloomed on trees in the parks, their sweet smell permeated, fighting with marine scent of the sea. The air was light-jacket crisp, the sun a yellow molten ball in the bluest of skies.

Tristano lifted his giggling bride in his arms and carried her, her laughter ringing giddy with joy up the walk to the ferry with the well-wishers surrounding them. He carried her to a small cabin on the ferry he'd reserved. Over the threshold, he didn't set her down but traipsed to an overstuffed chair and settled her on his lap.

On a table sat a wine bucket, a bottle of champagne poked out of it, two glasses were on a tray beside it. In a basket was an assortment of chocolate truffles. Tristano cuddled his new wife, salted her face with kisses. "How does it feel to be Mrs. Tristano Koffi?"

Jesa cupped his face, kissed him, said, "It feels wonderful. How does it feel to be Mr. Jesselin Judan?" They laughed together.

"The best, baby, the best, just like you." His fingers fumbled at the pearl buttons of her gown. "I need to get this white fluff off you and consummate our marriage. I can't wait any longer." He tugged the gown down her body, set her on her feet in front of him, then sat back with a wolf whistle.

"Hot damn, Wife, you are the sexiest, hottest creature I have ever seen!" His gaze burned over the curvy little body standing shyly in front of him. She wore white heels, white stockings with a white silk garter, tiny pink panties and a silky bra.

"Hmm," he pondered, tapping his fingers on his chin. "I can't decide what I want to leave on, or take off. I think the stockings and garter and heels stay on for now, the rest goes."

He swiped a hand out to grab her- with a squeal Jesa tried to run from him. He easily caught her, swooping her up in his big arms he dropped her on the small bed, then climbed atop her to nestle between her legs.

"You can run from me, little wife," he threatened with a grin as he unclasped her bra, smiling at her giggles. "But I will always catch you. Always."

The evening was spent making love and drinking champagne, munching on truffles until they passed out exhausted in each other's arms.

Hours later, Jesa jumped at the horrible sound, sat up straight in bed. She heard rumbles, and a low roar, cursing. Next to her, Tristano was thrashing, his fists punched out, he shouted, "No! I didn't kill them, it wasn't me! My shot hit the general, it was Jasper's bullet that killed that girl! No! Get off me, I'll fucking kill you all!"

"Tristano, baby, it's me, Jesselin, wake up." She gently prodded his shoulder ducking his swinging fists. She kept calling to him until her voice filtered in and he started to calm. His eyes drifted open, he peered at her through slits, sweat glistened at his temples, his chest pumped, panting roughly.

"Jess- Jesselin," he rasped, "what the hell-"

Jesa soothingly stroked his hair, cooed softly, "It was a dream, baby, you were having a nightmare." She smoothed his hair off his damp face, caressed his arm, his chest until his breathing grew shallower, his chest slowed its rise and fall.

Rubbing his eyes, Tristano labored to sit up, reclining back against pillows Jesa stacked. Shoulders humping forward, he pulled his knees up under the sheet and dropped his forearms on them, lowered his head. Jesa pet his huge shoulder, murmured gently, "Tell me about it, Tristano."

Shaking his head, he grunted. "No. It's an old nightmare. Reoccurs every so often. Memories of a bad time." A shudder visibly rippled through him.

"You'll feel better if you talk about it, baby." She kissed his bare shoulder.

"No, it was gritty, grisly, hell on earth, not for ears like yours."

She frowned at him. "We promised to never keep secrets from one another, Tristano. Tell me about it."

His head turned towards her, long black lashes shaded his dark eyes as he studied his wife. The best thing that ever happened to him. A sigh eased the horror of the nightmare. He plumped the pillows behind him, sank back against them, reached for her and drew her up to snuggle under his arm.

Exhaling the devastation from his lungs constricted with the vivid dream, he said, "I was in the Marines. A sniper in the Marine-Ground Task Force. We were part of a primo squad sent in Afghanistan to take out a specific nasty, deadly pocket of infidels.

"These men were raping and killing, torturing and maiming their way through a town. A group of us were stashed high up, literally, hidden in the trees half a mile away, waiting for them. Our Intel told us they were on this dusty scrub ridden road, headed our way. We waited, hours, but that was okay, we were trained for it."

Jesa turned slightly to face him, set her palm over his heart, felt it beating slowly, then it sped up as the memories flowed.

"They came, they were rowdy, drunk, their leader, General Hasmin leading, the loudest. There were women and children swirling around them. They used them as shields. We were prepared for it, we'd practiced shooting in darts and dashes to not hit the innocents. We had planned that we would wait until they were only 50 meters from us and then we'd start firing, that would ensure none of the civilians would be hit."

Quietly, Jesa commiserated, "Must have been pretty scary."

"It was the waiting, it keeps the adrenalin flowing, revs you up. Unfortunately, it also pushes you to react too soon. My major, Darren Jefferson didn't have the greatest reputation. There were complaints that he could be reckless in his impatience. He wasn't really a very nice guy who drank heavily and that led to trouble when on base.

"He'd get into fights in bars and shit. Heard he slapped his woman about while sleeping around with others. No one wanted to be under his command, but you didn't get to choose your own assignment." Tristano's eyes closed, anguish flickered across his lids.

"Go on, baby," Jesa murmured, her hand on his arm.

Keeping his eyes closed he said, "So, the infidels came closer, they grew louder, some of the women whimpered from the men's abusive behavior. Children were kicked for no reason. Jefferson and I were the closest, hunkered down in the same enormous tree. I could see his hands shaking, not a good sign.

"His agitation was skyrocketing, he shouldn't have been given the mission, the man wasn't equipped to handle high stress situations. His father was a high ranking decorated colonel and he was instrumental in getting Jefferson promoted again and again. He also made his errors and complaints disappear."

"Doesn't sound right, sounds like it could be dangerous in the long run." She rested her face on his chest and looked up at him.

His eyes opened, they lowered to her. "Yeah. It was. The closer the infidels got the more he panicked. I wanted to tell him to chill but we had to maintain silence.

"Anyway, when the group got to 75 meters, he couldn't hold it together, he barked out the order to fire. I hesitated, which is wrong, insubordinate, a dishonorable dischargeable offense, but hell, Jesselin, it was too soon, they were too far away. He ordered again, louder, fire! I had no choice, we started shooting.

"We both had M110 semi-automatic sniper weapons. I was a Marine Corps Scout Sniper, trained in the use of the weapon, Jefferson was not. He had no business firing it. I took out the general of the infidels, but then all hell broke loose. Jefferson was firing wildly, the people started scattering, fleeing in screaming panic. Our other soldiers in the trees fired.

"When the smoke settled, we jumped out of the trees and surveyed the damage. A woman and three small children were among the dead. It was heart-wrenching, ghastly, their bodies riddled with bullets, blood everywhere. We managed to kill all of the insurgents but, there was civilian loss." His head tilted back, he closed his eyes again, and grew silent.

Jesa sat beside him, there was nothing she could say that would be helpful, so she just sat with him. Some time passed, her voice gentle she asked, "What happened next?"

Wiping at his eyes, he pinched them, then looked at her, agony streamed through his dark eyes, his pain tangible. With a groaned, "Ah," he combed his hair back off his forehead, sighed, the pain vanished, his normal iciness chilled his eyes back to cinders.

"Jefferson blamed the civilian killings on me. We weren't allowed to take the bodies for examinations, analyze the bullets, see whose weapon they came from, although," he snorted drily, "I damned well knew who shot the civilians.

"But, I had no proof, and his father was a big shit, and had friends that were higher up, bigger shits. He managed a huge cover-up, and made me take the fall. I was given a general discharge and warned not to fight it. Said that the JAG, you know, Judge Advocate General's Corps, military prosecutors would guarantee I was court-martialed. So," he shrugged indifferently. "I was booted. I was lucky to be able to get hired with the FBI. I had special...talents, skills, that they desired so they overlooked the discharge."

"You are so strong, to get through all that, Tristano. You must be seething inside, all the time. Enraged, wanting revenge but can't get it. Your beloved career taken from you. How do you control the rage?"

He shrugged dismissively again. "At first I drank a lot, all the time. Got into brawls, just like that idiot Jefferson used to, to work off the strain, the blistering pressure keeping me on the edge of rupturing, and the fury that ate at my gut all day, every day, every night. Only thing I ever wanted to be since a young boy was a Marine."

Jesa stroked her hand up and down his arm, soothing, comforting, supporting him. "How did you get past it? I mean, you're so calm, always in control."

"Huh, sure. When I saw how my hands started shaking and I knew I couldn't shoot a gun like that, I learned to jam it way down deep, bottled up the rage and covered it with mental bricks. Suppressing it kept it controlled, but it also hardened my heart, I got to the point where I cared about nothing, no one. I had a good friend in Texas where I landed at first. Brogan Dillon," he chuckled, "a real cowboy who had been in my unit.

"He was caught up in the whole clusterfuck. He tried to kick off an investigation, but," he shook his head, "he was shut down and tossed out on his ear too. I went to Texas and spent time with him. We boxed, primed our martial arts, went to the shooting range, hunted, and talked. He helped me burn off the volcanic fury; he saved me from arrest or worse.

"Brogan allowed me to vent, to scream, to roar, and to fight, safely, with him, and vice versa. Brogan hired on as the sheriff of a Texas town to fight his demons, and I joined the FBI and they transferred me to Georgia, which," he picked up her hand, pressed it gently, "led me to the love of my life, and my second savior."

"What?" she burst out laughing. "Why do you say that?"

He lifted her hand to his mouth and kissed it, smiled with his lips on it. "Because when I'm with you I truly feel the calm, real peace. It's not just suppressed, I don't feel the rage, I just feel, love for you. Except," he waggled his eyebrows making her giggle, "when you're in danger. Then the tiger is out of the cage and I don't care how badly I hurt that person."

"I've noticed," she said drily.

"Anyway, I've received word someone has stepped up and is speaking the truth. I'm to have a hearing regarding the entire incident."

"That's wonderful, Tristano! Your name will be cleared."

"We'll see." Tristano rolled towards her, shifting his body to curl over her, his arm around her, he brushed strawberry tendrils off her cheek. "You know what else calms me, Bitty bit?"

"No, what?"

"This." He grabbed her waist and pulled her down the middle of the bed, moved between the cradle of her hips, and wed their mouths, a prelude to uniting their bodies. "Making love to my beautiful wife."

With a soft groan of desire, Jesa's hands went to his biceps, the huge muscles flexed as he moved her, fondled and caressed her sweet body. Loving the feel of their strength, their contour, his big hard hands strumming the music of her body, making it flame and throb with thrilling, piquant desire, Jesa surrendered to her husband.

2nd Epilogue

Even with the parachute he landed rough, hit the ground hard, the chute dragging him over abrasive ground teeming with thorny scrub and sharp rocks. By the time he stopped dragging, his body was littered with lacerations, bruises, his ankle stung, likely sprained. Fuck. He had headed as far south as he could manage before bailing. Last thing he wanted was to hike his way out of a snow covered cavern. Still, by his estimations, he was a long way from the closest town.

Favoring his right ankle, he trudged over the uneven ground, slogged through heavy snowdrifts. By the time he reached a road, frostbite had become a serious concern. Rubbing his arms to keep his hands and body warm, he plodded along, struggling to stay upright. If he fell he'd be done. He had no weapon to fight off wild scavengers.

Finally, after hours and hours of trudging through the bitter cold, forging over the harsh land stippled with bare trees, he emerged shivering from the woodlands, and in front of his grateful eyes was a road. The most magnificent thing he'd ever seen in his life.

Once his boots hit the asphalt, he stuck his thumb out. Another hour passed and an eighteen-wheeler pulled over. He opened the passenger side door and poked his head inside. A cheery, husky man greeted him. Chewing tobacco, he said, "How far ya goin' son?"

As he climbed in and dropped heavily onto the leather seat with a grunt of relief, he muttered, "I'm heading to Texas."

The End

Isle of Orainn

www.ingramcontent.com/pod-product-compliance
Lightning Source LLC
Chambersburg PA
CBHW020825180626
46814CB00001B/110